# THE Damning STONE

## TJ Klune

*NEW YORK TIMES* BESTSELLING AUTHOR

**The Damning Stone**
Copyright © 2022 by TJ Klune

Published by BOATK Books
http://tjklunebooks.com
tjklunebooks@yahoo.com

Cover Art by Reese Dante   https://reesedante.com

Published 2022.
Printed in the United States of America

ISBN: 978-1-7367186-9-8 (paperback)
eBook edition available

# PROLOGUE
## Teachers Should Not Have Sex with Their Students

"AND NOW, I WILL TELL YOU of my plans to take over the kingdom," the evil wizard and total douchebag Sam of Dragons said with a cackle.

"Release me now," I snapped. "I am the godsdamn Prince of—"

"Silence!" Sam bellowed, eyes ablaze. "You're my prisoner, and you'll listen to my villainous monologue about how I have unresolved issues involving my father which led me down the dark path of no return." He blinked. "Whoa. That came out better than I thought it would. Maybe there's something to this after—"

"Boring," the unicorn said, little sparks of pink and violet shooting from his flared nostrils. He stood next to me, all four legs bound by vermilion root. I was still perturbed by how much he'd groaned that the ropes needed to be *tighter*, Sam, honestly, this isn't my first time being tied up, for fuck's sakes, make me *feel it*. Unicorns were more trouble than they were worth. "Cupcake, we've talked about this. If you're going to make a good villain, you need to be *believable*. It needs to be fresh and exciting. What's the point of doing this if you're going to rehash the same moments we've already lived through?"

Sam glared at him. "Gary, I told you—"

Gary coughed.

"Gary, would you shut—"

Gary coughed harder.

Sam threw his hands up in the air. "Fine." He took a step further into the cave, his shadow dancing along the wall. "The Artist Formerly Known as Gary the Hornless Gay Unicorn, we agreed that you wouldn't give me notes about my performance until after I was done."

Gary batted his eyelashes. "There, that's better. Was that so hard?"

"Yes," Sam said. "It was. That's a ridiculous name and you should feel embarrassed."

Gary rolled his eyes. "You got to change your name. *Twice*, in fact. Sam Haversford became Sam of Wilds who became Sam of Dragons. You didn't hear me complain about any of that."

"Uh," Sam said. "You did complain. Like, all the time. You complained on the way *here*. You said I was obviously confused about my identity, and that I really needed to pick one and stick with it."

Gary sniffed. "Where's the lie? And becoming the Artist Formerly Known as Gary the Hornless Gay Unicorn was something I've always dreamed about, ever since I was a young foal." His eyes filled with tears. "Would you take that away from a poor, magical creature protected by an absurd number of laws? My word, Sam. That's a hate crime, punishable by life in the dungeons. You know you wouldn't do well in the dungeons. You're too...well. Not pretty, but you're identifiably human, which some people seem to like."

"I have no idea why," I muttered, struggling against the ropes encircling my wrists. Whatever else Sam was—a blight on the world, an annoyance capable of making even the strongest of men beg for the sweet release of death—he knew how to tie a knot. Perhaps I could finally be free of him if I was able to convince Dad to make military service mandatory. Sam would be shipped out to sea, working the decks so I'd never have to be pseudo-kidnapped again as part of his stupid drills.

"I'm delightful," Sam said, pushing a lock of dark hair off his forehead. He'd allowed it to grow out longer, tips beginning to curl, tying it back with a piece of rawhide. It suited him, though I would never tell him as much, especially after he told me (apropos of *nothing*) that a certain Knight Commander like to pull on it when they were... ugh. Whatever. "Everyone thinks so."

"I don't," Gary and I said at the same time.

Sam began to pace, his robe swirling around his feet. The cave was hot and humid, and I could think of at least a thousand places I'd rather be. Verania was in the throes of summer, and I was *supposed* to be in Castle Lockes, taking meetings with my father. In fact, I'd been heading toward Dad's chambers when a half-giant of alleged ill repute had smiled at me, said hello, and then threw me over his shoulder, crowing as he stole me from the castle. No matter how many times I demanded he put me down, he hadn't listened.

But then none of them listened, much to my consternation. What was the point of being a prince when my subjects refused to do what I told them?

"We have to be prepared," Sam said. "Just because the Dark wizards are all locked away doesn't mean there aren't stragglers out there, preparing their revenge against our badassery in saving the Kingdom of Verania."

"Let them come," Gary said, tail swishing. "It's been ages since I've stabbed someone with my horn."

"You know," I told him pleasantly, "after all the bluster and noise about getting your horn back, I honestly expected more from you."

Gary turned his head slowly toward me, eyes narrowing. "What was that?" he asked sweetly, a sure sign I was treading on thin ice.

"Uh oh," Sam said.

I shrugged. Gary was getting pissed off, and I'd been told time and time again that one should never upset a unicorn. But cave water had just landed on my face, and it smelled terrible. If I could get Gary going, maybe he'd go on a rampage and we could all go home. "I'm just saying. You got your horn back and what's changed? You're still pretty much the same."

"Sam."

"Yes, Gary."

"*Sam.*"

Sam sighed. "Yes, the Artist Formerly Known as Gary the Hornless Gay Unicorn."

"A question, if I may."

"Keep it short. I still have a whole speech I have to give about—"

Gary craned his neck toward me. I didn't flinch as his snout rubbed against my cheek, his massive horn brushing against the top of my head. "Isn't it true that anyone who insults a unicorn is automatically earmarked for death?"

"No?" Sam said. Or asked. He didn't sound sure. "I mean, if that was the case, you'd be a serial killer because plenty of people have insulted you. *I've* insulted you. Like, hundreds of times."

"Yes," Gary said, nibbling on my ear until I jerked my head back. "You have. And don't think I've forgotten any of the snide remarks you've made about my beautiful existence. I told you once that when you least expected it, you would find me standing above you, and that I'd be the last thing you'd ever see. Maybe not today, maybe not tomorrow, but one day. A unicorn never forgets. Which brings us back to our prince here. He insulted me. I demand recompense as a magical creature protected under Lockes Statute four nine six dash seven A, subsection C, paragraph four."

I squinted at him. "That statute is about bean farmers. And beans."

"I don't have *time* for your silly laws!" Gary trilled, his horn beginning to take on an unworldly glow. "I want to kill!"

"No killing," Sam said. "You promised you'd let me pretend to be a villain without interruption."

"With *minimal* interruption," Gary corrected. "Like I would ever agree to not provide feedback. It would be hypocritical because I'm always open to constructive criticism. It's why I don't talk about wind r—er, assault anymore, nor do I say that someone attempting to ride me is racist because people were offended by it. It's also why we don't call your mother's family Gyp—"

"Shut it!" Sam said, eyes wide. "You know we can't say that anymore. People might leave bad reviews on the City of Lockes community boards because they don't like the connotations behind that word which, okay, fair point because it *is* mired in racist ideology." He looked around wildly as if to make sure we were alone. We were. I hated everything. "I don't need another editorial written in the newspapers about how we're not as politically correct enough as the faces of the new Verania. Twenty-six times was enough."

Resigned to my fate, I said, "You're not going to let me go, are you."

Sam shook his head. "Not until I'm finished." He turned away from us toward the mouth of the cave. I couldn't see what he was doing, but it looked like he was staring down at his hand, muttering under his breath.

"What's happening now?" I asked Gary.

"He wrote the script down on his palm," Gary whispered back. "He was nervous about his performance. Doesn't take stage direction too well, that one. I thought about recasting his role, but I didn't have the time to hold auditions to replace him. We'll talk about it for next time. I'm thinking of a sexy centaur named Hidalgo, except instead of being top man, bottom horse, it'd be top horse, bottom *man*. How amazingly dirty would that be?" He laughed as I grimaced. "We don't kink shame. Some of us have unique tastes that should be celebrated rather than denigrated."

"You have a husband. Who is a dragon."

Sam threw his head back and laughed evilly. It sounded like an angry weasel getting shaved with a blunt razor. "You fell right into my trap, and now, you'll listen to my woes. It all started when I was a child. My father left one day for a pack of cigarettes and never came back." He stared off into nothing as if filled with memories that absolutely did not happen. "My mother tried to raise me on her own, but I proved to be too difficult."

"Now that I believe," I mumbled.

"Why are you trying to be funny?" Gary asked me. "You're the Ice Prince. You're not supposed to have a sense of humor."

"So she sold me," Sam continued, "to a diabolical mistress known as Mama, who took me under her wing—"

"Yesss," Gary hissed. "Cameos. All the cameos. Make me *yearn* for stories past."

"—and taught me the ways of the body. I used my slender frame as currency, selling myself and sexing the most powerful men in Verania. I was a lost soul, dreaming of something more than a man with a mustache grunting in my ear."

"Backstory is important," Gary told me. "Really gets the audience invested."

I glared at him. "*What* audience?"

"But then I realized I was meant for something more," Sam continued, hands curling into fists. "Something greater. Something *darker*. Which is why I have kidnapped the Prince and brought him here to this cave in order to exact my revenge." He shaved-weasel laughed again. "I will trade the only son of the King of Verania in exchange for the keys to the kingdom. And once the kingdom is mine, I will rule over it with an iron fist and everyone will know the true meaning of the word *suffering*."

"Whoa," Gary breathed.

Sam startled. "What? What is it? Is it me? Are you getting chills because I'm so believable monologuing as a villain and you're trembling with fear as you know that I'll do whatever it takes to ensure my plans succeed?"

"What?" Gary asked. "No. Of course not, you're pretty bad at this. Like, I know you're trying to be malevolent, but I'm not really feeling it. Maybe it's because I've seen you naked. Why don't you have chest hair? It's like you're twelve. Anyway. That's not what I was talking about."

"Fuck you too," Sam retorted. "Why'd you stop me?"

"That," Gary said, nodding toward the cave wall. "I think there's part of Lartin the Dark Leaf still embedded in the rock."

"*What*?" Sam demanded. He hurried over to the side of the cave, stopping in front of a wet *something* hanging off the wall. "Holy shit, is that a liver? Do I even know what a liver looks like? I don't think I do."

"A*ha*!" Gary cried. "You fell for it. It's just cave moss, you bitch! Now *I* will enact my plan for the destruction of the Kingdom of Verania!" And with that, he lowered his horn toward the vermilion root. His horn flashed brightly, and the root turned to dust, which should have been impossible but I'd long given up trying to understand anything.

Sam gasped. "*Double cross.*"

"That's right," Gary snarled, prancing in place, his hooves clicking along the rocky floor. "You were so concerned with the prince that you never saw me coming. It is I, the *true* villain, here to bring pain and death to all those who stand in my way!"

"This is so stupid," I said to no one at all.

"How dare you!" Sam bellowed. "You'll never defeat me. I am Sam of Dragons, the most powerful wizard in an age!"

Gary broke character, eyeing Sam up and down. "You really let that go to your head, didn't you?"

Sam shrugged. "Standing in front of a star dragon god who tells you you're the savior of the entire world has that effect."

"Huh," Gary said. "I never thought about it that way. Well. Color me impressed. Annoyed, but impressed. But I will *not* allow all that cosmic nonsense to go to your head, Sam. I really won't. Your ego is inflated enough as it is. Why, I've never seen such a travesty in my—"

A nine-and-a-half-foot-tall half-giant burst into the cave, causing the ground beneath our feet to rumble. "*TIGGY SMASH!*"

"Hurray!" Gary cried. "I'm saved! Dearest Tiggy, destroy the humans. They have taken me captive and were planning on using my voluptuous body for their nefarious deeds! And even though I probably would have been an active participant, now that you're here, we don't have to find out."

"Hi, Gary!" Tiggy said as he waved, hand opening and closing. His dark hair hung in loose waves atop his head, the muscles in his arms and chest bulging underneath a blue tunic. His large, tanned feet were bare, leaving behind footprints in the soft soil on the floor of the cave.

Gary grinned. "Hi, kitten. It's lovely to see you as always. It's been ten minutes since I saw your perfect face, but it felt like years. We'll discuss how you came in too early later. Your cue wasn't supposed to happen for at least another hour."

"Boring outside," Tiggy said. "Hot. Cave wet. Smash Sam?"

"Yes," Gary said. "Smash Sam."

"No smashing Sam!" Sam said.

"Aw," Tiggy said as he deflated. "Tiggy never gets to smash." He scuffed his hairy foot against the floor.

Sam melted, as I knew he would do. "Okay, big guy. You can smash. You can smash all you want. Just not me. Or Gary." He waited a long beat. "Or Justin."

"Tiggy smash!" he yelled, punching the wall, causing a large crack to rise toward the top of the cave. "There. Better. Yay Tiggy!"

"Smashing?" a thunderously deep voice said. "I didn't know this was going to be *that* kind of kidnapping party." A gigantic black reptilian head filled the mouth of the cave, his breath increasing the interior temperature tenfold. "I approve. I can see that everyone is still wearing their clothes, which means the party is just getting started. What are we going to do to each other? Tongues in butts, or….?"

Gary pranced by Sam, stopping in front of the dragon, rubbing his horn against the dragon's scaley cheek. "Kevin, my love. I told you that you can't always suggest rimming as the first sexual act. Some people don't like that sort of thing."

"My tongue is seven feet long," Kevin said, eyes glittering. "Everyone should like that sort of thing."

How we became the saviors of Verania, I'll never know.

"Sweet molasses," Sam whispered. "That's so gross." He shook his head. "Why are you here? I told you to wait outside."

Kevin snapped his enormous jaws, teeth like spikes as his forked tongue slithered out between his lips, flicking up and down. "Like I would ever miss my son's performance. What kind of father do you take me for?"

Great. This again. Just what the situation was missing. And knowing Sam, he was going to fall for it like he always did.

"You're not my dad! Gods, how many times do I have to say that?"

There it was, right on schedule. "Leave me out of it," I groused, grimacing at the way the ropes rubbed against my wrists. "And while you're at it, untie me at once. I've had enough of this."

"But I haven't even gotten to the part where I tell you what my plans are!"

"I don't care," I snapped. "This is pointless. No one is coming for us. I don't know why you think we need to run these ridiculous drills. We're safe. Verania is safe." I sighed as Sam frowned. "Look, I appreciate your concern. What we—*you* went through is enough to drive anyone mad. But it's been a year. We're okay. I promise."

Sam raised a hand, fingers wiggling. A whisper of magic rolled over my arms, familiar and cool, causing gooseflesh to prickle. My binds loosened, falling to the floor. I rubbed my wrists as Sam shook his head. "Sorry," he mumbled.

I swallowed down a retort. "It's fine. Just...tell me about these things beforehand. We can always do this in the castle, if you think it's necessary."

He nodded but still wouldn't look at me. Tiggy reached over and patted the top of his head. "Pretty Sam," he rumbled. "Good, pretty Sam. My favorite Sam."

Sam rolled his eyes but leaned into Tiggy's hand. "I'm your only Sam."

"Unhand the prince!" a voice cried. "Prepare to taste steel, villain!"

Then my ex-fiancé burst into the cave, sword at the ready. Knight Commander Ryan Foxheart flourished the blade, spinning it expertly in his hand, his thick, wavy blond hair bouncing on his head. He wore his practice field armor, dinged and dented from scuffles past, though polished so that it shone even in the low light of the cave. He looked as handsome as ever, even if he was still more than a little ridiculous. At least he'd gotten rid of the stupid beard.

His sword drooped a little when no one exclaimed in wonder at the sight of him. "Uh, what's going on?"

"We're making memories," Gary said.

"I smashed a wall!" Tiggy exclaimed proudly.

"Apparently, there won't be any rimming," Kevin grumbled.

"Get me the fuck out of here," I growled.

Ryan sighed as he sheathed his sword. "That's…pretty much how I thought this was going to go. Of all the motherfu—"

"I dare you," Sam said in a low voice, "to finish that sentence without thinking of all the children's lives you're ruining."

Ryan made a face. "Fine. Mothercracker it is. Let's get on with the drill. Should I enter again and let everyone really take in my presence? I'm pretty sure I can do it better than—"

"Drill's over," Sam said, waving his hand dismissively. "They failed and everyone died because no one will take this seriously. I'm a spectacular villain, and my fake plans were perfect. And *no*, Gary, I'm not looking for feedback, constructive or otherwise."

Gary snapped his mouth closed.

Muttering under his breath, Sam stalked toward the mouth of the cave, only stopping to kiss Ryan. Kevin's massive head still blocked most of the cave, and Sam had to press himself against the rock to squeeze by him. Kevin, for his part, didn't move to make it easier.

"That didn't go well," Gary said. "Honestly, all of you. Is it too much to ask that we play along with Sam's little game? I have so many notes. Kevin, you didn't even breathe fire."

"So cliched," Kevin said. "I'm more than breathing fire. I am a flying, talking reptile who—"

"Tiggy, you missed your cue."

Tiggy smiled. "Hi, Gary! I found squirrel. Gave it nuts."

"Ryan, you look dumb."

"Hey!"

"And Justin," Gary said, swinging his head toward me, the tip of his horn glittering. "You were an angel. Your command of the stage is unparalleled. A vision such as you has never before—"

"For the fifty-seventh time, I'm not going to petition for National Gary is Perfect Day, so don't ask."

"Then what's the point of you being alive?" Gary snarled. He blinked. "Oh my. I apparently have issues I need to work through. Thankfully, my performance was pitch perfect so I can start focusing on myself. It will be a strange, new world because I always put others first. But now it's Gary's time."

"Ooh," Kevin breathed. "Talk about yourself more in third person. You know what it does to me."

"Gary's gonna bring the pain," Gary purred as he slunk toward his husband. "You've been a bad, bad dragon. You didn't turn in your homework when you were supposed to, and now I need you to stay after class to discuss...extra credit."

"Maybe we should order takeout from the bakery when we discuss...extra credit," Kevin said, forked tongue slithering out from between his lip. "I'm hungry for a donut. A *glazed* donut."

Gary's horn began to glow. "You would be," he said rather aggressively. "And I hope you're ready because I'm going to donut all over your entire *face*—"

"Nope!" Ryan said. "Nope, nope, nope. Not today. Not again. Fool me once, shame on you. Fool me twelve times, shame on me." And with that, he pushed by Kevin and walked out of the cave.

"Gonna get wet," Tiggy said as Gary rubbed his entire body against Kevin's head. "Stay and watch?"

"No," Gary said. "You're far too innocent to see what's about to happen. I could never live with myself if you witnessed what I'm about to do to my enormous hunk of lizard. It would shatter all that you are and where would we be then?"

"Then maybe don't do it?" I asked hopefully.

"Too late!" Gary cried. "It's already begun! You bad student with your letterman jacket and cocky attitude who sometimes wears sweatpants to show off that dick like you don't know what it does to me. I'm trapped in a loveless marriage, looking for anything to light that fire in my loins I've been missing for all these many years. I'm going to sex that unentitled sense of accomplishment out of your entire body. Class is in, and I, as your teacher, am going to teach you a lesson about what to do with a butthole."

I stared in horror as Gary raised his tail and Kevin stuck his snout right in—

I tugged on Tiggy's arm. "Sack of potatoes! Oh my gods, *sack of potatoes*!"

And with that, the half-giant dropped his hands from his face, grabbed me by the waist, and threw me up and over his shoulder. With a triumphant bellow (and the sounds of wet *something* happening somewhere near us) Tiggy ran from the cave, knocking against Kevin but managing to get us free before the cave devolved into a den of sin.

The last thing I saw as we left them behind was Kevin's wings fluttering as he rumbled, "I didn't even get my mom to sign my report card, what is *up*?" and Gary snarling, "Oh, you're in for it now, you ferocious welp. You want me to give you an A? You better get up in *my* A."

All in all, a normal day in the Kingdom of Verania.

Unfortunately.

# CHAPTER 1
## Recounting Past Adventures for Backstory is Fine So Shut Up

ONCE UPON A TIME, in the City of Lockes, there lived a prince who only wanted to grow up to be like his father, a benevolent king who ruled the Kingdom of Verania with a firm yet kind hand. The boy prince lived in the castle, knowing his place in the world, and what his future entailed: one day, he would be king. Many people would look to him as their leader, to carry them when they were at their weakest, to lift them up in celebration when they were at their strongest.

"Being a king," this wonderful man said, "isn't about how much power he has, or the fear he can strike in the hearts of his enemies. A good king listens to his people, weighs the consequences of his decisions against the good of those he watches over. Every choice you make, from the smallest to the largest, will reverberate like ripples in a pond. The crown you wear is a symbol of a free world. It's a beacon, my son, drawing others to you. They will look to you as a weapon of hope. You will carry the wants and wishes of your subjects on your shoulders, and while there may be days when your burden will be heavier than you think you can bear, if you can take another step, you can keep going."

I was nine years old and taking in each word he said like gospel. "But what happens when I have to make a decision people don't like?"

Dad smiled at me. We sat in his chambers on the edge of his

bed, his arm around my shoulders. He'd taken off his robes, wearing only loose-fitting trousers and a billowy shirt. "Ah," he said. "Why wouldn't they like it?"

I frowned, squinting up at him. "Because they might not see how it's for the greater good."

"And what is the greater good?"

"That which benefits a majority," I said promptly.

"What about those it doesn't benefit?" Dad asked. "What would you say to them?"

I hesitated, unsure of how to answer. I wanted to impress him, to show him I could be who he wanted me to be, but I was scared of saying the wrong thing. "I…don't know?"

Dad nodded. "And that's okay. A king, regardless of his power, can't know everything. Believe me, I tried. I thought if I could predict every little divergence in the road ahead, I would be better off for it, and in turn, the people would be too. I was wrong."

A king admitting he was wrong was a big deal, and I stared up at him in shock. "Why?"

Dad smiled down at me. "Because that's not how life works. If we knew everything that was coming, we'd be so concerned with the future that we wouldn't stop and appreciate all that we have in the present. A king must be strong in his convictions, but not so much that he can't admit when he's made a mistake. Acknowledging your fallacies isn't a sign of weakness, Justin. It's the mark of a good person to know when you're wrong. But it can't end there. Just saying you're wrong isn't enough to fix the problems at hand. While your word will one day become law, you must learn how to listen, to hear all sides before handing down judgment."

"But how will I know I made the right decision?"

"You might not," Dad said gently, squeezing the back of my neck. "Not for a long while. But if you remember kindness, and if you remember that a king lives in service of his people, I know you'll do what's right, even if it sometimes feels like you're standing alone."

"But I won't be alone," I said quickly. "Because you'll be there."

Dad laughed, a deep, happy sound that never failed to fill me with joy. "I will. And I cannot wait to see the man you'll become." His laughter faded, and his smile took on a melancholic lilt. "She would be proud of you. Your mother."

Every now and then, she would spring up between us, a flower of grief blooming bright in the spring sun. From all that I'd been told, she'd been bright like a star, her beauty unrivaled, her laugh something the bards had written dozens of songs about. But it was her love of her people that was remembered the most, the way she'd held the sick, the wounded, the weary. She wasn't a typical queen. She'd rather have been in the streets of the City of Lockes instead of sitting on the throne. There was nary a day when she hadn't been out in the city, listening to anyone and everyone who needed their voices heard. It was because of her that more schools had opened in the Slums. It was because of her that shelters had been placed throughout the city to protect the homeless. It was because of her a generation learned how to read and write. She was the People's Queen, and though my father ruled over the most prosperous age Verania had ever seen, it was she who they adored.

And she had died while giving birth to me. There wasn't anything nefarious about it, as far as anyone could tell. These things sometimes happened, a dark twist of fate that no one could've prepared for.

Two weeks after I was born, I was presented to the people of Verania, my father holding me on a balcony of Castle Lockes that overlooked the city. Dad like to remind me (when he was a little deep in his cups) that I was dressed in all lace, blinking slowly at the sounds rising around us. I was told people cheered and cried at the sight, saying that I carried the spirit of my mother within me.

I didn't always make things easy, but I knew he needed me just as much as I needed him. Still, knowing she had died giving birth to me weighed heavily, an encroaching cold that numbed me from the inside out. As one might imagine, it made me...difficult, to say the least.

*****

"WHO IS THAT?" I asked, voice filled with derision. I was a teenager, which meant I was smarter than everyone else. It also meant I was an asshole.

I stared at a young, dirty boy, as he walked into the throne room, his eyes wide, mouth moving a mile a minute. He trailed after Morgan of Shadows.

The man next to me, a portly fellow with a sunny smile, laughed quietly. "His name is Sam," Pete said. "Pain in my arse, but he's a good kid. Tends to get in trouble more often than not, but a good kid nonetheless."

"Why is he here?" I asked, mouth twisting in disdain. "He better not touch any of my stuff. I don't want to get fleas."

Pete cuffed the back of my head. "Don't be a jerk, your Majesty. He's a handful, but he's not all bad. Morgan sees something in him the rest of us can't. And if Morgan says it, then it must be true."

I scoffed. "Wizards don't know better than the rest of us. And even *if* he does have magic, that doesn't mean he has what it takes to learn from Morgan and Randall."

"Perhaps," Pete said. "But this boy is different." He leaned toward me, dropping his voice. "Turned a bunch of bullies into stone in the Slums, my Prince."

I eyed the boy warily as he tugged on Morgan's sleeve, causing the wizard to bend over. The boy whispered in his ear, punctuating each of his words with wild waves of his hands. He looked…loud. I didn't like loud. I wasn't impressed, even if he had turned people to stone.

*****

"I'll never see the boy again," I told myself as he moved into the castle with his mother and father.

"I'll never see the boy again," I told myself as it was announced he would become a wizard's apprentice.

"I'll never see the boy again," I told myself as I ran into him in the halls of Castle Lockes for the hundredth time.

"Don't worry about him," I told Ryan Foxheart as I trailed my finger along his muscular forearm. "We won't ever see the boy again."

"I never want to see you again," I snarled at the boy when he kept staring at my boyfriend with a look of misplaced lust and awe. He squeaked and ran in the opposite direction.

"Well, this sucks," I said to no one after I was kidnapped by a sexually aggressive dragon. "At least I'll never have to see him again."

And as we stood atop the dragon's keep so far from home, I did what my father had taught me and spoke only truth, telling a knight that a certain wizard thought he was a cornerstone, the building block for all things magic, a tether to keep the wizard from turning Dark. A voice in my head—a small voice but there all the same—said I was *wrong*, that I was making things *worse*, that I was only lashing out because I felt threatened, and isn't that what my father had warned me about? Isn't this *exactly* what he said a king shouldn't do? Stabbing where it would hurt the most, spilling blood in the form of great secrets, letting the shadows melt away to pull the truth kicking and screaming into the light.

It should've made me feel better. The look of heartbreak on Sam of Wild's face should've been exactly what I was looking for. It was intentional, this, and while love and hope was a weapon, so was reality. So was the truth. It could hurt in expert hands, and I aimed to pierce his heart and leave as much destruction in the wake as possible.

My plan—such as it was—to destroy Sam of Wilds so he'd never again stand with his head held high in my presence, had finally been enacted. I didn't need him. I didn't need *any* wizard, no matter what my father said. Magic muddled everything. If I had my way, the line of King's Wizard would end with Morgan of Shadows, and I'd usher in a new age to Verania, an age of logic and reason and technology without the need for magic. We would become a glorious beacon for all the world to witness, and in the end, people would thank me for opening their eyes as to the truth of wizards.

Except Sam of Wilds didn't know how to *go the fuck away*.

Because for some godsdamn reason, this boy decided that I *needed* him, that he was going to be the best King's Wizard the kingdom had ever seen. And even worse—even more than stealing my fiancé—he became entrenched in the belief that I was going to be his best friend and therefore, needed to be everywhere that I was.

And maybe—*just maybe*—I could have ended it all. I could've figured out a way to finally be rid of Sam of Wilds, to make him so miserable that he left of his own volition, returning to where he came from, never to bother me again. Even if he made me laugh once or twice begrudgingly, he was still a walking catastrophe, more often than not putting us in impossible situations that defied all explanation.

And I would have gotten away with it too had it not been for that pesky thing called destiny.

I knew my destiny. I was to follow in the footsteps of my father and become King of Verania. It was what I'd been training for all my life. I knew the rules and laws of Verania like the back of my hand. I could speak in front of crowds of thousands without sweating. I could handle myself in battle, my sword an extension of my hand. I could fight for my kingdom, for that which I believed in, protecting the meek and the fearful, standing for those who couldn't stand for themselves. I knew what I would become. I knew *who* I would become.

But destiny is a fickle thing. It's indiscriminate, and even if the gods had the worst sense of humor ever created, it still called upon those whose future was written in the stars.

The ending of all I had planned arrived with a woman from the desert, a woman named Vadoma who came to Castle Lockes with an ominous warning. Darkness was coming to Verania, and we would know the true meaning of the word suffering unless the boy from the Slums rose up and answered the call of destiny.

And I was *pissed.*

I didn't know at who. Sam, definitely. Vadoma, absolutely. Her little idiot sidekick, Ruv? Hell yes. Dad for believing it, Randall and Morgan for already knowing more than they'd said, Gary and Tiggy and Kevin for going along with it like they always did.

And Ryan. Ryan Foxheart who took one look at Ruv, who was supposedly the true cornerstone to Sam of Wilds, and decided—in his infinite wisdom—that the only thing to do was to have a godsdamn *pull up contest* to prove he was better than his new opponent.

The world had gone mad.

I didn't believe Vadoma.

I was wrong.

Because as much as I hated the idea of destiny, Sam of Wilds hated it even more. I watched as he snapped and scoffed through his fear and worry, always a quick retort in the face of something so ridiculous. I had to tamp down on the strange feeling of pride that roared through me. It wasn't what I was supposed to feel about Sam. And now he was being told that the future of my country rested upon his stupidly skinny shoulders?

Fuck that. And fuck him.

I felt torn in two as I silently cheered Sam as he denied his destiny. Why did I give a shit about what he did? If Vadoma was right, there was the potential that she'd take him away to the desert city of Mashallaha and that would be that. Problem solved. Sam would be gone, and we could forget that he'd ever existed.

And then he actually left, taking the others on a stupid adventure involving dragons and stars, the fate of Verania resting upon them. "Good riddance," I told myself as I watched them leave. "Never come back."

It started the next day, a quiet whisper at the back of my mind. I ignored it as best as I could, but it was always there, fluttering like a little bird. On the third day after their departure, I was walking through the castle, and the sound of footsteps came rushing up behind me. Without thinking, I snapped, "Sam, would you just leave me alone? I don't need you to follow me wherever I go."

Except it wasn't Sam. It was a maid on her way toward the kitchens. She smiled at me, a thin, wavering thing that didn't quite reach her eyes, nodding at the half-hearted apology I tossed at her. She rushed by me without a word, and it was then I realized something: I missed the boy I never wanted to see again.

A fluke, I reassured myself. A momentary lapse of judgment. That's all it was. With that, I tried to push Sam out of my mind.

It didn't work.

I was outraged; it seemed he'd somehow infected me to give a damn about him. He'd cast some sort of spell to make me care that he was gone. It was the only thing that made sense.

I went directly to Morgan in his lab, demanding he fix me by removing whatever magic Sam had placed upon me without my permission. "It's a violation," I snarled at Morgan. "I never wanted this. I never *asked* for this."

Morgan didn't speak a word, raising his hands, holding them a few inches away from my body as the tips of his fingers twitched, the skin around his eyes tightening. It felt like it went on for hours, and when he finished, he stepped back, lips quirking. "I've found the source of your problem."

I knew it. I *knew* Sam had done something to me. "What is it? Do you have a counter spell that can fix it? I swear to the gods, when he comes back, it's straight to the dungeons with him. How dare he think he could enchant me with—"

"It's your heart," Morgan said.

That…didn't sound good. "What's wrong with my heart?"

"You have one."

I blinked, unsure of what the hell he was talking about. "I know that," I said slowly, worried that Sam's deviousness had gotten to Morgan too, addling his mind.

"Do you?" Morgan asked. "Because I'm not sure you do. It's not magic, Prince. It's nothing Sam did, at least not directly. You've been afflicted by the same thing that seems to happen to people who come into contact with him."

I blanched. "Oh no. Is it fungal?" A million thoughts ran through my head, each worse than the last. He had to have gotten it from the Dark Woods. Always spending time in there, even though he knew how dangerous it could be. Hell, he'd gone into the woods and come back with Gary and Tiggy. Look how *that* worked out. "Am I dying? Beheading! We're going to bring back beheading, and Sam is going to be the first. I *knew* he was—"

"I'm afraid it's much more serious than a fungus," Morgan said gravely.

I slumped down in a chair, my legs unable to support me. "What on earth could be more serious than a fungal infection on my heart?"

"You're having feelings," Morgan said, and I swore he was trying his hardest not to laugh.

I jerked my head up, eyes narrowed. "Feelings? Is that wizard speak for something awful and dangerous?"

Morgan patted my shoulder. "Worse. Your heart isn't infected with fungus, Prince. You have found yourself—quite impossibly, given how hard you've tried to fight it—caring about your wizard. That ache in your chest, that little voice that never seems to go away? That's because you're human. It's not physical. It's emotional. You miss Sam."

I laughed, long and loud, unaware that Morgan of Shadows was attempting to moonlight as a comedian. I resented the fact that he was attempting to workshop his new material on me.

I stopped laughing when Morgan didn't join in. Instead, he arched an eyebrow.

I said, "What."

"Somehow, Sam has wormed his way into your heart," Morgan said. "He has carved a place for himself within you. And I think you know that."

I stood abruptly, the chair scraping along the stone floor. "How dare you," I said coldly. "I don't have *feelings* for Sam of Wilds." I paused, considering. "No good feelings, anyway. He's hotheaded, never takes things seriously, and always, *always* finds a way to drag me into whatever mess he's created, even when I proclaim quite loudly that I want nothing to do with him. Yes, he's sometimes funny in the same way that street dogs are when they perform tricks for food and *yes*, I've somewhat forgiven him for the whole getting me kidnapped by a dragon thing *and yes*, I might be a little worried about what's happening to him now that he's out of my sight because that idiot is likely to set himself and everything around him on fire, and who's going to put him out when he does? Gary? He'll just screech and moan while Kevin tells Sam he's never looked hotter, and Tiggy will try and smother the flames, but instead will most likely crush Sam, and *Ryan*. Don't even get me started on Ryan. He'll try to be dashing and immaculate and carry Sam toward the closest river to put him out when everyone knows Sam hates getting thrown in rivers when he's on fire and why do I know that? *Because it happens all the godsdamn time*. And I'm so pissed off that I have to stay behind while my best friend goes out into the world because of *destiny*."

"There it is," Morgan said, looking pleased with himself.

I choked on my tongue as I came to a terrifyingly stark realization: Sam of Wilds was my best friend. And not just a *normal* best friend. No. Somehow, against my will, Sam had become the one thing I thought impossible.

He was my Best Friend 5eva, capitalized so I knew it was true.

"What," I said faintly, "the fuck."

"Indeed," Morgan said. "You love him. Against your better judgment, against everything you know to be true, you love him. Your heart hurts because he's gone. That little voice in your head is there because you're worried about him. There hasn't been a time since Sam arrived at the castle—disregarding that business with Kevin—when the two of you have been apart for any length of time." He sighed. "He has a way of sneaking up on you. I saw him for what—*who* he was. Just a child, but capable of magic I'd never thought possible. I've watched as he's grown, leaving the trappings of childhood behind, becoming the man I always thought he'd be. And if Vadoma is right, he'll save us all. But it won't be without heartache." He hung his head. "He'll need you, Prince Justin, before the end. You have a part to play in all of this, and I fear there will be darkness before we once again step into the light."

"I never wanted this," I whispered. "I never asked for any of this."

"And yet it's there all the same," Morgan said gently. "Destiny isn't arbitrary. It'll find you, whether you want it or not. It has found Sam. He'll become who he's supposed to be."

"Is she right?" I asked. "Is everything Vadoma said true?"

Morgan did not answer.

\*\*\*\*\*

It almost didn't matter if Vadoma was right, or if I believed her. Because *Sam* believed her. Sam, who watched as Morgan was taken from him. Sam, who gazed upon his unconscious cornerstone in that billowing white room. Sam, who took it upon himself to enter the Dark Woods with the dragons of Verania, all in the name of the gods.

I didn't like to think about the eleven months that followed very much. The people we lost. The time taken from us. Our home—the *throne*—in Myrin's control. Morgan gone. Randall only gods knew where. My father imprisoned in the dungeons. And the people. *My* people.

My father was right: they looked at me to lead them, to guide them through our new existence. I didn't know what I was doing. It was as if everything I'd been taught had left me. I was terrified, more so than I'd been in my entire life. I was a child playing pretend. Nothing could have prepared me for this.

But I wasn't alone. I had Gary. And Tiggy. And Ryan and Joshua and Rosemary. Even Lady Tina and the contingent she surrounded herself with, women who I wouldn't dream of crossing as they had a tendency to be fanatically terrifying. I had the will of the people behind me, an undying spark that could never be extinguished, no matter what was thrown at us.

So we did the only thing we could: we gathered together, planning, waiting for the sign that it was time to rise up and fight back.

It came, eventually.

Nearly a year later, it finally came.

A wizard returned from the Dark Woods, but he was Sam of Wilds no longer.

Sam of Dragons had come home.

\*\*\*\*\*

That should have been the end. A happily ever after. The boy from the Slums had accepted his destiny and become a wizard of almost unlimited power, defeating the evil that had shrouded our home in shadows. We had suffered loss, yes, but those of us who remained would carry on their legacy with every action we took. Sam and Ryan were married. My father sat upon the throne, Morgan of Shadows at his side where he belonged. Tiggy had more brooms than he knew what to do with, and Gary and Kevin engaged in acts of sexual congress that broke at least sixty-seven laws. The City of Lockes—and all the cities and towns and villages touched by Myrin's darkness—would be rebuilt. We would see to it. The Great White returned to the Dark Woods. The ice dragons—Pat and Leslie—went home to the snowy north, proclaiming their feathers didn't do well being so close to the sea. Zero Ravyn Moonfire went back to sleep for a hundred years in the safety of the desert, the people of Mashallaha promising to watch over him as he slumbered.

All would be well. We would never forget the lessons we had learned, and we knew that no matter what was thrown our way, we would meet it head on. Together.

An ending.

But not *the* end, not by a long shot.

Because something else was coming, something much more diabolical than anything we had ever faced.

A king from a faraway land was coming to Verania, to the City of Lockes, all with one purpose: to have a promise honored, one made the day before my mother's death.

A promise of the firstborn of the King and Queen of Verania, to take the hand in marriage of the firstborn of the King and Queen of Yennbridge.

Which meant me.

# CHAPTER 2

# My Poll Numbers Are Bigger Than Yours, So Suck It

B UT THAT WOULD COME SOON ENOUGH.

This was now.

"My *hooves*," Gary groaned as we approached the gates to the City of Lockes. "Someone had better rub them when we get back or there is going to be a significant amount of bitching on my part. Fair warning."

Tiggy was back with Ryan, explaining just how brave he'd been, that he'd punched the wall so hard it'd cracked. Ryan seemed amused, telling him that all caves would now cower in fear at the sight of Tiggy. This pleased the giant greatly.

Sam hadn't said a word since we'd left the cave. I walked next to him, glancing over out of the corner of my eye. He looked lost in thought, his expression slightly vacant and slack. I wouldn't say that he'd grown quieter since his return from the Dark Woods the year before, but he'd...matured? Sort of. He wasn't as prone to announce every little thought running through his head, but when he smiled, it didn't always reach his eyes the way it used to.

I didn't push because I didn't know if it was my place. He had the others for that, intrusive little pests who knew too much about each other for it to be even remotely healthy. I was curious but didn't let it get too far. Curiosity led to disaster, especially when Sam was involved.

But still, I didn't like quiet Sam. I cleared my throat, deciding on what to say. "Did that go as you'd hoped?"

He startled. "What?"

"The kidnapping. Did you get what you wanted out of it?"

"I guess," he said. He frowned as he looked at his palm, his chicken-scratch writing smudged. "Didn't get to my backstory as much as I'd have liked, but that's okay."

"Because there's always next time, right?"

"Sure," he said. "Next time."

He was frustrating when he spoke too much, and frustrating when he really didn't say anything at all. I'd long given up on a happy medium between the two. "Just…give me a head's up, okay? I had meetings this afternoon with my father's council."

He laughed quietly. "Oh please. You were looking for any excuse not to attend. It's always boring as shit."

He wasn't wrong. Sitting in one of the meeting rooms, listening as stuffy men and women droned on about all the minute details involving Verania was enough to drive anyone mad. The gatherings could often go on for hours, and Dad was prone to falling asleep part way through as people shouted over each other, Morgan at his side, always watching. Anything Dad needed to know, Morgan would tell him after.

Dad had been inviting me more and more to these meetings, saying it was part of becoming a king. I needed to know everyone's name and their roles in the machine that was Verania. A king cannot be caught unaware, he'd said time and time again. When I reminded him that he'd been snoring the last time, he grinned at me. "A king must also get his rest when he's able."

"Maybe," I said to Sam. "Morgan won't be happy. You were supposed to be there too." I knew no matter what mood Sam was in, the mere mention of his mentor would be enough to chase away whatever Sam was feeling. Manipulative, sure, but I didn't care.

"Yeah," Sam said. "He's going to be so pissed. I can't wait. You think he'll yell at me?"

I sniffed as we approached the gates of the City of Lockes, the sounds of our home already washing over me. "Probably. And when they ask, you'll take full responsibility for all of this. If I hear you trying to put any blame on me, you'll be pooping into a bucket by nightfall."

Sam waggled his eyebrows at me. "Promises, promises. You'd miss me too much."

"Bullshit," I growled. "I'd finally get some peace and quiet. In fact, why don't we just do that now. Report to the dungeons, Sam of Dragons. I'll let you know when the trial date is set for the kidnapping of the Prince of Verania. It will not go well for you. I have at least seven people who will testify to the deficits of your character."

"Only seven? Man, I've been slacking off."

"You really have," I agreed. "Don't let it happen again."

He bumped his shoulder against mine. "Thanks, Justin."

I scowled at him. "I didn't do anything. And when we're surrounded by my subjects, you will refer to me as Prince Justin. Or Your Majesty. I'll even allow Your Excellency, if that suits you better."

"Oh, of course," he said, and I *knew* he was mocking me. "Why, the very idea of any familiarity with a man who I've seen shit in the woods is obviously a mistake. My apologies, Justin. Oh, *excuse* me. My apologies, Your Greatness."

Before I could stab him, the massive gates of the City of Lockes opened, groaning as they did so.

And there, standing in a shiny suit of armor, blond hair pulled back, arms folded across her chest as she tapped a foot impatiently, was the leader of my personal guard. A woman so fierce that the mere mention of her name was enough to strike fear in the hearts of anyone who knew her. A woman so strong, she defied belief. A woman who once ran the Ryan Foxheart Fan Club Castle Lockes Chapter with an iron fist, ruling over a group of fangirls who apparently wrote quite explicit fanfiction about Rystin and HaveHeart, two words I wished I'd never had to learn in my life.

A woman who had betrayed Sam, but then proved herself to be trustworthy in his absence. A tool, a weapon against the rising tide of evil. A woman who Sam was convinced (still!) was his most mortal of enemies.

Lady Tina DeSilva.

"*You*," Sam snarled.

She arched a perfectly shaped eyebrow. "Me," she said. "Thank you for recognizing my existence. I can't say I'd do the same for you. In fact, I won't." She dismissed him immediately, much to Sam's outrage. "My Prince," she said, bowing low, her armor clanking. "Your leaving the castle was not on the schedule. I assume it was because of the wizard. If you approve, I can have him drawn and quartered by nightfall. There are protocols in place, and a certain individual ignored them all, putting you in jeopardy. Again."

"Ha," Sam said. "Shows what you know. Justin loves me too much to ever allow you to kill me. Right, Justin?"

I picked a fleck of dirt out from underneath my fingernail.

"Justin?" Sam said again. "Right, Justin?"

I smiled at him. "The day isn't yet over. Why don't we table that for now and bring it up should the need arise?"

Lady Tina snorted obnoxiously.

"Sam gonna be quarters?" Tiggy asked.

"Probably," Gary said. "We should say our goodbyes now. Bye, Sam! Goodbye! It was so nice knowing you. Have fun being dead." He paused. "And after you die, you can't come back and haunt me. I have a fragile constitution. I wouldn't be able to stand Ghost Sam trying to keep me awake at night. You *know* I need fifteen hours of sleep in order to look as wonderful as I do."

"Lady Tina," I said through gritted teeth. "Report."

She snapped to attention. "Your guard has spent the morning training. I left them in the training fields when I was notified of your return to the castle."

"Your guard," Sam muttered as he made a face. "How fun."

Lady Tina glared at him. "The women have proven themselves time and time again. If they're good enough for the Prince, then they should be good enough for someone like you."

Uh oh. While mostly true, that probably wasn't the best thing to say. I could see Sam open his mouth to issue something he'd consider devastating but in actuality was mostly petty, so I stepped between the two of them. I faced Sam, pressing my hand against his chest, holding him back. "No."

"But—"

"Sam."

He deflated, rubbing the back of his neck. "Fine. But she's the worst, and you know it."

I didn't blame him for thinking that way. I wrestled with it for a long time, struggling to reconcile Lady Tina's actions with her perceived guilt over what she'd been a part of. In the end—unsure if Sam was ever going to come back—I'd made a deal with the devil, allowing her to remain free. Keep your friends close, keep your enemies closer.

It didn't hurt that Lady Tina proved to be good at what she did. Perhaps too good. She knew her way around a sword and had the uncanny ability to cement herself as a leader, even if her followers were more akin to a tittering cult than a group of knights. She'd earned my trust. She, along with her assassins, had taken out multiple high-ranking Dark Wizards, all without losing a single member of her team. They were utterly terrifying when they wanted to be (especially when Ryan Foxheart appeared; the youngest, Deidre, had a tendency to get what Sam called the "crying-vomits" which, unfortunately, was exactly as it sounded) and had transformed into an elite unit. I weighed the pros and cons, but in the end, decided that they had deserved a place at my side. Lady Tina knew quite clearly that the moment she stepped out of line I would see to her myself.

And here we were, a year later, and not much had changed. They sniped at each other whenever possible, Sam usually the aggressor. And while Lady Tina certainly didn't do much to hide her disdain for my wizard, she rolled with the punches, knowing that Sam had a point. I had to believe he could one day understand that Lady Tina wasn't the enemy, not anymore.

"I get it," I told Sam quietly, Lady Tina glaring at the both of us. "But I need you to back off, Sam."

Something flashed across Sam's face, something hard and black, but then it dissolved as he sighed. "Fine. But I reserve the right to bitch and moan to you later for at least an hour."

"And that would be different how?"

Sam shoved me away. "Asshole."

How we'd ever found ourselves in the position where he could call me that without fear of retribution, I'd never know. It certainly wasn't anything *I* did.

Lady Tina cleared her throat. "As much fun as this is—and believe me, so fun—I'm here for a reason." She reached into the sleeve in her armor, pulling out a scroll. She unfurled it, the edges curled, her writing on the scroll a ferocious shade of pink. "The latest poll numbers are in."

Gary rushed forward, almost knocking me down. "Yes, *yes*. I've been waiting weeks for this. Tell me everything people are saying about me. Except if it's bad. The only thing I'll need from you then are the names, physical description and addresses of those polled. So I can murd—I mean, so I can ask them how to be a better unicorn." He shifted his eyes side to side.

"Start with them," I said, waving my hand at Tina.

She grinned at me. "With pleasure." She looked down at her scroll. "Of the five hundred and twenty-seven people polled, eighty-six percent believe that Ryan Foxheart is the dreamiest dream to have ever been dreamed."

Ryan chuckled as he scratched the back of his neck. "Aw, shucks. That's too kind of them. I'm humbled by their support. Gosh, this is so sudden. I don't even know how to respond. I'm literally speechless. Did they say anything about my hair?"

"They did," Lady Tina said. "Seventy-two percent admitted to having fantasies about running their hands through it."

Ryan frowned. "That's lower than it was last time. Wow. That... uh. That hurts more than I thought it would."

Lady Tina continued, though her mouth twisted into a sneer. "Eighty-nine percent of those polled think that the unicorn is not a horse, and now that he has his horn back, ninety-*two* percent believe he should not be killed."

"Ha!" Gary crowed. "You hear that, Foxheart? I'm more popular than you! Suck it!"

"That can't be right," Ryan said. "Let me see the numbers. You probably wrote them down wrong."

Lady Tina pulled the scroll back. "I assure you the numbers are correct. Seventy-five percent of those polled agree that Kevin has hit on them at one point or another. A smaller percentage said they were flattered. One person polled said he did not regret the three-way he had with Kevin and Gary, though he does have questions about where to submit the invoice for property damage."

"Ah," Kevin said. "That would be Miguel. Feisty fellow. Quite a good dicking, if you ask me. He didn't seem to mind that I destroyed his farm while he was riding my—"

"One hundred percent agree that Tiggy is made of literal sunshine and must be protected at all costs."

"Hard out there for a pimp," Tiggy said as he—inexplicably—fist-bumped himself.

"And Sam," Lady Tina said, voice sticky sweet. "Would you like to hear your numbers?"

Sam played it cool and aloof. "Doesn't matter to me one way or another. I know my self-worth. I'm a wizard—"

"Apprentice," Gary coughed. Then, "Oh. Wait. Right. That's not true anymore. Yet another pleasurable thing taken from me because of him, not that I'm keeping track. That was a lie. I'm definitely keeping track."

"Sam has a forty-two percent approval rating," Lady Tina said gleefully, and I *knew* blood was about to be spilled. "Most polled agreed that Sam is loud, obnoxious, makes too many jokes about sex, and is a little too similar to characters they'd read about in a book called…hold on. I have it—ah, yes. *The Butler and the Manticore*. Sounds positively dreadful. Oh, and that his sense of humor was only enjoyed by a select few, most of whom have questionable judgment. How curious."

"*What?*" Sam demanded. "What the hell are you talking about? I'm hysterical! Everyone thinks so!"

"There, there," Gary purred, rubbing his snout against Sam's cheek. "You certainly are acting hysterical. And just because almost everyone thinks I'm better than you, doesn't mean it's true. Ha, just kidding. That's exactly what it means. It's in a poll, and everyone knows poll numbers are completely accurate and can't be questioned."

"And Prince Justin," Lady Tina said. "I have your numbers here too."

"Go ahead," I said, though I was nervous. I'd never really paid much attention to polling, but Dad said it was important that I understand the will of the people, fickle though they could be.

She cleared her throat uncomfortably. "Perhaps we should do this alone."

"It's fine." It was not fine.

"Your…ah, numbers have dropped a little. Um. Let's see. Of those polled, you have a…ahem. Thirty-two percent approval rating."

What the hell? That was a fifteen-point drop in two months, and I hadn't even *done* anything.

Lady Tina winced. "The majority of those polled indicated that the Prince Justin who led the resistance in the Port is not the Prince Justin they see now. They see you as cold and calculating. They're… worried that when the time comes for the King to step down, you won't be ready to take his place. There might have even been a few that said they thought you'd make things…well. Worse. But!" she added quickly. "Your father has a ninety-six percent approval rating, so, silver lining?"

"It's okay," Sam said, patting my shoulder. "They don't know what they're talking about. Neither does Tina, but then she never does."

I shrugged his hand off in anger. I didn't have time for something as ridiculous as poll numbers. The people didn't always know what was best for them. I did. I'd led them once, and I could lead them again. I'd show them. I'd show them all, and when they apologized, I'd be magnanimous and only make them beg for my forgiveness for three weeks. "Thank you, Lady Tina. That will be all."

She nodded as she rolled up the scroll, sliding it back into her sleeve. "Your father wishes to speak with you, Prince. He's in the castle, overseeing the preparations for tomorrow's Liberation Day Ball."

Liberation Day, the new national holiday to celebrate the anniversary over the defeat of Myrin. Dad thought it would be good to allow the people to have a day off and come together in order to celebrate their accomplishments over the last year. The City of Lockes was mostly restored, with the repairs of Meridian City and Mashallaha scheduled to be completed by the end of the year. We'd worked our asses off to bring back Verania to its former glory. It'd been hard work, and I'd spent weeks helping to clear the rubble of Myrin's wrath, joined by countless people who wanted to once again feel safe in their homes.

(But apparently not hard enough to make them like me, what the fuck.)

Dad loved parties. I could live without them, but he said they were important, especially this one. It would be the first time we'd all come together, delegations arriving from all over the country in order to hear the words of their king. Dad was going all out, and the wine would flow, the food plentiful, music and dancing going on late into the night. Dad had hired all the chefs in the City of Lockes, having them prepare the largest feast the city had ever seen. All the people of Lockes would be included.

"Noted," I said. "I'll return to the castle in a moment. Lady Tina, you're dismissed. Tell the guard that I'm proud of their hard work, and that I'll be by later this week to check up on their training."

Lady Tina flushed as she bowed, one hand curling into a fist and tapping against the armor covering her chest. "Thank you, Prince. They'll be overjoyed to hear it." She whirled on her heels and disappeared into the crowd.

I turned back toward the others, only to find Sam and Ryan in a whispered conversation. Ryan looked perturbed, though he tried not to show it. Sam shook his head, squeezing Ryan's hand before taking a step back. "I'll be fine."

"I know that, Sam," Ryan said. "I can go with you, if you want."

"Nah," Sam said, going for breezy and not quite getting there. "I'll be back later. Tell Morgan that I'll meet him in the labs when I come home, okay?"

Ryan looked like he was going to argue but nodded instead. "Sure. Anything you want."

"Thanks, boo," Sam said, smacking a kiss on Ryan's cheek. He waved at me before leaving, his head bowed.

"We'll go with him," Gary said. "Keep an eye on him, make sure he doesn't get seduced by a man with a higher approval rating than you. Like myself."

"And me," Tiggy said cheerfully.

"And also me," Kevin said.

Ryan squinted up at him. "You…you do know how numbers work, right? Mine were higher than yours."

"Aw," Kevin said. "Look at you. A big, brave knight who thinks he's special. Who's a big brave knight? Is it you? Is it *you*? You dumb puppy with your stupid hair."

"Don't listen to him," Gary told Ryan. "If it makes you feel any better, I think your hair is divine."

"Really?" Ryan asked, puffing out his chest.

"No," Gary snapped. "It looks like a mangy dog died in an explosion that blew off all its legs. Honestly, Ryan, your neediness is unbecoming of a Knight Commander. Have some self-respect." He rolled his eyes as he looked at Kevin. "Can you believe this guy?"

Tiggy patted Ryan on the head. "I think you're pretty."

"Thank you, Tiggy—"

"You'd be lost without us!" Gary called back as they began to follow Sam. "And don't worry, we're not going to talk about you behind your back! Lolz, I'm kidding again. We're so going to do that. In fact, we'll start right now. Did you *see* Ryan's hair today? My gods, someone should really talk to him about it before we need to have an intervention."

And then they were gone, leaving only Ryan and myself.

"I love them," Ryan said.

"I know."

"They make me want to punch a wall."

"I know that too. Come on, I don't want to leave my father waiting."

Ryan fell in step beside me as we headed for the castle.

\*\*\*\*\*

IN PREPARATION FOR the Liberation Day Ball, the City of Lockes had been transformed. Banners hung from buildings and lampposts, my father's face smiling down. New flowers had been planted along most of the walkways, bright bursts of green, gold, indigo and blue. Vendors were already setting up their wares, hocking trinkets and baubles, sweet breads and frozen treats. Many had posters with my likeness on them. I'd posed for the painting a few weeks back, the artist demanding that I look as royal as possible. "I need ta zee da *true* Prince," he cried in his melodic accent, brush flying, paint splattering his face and the floor. "Give me vat dey desire. Make me *believe*."

I hadn't known what the fuck he was talking about, so I'd winged it as best I could. It hadn't turned out too bad. I stopped at one of the booths, eyeing the poster. In it, I wore tight black trousers, and a buff jerkin made of the finest leather. My sword was in my hand, silver crown atop my head. Perhaps he'd made my jawline too severe, my brown hair a bit too long (and I definitely wasn't as muscular as he made me out to be), but it wasn't bad. There'd certainly been worse.

"Looks good," Ryan said, coming to stand at my side, the vendor looking like he was about to faint at the sight of us. I smiled at the vendor, causing him to stumble back against the wall behind him, hands on his chest.

"It is what it is," I said. I turned away from the booth with a nod at the shocked man. "I don't have time for such things."

Ryan snorted. "Of course not. What was I thinking?"

"You weren't," I said. "But that's to be expected. I'm sure Sam has rattled your mind to the point where it's nothing but a gelatinous mess."

"You wound me, Justin."

If you'd told me a few years ago that I'd be walking through the streets of the city with Ryan at my side, talking the way we were, I'd have thought you were out of your godsdamned mind.

But life has a funny way of showing what was most important when you least expect it. After all we'd been through, I'd let go of old grudges. They seemed petty and insignificant in the face of the darkness that had almost swallowed Verania whole.

Which is why I asked, "Is Sam all right?"

Ryan hesitated before shaking his head. "He's…Sam."

"I know. That's why I asked."

He looked around as if to make sure we weren't being overheard. Smart that, as people tended to gossip. Even now, I could see people staring at us, whispering behind their hands. Part of it was them still getting used to seeing me out and about in the city, something I hadn't done much in the past. Instead of hiding away in the castle or out at the training fields, I'd taken to walking the streets of the city, trying to learn all of its secrets, all the little nooks and crannies that I would one day rule. Dad had suggested it over and over when I was younger, but I hadn't understood the importance. I did now. The city was alive in ways I hadn't expected, the people its blood, the castle its beating heart. If one part of the whole failed, we all would.

"He's having a hard time," Ryan admitted. "It's gotten a little better, but he still has nightmares at least once a week."

I frowned. "About what?"

"Me," Ryan said in a low voice. "And what he thinks himself capable of."

"Meaning…"

Ryan studied me for a moment. "Has he told you much about what happened with Myrin and the Darks?"

Bits and pieces, enough for the picture to start to take shape. I never pushed, sure that when Sam was ready, he'd speak up. He always did, even if the situation demanded his silence. "A little," I said. "I know you…died."

Ryan winced. "Yeah. Still not quite used to hearing that. But it's a bit more than that. He…" He shook his head. "Between you and me?"

"Of course."

"There was a moment when he…that level of power in him, I don't know if any one person was meant to have it. But he does, and while he's used it for good—"

I coughed.

"*Mostly* good," Ryan amended, "but he almost lost control. He came close to wiping out all the Darks at once. Not just Myrin. Not just Ruv. All of them. Every Dark in the city. Maybe all of the Darks in Verania."

I stopped in my tracks, my stomach dropping down to my feet. "Seriously?"

"Seriously."

"And that's bad because…"

"Because that would've been a form of genocide," Ryan said, not unkindly. "Regardless of what they'd done, Sam isn't the type of person to murder large groups of people indiscriminately. But with all that happened to him in the Dark Woods, there was a moment he said that he almost lost control. It was there, in the back of his mind. He said it would have been easy. All it would've taken was a little push, and he could have killed them all." His throat bobbed. "And when we were in that weird cosmic plane with Myrin and the Star Dragon, I could feel his anger, his despair. He almost gave in to it."

"Gods," I breathed. "What stopped him?"

"He says it was me."

I looked over at him. "Do you believe that?"

Ryan shrugged awkwardly. "Maybe. At the very least, I was part of it. But I know Sam. I may have gotten through to him in the end, but he made the choice to pull back his power. There's a reason the gods chose him as they did."

I scoffed. "Screw them. Screw all the gods. They could have chosen to finish this long before it ever came to that. And Morgan and Randall should've told him the truth ages ago. They knew what he was. They knew what he'd become."

"You don't like them much, do you?"

I did and I didn't. Morgan, I could get a handle on, mostly because he'd been my father's wizard long before I was born. Randall, on the other hand, was an irritating enigma. What they'd done in order to stop Myrin was tragic, but it was still no excuse for keeping the truth from Sam. I hadn't quite found forgiveness for that. Morgan knew it too, though I'd never told him directly. Randall didn't give two shits either way.

"It's complicated," I said lamely. It felt like an excuse. "I know they thought they were doing right by him, but I question the choices they made."

"Yeah," Ryan said. "You're not the only one. I was pissed at them too but maintaining that level of anger drove me crazy. And then Morgan came back and I just…I don't know. I had to let it go, for myself, but mostly for Sam. Losing Morgan like that almost killed him."

"He's in control now?"

Ryan narrowed his eyes. "He is. You don't need to doubt him."

"I don't," I said honestly "But I have to make sure he's all right."

"Why?" Ryan asked.

Why, indeed. "Because he's my wizard."

"Annnnd…"

"And that's it," I said stiffly. "A King's Wizard is one of the most important positions one can have. I can't have someone at my side who's going to take me down with him."

"You love him," Ryan said, and I considered going for his sword. "And without capitalizing it, he's your best friend. You said as much when things were crazy. You need someone like him. And he needs someone like you. I can't be everything to him. That's not how relationships work. And yeah, he has me and his parents and the king and Gary and Tiggy and Kevin and Morgan and Randall and a bunch of dragons, but we're not you. You give him something we can't."

"And what's that?" I asked without meaning to. "Not that I care one way or another."

Ryan wasn't fooled. For all that he was—a bit of an imbecile, his attraction to aggravating wizard twinks a mark against his character—Ryan could still surprise me. His insights, while rare, often cut through to the heart of the matter. "You're two sides of the same coin." He held up his hands as I snarled at him. "Oh, stop it. You know it, I know it, we all know it. And the sooner you can admit it to yourself, the better off you'll be. He needs us, Justin. Now, more than ever."

I softened at the wistfulness in his voice. "For how long?"

"Probably forever. Or however long our forever will be. Don't you see? He had the option to live hundreds of years. He didn't want that. He didn't want to watch the rest of us grow old while he stayed the same. He'll age, just like you and I will."

And that was the decision that surprised me the most. Choosing mortality over a form of immortality. He wished for it, almost more than anything. It impressed me more than I cared to admit. I didn't know if I would have chosen the same if I were him.

"Forever is a long time," I groused.

"It is," Ryan agreed. "But as long as we're together, all of us, we'll make the most of it. We're the future of Verania."

I sighed. "Well, that seals it. We're fucking doomed."

He laughed, and after a time, I joined in. Screw the poll numbers. We were alive and together, and that's all that mattered. We wouldn't be caught off guard again.

Famous last words.

# CHAPTER 3

# Annoyingly Attractive Men with Beads in Their Beards

WE PARTED WAYS AT THE CASTLE, Ryan saying he needed to check on his knights to make sure they were ready for Liberation Day. My plan was to make an appearance at the celebration and then leave as soon as I could, stealing away out into the fields so I could hack and slash against the wooden practice dummies, keeping one eye toward the sky to make sure I wasn't kidnapped by another dragon.

The castle was abuzz, the staff working hard in preparation, their excitement palpable. People hurried by, almost crashing into each other as they carried crates of fruits and vegetables, large hunks of meat. Others hung banners along the walls, garland around banisters, flowers on almost every available surface. The air was thick with the stench of wet paint and dust, dozens of men and women scrubbing every chair, table, and floor tile until they sparkled.

Everyone who saw me smiled and bowed. And even though I didn't care much about poll numbers, I complimented as many of them as I could, relishing in the flush of their faces, eyes sparkling as they thanked me profusely. The castle was a well-oiled machine, and everyone in our employ was well cared for. Positions in the castle rarely opened up, as most who were hired stayed with us for years.

I made my way to the main ball room and found my father standing near the far wall with his hands on his hips, issuing directions to a man trying to hang an oversized painting. It wasn't until I got closer that I saw what the painting was: a Sam Special, my father a three-breasted giant towering over the City of Lockes, a thunderous expression on his face. Next to it was another painting with a cloth covering it.

"I thought you destroyed that," I muttered as I stopped next to him, nodding at my father's painted boobs.

Dad chuckled. "I'm never one to stifle artistic expression. It'll certainly be a topic of conversation."

That was an understatement. My father did not look good with breasts, especially three of them. Sam's mind was a scary place.

Dad wrapped an arm around my shoulders, tugging me close. My father had always been affectionate with those he cared for, but it'd taken me a long time to appreciate this. It wasn't until he'd been taken from me that I realized how much I'd lost. Seeing his dirty, scraggly face when we'd rescued him from the dungeons had almost been enough to break me completely. I swore right then and there that I'd never let a day go by without hugging him at least once. I'd kept that promise.

I breathed him in as he brushed his bearded chin against my forehead. "How'd the kidnapping go?"

I groaned. "Of course you knew about it."

"I did," Dad said, and I could hear the smile in his voice. "Thought you could use a day out of the castle, at least for a little while."

"This was the fifth time! In *three weeks*."

"It makes Sam feel better," Dad said, squeezing my shoulder. "He wants to prepare for any eventuality. It went well, I assume?"

I snorted. "Gary complained, Tiggy punched a wall, Kevin was obscene, Ryan didn't save me, and Sam monologed."

"Very well, then," Dad said. "Where is Sam, anyway?"

"The Slums. With Gary, Tiggy and Kevin."

Dad frowned. "Again? What's he doing there?"

I shook my head. "I don't know. Reliving past glory? Reminding himself where he came from? Slacking off on all his responsibilities? Take your pick."

"I don't believe that, not for a minute. I don't think you do, either."

No, I didn't. But it was easier to say. Remembering what Ryan had told me, I said, "He's all right. For now. If something changes, I'll let you know."

"Do that," Dad said. "I'll keep my eyes and ears open as well. If you think the ball would be too much for him to handle, we could always postpone."

As much as I wanted that—indefinitely—I knew it was better to get it done and over with and not have to worry about it for another year. "It'll be fine. He can survive one night with a smile on his face, especially since I have to do the same."

Dad chuckled. "You never did like all the pomp and circumstance. Always with your nose in a book, learning all that you could about being a king."

"I don't understand the point of it," I admitted. "We know what we did. Why do we have to put on a display?"

"Because it's not about us," Dad said. "It never has been. Such things are for the people, who need moments of happiness, to celebrate their triumphs. It's why I put so much money into the reconstruction of Verania, specifically into the Slums. They sustained most of the damage. It's high time they be lifted from poverty and be allowed to have hope, just the same as the rest of us."

We had wealth—perhaps too much of it—and the City of Lockes, for the most part, had never been left wanting. For the longest time, I thought we needed the poor and destitute to act as a balance, to keep the scales from tipping too far in one direction. Where there was the wealthy, there'd always be the poor. But in the last year, Dad had launched an initiative with Sam to revitalize the Slums, not only repairing the damage Myrin and the Darks had caused, but to give the people a chance at a better life. It was slow going, and mistakes were made; there were people who'd lived in poverty for so long, they didn't trust a hand reached out in an act of delayed kindness. But Dad had made the smart move of making Sam an ambassador of sorts, the face of the initiative.

And it'd worked. Not at first, but eventually. Sam's parents had gone with him, both of them well known throughout the Slums. Joshua and Rosemary Haversford led a group of healers and construction foremen, chefs and bakers, teachers, farmers whose crops had survived the fall of Verania. Every mouth was fed, every purse filled, homes rebuilt better than they were before, new schools opened, jobs given in the castle and throughout the city. Most had been grateful. Some had not, asking why it'd taken the coming of Myrin for the King to give a shit about them. They weren't wrong, and it wasn't until Dad himself had shown up a couple of weeks later, dressed in work clothes ready to give a hand, that they began to see he was serious. He spent weeks there performing back-breaking work, saying that while he was there, he wasn't royalty, he was merely a worker, taking orders from nervous people who couldn't quite believe the king of all people wanted to help lay brick.

They loved him, more than I thought possible. My father, though human and therefore capable of making mistakes, gave himself to his people every day. I aspired to be like him, but I didn't have the selflessness he had, the breadth of knowledge he carried from years of service to the crown. I didn't think I'd ever be as strong as him. How could anyone hope to live up to his legacy?

"For the people," I repeated slowly.

"For the people," Dad agreed. "The will of the people is the most important thing a king must acknowledge."

"Another lesson," I said, amused.

"We're always learning, Justin," Dad said. "Every minute of every day. We're always learning how to do better, to be better people. And yes, mistakes will be made, but so long as we learn from them, allow them to help us grow, then it's possible to avoid making the same mistakes in the future."

"Only to make new ones," I muttered.

"Saw the poll numbers, did you?"

I groaned. "I don't know what I'm doing wrong."

Dad shrugged. "No one ever said it was going to be easy. I wouldn't worry too much about it. You'll turn it around." He lifted his head, and I followed his gaze and watched as a woman climbed a ladder, rag in hand to polish the gilded sconces that hung along the walls. She grinned down at the man holding the base of the ladder. "They are the future of Verania," Dad said quietly. "Even I need to be reminded of that, every now and then. We must make the most of the time we have in this world, because if we don't, what's the point?"

I didn't know how to answer that, so I said nothing at all.

*****

THAT NIGHT, I SAT AT THE DESK in my chambers, staring out the window to the castle grounds below, lights from the City of Lockes flickering in the distance. The stars were bright. When I was young, I heard the stories of the heroes that had earned their place in the sky, diamond chips that flickered coldly. I'd wondered if I'd ever join those who had come before me. My father told me the gods were always listening, that I need but whisper my wishes to the stars, and all would come true. It seemed trite, this. Why would I need to ask for something when I had all I could ever want?

When I told my father this, he'd laughed. "Everything, you say? Don't you want to wish for impossible things?"

"Nothing is impossible," I said, twelve years old and already beyond such frivolity. "If you spend all your time wishing, you'll never accomplish anything. It's pointless, and worse, it's a waste of time."

"Pragmatism is the death of imagination," Dad said, amused. "You don't need to be so serious all the time, Justin. Allow yourself to be a child. The world will still be there waiting when you're older."

And now, here I was: older, and the world waited. I had a speech to give that was only half-written. Dad had offered the use of his personal speech writer, but I'd declined. I didn't like speaking another's words. If I was going to be king, I needed to have my words be my own.

The *problem* with that was everything I'd written so far had come out flat and banal. I'd been working on the speech for weeks, trying to remember how I'd felt when I'd spoken to my people in the Port, Sam having returned to us, the future still hidden in shadow. Hope, I'd said, was a weapon. *That* Justin had been pissed off and more than a little scared but refusing to show it. He'd been strong, capable. A leader. One might even say a king. I'd spoken from my heart, though it felt like a lie, a child playing dress up and pretending to be more important than he actually was. An imposter who people glommed onto because if they didn't, they'd be lost.

And now? How fickle their loyalties. Fucking poll numbers.

I sighed and dropped my pen, the ink splattering on the parchment. I needed a break, something to distract me. Tomorrow I'd find some visiting dignitary, someone with heated eyes and a knowing smirk. Someone to take to my bed and fuck all the doubts away, at least for a little while. It'd been too long since I'd allowed myself a moment of self-satisfaction. I might even remember his name when it was over.

And it wasn't as if I'd been celibate since my failed wedding. I was human, after all, and only twenty-seven years old. Shortly after Myrin had been defeated, I'd met a cocky lord with curly hair and crooked teeth. He'd bowed before me, bringing my hand to his mouth, lips scraping against my skin. It'd been at one of Dad's parties, and though I'd never seen the lord before, he made his intentions known almost immediately. We'd danced twice, Dad watching us from the throne with a small smile on his face.

I'd fucked that lord three times that night, his groans low and guttural. When we'd finished, he'd rolled over, chest heaving and slick with sweat. He'd grinned up at me, eyes sparkling. "That was good."

"I know it was," I'd said. "Do you see the door over there?"

He'd lifted his head, confused. "The one we walked through? What about it?"

"Use it," I'd said. "And speak not a word of this. Not that anyone would believe you."

He'd gaped at me. When I didn't speak again, he'd risen, gathering his discarded clothing. "I see they call you the Ice Prince for a reason."

I'd grinned at him, knowing it was mean. "What did you think would happen here? That I'd let you stay the night, and tomorrow, we'd get breakfast and make plans for the rest of our lives? You can't be that stupid."

The man—Elliot? Eduardo? Something like that—snorted, shaking his head. "I've been accused of far worse. But what if, Prince? What if we could be something?"

"You think too highly of yourself," I'd said, tone clearly indicating that I was over this conversation. "I don't have time for such things."

"You don't have time for love?"

I'd laughed, wild and bright. "That's what you think this is?"

"Of course not," the man said. "But what about what it *could* be?"

I'd waved him off. "I guess we'll never know. Of all the damnable luck. Don't forget your socks."

He had left soon after, muttering what I was sure were compliments under his breath.

There had been a couple of others, but I'd kept to a promise I'd made myself. I would never let anyone close like I'd let Ryan. It was too easy to have it blow up in my face. It was better to go it alone. Dad didn't agree, but then he'd been alone for years after the death of my mother. I'd never known him to take a shine to anyone in a romantic light. If he could do it, so could I.

And if that made me the Ice Prince, then so be it. The people would accept me as I was, or they wouldn't. It was that simple.

I stood from my desk, ready to dress for bed when a sound stopped me. I frowned, turning toward the door.

The knob creaked back and forth, as if someone stood on the other side, trying to gain access. I'd given my guards the night off, knowing they'd be too busy tomorrow to properly enjoy the festivities. My bedroom door was locked, but it appeared someone didn't quite get that message.

I moved quickly to a large armoire near my bed, pulling open the doors and grabbing my sword, letting the scabbard fall to the floor. It was late, nearly midnight, and the castle should've been silent. If whoever was on the other side of the door was up to no good, it'd be the last thing they did. Like Gary, it'd been too long since I'd stabbed anything.

I went to the door, sword at the ready. If they thought they could assassinate me in my own chambers, they were sorely mistaken. I would spill their blood, and then I'd find whoever sent them, and spill *their* blood too. They would regret the day they'd ever even considered such a foolish plan.

In one smooth motion, I lifted the lock and opened the door, knuckles white around the grip of my sword.

And there, standing on the other side in the hall, was a man.

His eyes widened as he stumbled back, tripping over his feet and almost falling. He didn't carry a weapon that I could see, but that didn't mean it wasn't hidden away. Or if he was a wizard, he wouldn't need a weapon. He could be gathering his magic, ready to curse me somehow, or turn me into a sheep. It'd happened once before. Quite by accident, Sam had said, though he was laughing too hard for it to be remotely believable, and it'd been made worse when Gary had suggested that I should be shaved, my wool to be used to knit him a new scarf.

"You're not going to turn me into a sheep," I snarled at the man, pressing the point of my sword against his throat, the skin dimpling.

"What?" the man croaked out. "I'm not trying to do that! Bro, stand down. Legit!"

I looked left and right quickly. The hallway was empty, the firelight flickering in the sconces. If this man was an assassin, he appeared to be working by himself. That annoyed the hell out of me. Did they really think it would take only one person to kill me? Fucking amateurs.

I pressed the sword into his throat just a *little* bit harder. The man swallowed thickly, Adam's apple bobbing up and down. "What are you doing here?"

"I'm lost," the man spluttered. "I got turned around trying to find—"

"Spoken exactly like an assassin trying to catch me off guard," I said flatly.

The man's eyes bulged. "An *assassin*? I've never assassinated anyone!"

I scoffed. "Likely story. Who are you? What are you doing here?"

"I'm trying to find the bathroom!"

"The bathroom," I repeated slowly.

He nodded, head jerking up and down, chin hitting the blade of my sword. I'd never seen him before, so I didn't think he was staff. Even if I didn't know all their names, I knew their faces. I took a step toward him, bending my arm to keep from running him through.

The man looked to be a few years older than me, perhaps thirty or thereabouts. His black hair was shorn on the sides of his head, leaving a longer length on top, pulled back into a messy bun held together by a metal clasp inlaid with milky pearls. The lobes of his ears were lined with earrings, a half-dozen small silver hoops linked together by thin chains. A similar ring—though larger—hung from his nose, the ends curling up through his septum. His olive skin reminded me of Rosemary, Sam's mother. He had a beard, the ends braided with white lace and colored beads that clanked against my blade. His strange, brown-and-gold eyes were adorned with smoky makeup, dark smudges that gave him the appearance of a warrior. His clothing was simple: muddy boots over white trousers and a vest that left his strong chest exposed, stomach soft and covered in curly hair, bulging against the vest and hanging over the hem of his trousers. His arms were thick and covered in dark hair and tattoos that extended from his biceps down to his forearms: a forest with black trees around his left and what appeared to be a mountain range on his right, a thin line bisecting the peaks like a river.

Slightly mysterious and annoyingly attractive, a combination I didn't like. If this was the best they could send, then they'd already failed. I wouldn't be distracted by pretty things.

"There isn't a bathroom for you in this wing of the castle," I said, trying to keep my voice even, my gaze firmly planted on his face. "You shouldn't even be here."

"I told you I got lost, my guy," he said, and it was only then I detected the hint of an accent. Nothing pronounced, but I could hear it in the curl of his words. "Just need to take a leak."

I backed away slowly, keeping the sword pointed at him. "So, you're not here to kill me."

"No," he said, rubbing his throat.

"Then you're just an idiot. Good to know. Are you here for the celebration?"

He stared at me with the look of an abandoned puppy, which is to say pitiful. He squared his shoulders and puffed out his chest. I was not impressed. "I'm here to meet my future husband. I'm to be presented to him at the ball. Pretty rad, right?"

No. No it wasn't. "Sucks to be him," I muttered. Then, "I hope you make a better first impression than you did here. The ball starts at seven." It started at six. You had to make your fun whenever you could. "Take the stairs back down to the second floor. There's a bathroom first door on the right. Don't let me catch you up here again."

"But—"

"Leave," I commanded. He looked like he was going to say something else but shook his head instead. Without turning his gaze from me, he backed down the hallway slowly, hands raised in front of him. I snorted when he tripped over his feet, colliding with a closed door. Graceless. Annoying and graceless. It took all kinds.

I was about to head back into my room when he said, "Can I at least know the name of the bro who tried to kill me, even if he's being a butthole about it?"

I paused, turning my head toward him, teeth bared. A *butthole*? What was he, twelve or Sam? He blanched, and I said, "Tried? Oh, if I wanted you dead, you would be. You'd do well to remember that." I walked into my room, slamming the door behind me and locking it again for good measure, hoping he heard the finality of it. I pushed him out of my mind. Knowing the amount of people who had come to the City of Lockes for Liberation Day, I knew I'd most likely never see him again, which was fine by me. I felt sorry for whoever it was he was here to woo. They were in for a rude awakening.

"A butthole?" I mumbled to no one at all. "Seriously, fuck that guy. Fuck him right in his stupid face."

When I slept, I didn't dream.

# CHAPTER 4
# It's My Party and I'll Cry if I Want To

AT SIX ON THE DOT the following evening, crown atop my head, I stared out at the mass gathering before us. People were laughing and smiling, wearing brightly colored suits and dresses. Everyone seemed to be in a festive mood as they gathered in the ballroom, the air filled with excitement as the royal announcer bellowed name after name, the rich, the poor, the strong and the infirm, the heroes of Verania who had fought in the name of the king. Dad had held a lottery where everyone was invited to participate in hopes of winning a ticket to attend the celebration in the castle. Those who weren't selected were still being taken care of in the streets of the city where wine flowed as much as it did in here. No one was going without, not today, and the party was only getting started. Knights had been deployed to make sure things didn't get out of hand, but at the last report, everything was going smoothly, with only an exuberant hiccup or two in the form of men and women already sloshed.

Here in the ballroom, tables lined the right wall, stacked high with meats and cheeses, fruits and vegetables, all waiting to be consumed under the watchful eye of an ice sculpture that was supposed to be of the Great White, but looked like a diseased tree. In one corner, musicians were tuning their instruments, ready to provide the evening's entertainment. Against the wall behind a group of knights hung a large cloth, ropes hanging down on either side next to the painting of my many-breasted-monster father. I wondered at it briefly again, not knowing what was hidden behind it.

Dad sat next to me, smiling widely and speaking to everyone who bowed before him. They moved on to me, and I nodded at whatever they said, barely listening. Behind us, Gary and Tiggy stood with Kevin, his massive head poking through the doors. He didn't like to be left out, so we always tried to accommodate him. Ryan was inspecting his knights, making sure their swords and armor were polished until they shone, wanting to make the best impression. Lady Tina and her contingent moved throughout the crowd, keeping an eye on those already trashed so they didn't make fools of themselves. I thought I saw a man named Todd, his ears sticking out from the sides of his head, holding onto the pocket of a man I never wanted to see again, a man who had tried to make me call him Sir, all thanks to a stupid wizard who didn't know when to stop interfering in my business.

"It's lovely to see you, Prince Justin," a simpering lord said, practically licking my hand when he brought it to his lips. "You're looking divine."

I pulled my hand back with a grimace, wiping it against my dress trousers. "Thank you. You may go now." I pulled my hand back and stared at him pointedly. He'd do in a pinch, but I had my sights set higher. If I had to sit through this, then I was going to make sure my reward was justified. He wasn't it. His squire, however, looked dangerous and rough with hands almost as big as Tiggy's. When he took my hand and bowed before me, I made sure to let my fingers linger against his. His breath hitched once before he looked back up at me, a knowing heat in his gaze. Yes, he'd do just fine.

"Really?" Dad said next to me as the lord and squire melted back into the crowd.

"I have no idea what you're talking about."

Dad snorted. "Uh huh. I don't have a problem with you having a bit of fun, just go easy. You don't want to burn bridges before they're finished being built. There's sowing your oats, and then there's shitting where you eat."

"Spoken like someone who knows what he's talking about," Morgan of Shadows said. He stood next to my father, his long beard oiled and glistening, hair swept back on his head, his robes a brilliant blue with lines of white almost like lightning. He placed a hand on my father's shoulder, squeezing gently. Dad reached up and patted his hand, and I squinted at the way his fingers seemed to linger before falling back into his lap. Morgan didn't move his hand for a long moment, not until another person stepped forward, extolling Dad and Verania and blah, blah, blah. Briefly, I wondered what Randall was doing right at this moment. He'd been invited to the celebration. Though Sam and Randall had come to a strange understanding, Randall had said he'd rather bend over and expose his own asshole than stand in front of yet another group of people.

Bored, I looked out at the people. I didn't see the man from the night before. Either I couldn't find him, or he wasn't coming until seven like I'd told him. By then, the celebration would be underway. How embarrassing for him.

Not that I cared. The squire I'd set my sights on stood next to his lord, glancing my way like he thought I couldn't see him. I grinned at him—all teeth—when our gazes met. He blushed and turned back to his lord. Yes, easy pickings tonight. I hoped he liked getting fucked because I was going to ruin him for all others. He would never walk right again.

I startled from the filth in my head when Dad rose from his chair. The people turned toward him and began to cheer. It bowled over us, the sound ferocious as it bounced off the stone walls and ceiling. Dad let it go on for at least a minute before raising his hands, a wide smile on his face. "Thank you all for coming," he said, voice booming as it carried out over the people. "We have much to celebrate this night. The might and will of Verania is as strong as it's ever been. The trials we have faced in these last years have only shown me that we, as a country, have traveled through the dark and once again found ourselves in the light. I have much to say on the matter, but before I begin, I received a request from one of our great citizens. I've heard tales of his musical abilities, capable of creating earworms so profound, they can never be unheard once the words leave his lips."

"Oh *come on*!" I heard a voice cry, and I wasn't surprised to see it was Sam. He pushed his way through the crowd, people muttering at his temerity as he climbed onto the dais. He pulled himself up with a grunt, ignoring me as I stared pointedly at the stairs that he could've used. He stopped in front of Dad, glaring at him. "I told you not to invite him!"

Morgan sighed as Dad said, "And I took your counsel as I always do. I listened, weighed the pros and cons, and decided that this time, I was going to ignore you and do what I wanted."

"You're lucky I can't be king," Sam told him, as the people within hearing distance gasped. "Otherwise, there'd be a whole lotta changes around here."

"I tremble at the thought," Dad said. "We're very lucky you're a wizard instead."

"Damn right—hey!"

I reached around my father, gripping Sam by the wrist and pulling him toward my chair. "Would you shut your mouth for five seconds?"

"I tried that once," Sam said. "It didn't take, so."

"That's my son!" a voice cried from the crowd. We looked out into the audience to see Joshua, face slightly splotchy, raising a goblet toward Sam. Rosemary stood at his side and did nothing to try and stop her husband. "I love you, son! Wizards are the best!" He tilted his head back and howled, a jubilant sound that caused people near him to wince.

"Oh my gods," Sam mumbled. "He's so embarrassing. I mean, it's true, but still."

Morgan chuckled as he rounded the back of the chairs. I let go of Sam as he went for a hug, something he did whenever Morgan was around, even if the situation didn't call for it. I didn't blame him for that. What was once lost had been found, and if Sam needed to remind himself, then so be it. I glared at anyone who dared to try and whisper about it in the crowd. Their mutterings dissolved on their tongues as they shuffled their feet.

"Just one song," Morgan said as Sam pulled away. "Consider it penance."

"For what?" Sam demanded.

Morgan arched a bushy eyebrow.

"Right," Sam said quickly. "For a lot of things. Fine, I'll allow it, but tomorrow, I'm lodging a formal complaint. Bards are the worst, and their songs are stupidly pointed, even if no one asked for their opinion."

"I'll make sure to hear your complaint," Dad assured him. "Just as I've heard the last six hundred of them."

"I have a lot of ideas," Sam said.

"And half of them end up with putting my life in danger," I reminded him.

Sam shrugged. "Gotta keep you on your toes, dude. Speaking of which, if you find yourself suddenly kidnapped in the next week, just know that Gary has written a new script, and it's waaayyy more sexual than anything I ever came up with. It calls for the secret menu at his bakery. I didn't even *know* there was a secret menu. Now that I do, I wish I could scoop out my brain. Fair warning."

"You just *wait* until you've tried my custard," Gary said. I'd never been threatened with confectionaries before. Desserts had been ruined forever because of him.

"It's banana flavored," Kevin announced grandly. "And by bananas, I mean—"

"Happy place!" Tiggy cried, giant hands covering his ears. "Go to happy place!" He began to hum as he rocked back and forth.

"Yes," Dad said, his smile only growing. "This is what we've fought for. This is why we're here. To be allowed to have moments of levity, of joy and happiness. Regardless of whatever else our future holds, this cannot be taken from us. Bard, if you please!"

The crowd parted, and a slender fellow stepped forward. He wore a soft tunic under a leather vest, his hair slicked back, his mustache curled at the edges. He bowed dramatically in front of us, one hand across his chest, the other folded behind his back. "My King," he said, voice loud and clear. "My Prince. I am honored by your invitation. I'm the singer of songs, the keeper of truths, the voice of a generation. I have traveled near and far, explored the borders of Verania and beyond! I have seen the beating heart of this country, and I have never been filled with more hope than I am at this moment. I am Zal the Magnificent, and tonight, I do not bring you songs of cheesy dicks and candlesticks—the lyrics of which are on sale at a deeply discounted price after my performance so you can have it in your own homes!— but instead, a tale of the strength and power of our victories over those who would defy us. But first, a word from our sponsor."

A sweaty man appeared out of nowhere, skull gleaming under his thin combover. He held a parchment in his hands. Without looking up at the crowd, he began to read quickly and in monotone, barely taking a breath. "This performance of Zal the Magnificent is brought to you by Perry's Peculiar Potions and Antiquities. Do you have a mole the size of a child on your back? Are you losing your hair? Is there an invasive garden gnome in your flowerbed? Do you require an ancient tome that will allow you to summon demons in order to take revenge against your neighbor who won't stop singing sad songs at three o'clock in the morning because his wife left him after he was fired from his job for embezzlement? Take it from me, Perry's Peculiar Potions and Antiquities has a solution for you. I began to lose my hair at the age of fifteen, and now, my gorgeous locks are full of bounce and vibrancy, all thanks to a potion from Perry. I'm also gnome free and have a demon named Bloody Bridgett who won't go back to the hell dimension from whence she came. Please, someone help me. The demon won't leave me alone. I see her everywhere, even in my dreams. She's here now. Oh my gods. She's getting closer. Perry's Peculiar Potions and Antiquities uses organic ingredients, so you know it's safe. There's even a potion to give to unruly children, which will put them right to sleep for at least six days. Perry's Peculiar Potions and Antiquities is not responsible for loss of life, burning sensations that never end while urinating or delusions of grandeur that involve the belief that one can fly. Perry is required to say that he is not a medical doctor, has never gone to medical school, and makes all his potions in a cave behind his shack that is potentially haunted by the ghosts of those he tested his wares on. Perry's Peculiar Potions and Antiquities, for the moments when life tends to be a bit...peculiar."

Eight people clapped. I was not one of them.

The man stepped back down off the dais as Zal reappeared. "Thank you, Jerome. That was most illuminating. You might want to check the instructions about hair rejuvenation because it doesn't appear to be working."

Jerome flipped him off.

Zal clapped. "And now, good people of Verania, I am pleased to present to you a new song, one born of strength and heartbreak, of love and loss, of the power of fate written in the stars." He nodded toward the musicians, who held their instruments at the ready, waiting for his cue. "Listen well, for this song is one of my very best. It's called... Destiny, Fuck Yeah!"

"What," Sam said.

"What," Ryan said.

"What," Gary said.

"Butt!" Tiggy yelled.

"Hella cool," Kevin rumbled. "Hella, hella cool."

Morgan put his face into his hands.

I slumped down into my chair, wishing I could be anywhere but where I was.

But it was already too late.

Sweet notes trembled from the strings as the bard began to sing, slowly at first, then picking up speed.

*There once was a child raised in the Slums*
*who dreamed of life so free,*

*Chased by boys with malice in their hearts*
*into a wet and darkened alley.*

*He stood alone, back against the wall*
*and though his bravery was true,*
*it wasn't until the boys were turned to stone*
*that he realized what he could do.*

*A wizard came with pointy pink shoes*
*and told the boy he was special.*
*Filled with magic to an untold degree*
*and with this he did start to wrestle.*

*Because you see, and I do agree*
*his fate was written in the stars.*
*For he would be the savior of us all*
*this boy with the lightning-struck scars!*

"It's lightning-struck *heart*!" Gary yelled. "Know your source material!"

*Because...he had...a...*

*Destiny! Fuck yeah, he had a destiny!*
*The gods had deigned and chosen him*
*for reasons quite unknown!*
*But he rose to the challenge with fire in his heart,*
*and the Dark Wizards cowered all alone!*

*The King's wizard had a secret,*
*of a brother turned to shadow.*
*The Head Wizard had one too*
*for the brother was his beau!*

*They tried to keep the evil away*
*by locking it behind a seal of magic.*
*But unbeknownst to all involved*
*the story would take a turn...most...tragic...*

I was stunned to see a tear trickling down Zal the Magnificent's cheek. The ball room was silent as a tomb as everyone watched and waited. He looked out at the crowd for a long moment before turning to face us. "I apologize. There's more, so much more, but I don't know if it matters. Not when..." He sighed, looking from me to my father, to Morgan. And then his gaze settled on Sam, who glanced around as if he thought Zal was staring at someone else. Zal took a step toward him, and Sam flinched slightly when the bard cupped his face.

"You," Zal said. "You are the reason I can be who I am, the reason *all* of us can be as we are. Don't you see that, Sam? Ever since I met you in Arvin's Crossing, I knew you were someone special. I knew you were meant for great things. But even I didn't know just how great you would become." He took a step back, letting his hands fall away. The crowd gasped when he fell to his knees in front of Sam. Zal ignored them, eyes only for Sam. He took Sam's hand in his own. "Has anyone thanked you for all that you've done? Has anyone said, Thank you, Sam. Thank you for fighting for all of us. Thank you for believing in us." He looked at Tiggy and Gary and Kevin. Then to Ryan, standing just off the dais. Finally, he looked to me, and he didn't try and wipe away his tears. "To all of you. You brave, you true, you mighty warriors. Thank you for all that you did, for all that you sacrificed. Without you, we would have been lost. It's not about destiny or fate or whatever else the gods decreed. It was about the strength within you. And no one, not Darks, not villains, can ever take that away." He kissed the back of Sam's hand.

It started quietly, at first. One guy clapping in the back of the crowd. "Oh, come *on!*" he cried. "Don't make me be that guy who slow claps by himself in hopes that others will join in, you dicks!"

Others joined in. Many, many others, until the sound of their applause rolled over us like a cascading wave. I couldn't breathe, much less move. I thought it would never end, but then my father rose, raising his hands to silence the cheers.

"Thank you, Zal," he said. "Your words have once again proved to be enlightening. Especially since you're correct. We stood together in the face of shadows, but there were a few of us who rose above everyone else." My father stepped past Morgan and jumped off the dais, approaching Tiggy and Gary and Kevin. He drew his sword, the steel glinting in the firelight.

"Kneel, Tiggy," he said.

Tiggy did immediately, though he was still taller than my father, even on his knees. He looked at Gary, who nodded, mane bouncing. Tiggy turned back toward my father. "Hullo, King."

"Hello, Tiggy," Dad said. "Or should I say, Sir Tiggy." He placed the flat of his blade first on Tiggy's right shoulder, then moved it up and over his big head to the right. "You have proven yourself beyond measure, my tall friend. In the eyes of all of Verania, you are now a knight."

"Holy shit," Ryan breathed. "Seriously? Yes! Tiggy, I'm going to get you the *best* armor, you don't even know."

"Tiggy a knight?" Tiggy asked in wonder.

"You are," Dad said. "The first giant to ever become a knight, but hopefully not the last. It brings me joy to know our home will be under your protection in a more official capacity. In addition, tomorrow, I'll take you to a room in the basement where I've gathered every broom I could find, all for you."

"Brooms for Tiggy?" the half-giant whispered.

"All the brooms," Dad agreed.

Tiggy grinned.

Dad moved on to Kevin. "And you, dragon. You followed your hearts, even as they were breaking, knowing all that you left behind."

He raised his sword, pressing it to either side of Kevin's head. "To you, Kevin, I bestow the title of official envoy of Verania. Anyone who desires a meeting with the king shall speak to you first, because your council has proved to be most valuable."

"Wow," Kevin rumbled. "That sounds important. Question: what if the person who wants to meet with you are three sheep wearing a trench coat trying to pass themselves off as a human? Do I have permission to chase them and make them scream?"

Dad's lips twitched, but he somehow managed to maintain control. "Yes. You may. In fact, I insist upon it. Should there be three sheep in a trench coat trying to pass themselves off as a human, you may deal with them as you see fit."

"Hell. *Yes*. I accept. I accept so hard."

Dad moved on to Gary, whose eyes were so wide, I thought they'd pop out of his head. "And to you, Gary, I—"

"Of course I will marry you and become queen of Verania!" Gary said as he burst into tears. "It's all I ever wanted. Imagine: Queen Gary the Tyrannical! My gods, it just rolls off the tongue." His tears dried immediately as he leered at my father. "And I bet you do too, King. I bet you'll roll all *over* my tongue. Fair warning, our marriage bed will most likely break the first night. I'm a power bottom, a power top, and I can do this thing with my horn that'll make you shriek in ways you never thought possible."

"I will also partake," Kevin said. "As the official envoy of Verania, it's my duty to make sure the King gives my husband the ol' what for."

"Or," Dad said evenly, "I can make you a lord."

To which Gary immediately said (eyes dry!), "I'd rather be a Lady."

Dad nodded. "Lady Gary, then."

"Lady Gary the Tyrannical. You forgot to say that part."

Sam sighed. "He capitalized it, so you might as well."

"Lady Gary the Tyrannical," Dad said, tapping his sword against Gary's shoulders. "Long may you reign."

"Ha!" Gary cried, glaring out at the thunderstruck crowd. "You hear that? It's *over* for you bitches. You thought I was insufferable before? You ain't seen *shit*!"

"This was a mistake," I mumbled. "Our entire lives were mistakes."

Dad was no longer trying to fight a smile as he moved on to Ryan, who stood ramrod straight, his armor gleaming brightly. "Knight Commander Ryan Foxheart. I have watched you grow from a headstrong boy into the man who stands before me now. You're already a knight. You're already a leader. Shortly after your wedding, you came to me with a request. Do you remember?"

He nodded stiffly. I had no idea what they were talking about. Ryan never mentioned anything to me.

"You knew at the time that our customs dictated that your name remain as is, that you were a knight, and therefore, would stay as Ryan Foxheart. You said that a name had power, and that you wanted to make something of yourself. You'd done that, and you were ready to take on a new name, one near and dear to your heart. Nox that was, Ryan Foxheart who he came to be, you will now and forever be known as Knight Commander Ryan Haversford, husband to Sam Haversford, also known as Sam of Dragons."

A sob burst from the crowd, and I looked to see Joshua Haversford crying as his wife rubbed his back. Ryan appeared stunned as they both shot him a thumbs up, even as Joshua—a big northern man who could knock anyone into next week with a flick of his finger—continued to cry.

Ryan grinned, wide and beautiful. "I…I'm Ryan Haversford?"

"You are," Dad said gently. "A fine name, one worthy of a man such as yourself. Own it with pride, Knight Commander, because it too is a powerful name.

Ryan wasn't able to get another word out, seeing as how Sam jumped off the dais, tackling him to the floor, armor clanging. Ryan didn't seem to mind, his hands in Sam's hair as they both laughed and laughed, Sam kissing every inch of Ryan's face. They only stopped their mauling of each other when Rosemary and Joshua burst through the crowd, Joshua scooping Ryan up and hugging him tightly, Rosemary with her hand on the back of Sam's neck as they formed a circle of just the four of them, talking excitedly.

Dad turned from their joy. He held out his hand, and Morgan helped him back up to the dais. A grimace crossed his face, there and gone before I could latch onto it. A droplet of sweat trickled down his forehead. He motioned for me to stand. I did so nervously, unsure of what he had planned. We hadn't discussed any of this, and I didn't know what he was going to say. I didn't like being caught off guard, but hearing Ryan and Sam's happiness, the way Tiggy kept whispering to himself, "I'm a knight, Tiggy a real knight with brooms" was enough to chase the worst of my fears away.

"And to you, my son," Dad said, voice carrying around the ballroom. "I have thought long and hard about what I can offer you."

"I don't need anything," I said.

Dad shook his head. "Always the same with you. Never asking for anything. Nevertheless, for you, my son, a gift, and one that cannot be taken lightly."

And with that, he raised his sword. For a moment, I thought he was going to try and knight me too, which wasn't possible. I was the King-in-Waiting, the next in line for the throne. Though I'd fought at the sides of my countrymen and women in many battles, I knew my place. I could never be a knight.

But that wasn't what my father intended. He turned the sword until it was horizontal, the tip of the blade pointed toward the audience, the hilt toward our chairs. "My sword, forged in fire by my great grandmother, a kind woman who ruled over Verania for decades with love and kindness. May her blessing be upon you and guide you toward your future. I have never been prouder to call you my son, and the people of Verania will know you are to be a true king, when you take my place."

I couldn't move. I couldn't breathe. This wasn't something I ever expected, something so outside the realm of possibility, it never crossed my mind. The sword was an heirloom, one of the most important still existing in our family. It wasn't meant for battle; though my father had maintained its sharpness, it was more ceremonial than anything else. It was a sign, a moment where the old generation stood down to make room for the next.

Panicking, I blurted, "I'm not ready to be king."

Dad laughed. "Soon, my son, but not yet. This isn't meant as an abdication of the throne to you. It is a sign of my faith and trust in you because I know in your heart you will be the king this country needs. For better, for worse, in the good times and the bad, you will meet every challenge you face with all that we've taught you. But you won't do it alone. You'll have your friends by your side, and long may you reign. Take the sword, Justin. It's yours now. Keep it safe, keep it whole."

I did as he asked, hands trembling. I'd held my father's sword many times before, knew its weight and heft, the way it felt in my hands. But this was different. I wasn't a child playing pretend, telling everyone I was going to be king and they had to listen to me. The blade was warm against my skin, the grip fitting my hand as if it were made for me. The crowd began to cheer as my father nodded at me. He leaned forward, his mouth near my ear, whispering, "For you, Justin, my love and my light. Always for you." He kissed my cheek as the applause washed over us.

My knees felt weak, but I somehow managed to stay standing, staring down at the sword. I jerked my head up when Dad said, "And last, but certainly not least, Sam of Dragons."

"Gold!" Gary yelled. "Ask for as much gold as you can carry!"

"No," Kevin said. "Ask for vacation passes to Meridian City where you can do anything you want and I can watch! I mean, where I can follow along to make sure you don't get into trouble." Then, quieter, "So much trouble, I'll be forced to break you out of jail wearing a disguise that makes me look like a sex god. Chaps. Yes, I will wear chaps. And you will *like it*."

"Brooms," Tiggy intoned. "Every broom. Ten million brooms. Knight Tiggy says it."

Dad stopped in front of Sam, who looked up at him with bright eyes. "There has never been one such as you," Dad said, and I agreed, though we probably meant different things entirely. "All that you've seen, all that you've lost. Time, love, immortality, all of it was taken from you, sometimes by choice, and other times not. And yet you persisted. You never stopped, even when your heart shattered. The blood of Verania runs through your veins, Sam, because you *are* Verania. And we all owe you a debt of gratitude that I don't think we can ever repay. We are here because of you. Not destiny. Not fate. Not the gods. You."

A few people began to mutter in the crowd, and even I was flabbergasted at my father's perceived blasphemy.

Dad ignored them. "You rose to face an impossible challenge, and I've spent weeks and months trying to think of a way that I could show my gratitude. Gold, I thought."

"Hell yeah!" Gary cried.

"But then I realized you wouldn't want that. It's not who you are. I thought of a new home, a manor fit for someone who has given so much for the rest of us. But you already have a home here, don't you?

Sam nodded, swallowing thickly.

"I wrestled with it, so much so that I thought I could never find something to show how much you mean to us all. But then it hit me like a stroke of lightning. And I knew what I could give you. Because even though we stand before you today, not all of us survived. We lived, yes, but many were lost to us, one in particular. A brave man who gave his life in your name, knowing that one day, you'd return and become the hero we so desperately needed."

"Pete," Sam whispered, a tear trickling down his cheek. "My guard."

"Pete," Dad agreed. "A wonderful man who saw you as you were and knew what you were capable of long before the rest of us did. A man who deserves to be memorialized forever." He lifted his head, turning toward the knights lining the wall. "Gentlemen and ladies, if you would."

Two of the knights spun on their heels, their movements fluid and quick. They reached for the ropes hanging down on either side of the of the cloth and yanked. The cloth fluttered to the floor.

Hung on the wall was a painting, one so lifelike, I thought it a real person. But then I saw who it was and knew it was wishful thinking.

Pete, in all his glory. He stood in front of a Veranian flag wearing a full suit of armor, one hand resting on the hilt of his sheathed sword. He was smiling in that way he did, the smile that only seemed to appear when Sam was around, soft and slightly flummoxed. Below the painting, engraved in a panel of gold, were the words:

*Knight Peter Duncan*
*Protector, Advisor and Friend*
*His Sacrifice Will Never Be Forgotten*
*May He Watch Over Us All*

"It will hang for as long as these walls stand," Dad said. "He shines down upon us from the stars, and we'll always remember what he gave. But for you, Sam, he was more. So much more, and this is my gift to you. A remembrance, not for what we lost, but for what we—and Pete—stood for."

Sam stood, open-mouthed, his chest hitching once, twice. Then, even though he was only a few feet away, I barely heard what he said next. "Thank you," Sam whispered as he looked at the painting. "It's…it's perfect." He hugged my father tightly, Dad's face in his hair as Sam clutched at him.

People applauded once more.

Dad pulled away from Sam, though he took Sam's hand in his. "And now, I present to you my son, Prince Justin, who will grace us with his words. Justin, if you please."

I slowly stepped forward to the front of the dais, my father's sword in hand, all eyes on me. I took a deep breath, letting it out slow. I hadn't finished my speech, so I was going to need to wing it. Trying to remember how I'd felt at the Port on the stage—powerful and strong and scared out of my mind—I opened my mouth to speak, praying to the gods that I didn't screw this up.

I never got the chance.

A loud din burst from the back of the room, shouts of anger and frustration. The crowd parted as they turned, the knights rushing forward and forming a line in front of the dais. Sam shoved Dad behind him as Morgan stepped forward, the air around him rippling as magic gathered. Kevin snarled, and Gary's horn began to glow. Tiggy cracked his knuckles, teeth bared. Lady Tina and her contingent jumped up onto the dais, surrounding me, swords drawn, their breaths light and quick.

The large doors at the back of the ballroom swung open, and the royal announcer appeared, flustered, face red, spittle on his lips. He looked momentarily stunned at everyone staring at him, but he recovered quickly. "My king!" he bellowed. "We have new arrivals!" He wrang his hands nervously. "I thought you'd been made aware, but it appears there was a break in communications. My apologies, King. I won't let it happen again."

Dad frowned. "What? Who is it?"

The announcer bowed before standing upright. He fidgeted as he cleared his throat. When he spoke, his voice bounced off the walls, echoing like the remnants of a dream. "May I present to you…the contingent from Yennbridge."

"Yennbridge," Dad said. Then he paled, the blood rushing from his face. He looked like a ghost. "*Yennbridge?*"

The hairs on the back of my neck rose. Something tickled the back of my mind, but I couldn't latch onto it. Yennbridge was a country to the north, far beyond the snowy mountains and Castle Freeze Your Ass Off. We didn't have much to do with them aside from years of trade deals. In fact, I couldn't remember the last time we'd met with any of their people, handling everything through couriers. And, I realized with a harsh flash of anger, they'd done nothing to aid us when Myrin had taken over Verania. They had to have known what was occurring within our borders, and yet they didn't even attempt to reach out and offer assistance. Verania was insular, but that didn't mean we couldn't have used their help.

And here they were, interrupting the festivities as if they had a place here. Hell no. If they thought they could just waltz in here without repercussions, then they were sorely mistaken.

A stranger appeared through the doors. He wore robes of gold, with black piping up the sides. His collar rose up around his neck, the tops of which brushed the earrings dangling from his ears. For the life of me, I couldn't quite figure out how old he was supposed to be. He seemed both young and old all at the same time, a dissonance that spoke of deep magic. His hair hung in black curls. On his face, a trimmed and neat goatee, inlaid with what looked like strands of gold that hung toward his chest.

"Wizard," Sam snapped. "He's a wizard." He raised his hands, fingers twitching. The air around him grew thick and heavy, the smell ozone-sharp and burning.

"Bah," the man said, voice carrying, deep and melodic. "Wizard? I am no wizard. I am a magician. I ask that you remember that as you stand down, boy. I am not here to cause harm. Quite the opposite, in fact." That tickle in the back of my mind grew more insistent. His accent was familiar, but I couldn't quite place where I'd heard it before. Not from him, but...

The man stopped halfway down the red carpet that led to the dais. He clasped his hands behind his back, looking at Sam and Morgan, then dismissing them almost immediately. I thought his eyes widened slightly at Gary and Kevin and Tiggy, but it could have been a trick of the light. He studied my father for a long moment, no one speaking.

And then his gaze fell to me.

His smile widened. "And you must be Prince Justin of Verania, the sole heir to the throne." He tilted his head in the approximation of a bow, though he remained upright. "I bring you tidings of great joy. I am Ramos the Pure, magician to the King of Yennbridge, here to claim what is rightfully his."

Dad's brow furrowed. "You're interrupting an important event. Surely you understand there are protocols in place for visiting dignitaries. You can't just barge in here when you feel like it."

"My sincerest apologies," Ramos said and strangely, he sounded as if he meant it. "But we sent word in anticipation of our arrival. It appears as if the message was lost. But I will remind you of the accord you and your wife signed with the King and Queen of Yennbridge, may they rest in peace." His smile faded. "Sickness ravaged them both. It was not without pain, but they have crossed the veil, and in their place, their son has assumed the throne. He is here to claim what you pledged to us."

"What's that?" Sam asked, still at the ready. I knew with one flick of his hand the man would turn to dust. I hoped that would happen sooner rather than later, I didn't like where this was headed.

"Why," Ramos said, "the hand of the Prince of Verania, of course. The firstborn of the King and Queen of Verania has been promised to the firstborn of the King and Queen of Yennbridge. They are betrothed. My king has come at last to claim his husband."

"Dun dun *dunnnnn*," Gary breathed. "Next time, on The

Househusbands of Verania: will Justin accept the hand of a strange man, or will he chop off the strange man's head? Tune in next week to find out these answers and more! And by next week, I mean right this second."

# CHAPTER 5
## What in the Actual Fuck

CAPITALIZED, SO YOU KNOW IT'S TRUE.

Because What in the Actual *Fuck*.

Chaos exploded like a bomb. People began to shout over each other, their voices melding and becoming nothing but a cacophonous bluster, the words lost but the ire clear. Dad was stiff as the dead next to me, Sam moving in front of me like he thought I was about to be attacked. Which, to be fair, it felt like I had been, like I'd been struck in the chest with the broadside of a sword, my lungs collapsing, throat closing. Ryan scowled as he unsheathed his sword, flourishing it expertly (and unnecessarily; if there was ever a time for him to *not* be dashing and immaculate, it was now).

The stranger—Ramos the Pure, a name that I didn't believe for a moment—wasn't bothered by the noise around him, standing stock still, watching me with dark eyes. He arched an eyebrow as people shouted their dismay, demanding to know who this man thought he was. "Villain?" I heard Tiggy ask, to which Gary replied, "Probably, kitten. This is so unexpected. We should probably see how it plays out before we resort to murder."

Of all the times for the damn unicorn to *not* want to murder someone.

Knowing it would go on and on, I stepped forward, pushing Sam to my right. He glared at me. I ignored him. I was used to it by now. I raised my hands, and the people fell silent. Lowering my hands, I studied the stranger who, in a few words, had made a mess of a royal celebration.

He barely blinked. A chill ran down my spine, but I kept it from my face, my expression carefully blank. To show weakness meant you had already lost. And I sure as hell wasn't going to lose to someone who called themselves a magician.

Before I could speak, another did for me. I was almost relieved.

"Ramos the Pure," Morgan said lightly, though I knew him well enough to know his mind was working overtime, taking the magician in, cataloguing every piece and part of him. I'd heard of magicians before, but only in Meridian City. They were street performers, moving cups with balls hidden underneath, slights of hand with decks of cards, conjuring bundles of flowers from their sleeves. Illusory entertainment, and nothing more. They didn't have magic. They weren't like Sam and Morgan and Randall. Hell, they weren't even like the Darks.

And yet, there was something about him, something that I couldn't quite put my finger on. He didn't feel like Morgan or Randall. And he certainly didn't feel like Sam, more magic than blood by this point. There was an air about him I didn't like, and the room seemed slightly darker since he'd arrived.

"Morgan of Shadows," Ramos said, tilting his head once more. "It is an honor, sir. The tales of your...adventures are known far and wide, including your apparent death and resurrection."

"The stories of my death have been greatly exaggerated," Morgan said. "Yes, I did die, in a way, but I was brought back by a wish granted from one to whom I owe everything."

"*That's* what you think is an exaggeration?" Dad asked. "Honestly, Morgan, we really need to work on your delivery."

"I'm afraid you've caught me unaware," Morgan continued, never looking away from Ramos. "You've heard of me, but I don't know of any Ramos the Pure."

Ramos laughed, a gruff sound that made me want to punch his square teeth down his throat. "Oh, I don't expect you would have. I'm afraid I am not at the level of someone such as yourself. And I certainly don't have the abilities as your young apprentice."

"I'm not an apprentice," Sam snapped. "I'm a full-fledged wizard."

Ramos squinted up at him. "Truly? So you've gone through the Trials, then. I hadn't heard. Congratulations."

Sam blanched. "Well...no. Not exactly. I mean, if we're getting down to brass tacks, instead of the Trials, I went with five dragons into the forest and then a bunch of stuff happened before I came back, kicked major ass, and now we're here." He frowned. "There's more to it than that, but Justin looks like he's going to dropkick me, so we'll just leave it alone for now."

Ramos nodded. "I see. So you *haven't* gone through the Trials, and yet you still call yourself a wizard." The corners of his mouth tugged down. "And all because of dragons, you say? How fascinating. We had dragons in Yennbridge, once." He glanced dismissively at Kevin. "They died out for good reason. Terrible creatures, they are. Nothing but animals."

"I feel like I'm being insulted," Kevin said. "But I can't quite put my talon on why."

"It can talk," Ramos said, though he didn't sound surprised. "I'd heard such a rumor but passed it off as nothing more than a tall tale."

"Sam talks to dragons," Tiggy said. "They all sound like grr and rawr when he gone, but when he close, they talk like, Hey, Tiggy. You smash because smashing good." He raised his hands, the right forming a fist that he punched into the palm of his left. "I smash goooood."

"Does he?" Ramos said, eyeing Sam with a new appreciation. "That's quite the feat. I've never heard of a wizard with powers such as this. What else are you capable of?"

Sam shrugged. "Many, many things, most of which you probably don't want to find out."

Ramos smiled. "No need for threats. I come in peace. Yennbridge is a friend to Verania, and while we've been the long-distance sort of friends, you've never been far from our thoughts."

"Isaac and Latisha are dead?" Dad asked, still slightly pale. He grimaced as he rubbed his arm, shaking out his hand as if it'd fallen asleep.

"They are," Ramos said gravely. "Yennbridge wept at the loss. For the last six months, our country has been in mourning, honoring our king and queen. Their bodies were on display in the palace before they were interred in the tombs of our forebearers. And while we will miss them terribly, time marches ever forward, waiting for no man or woman."

"You have our condolences," I said.

"Thank you, Prince Justin," Ramos said. "Your words are a balm that I will carry back to our people. But we are not here to grieve. The first and only child of our king and queen has taken his rightful place on the throne in our capital, the City of Light. I had been the King's Advisor for nearly two decades when he and Queen Latisha passed. I was honored when their son asked that I stay on in the same capacity. My life is one of service and serve I shall."

"And you decided to come here, now," Dad said.

"We have," Ramos agreed. "Because the King of Yennbridge cannot rightfully rule unless he has a spouse. Thankfully, on his death bed, King Isaac spoke of a pact between the two kingdoms, one that cannot be ignored. A pact about the firstborn child of Verania."

"A pact," I said slowly, turning to look at my father. "About *me*."

Dad was sweating heavily now, trickling down his forehead, dripping onto his cheeks like tears. "I...Morgan?"

Morgan stepped forward, hands hidden in the sleeves of his robes. "They were here, my King. They arrived shortly before our queen..." He sighed, shaking his head. "Before she passed beyond the veil. That being said, I don't remember anything about a pact."

Ramos clicked his tongue. "Because it wouldn't have involved you. It was a thing between kings and queens." He turned back to my father. "I suppose when faced with the loss of your dear wife, most everything else would have fallen away. But I assure you, an agreement was made, binding in all its glory. To renege now would mean an act of war, and I believe that's something we'd want to avoid at all costs." He looked around at the people gathered around him. Some rich, some poor, but all where they were supposed to be. "Especially since your people have been through enough."

I didn't like his tone. Apparently, neither did Dad. "We handled ourselves remarkably. Verania still stands, and so do we. And I don't remember any pact. If there is one, it was obviously agreed upon at a time of heightened duress. My wife was about to give birth, and the pregnancy hadn't been easy for her."

"Duress," Ramos said, chewing the word and spitting it back at us. He raised his hands, the backs of which were covered in blue tattoos, lines that stretched down each individual digit to his fingernails. On his right palm was an eye, the iris black, the pupil that of a cat. I startled when the eye *blinked*, and then Ramos clapped his hands together. When he pulled them apart, a scroll appeared out of nothing, his fingers curling around the ends. "I take offense to such a suggestion, though I'll let it pass. For now." He took a step toward us and was immediately met by Ryan and three of his knights, all with swords drawn. Ramos pursed his lips and held out the scroll. Ryan hesitated before snatching it out of his hands. He turned toward the dais, marching forward, bowing as he held the scroll up.

Morgan took it from him, unfurling it, eyes darting back and forth as he began to mutter under his breath. "The King and Queen of Yennbridge, along with the King and Queen of Verania... hereby agree to... the first born will...Yennbridge and Verania will be joined...for the future of both our countries...within the rights of..." He looked up, eyes narrowed. "I don't see my signature on this."

"You are not royalty," Ramos said. "As I said previously, this was only between kings and queens. Of course you wouldn't be included. You're merely an advisor."

Morgan didn't take the bait, instead handing the scroll to my father. "It's your signature, Anthony. I would know it anywhere. And Natasha's."

My mother.

Dad read silently, mouth moving. When he finished, he looked up at Morgan. "I don't remember this. Is it a forgery?"

"A forgery?" Ramos asked. "And here I thought we were done with the insults. It is not a forgery. That scroll is made from the skin of a sphinx. No lies can be written upon it, up to and including forging a king's signature. I assure you that King Anthony and Queen Natasha *did* sign it, and that we're here to have the agreement honored."

"He's right," Morgan said, gripping the edges of the scroll. A bright flash of light popped from underneath his fingers, followed by a dark wisp of smoke that curled up and smelled like undergrowth. "I can find no deception here."

Sam snorted. "Are we really going to take this seriously? Come on. We've seen shit like this before. For all we know, this dude is a villain and has plans to try and take over Verania. They're all the same. Give them an inch, and they'll be monologuing about how they hated their fathers while detailing line by line every step of their evil plan, and suddenly, things will be lit on fire and there will be running and screaming and maybe even some billowing robes, if we're lucky."

For once, I agreed with Sam. Not about the billowing robe thing, because that was stupid. "I didn't agree to anything. And since we're a progressive country, consent is everything."

"Damn right it is," Gary snapped. "You don't think we'll sue the crap out of you? Because we will. I know, like, six lawyers who—"

"A unicorn," Ramos said. "Your name, sir?"

"Lady Gary the Tyrannical."

"I see," Ramos said. "What a fascinating name for a unicorn. Tell me, Lady Gary, are you the only unicorn here?"

"I am," Gary said. "My brother Terry was here for a time, but everyone agreed his presence was pretty pointless in the grand scheme of things, so he went back to where he came from and will probably never be heard from again. Good riddance. Accountants really tend to bring the mood down. And my parents, Barry and Mary—"

"Your names all rhyme?" Sam demanded. "I know I'm probably going to regret this, but *why*?"

"Of course they rhyme," Gary said. "Everyone knows that unicorn families all have rhyming names. It's how you know we're amazing. Last I heard from them, they were on their swingers tour at the edges of the country."

"*Still?*" Kevin exclaimed. "My gods, the virility! The recovery time alone is enough to make my knees weak with anticipation."

"Dear," Gary said evenly. "We've talked about this. Magical creature swinger tours usually last ten years. And as much fun as reminiscing about my family tree is, for the first time in my life, I'm going to say that we're not here to talk about me." He winced. "Ugh. That was the worst thing that's ever come from my mouth."

I looked back at Ramos, who seemed content to let things play out as they were. "As interesting as this has been, I think it's time for you to leave."

Ramos arched an eyebrow. "Your father gave his word. I'm afraid we're not going anywhere. After all, my king has come to make his intentions known." He clapped once, the sound sharp and echoing flatly. "And now, I present to you, His Royal Highness, the Keeper of Peace, the Leader of Yennbridge—"

"Oh my gods, oh my gods," Sam muttered. "His name is gonna be so cool, I just know it."

"King Dylan," Ramos finished.

"Dammit!"

The doors parted once more, and a group of men and women slunk in, all carrying long sashes made of fine silk. They writhed as they practically floated down the center of the ballroom, a few doing backflips, others leaping into the air, twirling the sashes around them as they contorted their bodies into impossible positions.

The dancers reached the dais, dropping their sashes at the base as if in offering. They moved along the sides of the ballroom, stopping in front of the knights, who didn't appear to mind the attention. I needed to have a word with Ryan about the proper protocol of his knights.

The men and women turned as one, raising their hands into the air, fingers wiggling as they tilted their heads back.

And then the King of Yennbridge stepped into the ballroom.

"You," I said, stunned.

Him. The man who'd knocked on my door the night before. The man who'd been lost, searching for the bathroom. The man who I'd tricked into coming late to the celebration, only because I was irritated at the intrusion.

Gods*dammit*.

The man—Dylan, I thought, the word like a shooting star in the back of my mind—held his head high as he walked slowly toward us. He was dressed similarly as he'd been the night before. However, his boots were clean, his black trousers made of an expensive material that hugged his thighs. His vest was leather and carved into it was a vast forest that matched the tattoos on his arms. He didn't have an undershirt on, his skin on display, his gut sloping. The jewelry in his ears, nose and beard glittered, as did something I'd missed the night before: a piercing in his naval, the chain hanging down toward the top of his trousers.

Each step was slow and measured. He didn't turn his head toward the whispering crowd, his gaze solidly forward as he marched toward us.

He made it halfway when he tripped on the carpet. He stumbled but managed not to fall. "Aw, nuts," he muttered. "That wasn't supposed to happen." Two people rushed forward to help him, and when he pulled himself upright, his elbow bumped the goblet held by one of his rescuers, causing wine to spill all over a woman wrapped in furs with peacock feathers in her hair. She shrieked as she got drenched. "Frickin' heck," Dylan said. "That wasn't supposed to happen either. Are you all right, lady-bro?"

"These furs are *imported*!" she cried, furiously wiping her face.

Dylan frantically tried to take her furs from her—to wring them out? to have them dry-cleaned? fuck if I knew—and she brought the back of her hand to her forehead as she swooned. The people behind her caught her as she fell back, eyes fluttering.

Ramos cleared his throat pointedly. "My king, if you could focus on the reason we're here."

Dylan's head jerked up and down. "Yeah, yes. Of course. Uh. Right. Where was I? Ah, yes! I remember." He puffed out his chest and continued marching toward us. "One foot in front of the other, big guy," he muttered. "That's all this is. Yup. There we go. You got this, Dyl. You are thirty years old, and you learned how to walk a long time ago. You're a lion. No, wait. A *wolf*. Heck yeah, a wolf."

"Dibs," Kevin yelled. "I call dibs!"

Dylan *finally* made it to the front of the dais without further injury, either to himself or anyone else. He looked proud of himself, shooting a grin at Ramos before turning back to us. He started to bow, but aborted halfway through, as if remembering that he too was a king, bowing for no one. Instead, he straightened, eyes firmly planted on my father.

"Good King Anthony," he said, sounding rehearsed. "It is an honor to stand before you in your home."

"We welcome you with open arms," Dad said, and he was such a fucking liar. "So long as you come in peace, we—"

"Why don't you have a sword?" I asked without meaning to, and the silence that followed was so absolute, I could hear the rabbit-quick beat of my heart thumping in my ribcage. Interrupting the king while he held court was considered a faux pas, one that only I and a few others could get away with and not be immediately shot down. Still, I should've kept my mouth shut. Not only was it rude, it made it sound as if I were…interested. Which I wasn't. At all.

Dylan looked at me, mouth turning down. "I remember you, bro." It was not a happy memory, if the expression on his face meant anything. And *bro*? Who the hell did he think he was addressing me with such familiarity?

I waved my hand airily. "How nice for you. I asked you a question."

"Who are you?" He glanced back at Ramos. "An advisor, or…?"

I grinned at him, razor sharp. "I'm Prince Justin, the man your magician has said you've come to claim as your own. Fair warning: I've just learned about this travesty seconds ago, and I am not pleased. Your answer will dictate whether or not you're invited to speak again, or if you'll be sent packing to whatever backwater place you came from. Answer the question."

"Justin," Dad warned, but I only had eyes for the man before me.

Dylan choked on his tongue, and I thought his eyes were going to pop from his head and land at his feet. I felt a savage twist of satisfaction. It took him a bit to recover, though by the time he did, he was drenched with flop sweat. *This* was the man who traveled all this way to demand my hand in marriage?

"Prince Justin," Dylan muttered. "Of all the…" Then, louder (and still obviously rehearsed), "Tales of your beauty were not exaggerated. The word on the wind has spoken of you as a—"

"Has that line ever worked on anyone before?" I mused. "Rhetorical question. I really doubt it."

He squinted at me. "Are…are you sure you're the prince, bro? Because you don't seem like a prince."

The crowd tittered as I sat back in my chair, making sure I looked extraordinarily bored by the entire proceeding. "Pretty sure, *bro*. I mean, I've only been called the prince since the moment of my birth, so. But if you have to ask, then maybe you should have done your homework before clomping in here like a beast."

"Gods," Gary whispered. "I don't know how I forgot he could be such a bitch. I love him."

"It's true," Dylan said, looking slightly flustered. "I don't carry a sword. Yennbridge is a peaceful country and we Yenners are pacifists. There is more to life than fighting in a war. We believe in action through words, not bloodshed."

His people cheered as I scoffed. Without waiting for their obnoxious din to die down, I said, "Pacifists? Then what would stop me from ordering our army to invade your country?"

He squinted at me. "You'd do that? Aw, man. Weak. Super weak, even. Not cool, bro."

"Of course not," Dad said quickly, and I knew that tone. I'd pushed too far, and he wasn't happy with me. "Forgive my son. Justin has a tendency to be…exuberant."

Sam snorted. "That's the first time anyone has called him that." He winced when Morgan cuffed him upside the back of his head.

"Do you want to invade me?" Dylan asked.

"What would be the point?" I asked. "You don't know how to use a sword. I like a little competition. Gets the blood going. Just because something would be very, very easy, doesn't mean it should always be done."

"I never said I didn't know how to use a sword," Dylan said, obviously struggling to keep his voice even. I was getting to him, and I knew that with a little push, he'd most likely end up storming out of the castle, never to step foot into my city again.

"Then you wouldn't mind a demonstration," I said, rising from my seat, Dad's—*my*—sword in hand. "Ryan, hand our esteemed guest your sword." I unbuttoned the front of my jerkin, giving myself more room to breathe as I jumped down from the dais.

"Uhh," Ryan said. "What."

"Justin," Dad said. "Perhaps now isn't the time. We're all friends here."

I looked back at him. He was still pale, but all I could think about was that he'd promised my future away in the name of unity. Sam had a destiny written in the stars, and my own path was to become the husband to a man I had immediately despised? Fuck that, and fuck him. "I'm one of the most accomplished swordsmen in all of Verania. If I'm to be paired with someone, then I would expect they'd at least be able to have my back should the need arise." I walked slowly around Dylan, eyeing him up and down with forced disdain. Screw this guy for having a great ass. Thicc, as Kevin might say. For his part, Dylan never flinched and didn't turn to stop my perusal. "We haven't survived what we have through something as ridiculous as pacifism." I finished circling Dylan, stopping in front of him. He had a few inches on me, and at least fifty pounds. But as the old saying went, the bigger they were, the harder I would fuck them up. "Ryan, your godsdamn sword."

Ryan hesitated, but only for a moment. He stepped forward, flipping his sword expertly, catching it by the blade, holding out the grip for Dylan. He didn't take it right away, staring down at it, eyes narrowing. "What do I get when I win?"

When, not *if*. My approximation of him rose a margin or two, but since it was already as low as dirt, it didn't mean much. "If you win," I said lightly, "you can stay. But *when* you lose, you'll turn around and leave this place and not look back."

"Your majesty," Ramos said. "Perhaps we should talk about this—"

Dylan took Ryan's sword. He fumbled with it briefly, almost dropping it. "Heavier than it looks," he said as Ramos sighed. "Used to a lighter weight. I got this, though. Just need a second."

"I'm sure you do," I said. "But you'll find that here in Verania, we don't do things by half measures. Remember: if you choose to raise that sword at me, it begins. I won't go easy on you. I hope you've enjoyed your limbs while you've had them."

"No dismembering," Dad said, sucking the fun right out of the room.

"Then how do we know who wins?" Dylan asked, gripping the sword. "I didn't think I was going to stab anyone when I first got here. Not in the right headspace for that."

"First blood," I said. This was going to be over quickly.

"Okie doke," Dylan said. "First blood. Cool. Cool, cool, cool. I'm a pretty light bleeder, so I'm not too worried."

Great. Wonderful. This was going so well already.

People stepped away from us, forming a large circle, Dylan and I in the middle. I raised my sword above my head, people beginning to cheer. Gary was already working the room, taking bets as Dylan eyed me warily.

"Kick his ass, Prince Justin!" a voice cried from the crowd.

"Lop off his hand!"

"Shove that sword so far up his ass, he gargles steel!"

"We're a little bloodthirsty here," I said to Dylan. "Is that going to be a problem?"

"Nah," Dylan said easily. "You know what they say. When in Verania something something. Didn't really pay attention to that part." He looked down at the sword laying limply in his hand. "We doing this, then?"

"We are," I said, bouncing on my feet. I felt loose, in control. Perhaps this celebration wasn't going to be a bust after all. "Hope I don't embarrass you *too* much." Then, as an afterthought, I added, "Bro."

I didn't expect what he did next. Instead of fumbling with the sword more, or sputtering excuses about his abilities, he nodded. Taking a deep breath, he crouched low, one leg stretched behind him, the other bent in front of him. He leaned forward, chest almost pressed against his knee. With his right hand, he brought the sword horizontal over his head, the blade pointed toward me. His other hand stretched out toward me, palm toward the ceiling. And then he wiggled his fingers, beckoning me.

I was going to motherfucking *destroy him*.

I'd held my first sword at the age of four, a wooden thing, cracked and chipped. It'd taken me mere weeks to advance on to a metal blade, thin, yet deadly. From there, I'd only grown stronger, my teachers had been the best in all of Verania. If I hadn't been born a prince, I would have joined the knights. I sparred with them as much as I could, and aside from Ryan, I hadn't yet met anyone who could defeat me. Ryan was all flash and pizazz, moving slower, but making up for it with brute strength.

I was a snake, muscles coiled and ready to strike. Speed always won over force, and Dylan looked like the type to hack and slash. His blood would be spilled with my first or second blow.

Or, at least, that's how it should've gone.

Because I darted forward without warning, sword swinging out in a flat arc, meaning to slice against his stomach, but not so hard that I'd disembowel him. A flesh wound, enough to give him a clear indication of who he'd raised a sword to.

Except that's not what happened. Right before the blade cut into his skin, he lunged *backwards*, bringing his sword down on top of mine. Sparks flew as my blade was driven into the ground, bouncing off stone, the vibrations rolling through my arms.

Huh. That was unexpected.

"Holy shit," Sam breathed.

I pulled my sword back slowly, our blades rubbing together with a metallic shriek. I moved away from him, sidestepping to the left. He turned with every step I took, sword at the ready.

He was weaker on his left side. I saw it in the way he carried himself, how he seemed to favor his right leg. Meaning to exploit this, I attacked, going in low, swinging the blade toward his left leg. But instead of steel meeting skin and bone, he fucking *jumped*, my sword hitting nothing but air. I tried to correct, but the momentum knocked me off my footing, and I stumbled.

The crowd began to whisper as a trickle of sweat fell down the back of my neck. Okay. If that's the way he wanted to play it, fine. I was done going easy on him. He had tricks, sure, but they would only get him so far.

I went right. He fell for it, and I feinted left. I sailed by him, his face inches from my own, and I slammed the hilt of my sword into his back, knocking him forward. He took three hard steps, absorbing the blow with barely a wince. Without giving him time to recover, I was on him again, trying to remind myself it wouldn't be diplomatic if I ran him through. He raised his arm, and my sword went underneath it. He brought his arm down, pinning my sword against his body. He spun away, ripping it from my grip, the hilt scraping against my palms before I lost hold of it. The crowd gasped as Dylan lifted his arm, letting the sword fall the floor, where it bounced.

"Are you done, bro?" he asked, an obnoxious grin on his face.

I shook my head slowly. "I'm just getting started."

He took a step back as I lunged at him, crouched low, scooping up the sword off the floor and slicing upward. He parried neatly, looking like he'd barely broken a sweat. Our swords clashed together, sparks singeing my skin. I was furious for reasons I couldn't quite explain. He was good, and that made him a liar. He was here, which made him an enemy. And I knew how to deal with enemies.

He deflected every hit, and it took me a moment to realize he was always on the defense, never trying to lash out. An early lesson I'd been taught. If you allowed your opponent to always attack, they would soon tire, creating an opening when they began to lag. He was trying to use my attacks against me, and I'd fallen for it. Begrudgingly, I was almost impressed, though wild unicorns would never be able to drag that out of me.

I changed tactics, stepping back out of reach, waiting for him to come to me.

He knew immediately what I was doing, always keeping me in his sights. Poor bastard. I hoped he realized that I wasn't going to be made a fool, especially not in front of my own people.

Eventually, he couldn't take it anymore, just as I expected. He came for me, sword raised above his head, telegraphing his intent. I side-stepped him, and when he brought the sword down, it met empty air. But it didn't hit the floor like I'd expected. He managed to course-correct half-way, swinging the sword toward my side. I fell to my knees, his blade missing my head by inches, so much so that I felt the wind of his swing against my face. I saw the look of outrage he wore as I leapt up, his momentum causing his back to face my front. I pressed up against him. The heat of him was enormous, and I thought if he hadn't come here to destroy everything I'd built, I wouldn't have minded taking him to my bed at least once, perhaps twice if I was feeling generous. I brought my sword up to his throat, forcing his head to tilt back against my shoulder. I turned my head, mouth scraping against his ear. He smelled of wild spices, dusky and heady, a couple of his earrings dimpling my lips. "Got you," I whispered, tasting metal.

"Nah," he said as a quick flash of pain prickled my thigh, there and gone.

I reared back, looking down. There, in his other hand, a dagger, the tip of which pressed against my thigh. A stain began to spread, blooming like a blood rose. "Femoral artery," Dylan said almost conversationally. "Severed, and you'll bleed out wicked fast."

Stunned, I took a step back. The wound was minor; in fact, I barely felt it. In a day or two, it'd scab over, and in a week, it'd be gone. In the grand scheme of things, it was nothing.

Except it meant I'd lost.

Dylan turned around to face me, grinning wildly. The smile faded when he saw the blood on my leg. "Oh, shoot," he said. "I'm so sorry. Are you all right, bro? I didn't mean to do that."

"You didn't?" I asked, incredulous.

"Oh, well, I guess I did, but I didn't mean to hurt you." He took a step toward me. "Cripes, is that gonna stain? My mom always said to get blood out of clothing, you need to use cold water and a bar of soap. Scrub it good, and then a drop of ammonia, and you'll be right as rain."

"Ammonia," I repeated dubiously.

He nodded. "Doesn't smell very good, but at least you won't be bloody." His eyes widened. "Oh my sweet crud. You're *bloody*. Which means I won! Yes! Yes!" He raised his sword above his head as his people hooted and hollered.

"You cheated!"

He frowned, hand still raised. "What? Not cool, bro. I didn't *cheat*. No one ever said we couldn't have a secondary weapon. I always carry the dagger. Someone tried to assassinate me three—wait, no, eight times—and I figured it's always better to be prepared."

I gaped at him.

"I like him," Sam announced. "Justin, marry him immediately. If you don't, I will."

"You stay away from Sam!" Ryan yelled. "If you don't, I'll slice off your face and wear it like a mothercracking *mask*."

We all turned to stare at him. Literally everyone in the room.

Ryan scratched the back of his neck. "Too much? Yeah, I knew that as soon as I said it."

"The things I'm gonna do to you later," Sam breathed.

"Sam," Joshua said. "We talked about this. You can't say things like that when there are visiting dignitaries in the castle. It's not polite."

"Are you all right?" Dylan asked me, sword forgotten. He reached for me, flinching when I snarled at him. I was embarrassed that I'd been bested so easily, my face burning with shame. Who the fuck did he think he was, playing me like that? But even more, I was pissed off with myself that I'd fallen for it so easily, my ego so massive I thought there'd be no way I could lose. I should have known the dagger was there, but I'd been so sure I'd beat him that I'd fallen prey to my own misplaced confidence.

I turned away from him, needing as much distance as possible. I wanted to flee for the safety of my room, but I wouldn't give him the satisfaction. Dad smiled quietly at me, no doubt knowing I was castigating myself in my head. I approached the stairs, meaning to climb them and take my seat. Dad held out his hand for me, and I reached for it.

His fingers trembled. His chest hitched, once, twice.

"No," he whispered. "No. Please, not now."

And then his eyes rolled back into his head, skin clammy and white. His knees buckled, and he collapsed on the dais. Before his head could bounce off the floor, Morgan was there, catching my father, cradling him in his lap.

Chaos once again descended as the knights rushed forward, as people began to scream, as Sam fell to his knees at my father's side. Numb, disbelieving what I was seeing, I hit the floor next to Dad, taking his hand in mine. His eyes fluttered, his lips bloodless, and as I demanded he wake up, yelling at him to open his eyes, squeezing his hand so tight, I felt his bones grind together. Morgan gripped his face with his magic building and I wondered if this was it, if this was the end, if I'd wasted my last moments with my father in a stupid contest that never should have happened.

"Wake up," I muttered. "Please, please, wake up."

# CHAPTER 6
## This is the Dumbest Timeline

I RUBBED MY EYES. They felt gritty, too large in their sockets. I hadn't slept, angrily pacing outside the healer's quarters all night, demanding that I be let in, only to be told my father was being cared for and that once they knew what was wrong I'd be told immediately. I'd half-convinced myself he'd been poisoned, that Ramos and Dylan had used their entrance as a distraction to harm my father. I was almost to the point where I wanted to order Ryan to detain the entire contingent from Yennbridge, to ensure they couldn't escape while we were distracted.

But then one of the healers—an ancient man with liver spots on his forehead and a sharp tongue that brooked no arguments—came out as the sun began to rise, uttering two words that stopped me cold.

It wasn't poison. It wasn't magic. In fact, it wasn't anything nefarious. It was, in the end, something so mind-numbingly common that I didn't quite believe it at first.

Heart attack.

My father had a heart attack.

"He's not as young as he once was," the healer said flatly, eyeing Sam, Ryan and me with disdain. "I told him at his last checkup that he needed to take care of himself, watch his diet and cut back his intake of mead. Did he listen to me? Of course not! Bullheaded, he is. Ever since he was a child, telling me he'd have the large scar rather than stitches."

"But he's going to be okay, right?" Sam asked. Once, I might have bristled at the familiarity between Sam and my father but now, it helped to remind me I wasn't alone. Sam—and Ryan and Tiggy and Gary and Kevin and Morgan and all the people of Verania—loved my father just as much as I did. I didn't even complain when Sam held my hand most of the night, almost convincing myself it was for his benefit.

"He will be," the healer grumbled, and I exhaled so explosively it hurt my throat. "So long as he takes it easy for the foreseeable future. A heart attack is no laughing matter. It scars the heart. And if it happened once, it's easier for it to happen again. Stress, diet, genetics, all of it combines in a perfect storm. He's being cared for to the best of our ability. Morgan is overseeing his care. I don't put much stock in magic, but Morgan's potions have proven successful in the past, so I'm inclined to allow him to continue to treat the king."

"When can Justin see him?" Ryan asked.

The healer eyed me sharply. "When I feel the king is good and ready, and not a moment before."

A thought struck me, terrible and surreal. "Did…did I cause this?"

The healer sighed, shaking his head. "While your little display certainly didn't help, no. This wasn't about your actions, Prince Justin. Rather, it wasn't *just* about your actions. Morgan said that the king seemed off even before the celebration began. I fear this was inevitable, regardless of your fit of pique. Now, if you'll excuse me. I have other patients to care for, not just the king." He turned back toward the door, stopping with his hand on the knob. Without turning around, he said, "Decisions will need to be made, Prince Justin. I don't know if it will be in your father's best interest to continue on as he has been."

I was dumbfounded as he went through the door, closing it behind him.

"What's he talking about?" Sam asked, squeezing my hand. "What decisions?"

I couldn't speak. Thankfully, Ryan did for me. "Let's not worry about that yet. We don't want to do anything until we know more."

Hours later, the air already promising a sticky-hot day, the door opened once more. Sam was half-dozing, and startled when I jumped up, finally letting his hand go. Morgan stood in the doorway, and if he hadn't been smiling, I would've expected the worst.

"He's awake," Morgan said, stepping back and beckoning us in. "Grumpy as a pregnant manticore, but awake."

We hurried into the room, Sam and Ryan crashing into my back when I suddenly stopped. There, laying in a bed, blanket pulled up to his chest, was my father. He looked smaller than I'd ever seen him, dark circles under his closed eyes like bruises. For a moment, I thought he was dead until his chest rose and fell, and he opened his eyes slowly. Feeling like I was in a dream, I went to him, Ryan and Sam moving around to the other side of the bed.

Dad said, "I'm fine," his voice weak, face ashen.

"You're not fine," Morgan said, sounding irritated. "You will stay there, and if you try to give us any grief, I'll make sure it's the last thing you do."

"I just need a bit of rest, and I'll be all right. You'll see."

"Stop talking," I said hoarsely, not giving a shit at the way my voice cracked. "This is serious."

He sighed. "I know it is. But I'm not going to be taken out by something as trivial as a heart attack. When I go, it'll be when—"

"You're not going anywhere," Morgan said. "You're going to stay here, and you're going to *listen* to those of us trying to help you. Honestly, Anthony, your stubbornness is going to be the death of you."

Dad tried to sit up again, batting our hands away when we tried to help him. Seeing that he wasn't to be deterred, Sam took a pillow from the empty bed next to him, putting it behind his back to help him up. Ryan stood at the foot of the bed, hands on Dad's shins. He too looked worried, which only made things worse.

"I'm not going to die right this second," Dad muttered. "All of you, wipe those expressions off your faces. You're not helping."

I wasn't going to let him get off the hook that easy. "The healer said you—"

"Bah," Dad said. "I know what the healer said. He made it very clear, onerous man. Should have retired decades ago, but he doesn't know when to quit."

"Sounds like someone I know," Morgan said, hand on my father's shoulder.

Dad rolled his eyes. "I'm—"

"If you say you're fine one more time," I snapped, "I swear to the gods I'm going to have Sam magically seal your mouth shut."

"And I'll do it," Sam said. "I can even make your mouth disappear." He paused, considering. "I think. That's a little weird. Remind me to try that on Gary, just to see how it goes."

"Ryan," Dad said, sounding a little stronger. "I need you to do something for me."

Ryan snapped to attention, chin jutting out proudly. "Of course, Your Majesty. Anything for you."

"See to our guests," Dad said. "The Yenners. I don't trust them, not for a second. We need to make sure they have no ulterior motives. We're not treating them as the enemy, not yet, but we need to be prepared for anything. Keep an eye on them. Allow them free reign of the open parts of the castle, but never let them out of your sight."

"You have my word," Ryan said, bowing low. Before he left, he leaned over and kissed Sam. "I'll let the others know about the king. Kevin's threatening to eat everyone, even though he's a vegetarian."

"Tell Gary to keep things quiet," Sam said. "Well, *try* to tell Gary to keep things quiet."

Ryan left without another word.

"Should I go too?" Sam asked, fidgeting nervously. "If you want it to be just you and Justin, I can keep guard outside the door. Along with the dozens of knights who won't leave."

Dad chuckled. "That's not necessary. I want you here too. There are things we apparently need to discuss, and it involves the both of you."

"We can do this later," I said stiffly. "You need to sleep."

Dad frowned, brow furrowing. "I'm the parent here."

"Maybe if you took better care of yourself, I would agree. But seeing as how you're the one laid up in bed, I don't give two shits about what you say."

"Damn right," Sam said. "Dumbass. And I say that respectfully."

"Noted," Dad said dryly. He closed his eyes for a moment, a grimace briefly crossing his face. When he opened his eyes again, he seemed stronger, more in control. "Yennbridge," he said, chewing on the word. "How curious they've come."

"Is it true?" I asked. "Did you promise them…" I didn't know how to finish without it sounding ridiculous. I pushed through it. "Me?" Yeah, it still sounded ridiculous.

Dad sighed. "It's not…" He shook his head. "Things were different, then, Justin. The City of Lockes. Verania. Even the world. In the last two decades, we've become much more progressive than we used to be." He sighed. "That's still no excuse." He looked at me with sad eyes. "I never wanted to put you into a position where you couldn't make your own choices, but I've failed in that. And this isn't the first time. Telling you that you needed to be married by the age of twenty-five because that's what our laws dictated at the time. And now this. You have every right to be angry with me, son. I won't try and take that away from you."

"Damn right you won't," I snapped at him. "Of all the…" I collapsed into a chair next to Dad's bed, my legs no longer able to support my weight.

"I only want what's best for you," Dad said quietly. "But I've gone about it all wrong. I apologize, Justin, without reservation."

I bristled. "And that's supposed to make everything better? What the hell would you have done had Ryan and I stayed together? Or not even Ryan. What if I'd found someone else? What would Yennbridge have done? What would *you* have done? Forced me to break up with someone who could potentially be my future because of a godsdamn *pact* you made without my consent? You shouldn't have kept this from me."

"He's right," Morgan said. "And even if you'd forgotten with all that's happened since then, it's not something you can expect Justin to welcome with open arms. He deserves the truth, Anthony. In all things." It felt pointed, though I didn't know why.

But that confusion lasted for only eight seconds.

Because Dad looked up at Morgan, studying him. And then he broke my entire world when he took Morgan's hand in his, and in a calm, measured voice, said, "Morgan and I are in a relationship."

The sound Sam made when he collapsed on the floor in a heap was a mixture of a high whine and a weird snort, like he was a selkie in heat. Morgan rolled his eyes as he reached down to help Sam to his feet where he swayed, eyes wide and shocked. I was frozen, unable to breathe much less move.

"What happened?" Sam asked weakly.

"You swooned," Morgan said, trying hard not to smile. "I don't think I should've expected any other reaction, but apparently, I did."

"You're dating?" Sam squeaked. "The *king*?"

Stupidly, I said the only thing that crossed my mind. "But….but you're *asexual*."

"I am," Morgan agreed. "What does that have to do with anything?"

Nothing. It had nothing to do with anything at all. "He can't be my stepdad! He's a wizard!"

"Oh boy," Dad said. "I don't even know where to start with that."

"I'm not going to be your stepfather," Morgan said.

"Well," Dad said. "Let's not get ahead of ourselves. Who knows what the future could bring?"

"Not helping," Morgan told him, resuming his place at my father's side once he was sure Sam wasn't going to drop to the floor again. I watched as he took Dad's hand in his, their fingers intertwined. It wasn't awkward. They didn't fumble, which meant they'd done it before. "Justin, I would never try and take your father away from you. You are—and shall rightly remain—his first priority."

"But not my only one," Dad said. "You're old enough now to hear such things." He frowned at me. "And I won't have you denigrating Morgan because you're upset with me. He has proven himself as much as anyone here. But even more so, he has given me happiness, something I never thought I'd have for myself again."

"So you get to choose who you want to be with and I don't? How long has this been going on?"

"It's not new," Dad said carefully. "There…" He looked up at Morgan, and I was floored by the soft expression on his face. "There was always something there. I…pushed for it, in these last years, but Morgan was hesitant. He wanted to focus on Sam's training, and rightly so. Then Myrin came, and…" Dad let out a shuddering breath. "I thought Morgan was lost. When I was in the dungeons, my grief threatened to overwhelm me. The loss of Verania, the loss of my people and home, the loss of Sam. And you, Justin. I grieved for you, even though I knew that you would guide our people as their rightful leader. As a parent, you worry about every little thing, from the scrapes on your knees to carrying a sword in my name. But I also grieved for Morgan, knowing that I'd missed my chance. I wished for just one more moment with him, so he would know all that was in my heart." He blinked rapidly, his eyes shining. "And when he returned, when I saw his face again, I knew my wish had been granted, thanks to our Sam here. I was done with half-measures. I told Morgan in no uncertain terms that I cared for him, and that if he allowed me the honor, I would spend my days making sure he knew just how special he is."

"He was quite forceful in his conviction," Morgan said. "And who was I to decline such an offer?"

"He's not your cornerstone," I said, struggling to maintain control.

"No," Morgan said. "He's not. She…I loved her. For the entirety of her life, I loved her. And she loved me. I will never forget what she was to me, and all that she gave me. She is not your father. But that doesn't mean I have to spend the rest of my life alone."

"Your life," I muttered. "Your life that will go on for long after my father is nothing but dust and bones."

"We know that," Dad said, a warning in his voice. I was so close to crossing a line, and we both knew it. He was giving me the opportunity to pull back. I wondered if it was already too late. "But if you let something like semi-immortality stop you, then you've already lost."

"Gary's gonna flip," Sam said. "Like, I hope you're ready for all of that, because I can't say if he's going to cry, try to stab you, or attempt to seduce you both." He grimaced. "Is it too late to send him back to the forest, or…?"

Dad chuckled. "I look forward to his reaction. It will certainly be…well. It's Gary, so I don't know quite how it's going to be." His smile faded slightly as he looked at me. "Love is a light, a fire that will keep you warm when you think you'll never be warm again. It was you I thought of in the dungeons, Justin. You and Sam and Gary and Tiggy and Ryan and Kevin. But it was also Morgan, because even when I thought him gone forever, no one, not the Darks, not Myrin, not *anyone* could take his memory away from me."

I scowled at him, my head filled with a sharp buzzing sound. "What the hell does this have to do with the Yenners?"

"What if?" Dad asked simply.

I gaped at him.

"What if," Dad said, "you gave this a chance? What if you let down your guard, if only for a moment? What if this king could be someone important to you?"

"Did you *see* him?" I demanded. "He tripped over his own feet! He said cripes, Dad. *Cripes.* And then he made a mockery of me in my own ballroom by—"

"Well," Sam said, "let's be honest here. You started it by challenging him to a duel, so I don't think you can say it was all his fault."

I turned my head slowly toward him.

"Yep," Sam said. "Shutting up now."

I doubted that immensely.

"You never know unless you try," Dad continued. "Maybe it won't work out. Maybe you'll both find yourselves to be incompatible. If that's the case, we'll deal with it then. I won't force you into anything, Justin. If you're set in your convictions, then we'll turn them away. I can't say there won't be repercussions, but I need to do right by you more than I have."

"You'd go to war over me," I said, dumbfounded.

"I would," Dad said. "Because you're my heart, the very reason I get out of bed every morning. And not just because of who you'll be. Even if you weren't a prince, even if we were paupers without a cent to our name, I would do anything for you. You're my son, Justin. Nothing—no king, no magician, no wizard and certainly no pact—will ever change that. And yet, here we are, with me having failed you as a father again." He blinked rapidly as he looked away. "I wish... I wish for many things. Peace. Joy. Happiness. Not just for me or you. For everyone. But I've gone about it all wrong. I'm so sorry, Justin. You deserve better than what I've done."

"I do," I said evenly. "But I think the same could be said about me." I glanced at Sam before looking back at my father. "What would you ask of me?"

Dad eyed me for a long moment. "Are you asking me as your king, or as your father?"

I shrugged. "Is there a difference?"

"There is," Dad said. "One is borne of duty, the other of love."

I felt as if I was playing a game of chess where the rules had been changed without my knowledge. "What would the King ask of me?"

"To do what's right in your heart."

"And my father?"

He smiled quietly. "As your father, I want you to find the person or persons who make you think anything is possible. And perhaps that's Dylan. What's the worst that could happen?"

"Yeah," Sam said. "See, when you say something like that, it usually means the worst is going to happen, and pretty soon, we'll be trapped by a monologuing villain who's trying to awaken some ancient god that sleeps beneath Verania—wow. That's...huh. Are there any ancient gods that we should be worried about? Because that would suck."

"Sam's right," I said, for the first time and the last time. "We don't know anything about them. For all we know, Dylan and his stupid magician have devious plans to take over the City of Lockes, and where will we be then?"

"Well, at least you'll be able to say I told you so," Dad said.

I glared at him. "Stop trying to be funny!"

Dad rolled his eyes. "Trying, he says. Ouch. That's a blow to the ego." Before I could yell at him some more, he raised his hand, trying to placate me. "I know you're both concerned. You have every right to be. With all you've seen, all you've done, I wouldn't expect anything less. That being said you can't let fear rule your lives. We *survived*, Justin. We survived and lived to fight another day. But what's the point of fighting if we can't enjoy what we've fought for? I promised myself that if—*when* I was freed, I wouldn't let anything hold me back anymore. I was done playing it safe. Morgan knows how I feel about him because I could no longer keep it to myself. Sam found his happy ending. You deserve the same. If it's not with Dylan, then it will be with someone else, so long as you open yourself to it. For so long you've had this…this armor around you. It's kept you safe, kept you whole, but that's not all life is."

I laughed bitterly. "So because *you* think you've found something with Morgan, you want me to have the same."

"I don't think," Dad said sharply. "I know. And while I can appreciate your anger, Morgan's done nothing to deserve your ire. In fact, he's paid the ultimate price, all in our name."

Chastened, I mumbled out an apology.

"It's sudden," Morgan said, "at least for you. I realize that. We didn't keep this from you because of how we thought you'd both react. We did so because we wanted to make sure it was something that would last."

"Is it?" Sam asked.

"It is," Dad said firmly. "I love him. And he loves me. That's all you should care about."

I latched on to the only thing I could. "But he's a wizard. How is that going to work? Is he going to be…what, the King's Consort? Another king? Aren't there laws prohibiting such a thing? He can't be both the King's Wizard *and* the Consort. That'd be a conflict of interest, and one people won't be happy about, even if they love you both."

Dad took in a great breath, letting it out slow. "No. He won't."

I blinked. "I don't understand."

Dad looked at Morgan, who nodded. "It's time, Anthony. You know it in your bones just as much as I do."

I didn't like the sound of that, especially when Dad turned back to me, a thoughtful expression on his face. He glanced at Sam at the end of his bed. Then, he said, "I've done all that I can for you both. Between Morgan and I, we've prepared you for this eventuality. I'm getting on in years, and I want to enjoy the time I have left. I love being king, it's in my blood, and nothing has brought me greater pleasure, through the good times and the bad. In this last year, seeing how we've all come together to rebuild, to reclaim our lives, I've wondered if it was time for a change. A king isn't meant to rule forever. My sunset is coming, Justin, and though I plan on staying around for many, many years to come, the sun is rising on you."

No. No, no, nono*no*—

"Which is why I'm beginning to make plans to step down from the throne," Dad said with a finality like the slamming of a door. "You, Justin, will be king. Sam, you will be the King's Wizard. Morgan and I will remain as your advisors, if you'd let us."

"Holy fucking *shit*," Sam whispered fervently.

"You're addled," I said wildly. "The heart attack, the potions, it's all gone to your head and is making you talk crazy." I reached up and squished his cheeks together. "Don't go toward the light! Stay away from the fucking light!"

"I'll kill the light," Sam snarled. "Star Dragon! You hear me? You even *think* about bringing light, I will fucking destroy it *and* you!"

"This is going as well as you thought," Morgan said dryly. "Sprinkled with a bit of blasphemy for good measure."

Dad gripped my wrists, thumbs brushing against the backs of my hands. "This wasn't a decision made this morning or last night. I've been thinking this for a long time, ever since you told me about how you acted after I was locked away. It was a test, one I wish you'd never had to face. But you did, and you rose to the challenge with fire in your eyes and love in your heart. You had lost me, lost Morgan, Sam and your home. By right, no one would have blamed you if you'd collapsed in on yourself. But you didn't. You acted like a king, Justin. I've heard countless stories of your bravery, of your kindness, the way you cared for the people displaced from their homes and scared out of their minds. It wasn't just about Sam and his destiny. You played a part in it, and a big one at that. I knew then that you were ready. I wouldn't be telling you this if I didn't think you were. You acted like a king because you *are* a king, Justin Roth. And I couldn't be prouder of that."

"That's not—"

"Roth," Sam said.

We all looked at him.

"Your last name is *Roth*?" Sam asked, eyes bulging. "When the hell did you get a surname?"

Of course that's what he'd grab on to. My father was telling us that we were about to be in charge of an entire country, and he was talking about *last names* of all things. "Since I was born," I snapped at him.

He looked confused, which was normal for him. "What? Why didn't I know that? What else have you been keeping from me?" He paled. "Oh my gods, do you have a middle name?"

"You're an idiot."

"What is it?" he asked. "What's your middle name? Is it Gravedigger? No, wait. Tiffany? Potato? That doesn't make sense. Who names their kid Potato? Well, some people might. It's a fun word to say. Po. Tay. Toe. Fun fact! When we lived in the Slums, there were days when all we had to eat were potatoes. Dad knew how to cook them in a lot of different ways, so we could pretend we weren't eating the same things over and over and by the look on Justin's face, I really need to stop talking. Done and done!" Then, in a whisper, "Justin Potato Roth. Your full name is stupidly glorious."

"It's not *potato*," I growled at him. "What is wrong with you? It's Marcus."

"Justin Marcus Roth," Sam said. "Wow. That is…huh. That's weirdly sexy." He eyed me up and down. "Question: if Ryan and I don't work out and I suddenly find myself attracted to you for reasons better left unexplored, does that mean I get to be a King's Consort? Because I think I'd be pretty good at it."

Scandalized, I said, "In what realm of possibility would I ever consider marrying you?"

Sam sniffed. "Rude. I'm an amazing husband. Just ask your ex-fiancé."

"Sam," I said through gritted teeth, "in case it didn't get through that thick skull of yours, Dad just said I'm going to be king, and you the King's Wizard. Shut. The fuck. *Up*."

Sam squinted at me before turning toward Dad and Morgan. "Yeah, I'm pretty much with Justin here. Not with the shutting up part because when has that ever worked, but all the rest? You have got to be out of your godsdamn minds."

"We're not," Dad said. "I'm as clear-headed as I've ever been. Sam, Morgan, if you could please give my son and I a moment. I need to speak with him alone. And Sam, not a word of this to anyone. Not about Morgan and me, nor anything about you two taking over, not until we're sure."

Sam nodded. "Of course. To be honest, I'm still a little hung up on sexy Justin Marcus Potato Roth to worry about running a country, and it'll probably take me at least a week to recover from that, so, mum's the word!" He squeezed my father's feet through the blanket and then turned to leave. He stopped before he took another step, and I thought he was going to once again try and say my father needed to reconsider. Instead, he slapped my ass and said, "You got this, dude. I believe in you. And if I may, that thing has bounce. Good for you."

Morgan sighed. "Sam, we've talked about this. Just because you think something doesn't mean you need to say it out loud." He leaned forward, kissing my father on the forehead. Dad closed his eyes. "Go easy," Morgan whispered. "But listen. Hear him out. All will be well."

They left us, the door closing behind them.

I didn't know what to say, didn't know what to do. I was angry, perturbed and strangely filled with a roiling energy that caused my skin to vibrate. I stood from my chair and began to pace next to my father's bed, trying to put my thoughts in order.

Dad didn't speak, though I felt his gaze on me, watching every step I took. Finally, when I could take the silence no longer, I looked at him, shoulders stiff. "You're sure about this."

"Which? Morgan, or you becoming the king?"

"Both."

"I am," he said quietly. "I believe in both things in equal measure, which should show you how serious I am. I don't make decisions lightly, Justin. You above all others should know that."

"Why now?" I asked. "With all that's happening, why now?"

He winced. "Well, to be fair, I wasn't expecting the Yenners."

"Oh, yes," I mocked him. "To be fair."

"I deserve that."

"Damn right you do. Of all the things to drop on me, this is the worst."

"And you're entitled to your anger," he said. "If our roles were reversed, I'd probably feel the same way. I'm not going to try and take that from you. Come here." He patted the bed beside him.

I sat down begrudgingly and didn't try and pull my hand away when he settled his own on top of it. His touch was warm, familiar. And while it didn't destroy the storm in my head, the winds lessened, light peering through the stormy clouds. "Listen," he said. "Don't interrupt. I need to get this out now."

I didn't like the sound of that.

He looked down at our hands. "For a time, I thought I wasn't a good father."

Startled, I said, "Dad, you didn't—"

He squeezed my hand. "Hush. Please. Let me say what I need to say." Once he was sure my mouth was closed, he continued. "You were…not unkind, for the most part, but you were closed off, and I can't help but feel it's my fault."

Uncomfortable, I said, "That's not—"

He arched an eyebrow. "The truth? Correct? Don't relieve me of my responsibility, Justin. To become a better person, I must own up to my mistakes. I tried to do right by you, but even my best intentions led me down a path where I attempted to follow the rule of law rather than considering what your heart wanted. That is a terrible thing for a father to do, and I'm sorry." He raised his other hand as I tried to speak. "I don't expect your forgiveness, now, or ever. Your anger is justified."

I said nothing.

His fingers brushed against mine. "And yet, I wasn't lying when I said you had an armor about you, an armor that you'd fastened to yourself to shield your heart. I worried about you, wondering how I could get you to see that there was more to life than learning how to be a king. Though that played a large part, I couldn't figure out how to make you see there was more in this world than a crown atop your head." He smiled. "In the end, it wasn't me who showed you the way, though I still like to think I played a part in it."

"Then who?" I asked.

He looked at me pointedly. "Stop. You know who I speak of. You don't have to hide yourself from me. I'm not talking to you as your king, but as your father. Against all odds, you found yourself surrounded by a group made up of the most loyal beings a person could ever ask for. Sam. Ryan. Tiggy. Gary. Kevin. All of them have chipped away at your armor. They did what I could not: they opened your eyes, extending a hand of friendship and brotherhood. You did your best to slap it away, but they knew as well as I did that you needed them as much as they needed you. They'd go to the ends of the earth for you, and I know you'd do the same, even if you'd complain every step of the way."

"That's because they're idiots," I mumbled.

"Perhaps," Dad said. "But so are you."

"Hey!"

Dad rolled his eyes. "A father is allowed to say such things about his child, especially when said father can also have a bout of idiocy every now and then. I'm not perfect, but then I never claimed to be. We knew this day would come, Justin. It was only a matter of time."

"Dad," I whispered, unable to say more.

"And you won't do it alone. You will have your friends who have become your family. And you'll have me. Just because I'll step aside doesn't mean I won't be there for you. I've thought about this, perhaps more than anything else. Do you want to know what I discovered?"

I nodded.

"You," he said. "In all your glory. What you achieved during my imprisonment was beyond even my wildest dreams of what I knew you could do. You led our people, Justin. When you were scared and furious, you still rose to the challenge."

"There's another *but* coming, isn't there?"

"Yes," Dad said gently. "Because that Justin, the leader of the resistance, isn't the Justin that sits beside me today. In the last year, you've grown listless. Ever since Myrin's death, you've lost your spark, that great fire that burned within you. What are you doing with your life?"

A quick flash of anger mixed with shame roared through me. "The best I can."

Dad shook his head. "You're not. While you haven't reverted to the way you used to be, you've picked up the pieces of your discarded armor, trying to protect yourself once more. And for what?"

"Yeah, well, maybe that's what happens when your home is taken from you along with your father."

He sounded frustrated when he said, "I wish you could hear yourself. And I wish you would hear *me*. I'm not saying this as a slight against you. I'm trying to open your eyes to the truth. A king is not an island, cut off by a vast ocean. He can't be afraid to admit his mistakes, to look to others to help guide him. But he has to trust in himself enough to make decisions that others can't. And I don't know if you're quite there."

I threw up my hands. "Then why the hell are you telling me you want to step down if you don't think I'm ready?"

"Because I need to find a way to ignite that spark again, to see that same fire in your eyes. I don't. All I see is smoke, a hint of what once was. I was hoping this would be the push you needed, but now that the Yenners are here, I wonder if I need to rethink things."

"Then why tell me this?" I asked. "Why not just let things go on how they are?"

"Because you're growing complacent," Dad said quietly. "And bored. I can see it clearly as I see you now."

He wasn't wrong, though I hated to admit it. Ever since Myrin, I felt as if I were floating through life each day the same as the last. I *was* bored, and I didn't know how to stop it. "Fine," I mumbled. "Maybe you have a point."

"I do know what I'm talking about, sometimes. You are not an island, Justin. You try to be, but I assure you you're not. You are not alone." Dad turned my hand over until our palms rested together, his finger encircling my wrist, brushing against my thundering pulse. "They—and you—are the future of Verania. Idealistic, hopeful, and more than a little stupid, but that's necessary to get the job done. What if I'd told the Justin of five years ago about where you'd be today?"

"I'd say you needed to be put into an asylum and never released for your own safety."

Dad snorted. "Sounds about right. But here we are, all the same, regardless of what you once believed." He looked thoughtful before he said, "And perhaps the same could happen with King Dylan of Yennbridge."

I snatched my hand away as if he'd scalded me.

"This is not an order," Dad said quickly. "For all that I've taught you about listening to others, I've proven that I've failed to heed my own advice. The choice is yours, Justin. And I will support you in whatever you decide. It's the very least I could do. Consider him, or don't. And even if you *do* and it doesn't work out, we'll deal with the consequences together."

"And if it does work?" I asked slowly, angry at the thought.

Dad laughed. "Then it does. But you need to look within yourself and decide for yourself. Perhaps King Dylan could be the spark you've been looking for."

"You mean it."

"I do," he said simply. "And I know you'll be the king this country deserves, one day."

"How?" I asked helplessly. "How do you know?"

"Because you're my son. I love you more than I can say."

And because I couldn't not, I collapsed on top of my father. He grunted but made no move to push me off. Instead, he held me close, my face in his neck, his beard tickling my forehead. He stroked my back as I clutched at him. "I'm still angry with you," I whispered. "But you can't ever leave me."

"I'm not going anywhere," Dad whispered back.

*****

I WASN'T SURPRISED TO FIND SAM waiting outside the healer's room, pacing as the knights watched him. They snapped to attention when they saw me. I ignored them for Sam. He looked up at me, a question on his face.

I shook my head, grabbing him by the arm and pulling him down the hallway around the corner. Once I was sure we were alone, I did the one thing I swore I'd never do in this life, or the next.

I hugged him willingly.

He startled, his arms pinned underneath my own. For a moment, all he did was breathe.

"That's not how hugs work," I muttered against his shoulder.

"Oh," he whispered as if he thought speaking any louder would scare me away. Carefully, he pulled his arms free and wrapped them around me. "There," he said, hugging me so hard, my ribs creaked. "That's the ticket."

"Don't make this weird."

"Uh, dude, no offense, it's already a little weird. Not bad!" he added quickly as I tried to pull away. "Just…weird. You give good hugs."

I pushed him away. "You made it weird."

"You're the one covering me in your feelings!" he retorted.

"Why do you have to say it like that?"

He rolled his eyes. "Oh, because *I'm* the asshole here? You're the one who attacked me with affection!"

I made a face. "Gods, you're the worst. I don't know what the hell I was thinking."

Sam grinned at me. "You were thinking you looooove me."

"I don't," I said stiffly. "And never speak to me in such a way again. I'll have you pooping in buckets before you can even blink."

He punched me in the shoulder. "Just warn me next time, okay? The next hug is going to blow your mind."

"It won't happen again."

"Uh huh. Sure it won't." He frowned. "Your dad okay?"

I shook my head. "I'm convinced he's addled. He thinks I've lost a spark, whatever the hell that means."

Sam scratched the back of his neck. "Well, he's not *wrong*."

"What the hell are you talking about?"

"For real?" Sam asked. "You've been…not *bad*, but…off. I don't know, man. I have too, so don't get pissed off at me. I'm in the same boat as you, I think."

"We're not the same," I snapped at him.

He shrugged. "Sort of. We've both got these big responsibilities hanging over our heads and it can sometimes feel like a guillotine, you know?"

I did, more than I cared to admit. "That doesn't help me."

"Then what will?" He looked at me earnestly. "My job, the one I've been training for years to do, is to serve as your wizard. That means I need to help you whenever I can. And not just *need*. I want to."

"Why?"

Sam smiled. "Because we're going to be the best King and King's Wizard Verania has ever seen. I got faith, dude. But we need to remember to have that faith in ourselves, too."

I hesitated, thinking hard. A spark of a plan began to form in my head, and for the first time since the debacle that was the Liberation Day celebration, I had hope. The king stuff? Fine. It was always going to happen one day, and if that day came sooner than I expected, I'd still rise to the challenge. I'd find that spark again. I knew I could.

King Dylan, on the other hand…maybe there was something to it, just not in the way everyone seemed to think.

"I have an idea," I told him. "We're going to do something about Dylan."

Sam nodded eagerly. "You're going to go on a series of dates with him, each more romantic than the last until you realize you can't spend your life without him and then you bend him over the nearest available surface and stick your princely scepter in his royal carriage?"

I stared at him.

"Yeah," he said with a wince. "I'm really not proud of that, but it's out there now, so we can either let ourselves become mired in sexy shenanigans with a hot foreign king or move on. Guess what I vote? It's probably not what you're thinking."

I sighed. "Sexy shenanigans."

"Whoa," Sam breathed. "It's like you can read my mind."

He froze at the smile on my face, all teeth. "Not hardly. I'm going to make him wish he'd never heard of Verania, much less stepped foot in my godsdamn castle. By the time I'm done with him, he's going to curse the day he'd ever heard my name. And you're going to help me."

"Whoa," Sam said. "Dude, chills. I just got *chills*. But…"

"But what?" I asked, exasperated.

"But is that the right thing to do?" He flinched when I growled at him. "Look, I get things are crazy right now, what with your dad having a heart attack, a king from a faraway land coming here to sweep you off your feet, and your dad getting a taste of wizard for the first time and realizing what he was missing—"

"Sam!"

"What! It's *true*. You know what they say, once you go wizard, all the rest is… godsdammit. I can't think of a rhyme. Fuck Kevin for infecting me with his poetry!"

"What does that have to do with anything?"

He shrugged awkwardly. "I get being pissed about everything happening all at once. And you're scared with what's going on with your dad—"

"I'm not *scared*," I hissed at him.

"I am," he said, and I deflated. "I know your dad is going to be okay—better than okay, even—but it's still a little scary. I don't want you making any decisions that you'll regret later."

I snorted. "That's rich, coming from you."

"There's some good stuff that can come from this, though."

"Good stuff?" I asked incredulously.

"Good stuff," he repeated. "Think about it. Your Dad and Morgan are dating and they asked us not to tell anyone, so that means you and I will need to hang out all the time and talk about it so I don't accidentally let it slip to Ryan. Or Gary. Or Tiggy. Or Kevin. Or a random person walking by me who doesn't care at all, but I'll probably end up telling them anyway."

I groaned. "This is the worst day of my life."

He punched my shoulder. "You're not a jerk, dude. Seriously. I know you've got this whole I'm the prince, no one fucks with me thing going on, but is that the right way to go about this? Being mean is just taxing. What's the point of being a dick to people?"

"Lady Tina," I said.

"She's not a people," he said promptly. "She's a fire demon bent on perfumed destruction." He glanced over my shoulder, eyes widening.

I ignored him. "I don't give two shits about being *mean*. If you think for one second I'm not going to do everything in my power to make Dylan's life a living hell—"

"Ah," Sam said, voice slightly shriekish. "Maybe we shouldn't—"

I overrode him. "—then you're sorely mistaken. He's going to find out just how much of a dick I can be. I promise you that. He won't know what hit him."

"Yep," Sam said, nodding furiously. "Totally get that. Question: you know how in books and plays when two people—say a wizard and an almost king—are best friends, and the almost king is talking shit about someone without knowing that said someone is standing right behind them, and then the wizard tries to stop him from talking and the almost king comes to a realization and says, 'He's right behind me, isn't he?'"

"What the hell are you talking about?" I snapped.

"Wow," Sam said. "I thought that example was pretty applicable to our real-world situation and you'd get it right away. Huh. I don't know if that makes me look bad, or you. Probably you."

I froze, the hairs on the back of my neck standing on end. "He's right behind me, isn't he?"

"There it is," Sam said. "I knew you could do it."

I turned slowly.

There, leaning against the wall, arms folded across his chest, was King Dylan of Yennbridge. He arched an eyebrow as the blood rushed from my face.

"Romance," Sam whispered.

# CHAPTER 7

## Frat Bros and Sashes Made of Evil

"WHAT ARE YOU DOING?" I asked, suddenly furious at Dylan and Sam and myself for reasons that were *not* my fault. "Are you spying on us?"

"Spying?" Dylan asked, face bunching up like he was thinking too hard for his brain to handle. "I've been standing here for the last five minutes. You really didn't see me?" He looked down at himself. For some reason, he decided to flex his arms, muscles bunching up. I did not stare at them.

I sniffed. "It's not my fault you blend in with the walls."

Sam stepped forward until he stood next to me. He grinned so widely I thought his lips would tear. He looked at me, then at Dylan, then back at me, bouncing on his heels. "Ignore me," he said. "I'm just here to observe. Act naturally."

I glared at Dylan. "And *why* have you been standing there for the last five minutes?"

Dylan pushed himself off the wall, though he kept his distance. "I wanted to make sure your father was okay."

"Why?" I asked. "He's not on his death bed if that's what you're asking. So, if you thought you could steal the kingdom you should reconsider your plans. And also leave."

He looked confused. "Why would I want to steal your kingdom? I already have one of my own. Having two sounds like a lot of work. I can work hard, but it's better when I don't have to."

"Ooh," Sam whispered, glancing back and forth between us.

"Consider going back to your own kingdom then," I said. "In fact, why don't you leave now? Save us all some trouble. I can help you pack. Not that it looks like you have much."

Dylan smiled. "You're funny. They didn't tell me you had a sense of humor. Wicked awesome."

"*Ooooh*," Sam whispered even louder.

"I am *not*," I said. "Never call me that again."

He looked confused. It was not adorable, no matter how expressive his eyebrows were. I wondered if I could get away with shaving them off in his sleep. "Okay," he said. He cleared his throat. "So. How are you?"

I stared at him.

He winced. "Aw, nuts. Sorry, bro. Not the greatest question."

"Nuts," I repeated. "*Bro.*"

Dylan scratched the back of his neck, the ring through his nose catching the light from the sconce above him. "Yeah, should have thought that through more. Sometimes my mouth moves before my brain finishes thinking its thoughts."

"That might be the first honest thing you've said since you arrived."

He must have missed the point entirely, because he said, "If it makes you feel any better, I know what you're going through. Sucks, right? Totally sucks."

I scoffed. "I highly doubt you know *anything* about what I'm going through."

"Dude," Sam hissed. "Dead parents, remember?"

If Sam and Dylan thought we'd bond over parental angst, they were both out of their godsdamn minds. Even though I wanted nothing more than to crush him where he stood, I wasn't a *complete* asshole. "Whatever. I don't want to talk about it. My dad is fine, your parents aren't, and that's where we are."

Dylan nodded. "Yeah, that about sums it up. Hey, do you know what I do when I'm feeling sad?"

"No," I said. "And I don't want to."

"Sometimes I go for a walk," he said as if I hadn't spoken at all. "I'll find a really good tree and sit under it and not think about anything at all. Or even better, push-ups! Releases endorphins. Makes you feel really good. Do you want to do some push-ups with me?" And before I could stop him, he dropped to the floor, jewelry jangling. "One," he said, pushing himself up. "Two. Three. Four. Five." He glanced up at me as if to make sure I was watching. Then, without looking away, he folded his left arm behind him, and used his right to lower himself to the ground before pushing himself back up. "Six. Seven. Eight. Nine. Ten." He jumped up and clapped once, looking inordinately pleased with himself. "There, see? I feel better. You want to try?"

"Oh, my gods," Sam breathed. "He's a *himbo*. Yes. *Yes*. Where have you been all of Justin's life?"

Dylan frowned. "In Yennbridge. That's where I'm from, remember?"

Oh my gods. Sam was right. He was a godsdamn himbo. What the *fuck*. How did I even know what a himbo *was*? "As fun as this is, I have matters to tend to, so if you'll excuse us."

"Can I come too?" Dylan asked.

"Oh," Sam said, glancing down at his bare wrist. "Would you look at the time. I just remembered that I promised to give Ryan a massage that will lead to my face planted in his ass for at least thirty-six minutes. Justin, Dylan, have so much fun, you two! You've really earned it."

Before I could stop him, he hurried down the hall, glancing back at me with an obnoxious wink. He disappeared around the corner.

Only to reappear a second later, head sticking out.

I glared at him. "I can still see you."

He inched back slowly until only his cheek and right ear were visible. "How about now?"

"Sam!"

"Going! Bye, Justin! Bye, Dylan! Bye! Have fun falling in love even though you don't think you will right at this moment! Bye!"

And then he was gone, footsteps echoing as he left us alone.

All alone.

It was then I realized that Sam was the worst person in the entire world, and he would know suffering before the end of his life. Well, more suffering. Maybe I'd hold off on it for a little bit. I scowled at how soft I was getting.

Dylan grinned at me.

"I'm not going to do push-ups," I told him. "So get that out of your oversized head right now."

His eyes rolled up, and I thought he was about to faint. Alarmed, I stepped forward, only stopping when I realized he was trying to look at his own head. "Seriously?"

He looked at me again. "Is it really big? I didn't think it was any different than other peoples' heads. Is that a thing in Verania? One of your customs? I'll be honest, I tried to read up about your kingdom, but it was all in really small print and it made my head hurt." He paused, considering. "My really *big* head."

My gods, he was a walking, talking nightmare of epic proportions. Focus, I reminded myself. He's just a dumb, pretty face. I'd dealt with plenty of them before. Bedded a couple or six. I knew exactly how to handle him. "I don't like you." There. That would show him.

He wasn't offended. Why? *Why.* "That's okay. You don't know me. But once you do, I think you'll like me. I have a lot to offer."

Oh, this should be good. "Like what?"

He startled, eyes widening. "Okay, Dyl," he muttered to himself. "Just like you practiced. You got this. I believe in you." Then, louder (and so painfully rehearsed, the secondhand embarrassment made my skin crawl), "Hello. My name is Dylan Davidson. My friends call me Double D. I like—"

"They call you *what?*"

He frowned. "Can you please not interrupt me? It throws me off, and I have to start over." He waited a beat to see if I would speak again. Flabbergasted, I couldn't get a single word out. "As I was saying, my name is Dylan Davidson. My friends call me Double D. I like working out, long walks in the forest, dragonflies because their wings are amazing, dancing, singing—hey! I even know the theme song of Verania! Cheesy dicks and candlesticks, and everything you—"

"That's not our theme song!"

He wasn't to be deterred. "I also like eating steak—in fact, I'd eat it every day if I could—playing cards, drinking mead—but not to excess!—and the last time it snowed, I organized a group of four hundred people to have a snowball fight. I lost, but that's okay. Winning isn't everything. I'm just glad everyone had fun. Oh! I like having fun too, because when you're having fun, you can't be sad. I don't like being sad."

I gaped at him.

He looked down at his hand, mouth moving silently as he ticked off something with his fingers. "Right, and one more thing." He stood upright, chin jutting out. "I think you're handsome, and it would be my honor to get to know you. You seem nice. Well, maybe not *nice* nice, but that's what I practiced, so I thought I should say it. Okay, your turn."

"My turn for *what*?"

"To tell me about yourself," he said. "But before you do, I have a present for you. I meant to give it to you at the celebration, but then I stabbed you instead and your dad had a heart attack, so I forgot." He grunted as he reached into the pockets of his trousers, his big blunt fingers barely able to get into the tight fabric. I swallowed thickly as his trousers rode low on his hips, a little tuft of black hair peeking over the hem. If you'd told me yesterday that I'd be staring at a visiting king's pubes, I would have had you executed immediately.

He pulled out a small…stone? Crystal? Something gold that glittered in the low light. I tensed, sure this was going to be something magic, and that he was going to suck out my soul or turn me evil. He held it out to me, the crystal resting on his palm.

It looked like it'd been carved inelegantly. I wasn't sure what it was supposed to be exactly. Perhaps a deformed goat? I tried to remember what Yennbridge exported to Verania. Were there any deformed goats? That didn't sound like something we'd want, but then who did?

"What is it?" I asked despite myself.

"It's a heart," he said proudly. "I carved it myself. It took me thirteen weeks."

It looked nothing like a heart. "What's it for? Is it magic? Are you trying to trap me inside it so you can assume the throne and combine our kingdoms?"

He frowned. "Um, no? It's not magic. I don't know how to do magic. That's for magicians and wizards. It's a heart made out of citrine, which is a type of crystal, in case you didn't know. Ramos said that I should give you cows, but that's stupid. Why would you want a cow when you can have something I made myself?" He smiled. "When you make something yourself, it shows you were thinking about the person you're gifting it to."

"And you were thinking of me when you made that," I said dubiously.

He nodded, earrings jangling. "A gift of a heart from my heart to yours."

I snorted. "Wow. Has that ever worked on anyone?"

"I don't know," he said. "I've never tried it before."

Now that I believed. Not wanting to be *too* rude, I took the crystal from him carefully, wanting to avoid touching him. The heart (that looked even more like a deformed goat up close) was heavier than I expected it to be for something so small. It had a heft to it, and for a brief moment, I considered chucking it at his head. "Thank…you?"

"Oh, man," he said. "You're so welcome. Wow. I was really nervous about it. I thought you were going to love it, but one can't be too sure."

"I didn't say I *loved* it—"

"Wait!" he cried, and I stumbled at the forcefulness. "I have one more thing for you!"

I groaned. "You can't keep giving me things. It's not—"

He raised his arms like wings on either side of him. He spun in a slow circle once, twice, and then stopped, lowering his arms. "There."

I looked around, wondering what I was missing. "There what?"

"That's the official greeting of Yennbridge," he said proudly. "It's a sign of peace and charity and love. When you're feeling bad, sometimes you just have to spin in a circle for a bit and then you won't feel bad anymore. It doesn't always work, but when it does, there's nothing like it. You should try it, bro."

"I don't feel bad."

He squinted at me. "You don't? Because that look on your face either means you feel really bad, or you ate rotten ham. One time, my friends and I ate rotten ham without meaning to, and then we leaked from every hole we had for a week. It was crazy."

"This is my normal face," I groused, gripping the crystal in my hands.

"Oh. Well. Congratulations? It's a good face."

I rushed toward him. He stumbled, back hitting the wall. I stopped inches from him, our noses almost brushing together. "Whoa," he breathed. "It worked? Holy crud, I thought it was going to be a lot harder than that. Please be gentle with me. I know I'm big, but I like it when it's gentle."

"When *what's* gentle?" I said, teeth bared.

"The sex," he said. "That's what we're about to do, right? I'm okay with that. Sure, I'd like to get to know you better before that, go on a date or ten, and we'll probably need to have a conversation about hard limits. I don't like fluids. I'm not talking about the sex kind, but…other fluids." He glanced down between us as if to prove his point.

"I'm not going to piss on you!"

He looked relieved. "Good. Because even though I respect kinks, I also know what I don't like. I have a friend—his name is Digger, good guy—who likes that sort of thing. Not for me, but to each their own, you know? Who am I to judge when people want to be covered in—"

"We're not having sex," I said coldly. "Get that idea out of your head *right* now."

He nodded, looking relieved. "Not until we're married. Got it. I can respect your customs and boundaries."

Flummoxed, I stepped away from him. "We're not getting married."

He frowned. "Oh, man, did no one tell you?"

I shook my head. "I didn't even know you existed until you stepped into the ballroom."

"Sucks, bro," he said amiably, seemingly unaware that he was *this* close to getting my knee in his junk. "Sorry about that. It probably just slipped their minds. No biggie. We got this. I believe in us. Do you like bread?"

I felt like I'd been in a severe accident, one in which my entire body had been crushed to nothing but gristle. "Bread."

"Yeah. Bread." He tapped his finger against his chin. "I thought I remembered reading that you had a thing for bread." He shook his head. "Or was it cheese? Or doing backflips. Can you do backflips? I tried once on a dare, but I landed on my neck and had to wear a brace for three weeks. I got so much shit for it, but then everyone signed it and I felt better."

Was this real life? If it was, I was obviously cursed. If it wasn't (and I wanted to believe this more than anything) then perhaps this was Sam's doing. Yes, that sounded right. This was Sam's fault. Another one of his drills. I was trapped in a magical sleep, and this was a construct he'd created in order to test the limits of my patience. I didn't know if I was succeeding or failing. "Everyone signed your neck brace?"

He laughed. "It was pretty gnarly. My buddies were egging me on, and we were pretty hammered." He paled. "Not that I get drunk all the time! Just sometimes. And *this* time was special, because it was the six-year reunion for our fraternity."

Oh my gods. Somehow, it was only getting worse. "You're a frat bro."

"Yep! Omicron Upsilon, the biggest in Yennbridge. We have this cheer and everything, Omicron Upsilon! We've got it going on! Look at us, we're the best, we are better than all the r—"

"Please," I said weakly. "No more." I tilted my head back toward the ceiling. "Sam, if this is your doing, I'd really like to wake up now. I demand it."

Dylan followed my gaze upward. Then, in a whisper, "Does your castle talk to you? That's a little creepy. Verania is so weird. But not in a bad way!" he added quickly when I glared daggers at him. "Just... different."

"In what realm of possibility do you think a castle would *talk* to me?"

He shrugged. "You have a talking dragon. I just assumed that most things here talk to you. Is...is that not right?" He turned toward the nearest wall. "Hello, castle. I'm Dylan." He waited. Nothing happened. "Guess not. Ha, you were joking. Still funny. Rock on. I dig that. My friends say I'm the funniest person they know. You want to hear a joke?"

"No," I said. "I couldn't want to hear a joke any less than I do right at this moment."

He fucking *pouted.* Bottom lip stuck out, eyes sad, the whole shebang. And for a moment, I almost felt *bad.* But it was a negligible thing quickly snuffed out. So, imagine my surprise when instead of telling him to go the fuck away, my mouth instead said, "Fine. Tell me."

He brightened almost immediately. "What do vegetarian zombies eat?"

"I don't care."

"Graaaaaaiiiins," he said, arms out in front of him as he zombie-walked toward me.

It caught me off guard. Everything about him did. Sam was right; he was a himbo of the most spectacularly awful variety.

Which is why when I was startled into laughter, I tried to cover it up by pretending I was hacking up a lung. I'd lived with my idiots long enough to know that once they thought you were enjoying their ridiculousness, it would never end, and one day you'd find yourself with friends that you absolutely did not ask for.

"See?" he said as I struggled to breathe. "I knew you'd find that funny. I've got a bunch of them. Back at the frat, we used to have joke offs. I always won because I'm pretty much the best at everything I do." It wasn't said with ego, or artifice. It was strangely disarming, which only caused my hackles to raise. He had to know what he was doing, trying to worm his way past my defenses. I had news for him. I'd faced bigger opponents and always emerged victorious. Time to change tactics.

I laughed quietly, looking up at him through my eyelashes as I took a step toward him. He swallowed thickly, gaze darting to the roll of my hips, watching every step I took until I could feel his breath on my face. He licked his lips, and I made sure to follow the swipe of his tongue before meeting his eyes. "You think you can handle me?"

He nodded so hard his neck cracked. "Yeah."

I reached up and curled my fingers into the end of his beard, tugging on the lace and beads gently. "All of me?"

"Oh yeah," he breathed, his dark eyes glittering.

I leaned forward, my cheek scraping against his. He took in a shuddering breath as my lips brushed his earlobe. "I'm going to destroy you," I purred, letting a bit of Gary fill my voice. "And you will thank me for it."

"So thankful," he choked out.

I stepped away from him quickly. He blinked as I grinned at him, razor-sharp. A new plan was forming in my head. It'd been a long time since I'd had a bit of fun, and he'd do just nicely. He would never be my husband, but while he was here, I was going to use the fuck out of him. And when I finished, I'd send him packing and never think of him or Yennbridge again. A notch in my bedpost. That's all he'd be. And maybe it would give me the spark Dad thought I'd lost.

Without another word, I left him standing in the hallway, knowing he was staring after me. He didn't know it then, but we were at war. And I took no quarter. This was going to work out exactly how I expected it to.

*****

"WE HAVE TO *WHAT*?" I snarled.

Everyone seated at the table turned to stare at me, my father's advisors (who would soon apparently be *my* advisors), Dad, Morgan, Sam, Ryan, Ramos, Dylan, *all* of them looked at me as I slammed my hand on the table. I ignored Gary and Tiggy standing against the wall, Gary providing commentary that did nothing to help the situation. "That's his mad face," Gary said, voice carrying. "He has that a lot."

"Tiggy mad too," Tiggy said, crooking his fingers like claws. "Spittin' mad."

It was three days past the celebration. Dad had recovered enough to leave the healer's room the night before with the warning he needed to take it easy. Morgan promised Dad would do just that, his tone brooking no argument. Dad looked better than he had laying in the healer's bed, though he was still a little weak. The news had spread swiftly through Lockes, people rejoicing and praying for the health of their king.

I'd woken this very morning filled with an energy I hadn't felt since we'd battled against Myrin. I had a purpose, a plan, and I couldn't wait to enact it. I had managed to avoid Dylan and his entourage until this day, sending word through Sam that I wasn't ready to receive any guests when Dylan had asked after me. I had plotted out all the minute details, every little thing that could go wrong. Traps neatly set, pretty words or gifts of crystal, an offer of another duel, I went through as many eventualities I could think of, preparing for the worst.

And it had been going perfectly.

Perfectly, that is, until Ramos the Pure opened his fucking mouth and brought it all toppling down on top of me.

Ramos, for his part, didn't seem to mind my outrage. Or, at the very least, he ignored it. "It's part of our customs," he said for what felt like the hundredth time. "A courtship is a sacred thing in Yennbridge, and none more so than when it involves a king. We take this very seriously. I would hope you can understand that."

Certain I'd misheard, I said, "Say it again. Just so we can be clear."

He patted the folded cloth in front of him. It looked to be nothing more than a dirty rag, but appearances could be deceiving. Regardless, it wasn't the rag that concerned me, but what apparently lay hidden inside. "For thirty days, two members of royalty in a courtship will be bound together by the Sash of the Grand Hunt, for what is new love but a hunt? Those involved will be tied together for a month's time. Once the sash is tied to your wrists, it cannot be removed until the time has passed, or if one of you meets an untimely fate before then."

"Sounds fake, but okay," Tiggy said.

Sam, of course, asked, "What happens when Justin has to take a shit?"

I closed my eyes and breathed in through my nose, out through my mouth.

"Oh," Sam said. "Sorry. That was vulgar, especially in such esteemed company. I'll rephrase: what happens when Justin has to evacuate his bowels?"

My eyes snapped open. "How in the hell was *that* any better?"

"What?" Sam asked. "Oh please. We were all thinking it."

Most everyone at the table nodded. Once I was king, I was going to fire them all. And by fire, I meant directly into the sun.

"The sash is imbued with magic," Ramos said. "Nothing nefarious, mind you."

"When people say it's nothing nefarious, it usually is," Gary said to Tiggy. "Why don't they realize that?"

"Bad guys dumb," Tiggy said succinctly.

"It will bind the two together," Ramos continued, "and can only be removed once thirty days have come and gone. Given its magical properties, the sash can stretch to a distance of approximately twenty feet, which should allow both parties to…take care of their private needs. But I will caution you: once attached, any attempts to remove it will result in a breaking of the vow, and we will consider that a monumental slight against our country."

"You can't be serious," I said. "You really think I'm going to agree to bind myself to him? Why would I ever do that?"

"Because it is our way," Ramos said as if speaking to an unruly child. "I understand that our customs may be foreign to you, but I assure you this is how it has always been." He sat back in his chair, steepling his hands under his chin.

"Villains do that," Gary said. "The thing with his hands? Yeah, that usually means they're plotting our demise. That also comes from experience."

"People want to kill us?" Tiggy asked.

"All the time," Gary said easily. "It's mostly Sam's fault."

Ramos narrowed his eyes. "May I speak frankly, King Anthony?"

"I wish you would," Dad said. "We're all…well. Not friends here, but at the very least, we're listening."

Ramos nodded slowly. "Verania is...Verania. To put it bluntly, your country is a bit of the red-headed stepchild in the greater world."

"That's not very nice," one of my father's advisors grumbled. It probably had to do with the fact that he had red hair and his mother had remarried after his father had run off with a banshee. Why I knew that, I didn't know, especially since I couldn't even remember his name.

"I would choose your next words carefully," I ground out.

"I mean no offense," Ramos said in such a way that I knew he meant *all* the offense. "I'm merely speaking truth. Your country, though beautiful and strong, is considered a sort of aberration. Surely you know this. You have hundreds of wizards, most of which are Dark and now locked away in a prison in the desert. And don't get me started on all your dragons. It's...quaint, for lack of a better word, your faith in the gods. Yennbridge is a place of science and technology. We don't put much stock in religious dogma. While everyone is entitled to their faith, Yenners take a more practical approach. And that doesn't even begin to consider the fact that you almost lost your entire country to a madman who bested you at nearly every turn. A madman, who is— *was*, the brother to the King's Wizard."

"He was," Morgan said. "And he's been dealt with. He will never be a threat again." He leaned forward, tapping the table in front of him. "But that does beg the question: if you knew about the fall of Verania, where was Yennbridge? As you said earlier, you consider yourselves allies to Verania. Why did you not come to our aid?"

"We tried," Dylan blurted, much to the annoyance of Ramos, the skin around his eyes tightening briefly. "But by the time we heard, the borders to Verania had been closed off by Darks. While Yenners are pacifists, we still would've tried our best. But Yennbridge isn't like Verania. We only have a few who know magic. There were hundreds of Darks, maybe even thousands. They would've wiped us out. So. Um. We're sorry?" He nodded as if that explained everything. It did not.

"So sorry," Ramos said. "To our people, wizards are something to be feared, born of the fairytales we tell our children to teach them valuable lessons."

"But you know magic," Sam said. "You call yourself a magician."

"I do," Ramos said. "But the difference between you and me is that my magic is hard-earned, and extraordinarily taxing." He raised his hand, the tattoo of the eye on his palm facing me. "I can do what I do because of the marks on my skin. It grants me abilities that I would not have otherwise. Yours is a form of wish fulfillment, and that is a concerning thing."

"Why?" Morgan asked. He didn't sound angry, merely curious.

"Because if the stories I've heard are true, where is the line drawn?" Ramos asked. "What would stop your Sam of Dragons from letting the power consume him, shaping the world to his very whims? My people have walked the streets of your fair city. They have spoken with many of your subjects. Some—not all, but a good few—share our concerns. They saw what Sam did in order to—"

"Save us all because no one else was willing to help us?" I snapped. Dad settled his hand on my knee, squeezing gently. *Don't stop*, it said. *But tread carefully.* "Mind your words, magician. I won't have anyone speaking badly about my wizard. That's *my* job, and one I take seriously."

Ramos looked amused. "Is it? Tell me then, Prince Justin, since you take your job seriously, have you ever considered the possibility that Sam would turn on you? Has there ever been a moment where you've feared what he could do?"

Yes. Many times. All the time, in fact. But it was the little things: making my hair turn green or increasing the size of my tongue until I couldn't close my mouth around it. The idea of Sam turning Dark was laughable, even though it had apparently been close when facing Myrin and the Star Dragon. But Ramos didn't need to know that. That was a thing between Sam and the rest of us. "Never," I said firmly. "I trust Sam with my life."

"Can I get up from the table and hug him?" Sam whispered to Morgan. "Because I really think I need to after that. He just told everyone he loves me more than anything in the world."

"Perhaps save that for later," Morgan replied. "We're in the middle of an important conversation."

"Got it," Sam said. He leaned forward, looking down the table at me. "Pssst, Justin. *Justin.*"

I turned my head to look at him, my expression clearly stating he needed to shut the fuck up.

He ignored it, of course. "You're in for the hug of your godsdamn *life*," he whisper-shouted, eyes alight. "You thought it was bad before? Oh, man, just you wait."

To which Dylan said, "Aw. That's so nice. I like it when people care for each other that much. I'm having a great time. Best vacation I've been on since me and the boys went to the mountains and got so wasted we ended up lost in the forest for three days. I got frostbite on my toes, but then I put them in a fire, and I got to keep them all."

"The boys?" Gary asked.

"He's a frat bro," I muttered with disdain. "They call him Double D."

Gary laughed. When no one joined in, he stopped. "Wait, what? Seriously? Oh my gods, this is the best day of my entire *life*. Marry him, Justin! Marry him so fucking hard! If you don't, I will."

"Sweet," Dylan said. "My first endorsement. This is going well. Anyone else?" He looked at Tiggy who shrugged. No one else spoke. "No? That sucks. Ah well. I'll take it." He leaned back in his chair, stretching his arms behind his head. Making sure I was watching, he flexed his biceps. "Yep. There it is. Goooood stretch. Just stretchin', that's all this is. Not showing off or anything. Ah, that's awesome. Good stretch."

"Wow," Sam breathed. "Do you think you could lift me up with one hand or…?"

Without looking at him, I said, "Ryan, put your sword away."

Ryan muttered under his breath as he sheathed his sword.

"If we could get back on track," Ramos said. No one else spoke, so he continued. "In addition to asking about your wizard, we asked your people about the prince. Many were complimentary. Many were not. I even heard something about polls not going as well as one might hope?"

"Numbers change," Dad said. "As an advisor to the king, you should know that."

Ramos nodded. "Oh, I do. At least when I came here, that is. You see, back in Yennbridge, King Dylan enjoys a near one hundred percent approval rating amongst his people. That did not change as he moved from princedom to kinghood."

"I'm popular," Dylan said proudly. "Cool, right?"

"Very cool," Ramos said, though it looked like it taxed him greatly to say so. "And I mean no offense when I say that while a match between the prince and the king would benefit both countries, it would most likely do more for Justin than Dylan, given Dylan's standing."

No offense? I took *all* the offense. "I'm not going to sit here and let you—"

"Can I talk now?" Dylan asked. "Because I'd really like to talk now."

Ramos looked like he was about to argue, but for some reason, subsided instead, waving his hand at his king.

Dylan leaned forward, gaze firmly fixed on me. I didn't look away. Doing so would be a sign of weakness, and I wouldn't give him the satisfaction. "Look," he said. "I know this is sudden. Like, not for me because I've known about it for months, but for you? Sure. You didn't know. That sucks, but whatever. You all had a lot going on."

"By a lot, you mean fighting for our lives and trying to keep our people safe?" I asked sweetly.

He nodded as if he didn't know I was making fun of him. And now that I thought about it, he probably didn't. His brain was made up of mead, a misplaced sense of entitlement, and testosterone, a combination that made me want to pull my hair out. "Yeah, that. And I bet you didn't have much time to think of anything else. So, I'm not mad. *You* seem mad, but I'd probably be too if another country came marching in here, making demands about marriage and junk."

Okay, maybe not quite as dumb as he seemed. I'd do well to remember that. For all I knew his entire irritating existence was all an act to try and disarm me. "So why do it then?"

He shrugged easily. "Because I want what my parents had. They started out in an arranged marriage, but it wasn't long before it turned into the real deal. They cared for each other beyond measure, and I want the same thing."

"Then why not find another Yenner to take to your bed?"

"Been there, done that," he said. "Got the t-shirt and everything. Ha, just kidding. Could you imagine? That'd be gnarly. I'd have a lot of t-shirts." His eyes widened. "Not that I'm easy or anything! But even if I *was*, that would be okay because it's my body, my choice."

"We need to keep him," Gary said loudly. "We need to keep him and hold him close and never let anything hurt him." He started forward, but Tiggy stopped him. "Kitten, let me go! I need to cover him with my musk!"

"You no eat his flower," Tiggy admonished. "That Justin's flower."

"Justin gets everything fun," Gary mumbled. "And what do I get? Oh. Right. A dragon with a big dick and preternatural recovery time. Okay, never mind. I'm good. Sorry! Sorry, everyone. I have decided not to fuck King Dylan." Then, in a lower voice, "*Yet.*"

"We could do this," Dylan said earnestly. "If we tried. I know it. Maybe we're not bound by fate, or what you all call destiny written in the stars. But that doesn't always have to be important. We could try this because we *choose* to, and that's all I could ever want."

"Okay," Sam said. "I'm Team Dylan now, in case anyone was wondering."

"No one was," I growled. "Tell me one good reason why I should agree to this."

"Because you need us more than we need you," Ramos said. I had a sinking feeling in the pit of my stomach that I'd been played. "Most of our land is farmlands, and we export much of it to you. In addition, we've always had an open border policy, allowing Veranians to cross into our country whenever they wish, so long as they don't have malicious intent. It would be very easy to close those borders, and reconsider what we give to Verania. The effects might not be seen for some time, but mark my words, in the end, your people will suffer. And no, before you ask, that is not a threat. It's merely fact."

"That'd be a mean thing to do," Dylan said. "But it wouldn't leave us with much choice."

"You speak of choice," I said. "But then in the next breath, you try and take it away."

Dylan blinked. "Oh, hey, no, I didn't really mean it like that." He shook his head. "When a king comes to the negotiation table, he needs to know how to play his cards right. I can't just give and give without getting anything in return. Dad taught me that's not how king stuff works."

"Oh," I said, "because you give and give, you think that means you have the right to make demands of me."

Dylan nodded. "Yep. Wait. Nope? Hold on. Argh. Now I'm confused." He looked at Ramos. "I thought you said this was going to be easy. It's not."

"I thought they would listen to reason," Ramos said. "It appears I might have been mistaken."

Dylan frowned momentarily before he brightened. "I have an idea!"

"Great," I said. "I can't wait to hear it."

He grinned at me like he thought I was serious. "Okay, stick with me here. It might get a little confusing, so stop me if you need me to go over it again. I'm really good at explaining things, but it might be a lot. Ready?"

"We wait with bated breath," Dad said, and I couldn't love him more if I tried.

"What if," Dylan proclaimed proudly, "we did it anyway?"

We were all silent, expecting more.

There wasn't more. He sat back in his chair, crossing his arms, looking far too satisfied with himself.

"That's it," I said slowly. "That's the idea you thought might get a little confusing for me."

"Yeah," he said. "Was it? Did I do it wrong? Let me try again. Hmm. How to say it so I'm completely clear. Got it! Let's…just do it."

Dad snorted next to me, and I found I could love him a little less if I tried.

"How was that any better?" I demanded. "Of all the—"

"What have you got to lose?" Dylan asked. "It's not as if you have a boyfriend or anything." His mouth curved down. "You don't have a boyfriend, right?"

Before I could say that yes, I *did* have a boyfriend, the best boyfriend in fact, his name was Thaddeus and he was bigger than Dylan and the only reason he wasn't here right now was because he was fighting a group of sand mermaids in my honor, Sam said, "Nah. He doesn't. And not for lack of trying. I've set him up on at least fifteen dates, but they all usually end up with us running for our lives to try and avoid object insertion." He frowned. "Now that I think about it, that seems to happen all the time."

I banged my head against the table.

"See?" Dylan said happily. "So what have you got to lose? All I'm asking for is a chance to prove myself to you, bro. Because that's what this is. I came here to show you I could be the best husband anyone has ever had."

Ryan laughed. "Already got you beat there, bro. Pretty much the greatest husband in Verania." He pulled out his sword, flourishing it with deft fingers. "Yep. That's me. The best there is. Everyone thinks so. Oh look! they all say. Here comes Ryan Haversford, the husband we all aspire to be!"

"Bro?" Sam asked. "Did you just say *bro*?"

"Stop embarrassing me in front of the cool king!"

Sam rolled his eyes. "You're doing that enough on your own." He sighed. "But yes, you really are the best husband in the entire world, Dylan will have to be second best."

"Darn right," Ryan said, puffing out his chest.

"And that's it?" I asked, desperate for this to be over. "We'll be bound together for one month and when that time ends, you'll respect whatever decision I make? And *if* I decide not to marry Dylan, everything would stay as is, trade routes, borders, all of it?"

Ramos said, "I don't think that—"

"Yes," Dylan blurted. "You have my word."

"Done," I said before Ramos could speak again, much to the surprise of everyone on my side of the table. Dad's hand tightened on my knee, but I ignored it. Thirty days was nothing. In one months' time, the sash would be removed, and Dylan would crawl back to where he came from. I would see to it myself. A king must think of his people at all times. I could deal with Dylan for a month for the sake of my country. How bad could it possibly get?

Dylan reared back. "Wait, really?"

"Really. I will allow the Sash of Great Stupidity—"

"Sash of the Grand Hunt," Ramos said mildly.

"—to tie Dylan and myself together. And no matter what the outcome is, we will all agree to respect that decision, suffering no repercussions."

Dylan rose quickly, his chair scraping against the floor. He punched a fist in the air. "Heck *yes*. You're not going to regret it, I swear. It's gonna be so cool. You don't even know."

"So cool," I said, mocking him.

Either he didn't hear it (unlikely), or he didn't get it (extremely likely). "Best day *ever*!" he crowed. "You should know I tend to kick in my sleep, but as long as we put a wall of pillows between us, the bruising shouldn't be too bad. It's what happens when you've got strong thighs." As if to prove his point, he lifted his leg, putting his foot on the table. He bent forward like he was stretching, the muscles in his legs evident through his trousers.

"Okay," Ryan said. "I think we can all agree that your thighs aren't *that* strong. Sam, tell him. Tell him my thighs are stronger." He chuckled. "Obviously."

Sam shrugged. "I haven't had his wrapped around my neck like I've had yours, so I can't say for sure. I mean, it sure *looks* like it, but who's to say?"

"Ooh, girl," Gary said. "The pupil has become the master, and I couldn't be prouder."

"We should go to schools," Tiggy said. "Teach little ones about life."

"We tried that once, remember?" Gary said. "I'm not allowed within five hundred feet of most schools now, but that wasn't *my* fault. How was I supposed to know that telling children of the birds and the bees and felching wasn't part of the curriculum? Ugh. Youth. Go back to your safe spaces!"

"Stupid youth!" Tiggy yelled.

I dropped my arm onto the table, pulling back my sleeve. The sooner we got this over with, the quicker I could say goodbye to these idiots and move on with my life. I was going to be king. This was yet another bump in the road, but after all we'd been through, it was minor at best. And, it didn't hurt that people would see how compromising I could be. Win win. "Let's do it."

Ramos smiled. "And we have your word?"

I bared my teeth at him. "Yes."

"King Anthony?"

Dad hesitated, but it was brief. "If my son is in agreement, then he has my support."

"Good," he said. "I will hold you to that." He placed his hands on top of the rag in front of him. "All of you." His smile widened. "Oh, but there is just *one* more thing. A tiny little detail, but one that I'm sure we'll all agree is necessary." He began to unfold the cloth. "You see, while your word is all well and good, there have been moments in the past where people have tried to go *back* on their word, which is most unfortunate." He pulled back the last corner of the cloth. There, curled up inside, was a thin, blood-red sash with gold trim. In the grand scheme of things, it wasn't anything major. I didn't know what I was expecting from a magical binding sash, but it looked like something that could have been bought off a vendor on the streets. Magic had a certain feeling, at least in my experience. Randall's felt cold and vast, like the castle in which he lived. Morgan's was kind and warm. Sam's was familiar, but only because I'd had it thrust upon me more times than I cared to think about.

But this sash? I felt nothing from it. It looked to be just that: a sash.

"What happens when someone tries to remove it before the time ends?" Morgan asked.

"Death," Ramos said. "For both parties. But you might be thinking, what if you could find some kind of loophole? For example, one could ask a wizard they know and trust to try and remove it by magical means before the time ends. And you might succeed. Which is why there is a contingency plan in place, one that makes sure we are all on an even keel."

He lifted the sash from the cloth, revealing a flat, iridescent white stone underneath, oval in shape with shots of blue and green and yellow through it, like a rainbow. He lifted it carefully, letting it rest on the eye on his palm, barely covering it completely. He raised it toward us.

"What is it?" Morgan asked. He eyed the stone warily, which did nothing to make me feel better. Of course there'd be something else, I'd played my cards too early.

"Oh, this?" Ramos said as if it were nothing. "We're not on our own turf, and it will allow us to level the playing field so no one person will have an advantage over the other. You should know this, Morgan, at least by name. Such things are extraordinarily rare. I don't know that I've ever come across another. It is a moonstone, and while they themselves aren't necessarily unique, this one in particular is. It's been in Yennbridge for generations, protected above all other treasures. The fact that you're gazing upon it is a great honor."

"What does it do?" Sam asked nervously.

"I'm so glad you asked, wizard," Ramos said. "Because it will affect you specifically. You know of cornerstones, yes?"

Sam glanced at Ryan, who gave him a thumbs up. "I do," he said. "The building blocks of all magic. It helps a wizard to stay in control."

"Yes," Ramos said. "It does, however trite the notion may be. Think of this as a counter to a cornerstone. Instead of helping you control your magic, this removes it entirely. Yours. Morgan. Even your unicorn's. Why, he would be no different than a horse."

The reaction was instantaneous. Our side of the table exploded, everyone was shouting above everyone else, myself included. Sam sat stunned, Morgan leaning over and whispering in his ear fervently, though I couldn't hear what they said above all the noise. Dad removed his hand from my knee, curling it into a fist that he rested on the table. He raised his other hand, and everyone quieted down almost immediately, save for Gary, who shouted, "Say that again to my *face*, you twat! I dare you! You want a horse? Guess what. I'm gonna horse over your entire *body*."

Morgan was pale when he said, "The Damning Stone. I thought…" He shook his head. "I thought such things were lost."

"As you can see, it is not," Ramos said evenly. "The Damning Stone will store your magic within, and on the thirtieth day when the Sash of the Grand Hunt is removed, it shall be returned to you."

"You had that this entire time?" I asked through gritted teeth.

"We have," Ramos said.

"And yet you couldn't come to our aid given that the borders of Verania were patrolled by Darks. You couldn't take their magic away. And what of Myrin? People *died* because of what he did. You had a way to stop him this entire time?"

"It wouldn't have worked like that," Morgan said, sounding almost apologetic. "From what I understand, it takes consent. The magic isn't stolen. It must be given away freely. It doesn't work otherwise."

"Exactly," Ramos said. "I'm not a thief, and I resent the implication."

"Don't worry though," Dylan said quickly, wincing as I scoffed at him. "It's only for a little bit. And Ramos said it shouldn't affect Morgan or Sam aside from containing their magic. It won't be gone completely. Just…stifled until Justin and I fall in love and get married and live happily ever after."

"Love," I said scornfully. "I don't even *like* you, and you're talking about love."

He shrugged. "You'll get there. I believe in you because I believe in myself. Remember my friend Digger? The one into watersports?"

Dad choked next to me, and I wondered if this was the first time anyone had sat at this table and talked about piss-play.

"I really wish I didn't know that," I said. "But yes, I have the awful memory of you mentioning your friend."

"He says that all it takes to succeed is to believe in yourself. He's pretty smart. Well, mostly. This one time, he stuck a firecracker up his butt and lit it just to see what would happen. He was in the hospital for four days. But then he decided that he didn't want to be there anymore, so he went home, and now he's fine." He sat back in his chair. "Except for all the scarring, but guys, gals and non-binary pals really love that for some reason."

"And that is who you're taking advice from," I said flatly.

"Yep," Dylan said. "Oh! I just remembered. He wanted me to tell you that I'm super cool, and that I will…cripes, what was the rest?" His brow furrowed. "Super cool and…right! That I'm reliable and as long as I get eight hours of sleep a night, I can do anything."

"And who's going to keep the stone?" Morgan asked. "Forgive my reticence, but why should we give our magic away to you?"

"It wouldn't be to me," Ramos said. "I don't expect you to trust me with so much power, so I've asked for two intermediaries to oversee the transfer. They should be arriving…ah, yes. Here they are. Right on schedule."

It was about this time that a gaping hole tore the fabric of reality with a low thrum, and from it, stepped two beings I hadn't expected to see today.

The first was hunched over, a scowl on his ancient, craggy face as he glared at all of us, his robes wrinkled, his hair in wisps around his head. He grimaced as he stood upright, hands going to his back as it cracked loudly, his large nose twitching underneath narrowed eyes and massive eyebrows. "Not getting any younger," he muttered. "And Sam, if I hear you say a single *word* about getting sucked through my hole, I will crush your liver into so much paste."

"*Randall?*" Sam gasped.

And next to the ancient wizard, fluttering at his shoulder, was a six-inch tall naked man with wings and a terrible mustache.

"Yes," he said, his voice a high-pitched buzz. "It is I, Dimitri, the King of the Fairies and ex-fiancé of Sam of Dragons, here to make everyone's lives so much better than they were even just seconds ago."

We were so fucked.

# CHAPTER 8
# Dimitri is a Creep and Other Stories

SAM PRACTICALLY CLIMBED OVER the table to get to Randall. Misconstruing his intent, Dimitri flew in front of the ancient wizard, tiny arms spread wide as if he thought Sam was going to hurt him. Instead, Sam batted him out of the way, causing the fairy king to squawk angrily. Randall sighed as Sam latched on to him. Much to my amazement, he actually *hugged* Sam back, though he didn't seem happy about it.

Theirs was a relationship I didn't always understand. For the longest time, Sam was nothing but the bane of Randall's existence, and who could blame him? If Sam had turned *my* nose into a dick right before I was scheduled to officiate a wedding, I'd probably hold a grudge.

"That's enough," Randall muttered, shoving Sam off him. "I allowed it to go on for twenty seconds, but any longer and you're going to lose your arms."

"My turn," Dimitri said, flying toward Sam once more, arms open wide. "Sam, did I tell you I met someone? His name is Grundle, and he makes me happy. I've never been more in love than I am right at this moment. But if you want me back, say the word and I'll drop him like the insignificant speck he is."

"I'm good," Sam said, ducking the hug as Dimitri sailed over him. "Congrats on your new relationship. Grundle, you say? Sounds like a good dude or the skin between my balls and my asshole. Either way, many happy returns."

"It's casual," Dimitri said. "Means nothing. Please take me back. What does Ryan have that I don't?"

"Girth," Ryan said promptly.

"Dammit," Dimitri muttered. "I *knew* you were going to say that. That's speciesist, Knight Commander Foxheart. How very dare you."

"It's Knight Commander Haversford now."

Dimitri's wings drooped. "Well, when you die in some bloody battle, know that I'll be there for Sam to console him. And when sufficient time has passed for your memory to fade—say, three weeks—I'll pick up the pieces and rail your husband within an inch of his life."

"Probably need to find a few more inches before you try," Ryan said. "I don't have that problem. Right, Sam? Ha, like I even need to ask."

"I like us," Tiggy said to no one in particular.

"What are you doing here?" Morgan asked Randall, who moved around the table to our side. He and Morgan joined hands, foreheads pressed together.

"Summoned," Randall muttered as he stepped back. "For more foolishness, of course. King Anthony, you're looking well. I'd heard you'd fallen ill."

"On the mend," Dad said. "The healer said—"

"Healer," Randall said with derision. "Bah, medicine man who thinks he knows better than the rest of us. I'll see to you myself once we've finished here, and I won't hear a word of it."

Knowing it was pointless to argue with the ancient wizard, Dad nodded. "Thank you."

Randall waved a hand dismissively before looking across the table. "Ramos. You're looking alive."

"Randall," Ramos said as he cocked his head. "It's an honor to see you again."

"You know each other?" Sam asked as he sat back down.

"We've met," Randall said. "Knight Commander, does it look like I don't want to sit? Stop standing there with that gaping maw of yours and get me a chair."

Ryan moved quickly, grabbing the nearest chair and jerking it. The problem with that was it was occupied by one of my father's infrastructure advisors, the red-haired man with daddy issues. The man fell on his ass with a crash as Ryan carried the chair toward Randall and set it down next to Dad. Randall grunted as he sat down. "That's better. Ramos, first things first: I'm not impressed by anything about you, so don't expect me to say otherwise. I have no patience for one such as you. You came to me once, seeking guidance to become a wizard. The power you held wasn't enough to survive the Trials, so I turned you away, telling you not to meddle in things you could never understand."

"I remember," Ramos said blandly. "You were quite…forceful in relaying your opinion."

Randall's eyebrows bunched together. "Opinion? *Opinion*? I'm the Head Wizard. I oversee *all* wizards who want to move beyond an apprenticeship. My word is not an *opinion*. It's fact. You were not—and can never be—a wizard and yet here you are, having wormed your way into the grace of a king for reasons that aren't quite clear to me."

Ramos wasn't affected. "I assure you that I don't have any agenda aside from following the will of my king."

"I don't believe that for a second," Randall grumbled. "Anyone who says they don't have an agenda has exactly that."

"You sought an apprenticeship?" Morgan asked. The fact that he hadn't known didn't sit well with me. It meant that either Randall was to be believed when he said he didn't think there was anything to Ramos, or he was keeping secrets again. I hoped for the former but suspected the latter.

"I did," Ramos said. "But as Randall so plainly put it, I was rejected. However, I forged my own path and found a place where I could be appreciated for my talents. Yennbridge isn't like Verania. We don't discriminate. Wizards aren't the be all and end all."

"And there's his motivation," Gary told Tiggy. "The steepling hands, the evil smile under a ridiculous goatee, and now it's revealed he tried to become something he couldn't. Yeah, this guy's gonna do something villainous within the next four weeks. Count on it."

"Ooh," Tiggy said. "Foreshadowing."

"And where is your king?" Randall asked, looking around. "I thought he'd be here, especially since he's the reason I've come to Castle Lockes."

Dylan cleared his throat. "That'd be me, bro." He stood quickly, reaching his hand across the table toward Randall. "It's so great to meet you. I didn't know you existed until you suddenly appeared out of thin air. You crushed that entrance, bro. How'd you do that?"

Randall stared at the proffered hand but didn't reach to grab it. He leaned back slightly, speaking out of the corner of his mouth to Morgan. "Who is this man trying to grab me?"

"That's King Dylan of Yennbridge," Morgan said.

Randall snorted. "Very funny. Did Sam put you up to this?" He glared at Sam. "How many times have I told you I won't fall for that again?"

"Thirteen times," Sam said. "But this isn't one of those. That really is the King of Yennbridge."

Once he realized Randall wasn't going to shake his hand, Dylan pulled it back and sat back down, only to be immediately accosted by the fairy king. Dimitri fluttered in front of him, reaching out and poking Dylan's nose. "This is the King of Yennbridge? Impressive. I haven't been to Yennbridge in centuries, but if this is how they're growing them now, I'm going to have to make a return trip. Dylan, was it? Welcome to Verania. If there's anything you need to do that involves removing your clothing, I'm your tiny man. But don't mistake my size for weakness. You'd be surprised at the things I'm capable of. Have you ever had an entire person crawl inside your urethra? No? Well, that can be fixed quite easily."

"I thought you were involved with Grundle," Sam said.

Dimitri laughed as he alighted on Dylan's shoulder, rubbing his cheek with his small hands. "Ignore him. He's just jealous. I'm the one that got away. You know what they say, 'Once you go small, you'll feel it in your balls.'"

"Kevin really needs to stop giving advice," Sam muttered.

"I'm good, bro," Dylan said, shrugging his shoulders to try and get Dimitri to move. "Got my sights set already. But thank you for the offer."

"Your sights?" Dimitri asked, eyes narrowed as he lifted off Dylan and fluttered down to the table. "On the prince? Are you sure?" He glanced at me before looking back up at Dylan. "You've got strange tastes, King, but who I am to judge?"

Oh, for want of a flyswatter, the kingdom was lost.

"He does not," I snapped. "In fact, his tastes are just fine as they are." They weren't, far from it in fact, but I wasn't going to give Dimitri the satisfaction. I had little time for fairies, the pesky nuisances they were. But they were part of the fabric of Verania, and we'd long held a peaceful accord with them, even if they acted independent of the crown. Dad was always of the mind that it was better to have a fairy as a friend than an enemy.

"So you've agreed to the terms, then?" Randall asked, stopping me cold. "You will bind yourself to the king for thirty days?"

"You knew about this," I said. It wasn't a question.

Randall, for his part, wasn't taken aback by the tone of my voice. "I did."

"And you didn't think to tell us?"

"I did not."

I waited.

He didn't say anything more.

"*Why?*" I finally asked.

Randall shrugged. "Because I knew you would find out in your own time. Which you have. My life doesn't revolve around the wants and whims of a prince. I have much more important matters to attend to. Why, before I came here, I was involved in a rather bloody game of strip checkers with a dragon who seems to think that cheating is an acceptable means of winning. I was in my underwear within five minutes."

"Leslie," Sam said fondly. "I don't think she quite understands how to play board games."

"She doesn't," Randall agreed. "Seeing as how she decided to throw checker pieces at my head when I accused her of deception. I was about to turn her into a llama when I remembered I had places to be. I'd like to get this over with so I can return and punish her for her insolence."

"Pat's not gonna like that," Sam said.

"It was Pat's idea," Randall said. "But that's neither here nor there. My day has already been interrupted, and since my time is important, shall we move on with this? Prince Justin, have you agreed to the terms?"

"I have," I said evenly. "But that was before Ramos revealed there was more to it than just binding myself to Dylan."

"Always a catch, eh, Ramos?" Randall asked.

Ramos shrugged. "It's not my fault the prince was so quick to agree. He certainly seems eager."

Dylan waved at me. I didn't wave back.

Randall snorted. "I bet he was. You there. King Dylan, was it? Stand up. Let me take a look at you to see what we're dealing with."

Dylan promptly stood. "Should I take off my clothes? No worries if I have to. I've been naked in public a few times. I got nothing to hide."

"Yes!" Gary cried. "I *love* important meetings!"

I almost agreed until I remembered my place and who I was dealing with. Especially when the very person I was dealing with began to do lunges around the room. "And *one*. And *two*. And *three*. Do you want me to do a handstand?" No one wanted that. He did it anyway, walking on his hands, his vest hanging down around his face revealing miles of dark skin, his stomach jiggling, the chain from his bellybutton piercing bouncing against his chest.

And because he apparently didn't want to be left out, Ryan immediately did the same, armor clanking as he flipped over, walking on his hands toward Dylan. "Not that hard," Ryan grunted, face turning red. "Anyone can do that."

"Upside down bros!" Dylan cried, spittle flying onto the floor. "Let's fight with our legs!"

"I've had dreams that started just like this," Sam breathed as Dylan and Ryan started battling with their feet, each trying to knock the other over.

Ryan got a good kick in to Dylan's chest, causing him to land on the floor on his back. "Sam!" Ryan bellowed as he flipped back onto his feet. "Did you see that? Took him out with ease."

"I did," Sam said. "And I'm going to wreck you later for it."

"I'm okay!" Dylan said as he pushed himself up. He grinned at Ryan, holding his hand out. "Damn, bro, you've got moves. Proud of you. I don't even care that I lost because you're awesome."

"*Yesss*," Gary hissed. "Now kiss."

But instead of kissing (because *what*), Dylan held out his fist, which Ryan promptly pounded. Dylan made an explosion sound, fist opening, fingers wiggling. "I like you," Dylan told him. "You remind me of my friends. We should totally hang out later."

"Hell yeah," Ryan said. "We could go out, totally do some stuff, bro."

Sam cleared his throat.

"After I check with my husband," Ryan added quickly.

"Right on," Dylan said. "I get that. Have to keep your man happy."

He glanced at me before looking back at Ryan. "Maybe you could give me some pointers? I'm good with the whole sexing thing, but wooing? I could use some help."

"I got you, Double D," Ryan said loftily. "Especially since I used to date Justin. I can totally give you some pointers."

Dylan's jaw dropped. "Whoa, seriously? Holy smokes, you're spitting mad game, bro. Respect." Another fist pound. I wished they didn't have hands. "I didn't know knights could be so cool. Learn something new every day."

"Yes," Sam said. "Because I love hearing my husband talking about his ex- fiancé, who also happens to be my Best Friend 5eva."

"Which is not the same as being a regular best friend," Gary said. "Because that's what Tiggy and I are to him. Most agree that's even more important than being a Best Friend 5eva."

"We're complicated!" Tiggy crowed.

Dylan stopped in the middle of trying to teach Ryan a convoluted handshake. "Wait a minute. Hold up. Bro. Ryan. You *dated* the prince?"

Ryan blinked. "Uh, yeah?"

Dylan shook his head. "I don't know if I can do this, then. It'd break the bro-code."

Yes. Fine. That. Whatever that was, I agreed completely.

"The bro-code?" Ryan asked.

"Yeah," Dylan said. "You're a bro. You might even become *my* bro. And the bro-code clearly says that no bro may move in on his bro's man, especially when they've broken up. That's definitely not awesome."

"You're so cool," Ryan whispered fervently. Then, "Can we…oh, man, I'm so nervous. I just…King Dylan?"

"Yeah?"

Ryan took a deep breath and let it out slow. "Can we be bros?"

"Bro," Dylan said, sounding absurdly touched. "Can I tell you a secret?"

"Yeah," Ryan said, practically panting. "Of course."

"Watch this." Dylan walked around Ryan in a full circle. "Guess what I just did?"

"What?" Ryan asked.

"I just walked around my entire world. Because that's you, bro."

"Mothercracking *yes*," Ryan hissed.

"Tiggy bro!" Tiggy bellowed. "I be bro too! Gary! Bro me!"

And with that, Tiggy and Gary began their own complex handshake involving Gary's horn, a dance that lasted thirty-seven seconds, and Tiggy ending it all by doing a spectacular death drop he'd learned from Mama, causing the floor to shake.

"Whaaaaat is happening," Sam said.

"We're apparently devoid of any boundaries of normalcy," Randall muttered, to which I whole-heartedly agreed. "King Dylan, thank you for that display. If I were a hundred years younger, I'd consider taking you for a spin myself. But seeing as how I'm old and don't have time to teach you the ways of the flesh, I'll have to hope for the best for our prince here."

"Speaking of boundaries," I said through gritted teeth.

Randall ignored me. "A request has been made, to bind the Prince of Verania to the King of Yennbridge for thirty days. The request has been agreed upon by both parties involved."

Alarmed, I said, "Now wait a damn minute—"

"Is that wrong?" Randall challenged, arching an eyebrow.

"It's not," Ramos said. "He agreed to it. We all heard it."

Almost everyone nodded, including my father's advisors, the traitorous slugs. I'd remember this when I became king. I'd throw them out on their asses quicker than they could blink.

"That was before you mentioned the little fact of Sam and Morgan losing their magic."

"And Gary," Gary said.

"And Gary," I said. "Do you really think I'd agree to let you take that from them without their consent? And that doesn't even begin to cover that *you'd* still be able to keep your magic."

"I wouldn't," Ramos said. "Because I would also be giving up mine."

Stunned, I sat heavily back in my chair.

Ramos leaned forward, knowing he had trapped me neatly. "I told you that this would put us all on an even keel. That includes me. It wouldn't be fair if one side gave more than the other. All of us will give up something. And Dimitri and Randall will be the keepers of the stone to avoid any…issues that may arise until the month has passed."

I sneered at him. "You really think Randall and Dimitri will act impartially? They're Veranians."

"I can speak for myself," Randall snapped, rebuking me properly. "And while we *are* Veranians, we're magical first, which means we respect the process. This isn't something to be taken lightly. We can and will remain impartial. You would do well to remember that."

Struggling to find something—anything—to latch on to, I blurted, "What about Kevin?"

"What of him?" Ramos asked. "A dragon's magic isn't like that of a magician or a wizard, or even a unicorn. He won't be able to interfere."

"Where Kevin?" Tiggy asked, looking around.

"Who knows," Gary said. "Last I heard, he was supposed to be flying around the city to keep an eye out to make sure these chucklefucks aren't trying to distract us. He's probably trying to get people to give him shinies so that he may buy me the best anniversary present money can buy."

"Anniversary?" Tiggy asked, face scrunching up. "For wedding?"

"Nah," Gary said. "It's the anniversary to the grand reopening of our bakery, which is code for the time when I covered myself with butter and used him as a slip n slide in order to—"

"Oh!" Sam said. "I get why Justin was asking now. He's worried that Kevin won't be able to talk like he does because my magic will be gone."

Yes. That's exactly what I meant. Sort of. "And that's not fair to him. Who are we to take his voice away?" That didn't sound bad, now that I thought about it, but I'd never let *them* know that. "I care for all creatures, both great and small."

"Such a fucking liar," Gary whispered.

"So long as Sam's magic remains within the stone," Randall said, "and the stone remains in the castle, he should still be capable of speech."

"See?" Dylan said. "We've got it all figured out. You don't need to worry."

Dumbass. He couldn't think it was this easy, could he? "I need time to discuss this with those affected," I said. "I won't agree to anything unless I have their support. It's not just about me."

Dad patted the back of my hand. "Spoken like a king. Taking in all sides instead of jumping in headfirst."

"Of course," Ramos said, tilting his head in deference. "Except…"

Oh my gods, this fucking guy. "Except *what*?"

Ramos shrugged. "You already agreed to it. It's not my fault you decided before all the details were readily available." He placed his hands on the Sash of Fucking Stupidity. "Once agreed to, the binding must be in place within a few hours or else it will not work."

"Making it up as he goes along?" Tiggy asked.

"Of course he is," Gary replied. "But since we tend to do the same, I can't be mad at him. It makes things fun."

"How long do I have?" I ground out.

"Two hours, forty-six minutes," Ramos said. "And counting."

Dylan looked at me. "Plenty of time, right?"

I stood abruptly. "I will take that under advisement. Please leave now. We will summon you when we've made our decision."

Ramos stood slowly, motioning for Dylan to do the same. "Of course, Prince Justin. My King, if you'd come with me, we'll retire to your chambers and wait to be called."

"Can I say something?" Dylan asked. "Just one more thing."

Sighing, I waved my hand at him.

"I'm great," he said seriously.

"He is!" Ryan cried. "The greatest! We're bros!"

Dylan winked at Ryan. He fucking *winked*. "I know you might not think so, but you don't know me. All I'm asking for is a chance to prove how great I can be. I know I can do it. I may not be the strongest or the smartest or the best at—oof. Man, that doesn't sound good." Under his breath, he muttered, "C'mon, Dyl. Just like Digger said. Sell it. Make them *believe*." Then, as if we hadn't just heard everything he'd said to himself, he continued. "I am the King of Yennbridge. I have many things to offer. And I know that I can make you happy, because when I see you, you make my insides feel funny. But like, a *good* funny. Like when it's summer and the sun is shining and you go outside and do somersaults in the grass."

"I remind you of somersaults," I repeated.

"In the *grass*," Dylan said earnestly. "You can't forget that part."

"Even if I tried."

Dylan nodded. "Exactly. So, like, I know you probably have a lot to think about, but just remember one thing: we have the chance to be something cool, but you have to want it as much as I do. What's the worst that could happen?"

"You could be faking all of this in order to trick me into believing you and then once I'm distracted, you'll try and murder me and my friends and take over my kingdom for your own while imprisoning my subjects for your nefarious deeds?"

"We have trust issues," Dad said.

"Ruv," Ryan muttered. "That fucking dick."

Sam bristled. "Ryan, how many times do I have to tell you to think of the chil—you know what? No. I take that back. Ruv sucked ass. Fuck that guy. Never mind. Ryan, I'll allow it because I love you and you're the best thing that's ever happened to me."

Ryan preened.

"Forget all the rest," Dylan said to me. "All the other jerks who tried to hurt you. I'm not them. I don't want to take anything from you. Okay, that was a lie. There is *one* thing I'm want to take from you."

I *knew* it. This was a trap. They were coming here to ruin everything we had rebuilt. Ready to signal the knights to take them prisoner, I said, "Oh? And what's that?"

Dylan squared his shoulders, chin jutting out. "Your heart."

"Oh my *gods*," Gary moaned. "Tiggy, don't look at my erection. It's something I can't control and I don't want to talk about it more than we already have."

Tiggy covered his face with his hands, peeking out through his fingers.

"We'll leave you to it," Ramos said, rising from his chair. "Time is of the essence. We'll expect your decision shortly. King Dylan, let's give them a moment or two. King Dimitri, if you'll escort us, it would be appreciated. That way, each group will have a potential keeper of the stone with us."

Dylan stared at me for a moment before nodding, rising from his seat and followed Ramos to the doors. Dad motioned for our advisors to do the same. They grumbled but didn't try to argue, leaving us to it, Dimitri fluttering through the entryway. The doors closed behind them with a terrible finality.

Silence fell in the room. I sank back down in my seat, rubbing a hand over my face.

"Well, that was certainly interesting," Morgan said.

"I've figured it out," Gary announced. "A way to tell without a doubt if they're evil or not."

I dropped my hand, looking at him. "Really? Is it some sort of unicorn magic? Why didn't you say anything before?"

"Because I'm mysterious," Gary said as he came to the table. "It's simple, really. We dealt with Ruv, who we thought was good at first, but turned out to be evil, right?"

"Right," Sam said.

"Ergo," Gary said, "we can't trust people whose names begin with *R*."

"Ramos," Ryan whispered. "Oh no. Wait. *My* name starts with R."

Randall cleared his throat pointedly.

"Oh," Gary said. "Right. Huh."

"And Justin's last name is Roth," Sam added helpfully.

"What?" Gary asked, bewildered. "When did he get a last name? Shit. That ruins everything. Welp, there goes my idea. What's for dinner tonight? I'm feeling snacky. Curry? If I ordered curry, would everyone else have some? I don't want to be the only one eating."

"Chicken on curry?" Tiggy asked.

"Oooh, maybe! Or what about beef? It's been too long since we've had beef."

"Justin?" Dad asked. "What are you thinking?"

If I could get away with serial murder. I'd have to be careful, but I'd start with Ramos. Perhaps ask him on a walk to talk about Yennbridge customs. Once he was dispatched, I could move on to Dylan. If there was time, Gary. It would get bloody, but I knew a guy in the city who could dispose of any remains without asking questions, so long as he had enough gold in his pockets. He'd flip over having a unicorn horn.

"Sam," I said instead.

"Yeah?"

I looked over at him. "Thoughts?"

Sam shook his head. "I don't know, dude. I mean, it seems pretty straight-forward, what with a magical stone sucking up all our powers and making us—for all intents and purposes—like everyone else while you bind yourself with a magical sash to see if Dylan is your one true love."

"Yes," I said. "So straight-forward. That's not what I'm asking."

"Then what do you mean?"

Of all the stupid people I had to be stuck with, it had to be him. He was really going to make me say it. I looked to Dad for help, but he just smiled at me as if he knew what was going on in my head. No help, that one. "Gods," I snapped. "Are you going to be okay with losing your magic, at least for a little while?"

Sam squeaked, his hands going to his mouth. His eyes were obscenely wide, and I swore they glistened with unshed tears. "You really care about me," he said in a hushed voice. "You're worried about what it would do to me."

Godsdammit, that is *exactly* what I meant, but I didn't want anyone to know that. I didn't speak, knowing anything I'd say would only make things more terrible.

Sam dropped his hands, sniffling. "Yes, Justin. I'd be okay with it. It'd take some getting used to, but it's not forever, right? And so long as it doesn't have any side effects that hurt me or Morgan, I'd do it for you."

Touched (and mostly against my will, so therefore, *molested*), I nodded, unable to speak.

"It shouldn't," Morgan said thoughtfully. "Granted, I've never dealt with a Damning Stone before, but Randall seems to think it'll act as advertised."

Randall nodded. "It should. If it doesn't, it'll be the last thing Ramos does."

"The name of the stone doesn't exactly inspire confidence," Dad said.

"It's all about power," Morgan said. "Objects such as this often have names that don't make much sense for what their intended purpose is. And I feel infinitely more comfortable knowing Randall and Dimitri would be the keepers of the stone."

I wished I shared his belief, but it still felt wrong. To take away the magic of our wizards would be ridding ourselves of a major line of our defense. We had the largest army of knights in the known world, but we'd be foolish to take this at face value.

Dad must have been thinking along the same lines. "We can send word to the northern borders. Notify our people to keep an eye out in case anyone from Yennbridge tries to cross, especially if they appear ready for battle. I don't think Ramos or King Dylan would act in such a way, but it's better to be cautious."

"And if they do when Dylan and I are bound?" I asked.

"Then I would think it would render the pact null and void," Morgan said. "Randall and Dimitri would have no choice but to return our magic to us and allow you to break the bind between you and Dylan. This is serious business, Justin. While you would do well not to trust Ramos, I don't think even he would attempt to interfere with his king's desires."

"Ruv," I reminded them. "We trusted him and look where that got us."

"Fucking evil sexy twinks," Gary muttered. "Just when you think they're cool, they betray you."

"And he paid for his crimes," Dad said gently. "Ramos knows this. If he thinks he can try and harm us, then he's going to be in for the surprise of his life."

"I'm worried," I admitted. "Not about…Dylan. I can deal with him. I don't like the idea of us being defenseless."

"We won't," Tiggy said.

We all looked to him.

"How do you figure, kitten?" Gary asked.

Tiggy looked at each of us in turn. Then, "Have each other. Bad guys come and Tiggy smash and help friends. Friends help Tiggy so Tiggy not alone. Long time Tiggy alone, but then Gary find Tiggy, and Sam and Ryan and Kevin and Justin and King and Morgan and Randall. Tiggy never alone. Prince never alone. Has us. Has me." His brow furrowed as if he was thinking as hard as he ever had. "We powerful," he said slowly. "Because we together. Not magic. Not swords. Us. Never defenseless. Never, ever, ever."

"Thank you, Tiggy," Dad said. "That was well said."

"It really was," Gary said, rubbing his snout against Tiggy's chest. "My smart guy. I love you to the moon and back."

"Pretty Gary," Tiggy said, running his fingers through Gary's mane.

"Tiggy's right," Ryan said. "Even if Ramos turns out to be a villain—which, I highly doubt because Dylan is rad and I *know* he'd never hang out with someone who wants to kill us—we can handle him."

*Rad*, Sam mouth to me, rolling his eyes.

I turned toward the doorway. A page stood next to the doors, fidgeting nervously. "Bring me Lady Tina," I told him. He nodded and fled the chambers.

"You sure about this?" Ryan asked Sam. He took Sam's hand in his own, palms pressed together. "You've known only magic for so long, it's going to be a shock to your system."

Sam laughed, but it wasn't as bright as it normally was. "It won't be forever. And if this is what Justin wants, then I'm going to do what I can for him."

"It's not about *want*," I said. "And I hope you all remember that. I don't know who Dylan thinks he is, but I'm not to be trifled with."

"I would caution you, Justin," Morgan said. "Matters of the heart are far more powerful than you give them credit for. You might find yourself changing your mind before the end."

I scoffed. "I doubt it. I'll give them the thirty days they ask for. And when the time is finished, we'll forget this ever happened."

I wished I believed in my words more than I did.

The doors opened once more, and Lady Tina marched in, the scabbard that sheathed her thin sword bouncing against her armor. Her eyes widened briefly when she saw who was gathered before her, but it was brief; regardless of what Sam thought of her, she knew her place.

She bowed low, fist against her chest. "You asked for me, Prince?"

"Boooo," Sam and Tiggy and Gary said at the same time.

I ignored them. "I'm going to be bound to Dylan by a magical sash for thirty days while he tries to convince me to marry him. And while this happens, Sam and Morgan and Gary won't have their magic."

She coughed roughly, face turning bright red. "I'm sorry. *What?*"

"What happens when Lady Tina DeSilva thinks something is a bad idea?" Gary whispered to Sam. "Does that mean it's a good idea or the worst idea?"

"Who the fuck knows anymore?" Sam mumbled.

"I have a job for you," I said to Tina. "A top-secret assignment. Do not be noticed. Do not be caught. Keep your ears open at all times. I am assigning you to Ramos the Pure to act as his guard while he and his people are in Verania."

"Guard?" Tina asked, confused. "Why would I need to guard them?"

"Pretense," I said. "Be seen and not heard. Blend into the background. Never let him out of your sight. You and your contingent can work in shifts. Anything you hear that sounds unsavory, you let me know immediately. Make sure your group knows this."

Tina nodded. "Can we assassinate anyone? The only reason I

ask is because Deidre hasn't stabbed anyone in six months, and she's starting to get...difficult."

"Isn't she the youngest?" Morgan asked.

Tina shrugged. "She's very dedicated."

I shook my head. "No assassinating. This is purely reconnaissance. For now."

"Yes, Prince Justin." She turned to leave but stopped before she turned all the way around. "Prince, if I may."

"You may."

"Was this Sam's idea? Because if it was, you really need to reconsider. If you're looking for someone to marry, I know at least nine lords who would bend backwards—literally *and* figuratively—for you."

"Oh, fuck off, you diseased troll," Sam said. "Look at you, with your stupid face and your dumb hair and—"

"Idiots say what?" Tina asked.

Sam blinked. "What?"

She smiled. "There. That's settled forever."

"Hey!"

I narrowed my eyes at her. "Are you questioning me?"

"No!" Tina said quickly. "No. I wouldn't even *dream* of it. You are the picture of benevolence, the most handsome prince to have ever princed, the future of all that we hold dear—"

"Good," I said. "I'm glad you think so. Now do as you're told."

She bowed again before spinning on her heels and fleeing the chambers. She paused at the doorway and then, as if we all couldn't see her, flipped Sam off and then disappeared, blonde curls trailing after her.

"Justin," Dad said. "Are you sure about this?"

I rose from my chair. "No. I'm not. Because for all your talk of choice, you're not leaving me with much of one, are you?"

Dad winced. "I deserve that."

I sighed. "You did. And you do. But we'll deal with it as we always have."

"Kicking and screaming and begging for it all to stop while we find ourselves in increasingly bizarre situations that defy all logic and make no sense to anyone with half a brain?" Sam asked.

I nodded. "Exactly." Then, "Wait. What? No. Of course not. We will face it head on and emerge victorious. King Dylan wants a husband?" I grinned. "I'm going to absolve him of that notion so quickly, he's going to wish he'd never heard of Verania."

"I can't believe I left a game of strip checkers for this," Randall mumbled.

# CHAPTER 9
# Surprise! Things Don't Go as Planned!

I STOOD ON THE LARGE BALCONY that overlooked the front of the castle out onto the City of Lockes. My father stood at my right, hands raised to try and quiet the boisterous crowd of thousands who were relieved to see him on the mend. Sam and Ryan were to my left, hands clasped between them. Gary and Tiggy stood against the wall behind us. Morgan was on the other side of my father, and Randall next to him.

"Good people of Verania," Dad said, voice carrying out over the crowd. "I am filled with unparalleled joy to see all your faces. Thank you for your well wishes as I continue to recover. I'm under the best care, and though I will need to take it easy for a little while longer, I'm looking forward to getting back to work as soon as possible."

The crowd cheered.

"But today isn't about me," Dad continued. "As I'm sure you've heard by now given the Veranian rumor mill always seems to be in overdrive, we recently received guests from the wonderful country of Yennbridge. Their king, Dylan, has made a request."

*Request* was a bit of a misnomer, though I allowed it. I didn't want anyone to be pissed off at my father. That was my job.

"King Dylan has asked for my son's hand in marriage. Prince Justin has taken counsel on the matter and has agreed to a trial that will last for thirty days. During this time, as per Yenner customs, King Dylan and Prince Justin will be joined together by the Sash of the

Grand Hunt."

The crowd applauded, but it wasn't as loud as it'd been before. They were probably just as confused as I was. The devil was in the details. We wouldn't be announcing anything about our loss of magic, it was better to be safe than sorry. While I didn't think anyone listening would attempt a coup, we had to be prepared for every situation. I didn't know how we'd be able to keep it secret, but we had to try. That being said, the tabloids were going to have a field day with all of this. I could already see the headlines: SCANDAL IN LOCKES! PRINCE JUSTIN GETS TIED UP FOR LOVE!

Dad nodded at me as he said, "If, at the end of the trial my son finds true love with King Dylan, they will be married, joining our two great countries in an era of peace and prosperity."

"And what if they don't!" someone shouted from the crowd. "What if King Dylan realizes what he's getting into and wants to leave before his soul is consumed by the Ice Prince!"

I glared down at the man. He waved up at me wildly, telling everyone around him that the Prince knew he *existed*, can you believe it?

"If they don't find true love, then they will part and search for greener pastures," Dad said. "Nothing will be held against either of them for such a decision. And now I'll make a request of all of you: you may see your Prince and King Dylan around the City of Lockes, or other Yenners exploring what we have to offer. Make sure you welcome them with open arms and let them want for naught. I know that Verania will rise to the occasion as we always do."

The crowd was ecstatic. I had no idea why. This sounded like a bad idea in a long, long history of bad ideas.

"And now," Dad said, "may I present to you, the ruler of Yennbridge, King Dylan. And his advisor, Ramos the Pure."

He stepped back as Dylan and Ramos walked onto the balcony. My eyes bulged from my head as Dylan stopped beside me. His forehead was covered in a sheen of sweat, but that's not what captured my attention. No, it had to do with what he was wearing.

Or, to be more specific, what he *wasn't* wearing.

Oh, he still had boots on. He still had *trousers* on, thank the gods. But he was shirtless, his torso looking as if it'd been rubbed with grease, and it was only then I realized he wasn't *sweating*. No, he'd been lathered up for some godsdamn reason, looking like if I tried to touch him, I'd slip right off and fall to the ground. His strong shoulders caught the sunlight, his stomach swaying as he breathed in and out.

"Did he get *lubed*?" I heard Sam whisper, and I wondered what it would take for the balcony to collapse and kill us all.

But whatever else he said was drowned out by the screams from the crowd, women (and more than a few men) shrieking their pleasure at the sight of Dylan. He gripped the railing of the balcony, letting the sound wash over him. "Whoa," he said. "We don't have this many people in the City of Light. Crud. I wasn't expecting that. Ha, ha! Isn't it funny to find out I have stage fright right at this second?"

"It's *not* funny," I hissed at him. "Act like a king!"

He nodded. "Right. King stuff. I got this." He raised his voice. "Hey! Hi. Yeah, it's me. King Dylan! Thank you for that epic welcome. I'm so excited to be here. You look like a rockin' crowd. It reminds me of the time me and my buddies went on spring break and beads were thrown at us anytime we showed our butts. Do you have any beads because I can drop trou right here if you want."

In my short, albeit eventful life, I'd never had beads thrown at me. I didn't even know where people got beads from. But you would think they were the only thing ever created in Verania with the amount flung in our direction. Sam had to duck to avoid getting smacked in the face.

Dylan brought his hands to his trousers, getting ready to pull them down. We were saved when Ramos cleared his throat and said mildly, "Maybe now isn't the time for that, Your Majesty."

"Right," Dylan said hastily. "No one probably wants to see that."

"We do!" a woman shrieked. "We want that so bad! Show us what you're working with!"

Dylan grinned down at her. "Maybe next time."

I rolled my eyes when the woman swooned, falling back on her friends who caught her before she hit the ground.

"I'm grateful to be here," Dylan continued. "Your country is foreign to me, but we've been made to feel like we belong. That's gnarly. So, thanks and stuff. Oh! And I promise to make Justin the happiest he's ever been, so much so that he won't ever want to be without me, and when we get married, you're all invited!" He fist-pumped the air when the crowd exploded below us. "Heck yeah! You know what I'm talking about. Yeah, you, bro. The one doing cartwheels. Whoa, you almost kicked a baby in the face. Careful, dude!"

"Thank you for coming!" I yelled, trying to end this farce. "That's all. Go back to your homes and forget everything you saw here!"

I grabbed Dylan by the arm, meaning to pull him off the balcony before he could open his mouth and say something else we'd both regret. Unfortunately, even his fucking *arm* was lubed up, and I slipped and stumbled into Dad.

Dylan said, "Oh man, sorry about that. Ramos said that I needed to be shiny before going out in public. My bad."

"Your bad," I muttered. "I'll fucking show you *your bad.*"

"Stop flirting," Randall scolded me. "There will be time for that later. Honestly, Prince Justin. Show some decorum."

I stalked off the balcony. If they followed, fine. Great. Wonderful. If not, screw them all.

Apparently since my life was unbearably tragic, they followed, Dylan leading the way.

I didn't stare at the muscles in his back as he passed me by.

"Yeah," Sam said. "He's pretty hot, so congrats on all the sex you'll be having."

"I will straight up *end* you," I growled.

"Sure you will," he said, patting my arm. "Hey, question: since Dylan is all lubed up and ready to go, how long do you think it'll be before you put yourself inside him? Gary thinks three hours. I said there was no way it'd happen like that."

That made me feel a little better. "Thanks, Sam. I know—"

"I said it'd take at least two days," Sam said.

I glared at him. "You better not have made any bets on this."

"We did," Sam said cheerfully. "Winner gets bragging rights. You want to hear how your dad bet? He thinks it's going to take four—"

"Maybe we should save that for later," Dad said, pushing Sam into the castle. "Not everything needs to be said out loud."

"I will banish you all!" I bellowed after them.

"Ignore them," Morgan said. "I know it can be difficult, but you can't allow them to distract you."

"Thank you, Morgan," I said, relieved. "It's nice to know I have at least *one* person on my side."

"Morgan bet two weeks," Tiggy said as he walked by us. "Tiggy didn't bet because against religion. Joke. No religion because it's dumb. Tiggy no bet because Tiggy Knight of Brooms. Capitalized. True now."

They laughed at me when I began to sputter nonsensically.

I closed my eyes and prayed for death.

The gods did not comply.

*****

"PLACE YOUR HANDS UPON THE STONE," Ramos instructed. We all stood in a loose circle in the throne room, sunlight pouring in through the stained-glass windows, covering us in shades of green and gold and yellow and blue. Kevin wasn't part of the circle, but only because he couldn't fit inside the throne room. Instead, he stuck his head through the open doors that led to the gardens, tongue snaking out and flicking the air.

Randall stood in the center of the circle, the Damning Stone resting in his cupped hands, Dimitri on his shoulder, leaning against the old wizard's cheek. The fairy king wriggled his mustache as he peered down at the rock. "Once done, it cannot be undone until the thirty days have passed. If you do this, there's no taking it back."

Sam hesitated, looking at Ryan, who smiled quietly at him. "You got this. I know you do. It'll be over before you know it. And no matter what happens, I'll love you all the same."

Sam swallowed thickly. "Even if I can't accidentally turn your hair into live snakes?"

Ryan shuddered. "Especially then. That was a weird two hours." He sobered. "It doesn't matter to me one way or another. Magic or no magic, you're still my Sam, and I'll love you forever. I got my wish, remember? Because when I looked upon the stars, there was nothing I wished for more than—"

"Yawn," Gary said. "Been there, done that, and read the overblown, self-serious sequels. Stop trying to make this about the pair of you. Four times was enough. Even *I'm* fine with taking on a reduced role."

"What's he talking about?" Ryan asked.

"I have no idea," Sam said. "But yes, I'm sure." He glanced at me before looking back at Ryan. "It's scary, but it's for Justin. That means it's part of being Best Friends 5eva. He would do the same for me if our roles were reversed."

He wasn't wrong.

Sam hugged Ryan then began to approach Randall but stopped when Morgan placed a hand on his shoulder. "Perhaps I should go first," Morgan said. "Just to be safe."

Sam hesitated. "Are you sure?"

"I am," Morgan said. "Should something happen to me, you'll need to be ready."

Sam glared daggers at Ramos. "*If* something happens that hasn't been explicitly described, then I'm going to end them all, right here, right now. And I think they know I can do it."

A chill ran down my spine because I knew he was serious. Even more, I thought he could do exactly as he threatened. Not for the first time, I was grateful Sam was on our side and not an enemy. We would never survive his wrath.

"I assure you nothing untoward will happen," Ramos said. "So long as you give consent, your magic will be stored safely, returned to you once the ritual has been completed."

"Oh," Gary snarked. "Now it's a *ritual*. Funny how that changed in the last few hours."

Before Morgan could approach the stone, Dad stopped him. Morgan smiled at my father, but Dad didn't smile back. "I'll be all right, Anthony," Morgan said gently. "I have too much to live for to consider otherwise."

Dad nodded but didn't seem to want to let Morgan go. Eventually, he released his grip on Morgan's hand.

"You'll feel a little suction," Randall said as Morgan stopped in front of him. "And no, Sam, that doesn't need your commentary."

Sam snapped his mouth closed, looking disappointed.

"It shouldn't hurt," Randall said. "But you'll feel drained after. Unfortunately, there isn't much I can do about that, but it'll pass with time. You might not feel completely like yourself, but—"

"But I've survived worse," Morgan finished for him. "I trust you, Randall. I always have."

Randall startled but recovered swiftly. "I wouldn't let anything happen to you. You have my word as your former mentor."

"Former nothing," Morgan said. "I still learn from you every day."

"Something your own former apprentice would do well to remember," Randall said. "Place your hand upon the stone. Clear your mind. Allow nothing to distract you. The rest of you must remain absolutely silent."

Morgan nodded. He raised his hand. His fingers trembled briefly, and he curled his hand into a fist before opening it again.

And then he placed it upon the Damning Stone.

It immediately dissolved into liquid with a low *whoosh*, the air around us thickening with the stench of pure magic, ozone sharp and cloying. Randall muttered under his breath words that I hadn't heard in a long time, not since Sam had to use them to cast his magic: *che* and *rey* and what sounded like *lyor*. Morgan's head rocked back, eyes wide and unseeing as the cords jutted from his neck as the now liquid stone crawled up his hand, encasing it like a wet glove. His entire body shook as if a tremor rolled through him. It felt like years but lasted only seconds. A thick, wet *crack!* echoed around the throne room, and Morgan jerked his arm back as if scalded.

The stone had solidified once again in Morgan's hand.

Morgan stumbled, Dad rushing forward and catching him before he fell. Morgan laughed weakly in Dad's arms. "I'm fine," he choked out. "It's done. I…" He shook his head, allowing Dad to pull him back. For wanting to keep their relationship a secret, they sure as hell weren't trying to hide anything as Dad whispered soothingly into his ear, holding onto Morgan tightly.

Not to be outdone, Ramos pushed his way forward. He didn't pause before placing his on the stone. The skin around his eyes twitched as the stone turned to liquid, covering his hand. The same *crack!* sounded, and it was done.

"There," Ramos said breathlessly. "I have done my part."

"You all right?" Dylan asked as Ramos resumed his place in the circle.

"I'm fine."

"I love you, baby!" Kevin yelled as Gary approached Randall. "You're always a unicorn to me, no matter what!"

"Of course I am," Gary said, going for brave but missing by a mile. "I lived without my horn for years. I can do this." He leaned forward, studying the stone, snout inches away from it. Once he finished his inspection, he looked up at Randall. "You fuck with me, I'll end you."

"I wouldn't dream of it," Randall said dryly.

Gary touched his horn to the stone. It melted again, wrapping itself around his horn. He shuddered, the hairs of his tail hardening as if he were being electrocuted. The stone *dripped* off his horn back onto Randall's waiting palm, where it reformed as Gary sagged. "There," he said weakly. "I feel like a sex worker after buy one get twelve free."

"Come here," Kevin said. "Need to check and make sure you're still Gary."

Gary moved slowly toward him, head bowed, Sam reaching for him but pulling his hand back at the last moment. Gary stopped in front of Kevin, not looking at him.

Kevin bumped his head underneath Gary's jaw, forcing him to look up. "There you are," Kevin said. "Still as beautiful as the day I first met you."

Gary sniffled. "But I don't have magic."

"It doesn't matter to me," Kevin said. "You're the best unicorn I've ever met, and I've met *two* of them. I don't care if you don't have magic. I'll love you all the same."

"Really? But my horn is merely decorative now."

"Hey," Kevin said. "Hey. Guess what?"

"What?"

"You can still stab people," Kevin said. "And isn't that the most important thing of all?"

Gary nodded slowly. "It is. Just because they took away my magic doesn't mean I still can't murder. Thank you for reminding me of what's important." He rubbed up against Kevin. "You always know the right thing to say when my magic gets sucked up by a magical stone."

Randall cleared his throat pointedly. "Sam, it's your turn."

Sam startled, looking at Ryan who nodded. "It's like Kevin said. You don't need your magic to still murder people." He frowned. "Wait. That's not what I meant."

Sam snorted. "Thanks. You always know the right thing to say when my magic—"

"Stop stealing my intellectual property!" Gary shouted. "My magic is gone and I'm *not* amused!"

Sam sighed as he raised his head. He marched forward quickly. I thought he'd hesitate at the last moment—and the urge to tell him to stop bubbled furiously in my throat—but he didn't. He slammed his hand down on the Damning Stone.

Nothing happened.

Sam squinted down at the rock as he lifted his hand. "Huh. That's weird."

"Consent," Ramos said with a scowl. "You have to agree or it won't work."

"I *am* agreeing," Sam said, slapping the stone repeatedly. "Consent! All the consent!"

"Maybe it's broken," Gary said. "Took all my magic and now it doesn't work anymore. Guess that proves what I've been saying for years: I'm pretty much the greatest creature who has ever lived."

"Spank it, Sam!" Tiggy yelled. "Spank it hard!"

"I'm *trying*," Sam growled, hitting the stone again and again. "Work, godsdammit! Take all my—"

The stone exploded.

Or at least I *thought* it exploded. It broke apart when Sam slammed his hand down for the last time, turning into liquid. It looked sentient as it congealed, rising up between Sam's fingers, forming what resembled an iridescent tower. It glittered before collapsing on top of Sam's hand, covering his skin. Sam's head rocked back, and the moment before his eyes closed, I would've have sworn they glowed with an otherworldly light.

Sam stumbled back as the stone reformed in Randall's hand, though it wasn't quite the same shape as it'd been before. It looked lumpy and *alive*, the stone pulsing like it was breathing. Randall frowned as he looked down at it, Ryan holding Sam close. I opened my mouth to ask if he was all right, but Ramos spoke before I could.

"Quickly," he said. "The sash must be tied now while there's still time. Prince Justin, King Dylan, step forward now."

I swallowed thickly as I stepped forward. Dylan did the same, and we stopped next to each other, our shoulders brushing together. I flinched when Dylan grabbed my right hand with his left, our palms pressed together as he raised our arms toward Ramos. The magician didn't hesitate, pulling out the sash with a flourish, handing it over to Dimitri who gathered it as best he could in his tiny arms. Dimitri fluttered toward us, the material settling on our hands. It felt soft and warm. Dimitri began to mutter under his breath as he flew in circles around our wrists, wrapping the sash tightly, his wings flashing brilliantly, eyes black as coal. Dylan breathed heavily through his nose, his palm sweating against mine.

Once Dimitri had finished, he flew above us, inspecting his work. He nodded in satisfaction. "There, it's finished. Ramos."

Ramos stepped forward, resting his hand on the top of ours. His skin felt weirdly cool, and I had to stop myself from pulling away from him, not liking the eye tattooed on his palm against me, though it looked faded. He glanced between the two of us. "The Sash of the Grand Hunt has bound Prince Justin and King Dylan together. For the next thirty days, you will be joined in all things. You will use the time you have together to learn about each other, to find out if you have what it takes in order to be one. This will not be without danger: one of the most difficult things a person can do is allow others to see them at their most unguarded. Above all else, you must remember honesty, for what is love but an unvarnished truth?"

The sash tightened around my right wrist as if it were alive. It wasn't painful, but I couldn't ignore the fact that it was there. Dylan stared down at it in awe.

Ramos stepped back as I let Dylan's hand go, the sash trailing down between us. At most, it looked five feet in length, not the twenty we were told. Deciding to test it out to make sure Ramos wasn't a godsdamn liar, I backed away slowly. The sash stretched taut. And then, impossibly, it *kept* stretching with every step I took until I was about twenty feet away from Dylan, when it wouldn't move any further, Dylan's arm raising with my movements.

"That's it?" I asked, dumbfounded. "That's all that happened? I don't feel any different." Irritated, yes, but I'd expected the sash to explode or light on fire or *something*.

"You don't?" Dylan asked, sounding relieved. "Good, I was worried you wouldn't—"

"Ramos," Randall said. "The stone. Is this supposed to be happening?"

We all turned toward Randall, who was staring down at the Damning Stone. The surface of the stone rippled, concentric circles as if a pebble had been thrown into a lake. It flashed, once, twice, the same strange light that I'd seen in Sam's eyes.

"What's this?" Ramos asked, taking a step toward Randall. "I've never seen it move in such a—"

And then the stone *literally* exploded.

The shockwave slammed into all of us, knocking us off our feet. I flew back, closing my eyes as I braced for impact. The sash tightened around my wrist and I was then jerked *forward*, landing face down on the floor with a groan.

I blinked slowly as I struggled to lift my head, ears ringing loudly. Nothing seemed broken so far as I could tell. Anger flooded me, sure that this had been part of the plan, one meant to take us all out when we were at our weakest.

Thick, odorless smoke filled the room like a blanket of fog. I could barely see a foot in front of my face. I looked down as I sat up. The sash was still tied to my wrist, the length disappearing into the fog. I leaned forward, meaning to crawl along the sash until I found Dylan.

Before I made it too far, I heard movement.

I narrowed my eyes, wondering what horror was coming toward me. Steeling myself for an impending attack, I looked around for something that could be used as a weapon. Nothing. I was defenseless.

A small figure appeared in the fog, a black shadow that looked to be the size of a large dog. Confused, I reared back, wondering what beast had been awakened from the stone, sure it was going to be a snarling thing with razor sharp teeth and a penchant for human flesh.

It wasn't.

It was something much, much worse.

"What in the fucking *shit* is this?" a childlike voice demanded.

The fog parted slightly, revealing the terrible secret hidden within.

There, standing in front of me, was a baby horse, a foal on wobbly legs. The youngling was white with knobby knees and hooves far too big for such a little thing. Its tail swished angrily as the foal stared at me with the largest eyes I'd ever seen, eyelashes so long, they looked fake.

"Where did you come from?" I asked gently, reaching for it.

My hand stopped halfway, fingers trembling, when the foal lifted his head and I saw what stretched out from the center of its forehead.

A horn.

A fucking *horn*.

"What happened to me?" the foal screeched, voice high-pitched and wavering. "Where am I? Someone had better explain what the fuck is going on before I…before I…" It stopped, taking in a shuddering breath before promptly bursting into tears.

"*Gary?*" I whispered deliriously.

He froze, eyeing me warily, cheeks wet. "How did you know my name? Who are you? Did you kidnap me to try and have your way with my young, nubile body? Stranger danger! Stranger danger! I want my *mom*!" He began to wail.

"It's me," I said, trying to calm him down. "It's Justin. The Prince! I'm your…well, friend, I think?"

Gary peered up at me with wet eyes. "So you didn't kidnap me to try and have your way with my young, nubile—"

"Of course not," I snapped. "I wouldn't—holy shit. Gary, you're a *child*."

He was maybe three feet tall from the tip of his horn to his hooves, and perhaps two feet in length. For a moment, I almost said that he looked like a miniature horse, but I stopped myself before the words could get out, knowing they'd only make things worse. I was about to tell him to calm down, that we'd figure it out, but before I could, another shadow appeared above us in the fog, wings flapping.

Ducking my head—sure it was a rabid bat bent on revenge (for what, I didn't know, but fuck you because I was having a very strange day)—I gasped as the creature flew over me, the fog curling into wisps as the wings moved up and down.

And then it landed on the ground between me and Gary, and I thought my brain was broken. For there, no more than the size of the sheep he loved and hated in equal measure, was the Beast from the East, the dragon who'd once kidnapped me.

Except Kevin had never been this small, not in the entire time I'd known him. Somehow, someway, he, like Gary, had shrunk.

Gary's eyes bulged from his head as Kevin peered up at him, tail swishing back and forth. "Whoa," Kevin breathed as he stared up at Gary, and it took me a moment to realize his voice was higher than it'd ever been. "You're so pretty. Wow, wow, wowwy wow." He hopped around in a circle. "Hi! Who are you? I want to know everything about you. My name is Kevin. I'm a dragon! I can fly and *everything*. Do you wanna see?" He pumped his wings, rising a few feet off the floor before he crashed back to the ground awkwardly. "I'm okay!" he yelled. "I just did it so I can do it again!"

"Kevin?" Gary asked in a watery voice. "Were you kidnapped too? I like your name. It's very exotic."

"Thank you," Kevin said, puffing out his little chest. Then he deflated. "I want *crackers*. And a *nap*. And someone better hold me while I fall asleep or I'm going to light everything on fire!"

He reared back, throat working. A fiery glow began to appear in the back of his throat as he opened his jaws wide. I rushed forward, slapping a hand across his mouth, hissing at the immense heat. "No fire!"

Kevin's eyes bulged dramatically before he burst into tears, which made *Gary* start to cry again, both of them screeching as they huddled close together.

I stood slowly, dazed and disbelieving what I was witnessing. This had to be a dream. I was unconscious, laying splayed out on the floor, and dreaming terrible dreams. This notion was shattered a second later when a voice said from behind me, "Are you all right?"

I whirled around, the sash around my wrist fluttering. There, looking no worse for wear aside from the look of confusion on his face, was Dylan, moving through the thick fog. The sash was still tied to his wrist, shortening as he moved closer to me.

"What did you do?" I demanded.

"What are you talking about?" he asked. "I didn't do anything."

I jerked my head over my shoulder toward tiny Gary and Kevin. "Then how the hell do you explain *that*?"

Dylan peered around me, bending over and craning his neck. His eyes widened when he saw Gary and Kevin. "I didn't know you had a baby unicorn *and* a baby dragon. Bro, what is *up* with Verania?"

"That's Kevin and Gary!" I snarled at him.

He squinted at them. "Uh. What."

Before I could respond, the room filled with shouts as knights poured in through the doorway, swords drawn. Lady Tina led the charge, her face twisted in blazing anger as the fog began to clear. She saw me, eyes narrowing as she rushed toward me. "My Prince," she said, sounding breathless. "Are you all right? We heard an explosion."

"No," I snapped at her. "I'm *not* all right. It was a trap, just like I thought it was. Ramos did something. Take him into custody, and do it *now*."

She nodded and turned to do just that. She stopped, blood draining from her face as something caught her attention. I followed her gaze, the fog dissipating and revealing the horrible truth.

"Oh fuck," I breathed.

Ramos was fine, wincing as he sat up from the floor.

Randall stood, frowning down at the reformed stone in his hands, Dimitri standing on his shoulder, whispering furiously in his ear.

But they weren't what we were looking at.

Sitting in the middle of the room, struggling against oversized robes, was a child. A boy of about eight or nine, his complexion dark, his hair hanging down around his head in loose curls, his bottom lip wobbling. Next to him was another boy of approximately the same age with thick blond hair, buried in a mountain of armor that no longer fit him, sword laying discarded at his side. He reached down to pick it up, fingers barely able to wrap around the hilt. He grunted as he tried to lift it, but it was too heavy for such a little arm.

"Hey!" the boy in the armor said. "Are you all right?"

"No," the boy in the robes said. "I'm stuck and I can't get out!"

"I'll save you!" the boy in the armor yelled. He tried to stand but immediately fell over, armor clanging against the stone floor.

"Oh no!" the boy in the robes said. "You fell down!"

"I did *not*," armor boy said. "I did that on purpose."

"Liar!" robe boy said.

Armor boy began to sniffle, eyes welling. "*You're* a liar! I can do anything I put my mind to because I'm a *knight*. The bravest knight who ever existed!"

I choked on my tongue. Sam and Ryan Haversford had been turned into children, just like Kevin and Gary. I started toward them—meaning to do *what*, I didn't know—when an angry voice bellowed, "Tiggy *smash*!"

It was about this time that I was attacked by a six-foot-tall half-giant child. He landed on my back, and I staggered forward as his fists beat against my shoulders, his breath hot in my ear. "Tiggy!" I groaned as he wrapped his legs around my waist tightly. "Stop it! It's me, Justin."

Tiggy's knees dug into my hips as he held my chin, tilting my head back. "Justin?" he asked. "Who is Justin? I Tiggy! Sorry about smashing." He frowned. "A little sorry. Smashing fun. Tiggy smash!" He gripped me tightly, throwing his body forward. I couldn't support his immense weight, and I flipped end over end, landing on my back on the ground. Tiggy stood above me, his feet on either side of my shoulders as he grinned down at me. "There. Better."

I groaned as I sat up, pushing Tiggy back. He laughed as he reached down and grabbed my arm, jerking me up so hard, I almost flew over him again. Instead, I was wrapped in a bone-crushing hug. "I like you," Tiggy said proudly. "You smell good. Like…" His voice trailed off as he looked behind us. I turned my head to see what he was staring at. Gary. Kevin.

"Unicorn," Tiggy breathed. "Unicorn!" He shoved me away and headed toward Gary and Kevin. "Hi! Hi! So pretty." He began to stroke Gary's mane. "Prettiest ever. I Tiggy. I protect you for always."

"Tiggy?" Gary asked, tears still leaking from his eyes. "You really think I'm pretty?"

"Yes," Tiggy said firmly. "Name, please."

"Gary."

"Gaaarrrryyyy," Tiggy said. "My Gary." He picked up the unicorn, who hooked his chin over Tiggy's shoulder. Tiggy stroked his back, making soothing noises. "There, there. Tiggy got you."

"I want a hug too!" Kevin said. He crawled up Tiggy's legs with a grunt, claws piercing Tiggy's too big clothes.

I thought Tiggy would try and shove him off. He didn't; instead, he gathered them both up in his arms as best he could. "Got you. Mine, mine, mine."

"Bro," Dylan breathed. "This was not what I expected. Verania is *crazy*."

I ignored him, pushing my way through the gathering crowd, trying to find Dad. If anything had happened to him, I was going to kill Ramos. I didn't give two shits if that meant war. No one fucked with my father. I only made it halfway across the room when the sash wrapped around my wrist jerked me back. I glanced over my shoulder to see Dylan still standing where I'd left him, the sash stretched between us. Shit. I'd forgotten about that. We were still bound together. I thought about grabbing Ryan's sword and slicing the sash in two. The only thing that stopped me was Ramos's warning that it would mean our deaths. Instead, I grabbed the sash and pulled on it as hard as I could, causing Dylan to stumble toward me. Satisfied, I turned around, searching for my father.

A crowd of knights had gathered around Randall. I pushed my way through them, telling them to get the hell out of my way, Dylan getting dragged along behind me. The knights parted, and I saw Randall crouching on the ground. He heard me coming and turned his head. "They're all right," he said gravely. "Morgan and Anthony are fine."

And they were. Whatever magic had hit the others hadn't affected my father and his wizard. Morgan was helping Dad to his feet, his crown sitting askew on his head. "What happened?" he asked in a shaky voice. "Were we attacked?"

"No, my king," Randall said. "At least not from outside forces. That being said, it appears things are a mite more complicated than we expected."

Morgan blinked as Dad leaned heavily on him. "What do you mean?"

"Who the hell are all of you people?" Gary shouted from somewhere behind us. "I'm a strong, independent unicorn and I will *not take this shit.*"

"Oooh," Kevin and Tiggy and Ryan and Sam all said at the same time.

"He said a bad word," Sam whispered. "I'm going to do it too. Shit. Balls. Fucking sweet molasses!"

"Me too!" Ryan cried. "Damn motherfuck—"

"No!" Sam shouted. "You're a knight! Knights can't say bad things! It's the *law.*"

"Oh." His lip began to tremble. "Am I going to go to jail? I want my m-m-*mom.*"

And then they both burst into tears once more.

"What the fuck is going on?" I asked, sure this was a nightmare from which I needed to wake up.

"Nothing good," Randall said grimly.

Leave it to Randall to provide the understatement of the century.

# CHAPTER 10

## I Like When I'm With You

"IT MUST HAVE BEEN SAM'S MAGIC," Morgan said a short time later, looking down at the stone laying on the table in the labs. "He's not like other wizards. His gifts, while natural, were augmented to an untold degree during his time in the Dark Woods. When he poured his magic into the stone, it must not have been able to contain it all, causing a chain reaction on those he cares for."

I looked over at the other end of the labs. There, sitting with our friends now in miniature, were Rosemary and Joshua. Joshua was regaling the children with a story about the frozen north, the children staring up at him with wide eyes. Sam sat in his mother's lap, head on her shoulder as he struggled to stay awake. Ryan lay against Sam's knees, listening to Joshua's words like it was the greatest story he'd ever heard. Tiggy—still much taller than the others—had gathered Kevin and Gary in his arms. Sam's parents had been summoned, and though their reactions had been perversely comical, Rosemary had acted immediately, taking the boys away to get them into clothes that actually fit. Gary and Kevin had complained about not being included, which is why Gary now wore a sunhat far too big for his head, and Kevin wore one of Gary's scarves.

All in all, it'd been a supremely shitty day. And that didn't even begin to cover Dylan and Ramos, both of whom claimed to have no knowledge that such a thing could happen.

"I see your point," Morgan said, Dad at his side, watching the kids with a look of awe on his face. "It does make a strange bit of sense. That being said, why didn't it cause me to do the same?"

Randall shook his head. "I don't know. Perhaps your own magic?"

"Which is trapped in the stone," Morgan reminded him.

"I know that," Randall said, frowning down at the stone. "Still, that's the only explanation I have."

"And why didn't it affect me?" I asked. I was exhausted, and my eyes felt like they were filled with sand. The sash still hung from my wrist, binding me to Dylan.

"I don't know," Randall admitted. "I considered proximity, but nothing happened to the rest of us. Sam has Ryan, Tiggy, Gary and Kevin, which could explain why it involved them."

"That doesn't make sense," I muttered. "I'm just as involved as they are. It should have hit me too." I winced at how that sounded, like I was almost *jealous*. I wasn't, at least not in that I wanted to be a child too. I really didn't.

Ramos cleared his throat and looked as if he wanted to speak for the first time. I'd been about to order that he be shackled immediately, only stopping when Randall had shaken his head, telling me we needed to play this carefully. I'd agreed, begrudgingly, but that didn't mean I was going to let him off the hook. This was his fault. If he'd never come here, we wouldn't be where we were now.

"If I may," Ramos said. "First, I need to assure you all that Dylan played no part in this."

I arched an eyebrow at him. "Are you implying you did?"

"No," Ramos said evenly. "I'm merely wanting to absolve my king before anything else."

"Righteous," Dylan said. "Because honestly? I just came here to get tied to Justin. That's it. I didn't think it would involve making kids." He paused, considering. "At least not yet."

I rolled my eyes. "You really expect me to believe that?"

Dylan looked wounded. "I'm serious, bro. I wouldn't take things from you that aren't mine. These are your friends. That's not cool."

I made a face, mouthing the words *not cool* with disdain.

"And I didn't know this would happen," Ramos continued. "But then I doubt the Damning Stone has ever had to hold the power of someone like Sam. He's…"

"Different," Randall finished dryly. "Yes, we know."

"Then fix it," I said. "Give them back their magic. Reverse it now."

Ramos hesitated. "I cannot." I began to sputter furiously, only stopping when he raised his hand. The eye on his palm was faded, the ink looking as if it had been sapped away. "Once the sash has been tied and the magic taken, it must be allowed to play out for the allotted time. Removing it now would not only mean the deaths of Justin and Dylan, but there's no guarantee that it would—"

"This isn't about the stupid sash," I said coldly. "It's about the Damning Stone."

Ramos nodded. "And if I was allowed to finish, I'd tell you that the sash and the stone are bound together. Even if we decided to let it kill you and my king—which is *not* on the table—it doesn't mean that they would revert back to the way they were."

"Meaning what?" Dimitri asked, fluttering down to the table. He bent over the Damning Stone, which had returned into the small rock it had started out as. "They're trapped this way for the next thirty days?"

"Until midnight of the thirtieth day," Ramos said, and I was barely able to stop myself from reaching over and wrapping my hands around his throat. "I believe that once the ritual is complete and their magic returned, they'll revert back to their normal selves."

"You don't sound sure," Dad said.

"That's because I'm not," Ramos said. "I've never dealt with anything like this before."

As Tiggy once said, that sounded fake, but okay. "But what *are* they? Are they children again with no memories of who they once were? Or...?"

"Curious," Morgan mused. "They seem to have reverted back to how they were as children, in both mind and body. A test. Yes, a test." He looked over at the kids, raising his voice. "Sam?"

A tiny dark head peeked over Rosemary's shoulder. "What?" he squeaked. "Are you talking to me?"

"I am," Morgan said, sounding far more amused than the situation dictated. "Do you know me?"

Sam's face scrunched up, sucking on his bottom lip. My heart sank as he shook his head. "No. But I like you because of your beard and your face and your eyes and your—"

"And your wiener!" Gary yelled.

"Wiener, wiener, wiener," Tiggy said, giggling madly.

"I have a wiener," Kevin said. "I can show you if you want." He started to turn over on his back when Joshua stopped him, telling him we didn't show our wieners in public. Kevin looked like he was going to argue, but then got distracted by a fly, snapping his sharp teeth as he tried to catch it.

"Who is the boy sitting next to you?" Dad asked Sam.

Sam looked down at Ryan. "He's a knight. His name is Ryan, and he's the bravest knight to have ever lived."

"Whoa," Ryan said. "Thank you. I think so too."

"Do you know him?" Morgan asked.

Sam looked confused. "Uh, duh. He told me his name a little bit ago, so now I know everything about him. My mom and dad said I can't kiss him yet, but I'm going to when they're not looking!"

Ryan pumped his fists above his head. "Yes! Best. Day. *Ever.*"

"Sam," I said, trying to keep the fear from my voice. "Do you know me?"

Sam gaped at me before sinking back down onto his mother. He shook his head shyly as he whispered, "Hi. Are you famous? You're dressed like you're famous."

"Say hi to me too," Ryan said, pulling on Sam's trousers.

"I can't," Sam said. "I already said hi to the famous man and now I'm tired."

"Stupid famous man," Ryan said, pouting miserably. "He *always* gets people saying hi to him."

And then Randall said, "Myrin."

All the children stared at him in confusion. "Mirror-in?" Gary said with a frown. "Are we going into a mirror now?"

"I don't want to," Ryan said grumpily, crossing his arms over his chest. "That sounds dumb."

Kevin's head bobbed up and down as Tiggy stroked his back. "Yeah," the tiny dragon growled. "Mirrors are dumb and I won't go in one. There are *mirror* people who live in there, and they might eat our brains."

"No!" Gary yelled, prancing in place, his little hooves clopping on the floor. "No brain eating!"

Morgan sighed, shaking his head. "It's not a mirror. It's a name. Myrin. Do you remember Myrin?"

Surely they had to. He had defined so much of our lives, a dark monster who wanted nothing more than to leave destruction in his wake, no matter the cost. I would never forget him, the memory of his voice was seared into my brain like a brand.

So I was stunned when Sam shrugged. "No? I don't know mirror man." He tilted his head back up at his mother. "Do I have to go into mirrors and have my brain eaten?"

"No," Rosemary said gently. "No one will go into a mirror." She glanced helplessly at Joshua, who rubbed a big hand up and down Sam's back.

Sam looked relieved. "Oh, good. Ryan!"

Ryan looked up at him.

"Hi," Sam said.

Ryan grinned. "Hi! Oh my gosh, thank you! Hi, hi, hi!"

"Everything is terrible," I muttered. "So…what. All of it, all of their memories and history is just…gone?"

Randall tapped a finger against the stone, looking thoughtful. "It's…" He paled slightly, taking in a shuddering breath. He raised his hand above the stone, mumbling unintelligibly. The stone flashed brightly, and I steeled myself for another foggy explosion. It didn't happen. Randall sighed and dropped his hand. "Could it be…?"

"What is it?" Ramos asked, leaning forward eagerly. Too eagerly if you ask me. I narrowed my eyes at him. I needed to keep him in my sights as much as possible. Dylan also looked eager, but with the countenance of a quasi-intelligent golden retriever.

Randall sat back in his chair, folding his hands on the table in front of him. "Myrin was a tremendous source of trauma for all of us, but perhaps for none more than Sam. With the loss of Morgan, and Ryan's grievous injury, Sam had to leave them all behind to follow what he perceived to be his destiny."

"Perceived," I said derisively. "Is that what we're calling it now? Because I thought he *perceived* it that way only when you and Morgan and Vadoma filled his head with all that crap."

Randall's mouth twisted down. "Yes, Prince. We did, because it was the truth. Only someone like Sam could have ever hoped to stop him. Do you think we asked for this?"

I snorted. "You certainly hoped for *something*, seeing as how you and Morgan couldn't be bothered to handle your own shit. You had a chance, a choice, and you decided to lock Myrin away. A bandage over a dismembered limb filled with rotten infection." Oh, I was angry. At

Randall. Dylan. Ramos. "It wasn't until that infection spread out into the open that you laid all of your past mistakes on the shoulders of a wizard's apprentice."

"Justin," Dad said gently. "Go easy. He's not to blame any more than Morgan or I am."

"Bullshit," I growled. I needed someone to blame; Randall and Morgan would do just fine.

"Don't you think I know that?" Randall snapped. "Don't you think I live with it every day? Because I *do*, Prince. There isn't even a *second* that goes by that I don't regret all that took place."

"Sam has been struggling," I said coldly. "You may not have seen it since you fucked off back to Castle Freeze Your Ass Off, but I have. I've been here every day, and I've seen what it did to him. He's not the same as he used to be." I winced. "More than the kid thing."

Dad sighed but didn't speak.

Randall stared at me for a long moment. I held his gaze, daring him to try and refute it. To my surprise, he didn't. He sagged, shaking his head. "Then my theory is most likely correct."

"What's that?" Dylan asked, tugging at the sash around his wrist.

Randall glanced back at the others before turning to us, lowering his voice. "When Sam first placed his hand upon the stone, nothing happened. I think he couldn't quite agree to give up his magic. It's all he's known for so long, and the idea of losing part of his identity must have weighed more on him than we realized. Who he is, is so wrapped up in dragons and gods and an apparent unlimited reservoir of power. Part of him must have wanted to…forget. Forget all of the bad that had happened to him." He scrubbed a hand over his face. "Remove the trauma and revert back to a time when things were easier. A wish upon the stars that things could go back to the way they once were. But it was too much. Instead of just wiping out the memories of Myrin, he pulled the rest of them along with him, turning them into children." He scowled. "Mouthy bastards, but children nonetheless."

"You're blaming him," I said. "Seriously? You're blaming *Sam* for all of this? That's a shitty thing to do."

"Not blame," Morgan said. "And while it might not even be a correct assumption, we don't know how else to explain it. I've never heard of anything happening like this before, Damning Stone or not. Ramos?"

Ramos shook his head. "I'm afraid I'm at a loss as much as the rest of you. This was never supposed to happen." He looked at me. "Prince Justin, I know you don't believe that, but it's the truth."

"He wouldn't," Dylan agreed. "This is important." He tugged on the sash to prove his point. "We wouldn't have done this if we'd known what would happen."

I wanted to believe them. I really did. But they were strangers, and my friends were now eight-year-olds (something they had all told us quite proudly). Someone was at fault, and I wanted to lash out at all of them.

"So, what," I said. "They stay as they are until the month has passed? How are we going to explain this to the people?"

"We might not have to," Dad said. "It's only for a month. We can keep this quiet. I'll have to figure out something to tell the knights when Ryan doesn't report to work, but we can always say he and the others are out of the city on an errand for me."

"More secrets?" I asked bitterly.

"I know you're angry," Randall said. "And you have every right to be. But I'm asking you to *think*, Prince. Verania is still in the process of recovery, rebuilding. What would this do to morale if we announced the future King's Wizard and the Knight Commander had been turned into children?"

Anger. Fury. People would most likely begin to riot, riding on a wave of anti-magic sentiment, given how they seemed to dislike aspects of Sam. And me, too. It would spread like a disease, infecting anyone and everyone. And that didn't even begin to cover if our enemies found out. They might take it as a sign to attack, thinking us weak. As much as I hated to admit it, Randall had a point.

Backed into a corner, I could only agree. "Fine. We'll say they're gone for the time being. Thankfully, Dad isn't affected, so people won't question his word." I shuddered at the thought of how it'd be if *he* had been turned into a child. I would be expected to act in his stead, something I wasn't ready for. And as much as I hated lying, I could see no other way.

"I want to be king," Sam said. He looked up at his mom. "Can I be king and have a crown?"

She smiled down at him. "You can be anything you want to be."

"Can Tiggy have crown?" Tiggy asked.

"Yep!" Sam said happily. "We're all kings now!"

"I don't want to be a king," Gary said. "I want to be the queen."

Ryan laughed. "That means you have to get married to the king."

"No!" Kevin yelled, flapping his wings and rising a few inches off the ground. "Gary's *my* queen."

And then he breathed a small plume of fire, causing all the children to scream.

"Wow," Gary said as the fire dissipated. "I like it when boys fight over me."

"We're so screwed," I mumbled.

\*\*\*\*\*

As the sun began to set, I was more exhausted than I'd been since the days in the Port. Rosemary and Joshua agreed to house the kids in their rooms, Rosemary saying that she'd be delighted to watch over them. "I always wanted a big family," she told me, watching Joshua take turns with each kid, grabbing them by the arms and spinning them in circles. "It wasn't in the cards for us. We tried for a long time, but it never worked out. It wasn't until we had our little miracle that we decided one was perfect. We can handle this, Prince. It's not forever."

"I've told you to call me Justin."

She smiled at me, patting my arm. "Justin, then. We'll figure this out, okay? We always do. And I'll look over all of them as if they were my own, because that's what they are."

Touched, I nodded. "You need anything, just ask."

"I know," she said. "You and King Anthony have always provided for us, whether you wanted to or not."

My face grew hot. "It was…complicated."

"It was," she agreed. "But you moved beyond it and saw something in Sam that no one else could, not even Ryan. Though you fought it, you began to believe in him as much as he believed in you. Still does, in fact."

She had a point. The young version of Sam seemed inordinately fascinated by me, watching every move I made. But he seemed shy about it, hiding his face every time I looked at him directly. It should have rankled me more than it did. I wasn't…*charmed*, not exactly, but it was a mixture of exasperation and wonder at the sight of him as he was now.

"We'll fix this," I told her. "I don't know how, but we will."

"Of course you will," she said. "Because he would do anything for you. And I think you're starting to realize you'd do the same for him." She laughed when I tried to retort. "Stop that. You know it as well as I do. Forget the whole Best Friends 5eva thing, at least for a moment. He's your brother, Justin. Regardless of how much you've fought against it, you know it to be true."

I couldn't speak.

She glanced over my shoulder. "Dylan's cute."

I groaned, not turning around and looking back at the man bound to me. He still sat at the table, whispering furiously with Ramos, the sash stretched tight between us as far as it would go. "I don't have *time* for him. We have too many things to worry about now. And I don't even know if I can trust him."

"You'll figure it out," Rosemary said. "And don't use my son or the others as an excuse, at least not yet. They seem…"

"Happy," I whispered, watching as Sam and Ryan loudly plotted ways they could ride Kevin, to which the dragon yelled that *no one* was going to ride him except for Gary, causing Joshua to scold them gently that they were *kids*, and no one was riding anyone.

"Happy," Rosemary said. "They're not hurting. They're not in pain." She narrowed her eyes. "And this wasn't Sam's fault. At least not intentionally."

I waved her off. "I know. He's…"

"Sam," she finished, looking relieved. "Yes, he is, isn't he? Funny how just saying his name explains so much."

More than she could possibly know.

Before they were taken to bed (after gorging on a meal fit for *three* kings, Tiggy wanting to show everyone what the food looked like half-chewed in his mouth), they'd all come to me, hugging me and telling me good night.

Sam was last, yawning so wide, his jaw cracked. He still seemed shy but was determined to do what the others had before him. "Good hug," he mumbled as I bent down, his arms wrapping around my neck. "Can we be friends?"

"Uh…yes?"

He smacked his lips tiredly against my throat. "Justin?"

"Yeah?"

"You're a prince?"

"Yes."

He leaned back, gaze searching my face. "Are you *my* prince?"

I swallowed thickly. "I am."

"Yay. I like that." He reached up and squished my cheeks together. His brow furrowed momentarily. Then, "Funny."

"What is?" I asked as he poked my nose.

"It feels like I've known you for a long time."

Hope, bright and glassy. "Do you remember me?"

Sam started to shake his head but stopped. "I…don't know?" He scrunched up his face. "Ghost. Shadow. In my brain. There, but I don't like it."

I felt cold. I hoped that ghostly shadow was a locked-up memory of me, struggling to break free and not something insidious. "Don't worry about it," I told him. "You're all right."

"Gonna have a sleepover," he said. "With Ryan and Gary and Tiggy and Kevin."

"Sounds fun," I said, heart breaking, but not allowing it to show in my voice or on my face.

Distracted, I bid goodnight to the others, telling them I'd see them in the morning. Lady Tina waited for me at the door, but I told her to turn in for the night. She looked like she was going to argue but nodded instead. I had only made it partway across the room when my arm jerked back, almost knocking me down followed by the sound of a large crash. I whirled, ready to snarl at whoever had grabbed me.

No one had. Or, rather, no one *living*. The sash. I'd forgotten about the sash. Raising my head, I saw Dylan pulling himself up off the floor, righting the chair he'd been sitting in. Shit. *That* whole mess.

"Sorry," Dylan said quickly. "Didn't see you leaving. I, uh, guess that means I'm going too?"

For a brief moment, I considered finding the nearest sword and slicing the sash in two, consequences be damned. Instead, I said, "Let's go."

Without looking back, I stalked toward the doorway, tensing in case the sash pulled again. It didn't as Dylan hurried to catch up with me.

We didn't speak as we went through the castle, heading up the stairs toward my chambers. I was lost in thought, trying to parse through the events of the day.

Dimitri and Randall had agreed to stay for the duration of the ritual, both staying in the labs along with Morgan to see if they could find out more information on the Damning Stone. Ramos remained with them. I'd shot Randall a look, trying to tell him without words that he needed to keep an eye on the magician and that Ramos was not allowed to touch the grimoires. Randall had, of course, ignored me completely.

"So," Dylan said as we reached my floor. "That was crazy, huh?"

"Do you often say things you don't need to?" I asked without looking at him.

"Sometimes," he said easily. "Might as well be me."

"Maybe don't," I told him. "In fact, the less you say, the better."

I didn't notice he'd stopped until once again, the sash jerked against my wrist. I sighed, turning back around to see Dylan had stopped in the middle of the hallway. "What now?" I groused.

He frowned at me. "I didn't do this."

"You say that, and yet it wouldn't have happened had you not come here."

"Right," he said slowly. "But that doesn't mean *I* did anything." He paused, considering. "Or Ramos."

"I don't know you," I said coolly.

"Not for lack of trying," he muttered. Then, "I know you don't like me very much. That sucks, but it is what it is. I'm gonna change your mind, just you wait and see. All I ask is that you give me a chance to prove you wrong." He grinned. "Or right. Whatever. You know what I'm trying to say."

I sniffed. "I assure you I have no idea."

He took a determined step toward me, levelling me with a sharp gaze that I didn't think he had in him. "You do," he insisted. "I know everything is strange right now, but that doesn't change that we're bound to each other. Shouldn't we try and make the most of it?"

"What do you think is going to happen here?"

He squinted at me. "Were you…were you not listening to any of it? Oh, man, I totally get that. All the talking gets super boring after a while. Tariffs this, trade routes *that*, blah, blah, blah. Dad told me that being a king meant you had to listen all the time, but he didn't tell me how dull it could be."

He had a point. When I was a kid, the idea of being a king meant having a jeweled crown atop my head while everyone did exactly what I told them to do. Dad had absolved me of *that* notion rather quickly, much to my dismay. It wasn't all pomp and circumstance: being a king often meant hours and hours of listening to people drone on about everything and nothing all at the same time. It *was* boring.

It struck me then that I was finding common ground with Dylan. That simply wouldn't do. "Boring though it may be," I said stiffly, "we still have a responsibility."

"To the people," Dylan agreed. "Yeah, I know. Still boring, though. That's okay. I'm pretty good at it. I know you will be too."

Gods, I had been nothing but a dick to him, and here he was, still throwing out compliments like it was the easiest thing in the world. I wondered if he had been dropped on his head as a child. Repeatedly. Too tired to retort, I said, "Damn right I will be." I turned, expecting him to follow.

He did.

We reached the door to my room, and before I could open it, he said, "Hey, remember that time I didn't know who you were and you didn't know who I was, and I thought your room was the bathroom?"

"You mean three days ago?"

"Yep! Reminiscing is fun."

Grinding my teeth together, I opened the door and stepped to the side, allowing him to go in first. "Don't touch anything."

He laughed as he passed through the door. "Yeah, yeah." I followed him, closing the door behind us. He looked all around my room, taking in every little detail he could. I did the same, wondering what he saw. The room wasn't anything special. While it was one of the biggest bedrooms in Castle Lockes, I didn't spend much time in here. I was too busy with all my responsibilities, days filled with meetings and getting kidnapped.

And yet, my room was still filled with bits and pieces of me. The wall to the left was lined with different weapons: swords and halberds, a mace with sharp spikes and a black chain, a crossbow and a battle axe. Standing in the corner near the weapons were two full sets of armor, one I'd worn while battling in the port, the metal dented and scorched.

My desk sat in front of a window that looked out onto the City of Lockes. Next to the desk were doors covered in green curtains that opened out onto a small balcony that held two chairs, neither of which I'd used in a long time.

Books, many of which had come from Kevin's keep, lined the shelves against the wall to the right, shelves divided into three parts: left and right, floor to ceiling. The middle section of shelves only went halfway down the wall, stopping above my bed.

The only bed in the room.

I had made a terrible mistake.

"What's wrong?" Dylan asked, glancing back at me. "Your face is the same color mine was when I accidentally ate twelve Yenner peppers on a dare."

"Accidentally," I repeated dubiously.

He shrugged. "University, bro. We all do stupid things. I couldn't feel my tongue for two weeks after." He stuck the offending appendage out at me, flicking it up and down before pulling it back. "Works now, though."

I stared at him. "Are you hitting on me?"

Dylan laughed, a deep, husky sound that did absolutely nothing for me. "Nah. If I was hitting on you, you'd know it. You want me to show you?" Before I could respond ("Absolutely *not!*") he tilted his head side to side, cracking his neck. "Hey," he said. "You're pretty fly for a white guy."

Kill me. Kill me now. "You think *that's* hitting on me?" I asked, aghast. "How in the hell have you survived this long?"

"Sheer force of will. What, you think you could do it any better?"

"I *know* I can," I retorted, never failing to rise to a challenge, even as my brain was screeching at me to abort, *abort*. I walked toward him slowly, letting my hips roll, a twist of savage satisfaction roaring through me as his eyes widened, Adam's apple bobbing up and down. I stopped in front of him, that damnable sash ever present. Our bodies were so close together that I could feel the heat emanating from him. His brow furrowed, eyes dark and hooded. I leaned forward—not touching, never touching—my lips near his ear. "There's only one bed," I whispered.

He nodded frantically. "Yeah. Saw that."

"I'm thinking of putting it to good use."

"Are you?" he asked, turning his head slightly so that our cheeks *almost* brushed together. "What did you have in mind?"

"Oh," I breathed. "A conundrum, isn't it? Because a bed can be used for many, many things."

"Holy shoot," he whispered, and I barely kept from laughing in his face. Not because he was funny, I reminded myself quickly, but because he was an idiot who said things like *holy shoot*.

"Holy shoot," I agreed. "You want me to tell you what I'm going to use that big bed for tonight?"

"Ye-es?"

"Was that a question?"

"I don't know," he choked out. "My brain doesn't seem to be working."

"That sounds like a you problem," I purred. I clacked my teeth together, causing him to shiver. "Here's how it's going to go. You ready?"

"Oh yeah. Tell me. Tell me how it's gonna go."

I pulled back, beginning to move in a slow circle around him. He stood as if frozen, prey trying to hide from a predator. The sash wrapped around him, causing his left arm to be pulled tight against his chest, hand splayed against the skin through his open vest. I stopped in front of him again, grabbing my end of the sash. I grinned at him, all teeth. "First, I'm going to get undressed."

"Good first step. I approve."

"Then I'm going to brush my teeth."

"Oral hygiene is, like, so important. Are you gonna floss?"

I bit back a laugh. "I'm going to floss so *hard*."

"Yeah," he muttered. "Flossing prevents tooth rot and bad breath."

Oh my fucking *gods*. What the hell was I doing? "Right. That it does. Then I'm going to wash my face. Get it good and wet."

"Heck yeah, bro," he mumbled, flexing his trapped hand. "Get rid of all the oils that can lead to pimples."

I wondered if anyone would blame me if I threw him off the balcony. "And then you know what I'm going to do when my clothes are off and my teeth and face are clean?"

He coughed roughly.

"I'm going to go to sleep," I said. "Because I'm fucking tired after the day I've had."

I pulled the sash as hard as I could. He spun away from me, tripping over his feet and almost falling to the floor. I laughed at him when he looked up at me, confused and probably more than a little excited, if the bulge in the front of his trousers indicated anything. My blood was thrumming, but I ignored it as best I could. If he were someone else—*anyone* else—then I might have fucked him right here and now before sending him away, never to be seen again. Fortunately (or perhaps unfortunately; I did have eyes, after all) that wasn't going to happen. Thirty days. That's all I had to last. And not even thirty days, now. Twenty-nine and some change.

"Not cool, bro," he said, rubbing his wrist.

"Like I give two shits," I muttered. "Bathroom's through the door near the armor. If you have to use it, do it now."

Dylan glanced at the door. "Can I use your toothbrush?"

"Do you like your limbs attached to your body?"

"Uh. Yes?"

"Then, no. You can't use my toothbrush. There's a spare underneath the sink. In fact, why don't I get it for you." I grabbed the sash again, pulling it toward the door. He followed, and I slammed the bathroom door behind me, the sash thin enough that it didn't catch on the frame. I leaned against the door, taking a deep breath, trying to calm myself. My mind raced, a storm of everything that had happened today. Telling myself to get a grip, I pushed off the door and saw to my nightly ablutions.

Ten minutes later, I opened the door again, only to find Dylan's back to me, standing in front of my desk. He didn't act guilty like he'd been snooping. Instead, he was looking down at something in his hand.

"What are you doing?"

He glanced back at me. "You kept this?"

"Kept what?" I asked irritably.

He turned, holding out his hand. On his palm sat a stone in the shape of a deformed goat. Or, heart, as he'd so proudly claimed. I'd planned on throwing it away immediately but had gotten distracted and forgotten. That's all it was. It definitely had nothing to do with the fact that no one had ever made me something like that before, pitiful thing that it was.

"It's nothing," I said airily, trying to keep from sweating. "Forgot it even existed."

Dylan grinned. "Uh huh. Forgot it right on top of your desk. I dig that."

He was so insufferable I wanted to scream. I stalked forward, snatching it out of his hands, meaning to toss it in the small trash can next to my desk. But the staff hadn't emptied the trash yet, and it was full. If I tried to throw it away, it'd just fall off the top. So I didn't. "Go take care of your business," I muttered, shoving past him without looking at him. "I need to sleep."

He chuckled as he walked by me, his shoulder purposefully brushing against mine. I didn't turn around as the bathroom door closed behind me.

Trying to steady myself, I set the citrine carving back on my desk. Tomorrow. First thing tomorrow, I'd get rid of it. I could do it *now*, but I needed to use the time while Dylan was in the bathroom to change.

Working quickly, I started with my trousers, unfastening them and letting them fall to the floor. I started to pull off my shirt when I realized the sash would make that impossible. I frowned, wondering how the hell I was going to make this work. Cut the shirt off? Let it dangle on the sash? Wear the same damn clothes for the next month?

I worked my shirt off and for a moment, it did dangle on the sash. And then it went *through* the sash and fell to the floor.

"What the fuck?" I whispered.

I was still staring down at the floor when the door opened again.

"Whoa," Dylan said. "Nice underwear, bro. Are those crowns printed on them?"

Yes, yes it was. A gift from Sam for my last birthday, one that I'd glared at him for. I squawked, trying to cover myself. "Stop staring!" And it was about this time I realized Dylan had *also* taken off his clothes, standing there only wearing briefs that left nothing to the imagination. He was not circumcised, that much was clear. I quickly averted my gaze, finding something interesting to stare at over his shoulder.

He waggled his eyebrows at me. "Naked party. Nice."

"The shirt," I said stupidly. "It just...went through the sash."

"Well, yeah," Dylan said as if *I* were the moron here. "It has magical properties that try to avoid inconveniencing the people bound together. Did we forget to tell you that? My bad. You can get dressed or undressed and everything. Don't know quite how magic works, but hey, there's a lot of things I don't know about."

"I believe that," I mumbled, trying to avoid looking at the curly hair on his sloping stomach. I turned and went to my dresser, furiously pulling out sleep clothes. I normally didn't wear underwear to bed, but

I wasn't going to give him the satisfaction. "You'll sleep on the floor. I'll give you a pillow and a blanket."

"But your bed is so big," he said.

"Isn't it? If it makes you feel any better, the floor is even bigger. And besides, you said you kick in your sleep, and that would be assaulting the Prince of Verania, which is punishable by thirty years of hard labor." It wasn't, but *he* didn't know that.

Except apparently, he did. "Nah. It's six years in the dungeons plus community service so long as the prince doesn't lose a finger or toe."

I froze, my face trapped in my pajama shirt. "What."

"Read about your laws on the trip here. Pretty dry, but you know what they say. The more you know."

I pulled my shirt the rest of the way down, marveling at how it went *through* the sash before settling against my frame. I would never, ever understand magic. "Good for you. I know nothing about Yennbridge."

"Oh! That's no problem. I can tell you anything you want to—"

"That wasn't an invitation."

"Hey."

I turned around, ready to snap at him.

"Stop it," he said seriously.

I threw up my hands. "Stop *what?*"

He didn't look angry, not exactly. I wondered if he'd ever been angry in his life. But he wasn't smiling. Instead, his brow was furrowed, his eyes narrowed. "Being mean. I know you don't like this, but that doesn't mean you have to be a jerk about it and try and walk all over me. I'm a person, bro. I may be a king, but I have feelings just like everyone else, and you're hurting them. Not cool."

I bit back the retort bubbling in my throat. Weirdly, I felt something akin to shame, a sharp curl of embarrassment. I didn't want it, but I could do little to make it stop. Instead of replying, I went to an old wooden chest at the end of my bed. The lid creaked on its rusty hinges as I opened it. A pile of spare blankets and pillows lay within. I stepped back, not looking at Dylan. "Take your pick," I muttered. "Or you can use them all if you need to." Before I went to bed, I went around the room, blowing out all the candles, casting the room in bright moonlight filtering in through the windows, Dylan a vague, hulking outline in the dark. I walked around to the bed, climbing inside and pulling the comforter up to my chin. I closed my eyes and waited.

Dylan didn't move, at least not at first. Then he sighed, and the chest bumped against the end of the bed as he began to rifle through it.

I expected him to take his bedding as far away as the sash would allow. It's what I would have done if I was him. But since he was the most aggravating man I'd ever met, he went to the side of the bed where I lay, dropping the blankets and pillows to the floor. He frowned, hands on his bare hips, underwear sinking so low, it was almost obscene.

I squeezed my eyes shut before I got caught staring.

He grunted as he sank to the floor. I thought that was it for the night, that we'd both lie in silence, listening to each other breathe as we waited for sleep to take us. I didn't know if that would happen: my brain was on fire, a billion thoughts writhing in the flames. I didn't know what tomorrow would bring, if we'd be able to keep up this farce without anyone finding out what had been done to my friends and family. Someone was going to see Sam, Tiggy, Ryan and Kevin and put the pieces together. What the hell would we do then?

I rolled over, away from Dylan, feeling miserable.

Dylan said something I didn't quite catch. I gnawed on my bottom lip in indecision. Then, "What did you say?"

"Floor," Dylan said. "Not as hard as it looks. Not too bad. I've slept on worse."

An opening, if only one wanted to take it. I did and didn't. Dylan was right, in his own way: I was being an ass which was probably only making things worse. Even if I didn't trust him, I didn't think he'd done any of this intentionally. Ramos, on the other hand...

"Thanks," I finally said. "I'll let the builders of the castle know."

"Really?" Dylan asked.

"No. They've been dead for close to a thousand years."

"Ha," he said. "You tell jokes too. Awesome."

Of all the— "Where have you slept that's worse than a cold floor in a drafty castle?"

He laughed quietly. "Oh man, this one time—second year of university—Digger and I were on break and decided to go explore parts of Yennbridge we'd never been to before. Packed up a couple of horses with food and a bedroll for each of us and then got lost on purpose."

"Why?" I asked, confused.

He shifted on the floor. "Because you might end up seeing things you never expected to. We found this farm, right? Out in the middle of nowhere, miles away from any town. An old couple lived in this ancient house made of stone with moss covering the roof. They lived there with a few farmhands. They didn't have much room, but they welcomed us with open arms. Pretty rad, huh?"

"Rad," I muttered.

He took that as agreement. "Yeah, so rad. They fed us and told us all about their farm. It'd been in their family for hundreds of years, but the couple wasn't able to have children, so they were worried about the future of their farm. The house had been owned outright—had been for generations—but they'd had to sell off some of their land to make ends meet. It hadn't worked as well as they'd hoped, so they'd had to remortgage their house. They were getting by, but things were tough. They let us stay in the barn, and we slept with the cows."

I snorted. "That must have smelled awful."

"Oh, man, you have no idea. I even got to *milk* one of them. Have you ever milked a cow?"

"No."

"It's gross," he said, sounding gleeful. "It's warm and fleshy and when you squeeze it, stuff comes out."

I coughed roughly.

"Yeah," he said, smacking his lips. "That's what I thought too. Then Digger dared me to squirt milk in my mouth directly from the teat, but then I *double* dared him, and everyone knows that wins, so he did it."

I was horrified. "Seriously?"

"Oh, yeah," Dylan said in the dark. "It got in his eyes and everything."

"That's awful."

"Nah. It was hysterical. Then the farmer said that's not what cows were for, so we apologized and bought his farm."

I sat up quickly. "You did *what?*" I looked down at him on the floor.

He grinned up at me, teeth bright. "We bought his farm from him."

"What? Why? They *helped* you and you took from them?" I wasn't expecting Dylan to be capable of something so cruel. It reminded me that I didn't really know anything about him.

His smile faded. "Of course not. I paid off the mortgage for the house and the land and turned the title back over to them. It's not mine. I don't take things that aren't mine. They worked in honor of Yennbridge, backbreaking work they'd done their whole lives. I wanted them to have a measure of peace in their last years."

Layers. He had layers I hadn't expected. It didn't put me at ease as much as I thought it would. "What happened to them?"

Dylan looked strangely somber as he said, "They lasted a few more years, after. But they'd been married for so long, they didn't know how to live without each other. The husband went first, and his wife followed him a couple of weeks later. Can you imagine that? Loving someone so much that when they pass, your body knows it's time for you to go too."

Dad could have done the same. Morgan too, after the passing of his cornerstone. Randall and Myrin. Sam, seeing Ryan at death's door and making an impossible decision, even though his heart was shattered. All of these people could have chosen to lay down and die, but they hadn't. They'd known there was still work to do.

But it could have gone another way entirely.

I'd never known that kind of love. I'd loved Ryan, in my own way. I loved my father. And here, in the dark, I could even admit to loving Sam and Gary. Tiggy and Kevin. What would I do without them? Was that even the same thing?

"What happened to the farm?" I asked, lost in thought.

"They left it to me," Dylan said. "Crazy, right? In their will and everything. I didn't need the farm myself, but Yennbridge did, so I gave it to the workers at the farm, telling them to keep on keeping on."

"And you didn't ask for anything in return?"

He blinked. "What? No. Why would I? We all need to work together in order to live well. No matter who you are, royalty or pauper, everyone needs help, sometimes." Then, "Oh shoot. I lied. I *did* ask for something."

A*ha*. I knew it was too good to be true. No one was that magnanimous. "Let me guess. Profits from the output from the farm?"

He chuckled. "Nope! I don't need money, bro. I asked them to put together a program that allowed for underprivileged kids who wanted to learn to ride horses."

"Oh, *come on*," I said, slamming my head back down on the pillow. "You did not."

"I did," Dylan said. "They even let me name it. Dylan's School for Awesome Kids Who Deserve to Succeed, or DSAKWDS. There's a sign and everything."

"Capitalized," I whispered. "So you know it's true."

"What?"

"Nothing. Just…why?"

He rolled over, facing the bed. I turned my head, and I saw his earrings glinting in the low light. "I heard all the stories about how you and your Dad helped put your city back together after…well. You know. Why did you do that?"

I hesitated. "Because it was the right thing to do. They'd suffered because of our mistakes, and we needed to make things right."

"Exactly," Dylan said. "Because when we all work together, we can do anything. I have a poster hanging on the wall in my room that says exactly that. It's there to remind me in case I ever forget."

We fell silent. I was drifting, lost in the sounds of his voice in my head. I was on the cusp of sleep when he spoke again.

"You're not so bad," he said quietly. "You try and act like you are, but you're really not. That's cool, bro. I'm glad we're doing this, aside from all your people being turned into children and you not wanting this at all."

I thought I laughed, maybe, but then I was asleep and dreamed of stars.

*****

I WAS AWOKEN SOME TIME LATER, the light from the moon having shifted across the room, casting everything in shadows. I breathed in and out, waiting to see what had woken me up. The door. The door was closing. Movement in the room. Whispers. I reached under my pillow, grabbing hold of the dagger I've kept there ever since Myrin had been destroyed. Better to be safe than sorry. And good doing too, now that assassins had entered the room. I clutched the dagger, ready to swing it out in a flat arc. Carotid artery in the neck. That's all it'd take.

I tensed, ready to move as the whispers grew louder.

"Be *quiet*," a voice hissed. "They'll hear us."

"I *am* being quiet," another voice replied. "You're the one who's stomping around!"

"I don't stomp! You take that back!"

"No!"

The sounds of wrestling filled the room as I put the dagger back under my pillow.

Before I could speak, another did for me.

Dylan said, "What are you two doing?"

The sounds of the scuffle stopped. I raised my head slightly to see two kids—both in small pajamas—standing near the edge of the bed. A feeling of unreality washed over me as I realized it was Sam and Ryan. Ryan must have thought they were in trouble, because he shoved Sam behind him, standing as tall as he could, his thin chest puffed out. "We couldn't sleep," he said, sounding defensive.

"Yeah," Sam said, peering over his shoulder down at Dylan. "We couldn't sleep and it was *boring*. My dad snores and Gary pooped rainbows on the floor and made everything smell like cookies."

"And then we got hungry," Ryan said. "So we wanted to go to the kitchens."

"*Yeah*," Sam said. "But then I said I wanted to see Justin because he's a prince and my best friend."

"What about me?" Ryan asked. "Am I your best friend too?"

"No! That's only Justin. And Kevin and Gary and Tiggy.

Ryan's bottom lip began to wobble. "But what am I, then?"

Sam smacked a kiss on his cheek. "You're my *boyfriend*."

"Wow," Ryan breathed. "That's so much better. I get to be your boyfriend and they only get to be your best friends."

"And now we're here," Sam finished. "The end. Can we stay? I don't like smelling Gary's poop cookies. Kevin does, and Mom had to spray him with a water bottle when he kept trying to sniff it."

"It was oatmeal raisin," Ryan said, making a face. "Raisins are dumb."

"So dumb!" Sam yelled.

"Shh," Dylan said. "Justin's sleeping. You can stay if you promise to be quiet and go to sleep."

"So quiet," Sam whispered loudly.

"You won't even know we're here," Ryan agreed. "But we are."

"You go on the floor with Dylan," Sam told Ryan. "I'm going to get into bed with Justin."

That was something I never expected to hear from him. For a moment, I thought Ryan would argue. He didn't. "I get to have a sleepover with the cool king?" he whispered in awe. "Wow. Bro. Hey, bro! I'm gonna sleep with you!"

"Oh dear gods," I mumbled. "This is a nightmare. That's all this is."

Ryan practically collapsed on top of Dylan as Sam grunted, climbing up onto the bed. He kicked nearly every single part of my body as he moved over me. Right when he settled next to me, Ryan sat up, head peeking over the edge of the bed. "Sam?"

"Yeah?" Sam asked.

"I like you," Ryan whispered.

Sam gasped as he looked over me at Ryan. "I like you, too."

"Good," Ryan said. "Have fun in bed with Justin. I'm going to lay down with King Dylan and talk about bro stuff."

"For five minutes," Dylan said. "And then we go back to sleep. No arguing."

Ryan grumbled as he settled down next to Dylan.

Sam nearly elbowed me in the chin as he pulled the blanket over us. I turned my head toward him, and he squeaked when he saw I was awake. "Sam," I said.

"Hi," he said. He lay his head on the pillow, his hair brushing against my face. "Gary pooped cookies and then we—"

"I heard."

"Oh. You're not mad, right?"

I shook my head. "No. I'm not mad. But next time, you should—"

Sam smiled at me. "Good. I like when I'm with you."

And just like that, I was disarmed. He said it with the innocence of a child who'd never known pain, never known suffering. But he *did*. He knew all those things, even if they were somehow locked away in his head. This Sam was still my Sam, current appearances be damned. I swallowed past the lump in my throat. "I, uh. Me too?"

He blinked sleepily at me, reaching out and poking my cheeks, my nose, my chin. He yawned widely, his breath smelling like toothpaste. "Yay," he mumbled. "That makes me feel better." And then he lay his head on my shoulder, his hair in my face. A moment later, his breathing evened out, and I knew he was asleep. Just like that. As if it were that easy.

I closed my eyes, listening to Dylan and Ryan whispering to each other, Ryan cackling at one point so loud, Dylan covered Ryan's mouth with his hand.

And maybe, just maybe, before I fell back asleep, a thought crossed my mind, one so foreign it was as if I'd been electrocuted.

The thought?

Things would be okay. One way or another, things would be okay. We were together, still, even with all that had happened. Gods and the might of villainous men had tried to come between us, but we were still here.

And I wasn't going to let anyone take that from me again.

# CHAPTER 11

## In Which the Knights of Verania Dismantle the Patriarchy

TWO DAYS LATER I wished for death. Peaceful, horrible, any death would do. At least dying would give me some godsdamn peace and quiet.

"Gary!" Sam screeched. "Look at me! I'm swinging from the chandelier!"

He was. I didn't even know how he'd gotten up there, ten feet above the floor. From the way Tiggy was trying to hide behind my father's desk, I thought he was to blame. I watched in stunned silence as Sam swung back and forth, legs dangling, Ryan moving underneath him, promising to catch him if he fell.

I'd spent the morning in meetings with Dad and his advisors. Dad had told them that he'd sent Sam and Ryan on a mission, one that was only need to know. Kevin and Gary and Tiggy had joined them. Dylan sat next to me, obviously bored out of his mind. I was too, but I knew better than to show it.

We'd been in the meeting for close to two hours when Lady Tina entered the room, quickly moving toward me. She bent over, whispering in my ear. "We might have a problem."

I kept my face carefully blank as I turned my head toward her. "And that is?"

She blanched, looking up at the others at the table to make sure they weren't listening in. They weren't, most caught up in a stimulating conversation led by the red-headed man about filling in potholes that had cropped up around the City of Lockes. Morgan and Dad, however, were listening in to Lady Tina, even though they pretended not to.

"Well," Lady Tina said, "it's…nothing catastrophic?"

I closed my eyes. "Is that supposed to make me feel better?"

"Yes," she said promptly. "Did it work?"

"No," I said. "It really didn't. Out with it."

"Well, you see, I *tried* to do what you asked. I offered to help Rosemary and Joshua with…our unexpected guests, but then a certain boy who shall not be named told me I was a monster with stupid teeth. He told the others to look at my teeth, and then a…big lizard breathed fire when he sneezed. But it's okay!" she added quickly when I turned to stare at her. "We put it out." Now that she mentioned it, the ends of her hair looked slightly singed. "But then…" She cleared her throat as she lowered her voice once more. "But then a unicorn decided to tell the others about how…uh, how *fornication* works, and they all started screaming and Joshua and Rosemary asked—if you weren't busy, of course—if they could inquire about your assistance."

She looked pleased with herself.

I was not impressed. "What."

"I don't *like* children," she hissed at me. "I'm not a godsdamn babysitter!" Her eyes widened. "With all due respect, my Prince."

"Can I whisper with you too?" Dylan asked, leaning over. "What are we planning? A rager? I can get kegs if you want."

"We're not planning a rager," I muttered. "It's worse than that."

"Oh," Dylan said. "Super rager. Rock on. I don't do drugs, but respect. Your body, your choice."

"Stop talking about ragers!" I growled, louder than I meant to. Everyone stopped mid-conversation to look at me. I glared at them until they resumed. "Lady Tina, I asked you to *handle* this."

"I tried," she said, sounding wounded. "But you don't know what it's like being surrounded by those monsters. They're the *worst*. Kids are mean! Why can't you just lock them in a room until this is all over? I can make sure they have bowls of water and newspaper laid out on the floor."

Gods help any children she may one day have. But it wasn't like she was wrong. I could admit to having similar thoughts, especially when I woke up that first morning to find Sam drooling all over my shoulder in his sleep.

"Fine," I snapped at her. "I'll deal with this since I have to do everything around here." I stood from my chair. "If you'll excuse me," I said blandly. "A matter has come to my attention that I must see to immediately. Carry on. I'll catch up later. Dad, Morgan, I'll handle this like I handle *everything else.*"

"I'll come too," Dylan announced, as if we weren't tied together by magic. "Good talk, everyone. I'm super impressed by all of you."

The advisors smiled at him gratefully. Not to be outdone, I said, "Yes. What he said or whatever. Bye."

We left them behind, staring after us.

And five minutes later, in my father's office: "Sam Haversford, you get down from that chandelier *right this minute.*"

"No!" he shouted at me, swinging back and forth, the chandelier creaking precariously. "I'm *flying.*"

"Like me!" Kevin said, wings rising up and down as he lifted up off the floor. He flew around the room, the wind from his wings buffeting against my face.

Joshua grinned at me, laying on the floor and covered in sweat, as if he'd been playing with the kids since I'd left them earlier. Knowing him, he probably had.

"We had a handle on it," Rosemary said apologetically. "But then Gary said something he shouldn't."

"Where is he?"

Rosemary nodded toward the far corner of the room. Gary sat facing the wall, head drooped, horn scratching into the wood. He moved his head to the side, and I saw he'd carved the words DIE DIE DIE into the wall. That couldn't be healthy by any stretch of the imagination. "Time out," Rosemary said. "He's not very happy with us."

"I'm going to murder everyone," Gary muttered.

And then Sam fell before we could reach him. Ryan yelled, "I got you!" as Sam crashed into him, causing them both to collapse to the floor. I panicked, sure there'd be broken bones or missing teeth. I rushed toward them but stopped when they both sat up, looking dazed.

"You're heavy," Ryan said.

"Nuh uh," Sam said. "*You're* heavy."

I startled when Dylan clapped his hands behind me. "Everyone up!" he bellowed.

Surprisingly, everyone did just that. They formed a line in front of us, Ryan standing at attention like a little knight. Kevin landed clumsily, legs akimbo. "I'm all right!" he said as he righted himself.

"That means you too, Gary," Dylan said.

Gary looked over at us distrustfully. "I'm in time out."

"And why did you get put into time out?" Joshua asked, pulling himself off the floor.

Gary snorted, blue sparks shooting from his nose. "Because I told the others about penises."

"And?" Rosemary asked.

Gary sighed. "And how many someone could put inside themselves before their buttholes break." Then, defiantly, "The answer is *six*."

"Exactly," Rosemary said as if that weren't the most horrifying phrase ever uttered. "We don't talk about things like that. You have to wait until you're older."

"I don't understand," I said faintly. "Why can he remember that?"

"He's a unicorn," Joshua explained. "They're very carnal creatures. Also, magic? Who knows? Nothing about this makes sense, I gave up long ago trying to figure these things out."

"It's Verania," Rosemary said as if that explained everything. Unfortunately, there was more truth to that than I cared to admit.

"Gary," Dylan said sternly. "If you promise not to talk about grown-up things, you can come out of time out."

"For how long?" Gary asked suspiciously.

"For the rest of the day."

"Deal," Gary said as he joined the others. "Tomorrow, it's so over for you bitches, you don't even know. I didn't even get to the part of what happens when all those penises—"

"Hi, Prince!" Tiggy bellowed. "Hi! I have *brooooooms*."

Fun. Neat. Absolutely *fantastic*. "Hi, Tiggy."

"Guess what?"

"What?"

"Chicken butt!" the boy giant crowed.

They all dissolved into laughter as I struggled to keep from screaming. "What in the fresh hell—"

"Troops!" Dylan said. "I come to you with an important assignment. Will you listen?"

They all snapped their mouths closed, Ryan bringing up his fist to his chest and bowing. "Yes, Cool King Dylan. I will listen."

"Capitalized," Tiggy and Gary breathed at the same time.

"Suck up," Sam said before frowning. "My mouth says things my brain is thinking and I don't know how to make it stop."

"I'll help you," Joshua said, taking his hand. "If you think something, tell me first and I'll say if it's good or bad."

"That's my *dad*," Sam said proudly.

"I don't have a dad," Ryan said mournfully. "And Joshua said my mom is on a trip and that's why I can't see her."

Shit. I hadn't even thought of that, of course Ryan would want his mother. To him, at this age, she was still alive, somewhere in the Slums. She'd died right after Ryan had become a knight, holding on long enough to see her son achieve what he'd set out to do.

"That's right," Joshua said, shooting me a look of warning. "A long trip, but I promise you'll be okay because you're with me. I'll protect you as if you were my own son."

"Really?" Ryan asked with a sniffle.

"Yeah," Sam said. "He's your dad too. And since my dad is your dad, that makes you my brother. But since you're my boyfriend too, that means you're my brother-boyfriend."

"Brother-boyfriend!" Ryan chanted. "Brother-boyfriend!"

"Dylan," I said loudly, "if you're going to fix this, do it now."

"On it," Dylan said. He began to pace in front of them. "Troops, I have a dangerous assignment for you, one in which I can't guarantee your survival. Victory will be hard fought, but if we stick together, I know we can win. First, an inspection to make sure my troops are ready to proceed. Eyes forward. Chins up. Don't move. Don't talk."

They listened to him, each of them standing stiffly. Only Ryan looked like he knew what he was doing, but even he fidgeted as he waited his turn. Dylan started with Tiggy, straightening out the broom that lay against his shoulder.

"He's good with them," Rosemary whispered. "Makes you think, doesn't it?"

"I have no idea what you're talking about."

She laughed at me. "I'm sure you don't. Can I tell you something unrelated to anything that's going on right now?"

This coming from Sam's mother meant it was going to be just that: related to everything. I waved my hand at her, motioning for her to go on. Might as well get it over with.

"They like him," she said quietly. "And though you might not know it, children can sometimes be the best judge of character. They don't have a filter."

"Obviously," I muttered as Kevin stuck his tongue in Gary's ear, causing the unicorn to move his back foot like a dog being scratched.

"They see things others might not," Rosemary said, gaze too knowing for my comfort. "We can learn from them, if we only listen. It's not forever, but I admit to missing this." She sobered, brushing a lock of hair off her face. "I love my son more than anything, but I haven't seen him this carefree since…"

She didn't finish, but then she didn't need to. I knew exactly what she meant. "So it's a good thing?"

She shrugged. "It is what it is. I know Morgan and Randall are trying to find a fix, but if they don't, is it the worst thing in the world? Once your time with that sash ends, it'll hopefully go back to the way it was before."

"You sound like you don't want that."

Rosemary shook her head. "No, of course not. It's funny, but I already miss the man Sam had become. That being said, I'm relieved to see him happy. Not that he wasn't before, but it's…different."

"It's not a fix," I reminded her as Dylan told Ryan he was doing an amazing job. Ryan had stars in his eyes. "Everything that happened will be waiting for him when he returns to how he was."

"I know," Rosemary said as she sniffled. "And we'll do what we can to help him. All of us, because he needs that. We've all given so much to be where we are, but Sam most of all."

I wondered how long she'd had these thoughts, stunned they mirrored my own. She was his mother, of course she'd see it and worry. This was the first time I'd heard her speak it out loud. "So… what. We just let it go on as it is?"

"Would that be so bad? If his magic caused this to happen, it has to be for a reason." She wiped her eyes. "I don't think this was intentional, but what if this was the only way he knew how to deal with all he's done? Trauma manifests itself in strange ways."

I didn't know what to say, so I said nothing at all.

"I know about what happened. I know what he almost did." Her voice took on a sharp edge. "And I would love him all the same, regardless of if he'd done just that. If I were in his position, I don't know that I could have pulled back like he did. He's a fighter, Justin. Who are we to judge him?"

"No one," I said. "Because we shouldn't." Dylan moved on to Sam, adjusting his shoulders, tilting his chin up slightly.

"He needs someone like you," she said, hooking her fingers through my own. "And you him." She laughed when Sam nudged Ryan, showing him his parade rest. "I think we forget that, sometimes. We all go through life, wishing upon the stars. But it takes the brave and the bold to follow through with those wishes. Sam did. Can you say the same? What is it you wish for?"

"I don't know," I said honestly. "Not this, though."

"So we make the most of it," she said. "Do what we can with what we have. No one can or should ask us for anything more. Remember that, and I know you'll be the king you were always meant to be."

She left me, then, going to her husband, leaving me staring after her. Joshua wrapped an arm around her shoulders, hugging her close, whispering in her ear. She laughed quietly, shaking her head.

"Inspection complete," Dylan announced. "Good news, men. You're the best troop a king could ask for. Report in!"

"Remember the names I gave you?" Joshua asked. "Now is the time to use them."

"Knight Tiggy of the Brooms!"

"Lady Gary the Tyrannical!"

"Beast from the East, sir!"

"Knight Commander Ryan!"

"Sam!" His eyes darted side to side. "The...um." He deflated. "I can't remember."

"Sam of Dragons," Joshua said, and his son smiled so blindingly, I could barely take it in.

"Sam of Dragons," Sam said. "Yeah, that!"

Dylan looked at me.

I frowned at him.

He jerked his head pointedly.

"Prince Justin," I muttered.

"And King Dylan!" Dylan crowed. "Troops, follow me to battle!"

They all screamed as they charged.

With no choice, I followed them, looking back at Rosemary and Joshua. They grinned at me. "We'll stay here," Rosemary said.

"Need a nap," Joshua said. "Not as young as we used to be. Don't worry though, Justin. I'm sure you'll be just fine."

*****

I PROMISED JOSHUA WOULD PAY for his crimes against the crown when his son hit my shins with a wooden sword, causing me to hop on one leg and glare down at the pest that apparently lived to cause me pain.

"Take *that*," Sam said, hopping back, fumbling with the practice sword. We stood out in the training fields, the dummies set up as Dylan gave instruction. For a self-proclaimed pacifist, he seemed to know what he was talking about. That is until he paired up Sam and me, much to Ryan's dismay. As much as I wanted to whack Sam with my own practice sword, I held back, not wanting to hurt him.

He apparently didn't care either way, screeching a battle cry that sounded like a cat in heat as he charged once more. I deflected neatly, wanting to keep my shins intact. At least he hadn't yet aimed for my balls. Small favor.

Gary had decided that he didn't want cloth wrapped around his horn to keep from stabbing anyone in these drills, so he went to the nearest hill and got a running start, sliding down it on his side, Kevin taking flight and chasing after him. Tiggy apparently didn't understand what we were doing, choosing to spend his time sweeping the grass for reasons only known to him.

Leaning against the fence around this particular training ground were some of the dancers that had entered the celebration with Dylan. I'd learned a couple of days ago that they weren't just there to put on a show. They also acted as Dylan's guard, men and women who could move like liquid smoke. They were there to keep an eye on Dylan, but they smiled at his antics, laughing as if they didn't have a care in the world.

In the distance, the knights of Verania trained in an adjacent field. They all stared at us curiously, and I realized we were going to have a problem if we didn't think of something. We had been able to stave off questions about Ryan's whereabouts for the time being, but I knew the knights—whose lips flapped as much as a gossipy knitting circle—would start to wonder.

But that was a problem for later. Now we needed to worry about something far more serious: how to survive the onslaught of children with weapons.

"Hiiiii-*yaaah*!" Sam bellowed, clumsily swinging his sword at me. I brought my own sword up in an arc, knocking his out of his hands. It spun end over end before I caught it by the grip.

"Whoa," Sam said, eyes wide. "How did you do that?"

"Practice," I said.

He nodded. "If I practice, could I be as good as you?"

A quick flash of memory, and not a proud one. Me, leading Sam out onto the training fields, meaning to teach him a lesson about meddling with my fiancé.

I wasn't a good person back then. I was angry all the time with Sam being the focus of that ire. An interloper, one who'd been plucked from obscurity because of what he could do. But I'd only seen it as an affront to me. I'd been wrong, and I'd never apologized to Sam for it.

When he came back—because he would, I had to believe that—I'd tell him and ask for forgiveness.

I was startled out of my thoughts when Sam said, "Justin?"

I looked down at him as I handed him back his sword. "Yeah?"

He let the sword drop to the grass before raising a hand, a finger crooking back and forth, wanting me to bend over. I did. He studied my face with those familiar eyes. "Are you sad? You look like you're sad."

I forced a smile on my face. "No," I said, lying through my teeth. "I'm not sad."

He didn't look like he believed me. "You promise?"

"Promise. Why don't you practice with Ryan? I need to talk to Dylan. Just be careful."

Sam lit up as he crouched down, scooping up the sword and swirling around. "Ryan! Justin said we can fight each other so long as none of us bleeds and dies!"

"Hurray!" Ryan said, leaving Dylan standing with his own sword as he ran toward Sam.

I watched as they began to clash inexpertly, Ryan accidentally hitting Sam's hand and apologizing profusely. Sam held up his hand, and Ryan smacked a kiss against it. "There!" Sam said. "Better. Raise your sword, knight!"

"You cool, man?" Dylan asked as he came over to me. The sash shrank as the distance closed between us, and I was slightly perturbed how used to it I already was.

"I have no idea," I said honestly. "Just when I think I'm getting a handle on this, I remember that only a few weeks ago, things were… well, not *normal*, but not like this. Like, why does Ryan think his name is still Ryan?"

Dylan squinted at me. "Because it is? Why wouldn't he think that?"

Shit. Right. He didn't know. "He wasn't always Ryan Haversford. Before that, he was Ryan Foxheart. And before *that*, he was a kid from the Slums named Nox."

"Nox," Dylan said slowly, glancing at the boys. "Why did he change his name?"

"He wanted to be a knight more than anything," I said, a strange wave of grief washing over me. I wasn't sure who I was grieving for. Them? Myself? All of us? "He and Sam they…they knew each other when they were kids. Then Sam was taken to the castle when his magic was discovered to train as a wizard's apprentice, and Ryan says that he only followed because of his desire for knighthood."

"But you don't believe that," Dylan said.

I shrugged. "I don't know. I think it was part of it, but…"

"Sam was too," Dylan finished for me.

"Yeah. Maybe. Those two have always been drawn to each other. I hated it, hated Sam for a long time. Here was this kid, this loudmouth, annoying kid who was brought to the castle and charmed almost everyone right away."

"You were jealous." It was said without recrimination. Merely fact, and I appreciated that more than I could say.

"Yeah," I said, ducking my head as my cheeks burned. "I was. Looking back, it was stupid. I shouldn't have been, but I couldn't help but think I was being replaced. Why couldn't people like me as much as they liked him?"

"What changed?"

"Everything," I said. "Sam just…" Helplessly, I waved my hand. "He got to me too, somehow. Against my better judgement, against everything I thought I wanted, he got it stuck in his head that we were meant to be friends."

"Sounds like he knows what he's talking about."

I laughed quietly. "You'd think so, right?" I watched as Sam gasped when Ryan tried to do a backflip, landing on his back on the grass, blinking up at the sky. "He's...I don't know."

"He's your wizard," Dylan said.

"He is," I agreed. Enough with this. I didn't want to think about it anymore. It hurt my heart. "How are you so good with kids? I thought you were an only child."

Dylan scratched the back of his neck. "Oh, that? Yeah. I guess I am. I go to visit the orphanages in Yennbridge a few times a month."

I groaned. "Seriously? You visit *orphans*?"

He scowled at me. "They need hope like everyone else. Maybe even more."

I backtracked quickly. "No, that's not what I—of course you go to visit orphanages. You've got to be the most selfless person I've ever met."

He laughed at me. "Wow. That seems like it should be a compliment, but it sure didn't sound that way."

"You're perfect," I blurted. Face growing hotter, I added, "It's supremely annoying. You've got to have *some* faults."

"Oh yeah," Dylan said, a knowing spark in his eyes that I didn't like. "I've got a few."

Now that I believed, though for the life of me, I couldn't think of one aside from the fact that he existed at all. Strangely enough, it didn't seem as important as it had a few days ago. I told myself it was because of what had happened to the others, but that didn't quite feel like the whole truth. "Name one. No. Wait. Name *five*." There. That should be enough to put some distance between us. Metaphorically, at least.

He raised one hand and began to tick off each of his fingers. "I'm hardheaded. When I see something I want, I go for it."

I rolled my eyes.

He ignored me, second finger folding down. "When I get drunk, I like to hug people."

I stared at him. "Do you understand what faults are? Because I'm not sure you do."

"Third," he said. "When I was twelve, I ate bad seafood and vomited."

I threw my hands up. "Yeah, you have no idea what faults are, you—"

"Vomited all over the oldest woman in Yennbridge, who was the guest of honor at a celebration of her birthday." He looked at me solemnly. "She lived for another ten years, but I know she never forgot the prince who barfed on her face."

I gaped at him.

"Fourth," He continued, folding down his pinkie. "People think because I'm so nice, they can try and walk all over me. Which really blows so I'm trying to learn to be more assertive."

There. That was a little better.

"And finally," he said, curling his thumb inward, making a fist. "I..." He hesitated. Then, dropping his voice, "Can I tell you a secret?"

"If it involves pissing on Digger, I don't want to know."

He snorted. "Nah. Not my deal, as I said before." He levelled his gaze at me, taking a deep breath. For a moment, I feared what he'd say next, something so terrible, it'd destroy the good will he'd somehow managed to create thus far. "I don't know if I'm a good king," he finally said. "It's scary. Like, *super* scary. All those people counting on you, watching your every move. Dad tried to..." He cleared his throat, looking away. "They weren't bad people," he said dully. "My parents. People loved them, and they were good at what they did."

"But?" I asked.

His voice hardened. "Dad didn't think I had what it took to be king. Said it needed to be someone smarter, someone better. We didn't have the best relationship. I was a disappointment to the both of them." His eyes widened. "Not that they were jerks about it or anything! Just...I don't know. I wasn't what they expected me to be, and it showed. Sucks, right?"

It did, and terribly so. But even more than that, it showed we had more in common than I first thought. Not that Dad didn't think I had what it took—though the conversation after his heart attack still rang in my ears—but that Dylan was scared of being a king. I don't think there was anything I feared more. It would happen, one day, hopefully far, far into the future, and there was nothing I could do to stop it.

I didn't like how beaten down he looked. I wracked my brain, trying to find something to say that would make it better. "You're...

not so bad." I winced and hastily added, "I mean, you're still upright and breathing, so that has to count for something, right? Do you miss them?"

"All the time," he said. "No matter what, they were still my parents." He sucked in a deep breath, letting it out slow. "But then I remember how crappy it was sometimes, and I don't know how to feel. I know that's dumb."

"Not so dumb," I said quietly. "You...you're all right."

My chest hitched with how he brightened, his lips quirking. He bumped his shoulder against mine, causing my heart to stumble. "You too, bro."

"Bro," I muttered. "There's another fault. Consider working on that."

Before he could reply, Kevin apparently decided that he'd had enough of Gary sliding down the hill. He swooped down, closing his talons carefully around Gary's front legs, trying to lift off.

"Kevin!" I yelled, starting forward. "You put him down *right now*."

"No!" Kevin shouted back as he struggled to raise Gary off the ground. "He is a *treasure*, and since I'm a dragon, I'm going to take him to my hoard and keep him forever!"

"Oh dear," Gary said. "So many men fighting over me. What's a foal like me to do but allow it to happen?"

Tiggy tried to swat Kevin with his broom as Gary's back hooves left the ground, Kevin straining upward.

Dylan reached them first, managing to pull Gary back to the ground. Kevin snarled at him, rearing back as if he meant to light Dylan on fire. Before I could shout a warning, Dylan looked up at him and sternly said, "No fire, bro. That's definitely not cool."

Kevin choked before burping out a cloud of black smoke. He landed on the ground in front of us, glaring up at Dylan. "You're not my real dad!"

"Gods," I mumbled. "How many times do I have to hear that?"

"Justin!"

I whirled around at the sound of Sam's shout. He was pointing off toward the knights in the next training field.

I looked over, unable to see what had gotten him so riled up. The knights were gathered in a group, looking down at something that I couldn't see. "What is it?" I asked, confused. "Those are the knights.

You know that."

He shook his head wildly. "Ryan!"

The knights exploded in laughter as the crowd parted. And there, standing in the middle of them all, was a tiny Ryan Haversford, wooden sword raised as he said something I couldn't hear.

"Oh no," I breathed before taking off at a run.

Only to make it a few steps before my arm jerked behind me, the sash reaching its limit. I whirled around. "Dylan!"

He was already moving, gathering up Gary and Kevin in his arms, telling Tiggy to follow them. Tiggy agreed immediately, raising his broom above his head and bellowing wordlessly.

I grabbed Sam by the hand, pulling him along. He couldn't quite keep up, so I bent over in a smooth motion and lifted him, tossing him over my back. His knees dug into my spine as his arms wrapped around my throat. "Not so hard," I managed to choke out as he laughed in my ear.

"Faster!" he cried. "Go *faster*."

I did, the others chasing after us.

One of the knights heard the commotion coming toward them, turning to look over his shoulder. He gaped at us before shouting, "Atten*tion*!"

All the knights snapped into place, backs rigid. Including Ryan, fixing his stance to match the other knights.

I was out of breath by the time I made it to the group. I bent over, gasping for air as Sam cried, "Again! Again!"

"Never again," I wheezed, heart thundering in my chest. "I'm getting too old for this shit."

Sam slid off my back, rushing around me toward Ryan. "I didn't mean to tell on you," Sam told him. "I'm sorry."

Ryan didn't look at him, chin jutted up as he stood at attention.

Sam's face crumpled. "Are you mad at me?"

"No," Ryan said out of the corner of his mouth. "I'm a knight. I have to do what other knights do."

"Oh," Sam whispered, looking around at the other knights, most of whom seemed to be fighting back smiles. "I'll do it too." He walked around Ryan, looking him up and down before stopping and mirroring Ryan's pose, though not quite as good.

Ryan glanced at me nervously. I arched an eyebrow at him, but he must have taken it as permission because he broke rank, pushing against the small of Sam's back until Sam wasn't slouching. Then he resumed his position next to Sam. "Prince Justin," he said seriously. "Your knights of Verania."

I sighed as a few of the knights chuckled. "You can't just run off like that. You need to tell someone where you're going."

"Yes, sir!" Ryan said, staring resolutely forward. "Your wish is my command! May I speak freely, sir?"

"You may," Dylan said, setting Gary and Kevin down, Tiggy's broom still waving wildly as the half-giant began to sweep up grass clippings.

"Thank you, King Dylan," Ryan said gratefully. "As a knight, it's my duty—"

"Ha!" Gary said. "Duty."

"I don't get it," Kevin said.

"—to make sure my fellow knights are battle ready at all times," Ryan said. "And that they are the bravest people in all of Verania. It's part of the knight's code.'

"That it is," one of the knights said with a chuckle. "Who knows the code?"

"We know the code!" the other knights shouted.

"I don't know the code," Sam whispered, fidgeting nervously.

"That's okay," Ryan told him. "I can tell you. The code says that the knights will give everything in service of king and country, including their lives."

"Wow," Sam said, obviously impressed. "That's so cool."

"It is," Ryan said. "And only special people get chosen to be knights. They go through tests and stuff to make sure they have what it takes." He raised his wooden sword above his head. "For Verania!"

"For Verania!" the other knights bellowed back.

"I want to try," Sam said. "Can I see your sword?"

Ryan immediately handed it over.

"For Verania!" Sam cried, almost stabbing himself in the chin.

"For Verania!" the knights yelled.

"Tiggy too!" Tiggy said, shaking his broom. "For Verania!"

"For Verania!"

Gary blinked slowly. "Why do I like it when men yell?"

"When did we get another unicorn?" one of the knights asked.

"And another dragon," another knight said, squinting at the children before him. "I thought we only had five." He began to tick off his fingers. "The Great White. The teenage emo dragon. The two ice dragons. Kevin. Yeah, only five."

"And that boy with the broom is really big," the first knight said. "Like, what are they feeding him?"

"Meat," Tiggy said proudly. "And love."

This was a bad idea. Beginning to sweat profusely, I was about to tell the knights to forget what they saw and to go back to their drills when Ryan said, "I'm going to be a knight when I grow up, or my name isn't Ryan Foxheart!"

Silence fell as I closed my eyes. I waited for the knights to figure out what was going on, to ask question after question about how their Knight Commander had turned into a child. Mind racing, I tried to think of a plausible excuse that would explain away everything. I should have known that the knights would figure it out. They were a savvy bunch; Ryan saw to that. Only the best, and now we were screwed.

"Ryan Foxheart," one of the knights said slowly. I opened my eyes in time to see him frowning, brow furrowing. He was Ryan's second in command, the leader in their Knight Commander's supposed absence. Neil, I thought he was called. "Your name is Ryan Foxheart?"

"It is!" Ryan said. "Have you heard of me?"

Neil crouched low, staring at Ryan. "Oh my gods," he whispered. "I...can see it. It's so obvious. How the hell did we miss this?" He looked at Sam, then Kevin. Then Tiggy. Then Gary. "This is..."

Oh no. "It's nothing!" I said quickly. "There isn't anything strange and magical going on here! Everything is *fine*."

Neil shook his head as he stood. "It's not fine. Knights, I know what's happening. And it's something you won't believe."

Godsdammit. This was going to get out, and there was no way to stop it. Soon, all the rest of Verania would know. We should've stayed in the castle.

"What is it, Neil?" another knight asked. "What won't we believe?

Neil waved his hand at the children. "A unicorn," he said. "A large boy. A tiny dragon. A kid named Ryan Foxheart who wants to be a knight." He looked down. "And you. Your name is Sam, isn't it?"

Sam nodded excitedly. "It is! Oh my gosh, you know me too?"

I winced, unprepared for the inevitable.

"Knights," Neil said gravely. "Something has been kept from us, something so serious, I can barely speak it aloud."

I tried to gather up the children and take them away before Neil could ruin everything.

I was too late.

"But I *will* speak it aloud!" Neil cried as I tugged on Sam and Ryan's hand, much to their annoyance. "Can't you see what this is? Five children who appeared out of nowhere, two of which have the same names as our future King's Wizard and Knight Commander? Guys, it means…"

"What?" one of the knights asked, practically panting. "I can't stand the suspense! Tell me before I literally explode!"

Another knight snorted. "You won't literally explode. I told you to stop using that word. You *literally* don't know what it means."

"I literally do!"

"Huh," Sam said. "Has this happened before? Because it seems like it's happened before."

"Yes," I said, irritably resigned. "You figured it out. They're—"

"Sam and Ryan have *children*!" Neil yelled. "They adopted two boys from an orphanage and gave them their same names in order to pass along their legacy! *And* at the orphanage I previously mentioned, they also discovered a baby unicorn, a baby dragon and an oversized boy with a penchant for brooms, just like Gary, Tiggy and Kevin! Instead of leaving them at the orphanage, Sam and Ryan adopted all of them."

"What," I said.

"Wow," a knight said, a woman with perfectly plucked eyebrows and a battle scar running down her cheek. "That makes so much sense. I don't know why we didn't see it before."

"What," I said again.

"Exactly," another knight said. "It's *literally* so obvious, so suck on that, *Brad*."

Brad threw up his hands.

"Ryan and Sam adopted five children," Neil said. "And then when they were sent on their top-secret mission, they had to make the hard decision to leave their new family behind. But! They did so, knowing there was only one person they could trust to protect their progeny."

Okay, they were idiots, the lot of them, but there was a compliment in there somewhere about leaving me in charge. "Thank you," I said. "That's—"

"King Dylan," Neil said. "They left King Dylan in charge because they knew he would keep them safe."

"Long live King Dylan!" the knights yelled.

"Aw," Dylan said, blushing as he scuffed his feet. "Of course I'd watch their kids that I didn't know they were having. I'm just happy to be included."

I put my face in my hands.

"Those bastards," Brad said, smiling widely. "They should have told us they were making a family."

"They probably didn't want anyone to know right away," Neil said. "I *knew* Ryan was hiding something." He glanced at me. "Prince Justin, you tell him as soon as he gets back that we're throwing them a baby shower." He raised his hand as I started to sputter angrily. "Hey. None of that. While baby showers are rightfully meant for pregnant women, sometimes women aren't part of the fabric of a family, and that's okay. We really need to avoid toxic masculinity here and understand that preconceived gender roles don't always dictate happy events such as baby showers. Come on, Prince. You're better than that."

I wanted to punch something. But seeing as how most people here were either children or wearing armor, I decided to hold back. "Just so I'm clear," I said evenly. "You're telling me that you believe these are all Ryan and Sam's children."

"Exactly," Neil said. "And that you need to work on how you view the patriarchy. For too long, men—myself included—have thought of ourselves as the breadwinners, the brave and the true. But women are just as important. Times are changing, and it's essential that we recognize that and help facilitate said change. Everyone, magical or not, are created equally, which is why we now have women being granted knighthood, which should've happened ages ago. I'm a little disappointed in you, Prince Justin, for being stuck in the old ways." He shook his head. "What are you going to do when you and King Dylan have a girl, either through adoption or artificial insemination after interviewing dozens of applicants before settling on the perfect woman to carry your love child?"

I choked on my tongue. "When I have a *what* with *whom*?"

"Down with the patriarchy!" Brad yelled. "Except for the king, because he's pretty okay, I guess."

"Justin and I aren't having children," Dylan said seriously.

Finally, someone here with even an *inch* of common sense. *"Thank you, Dylan. I—"*

"We have to fall in love first before we get that far," Dylan continued, and I had to shove my fist in my mouth to keep from screaming. "And then we'll get married and talk about having children. A boy or a girl or somewhere in between, it's all good to me."

"You marry him," Neil told me. "You hear me, Prince Justin? You marry that man right this second. He's aware of your boundaries and isn't pushing. But one day, and one day soon, that wall you've built around yourself will crumble, and your thighs will quiver in delight when he puts his—"

"We're leaving," I announced. "And I *won't* hear any arguments."

Which meant everyone began to argue immediately, knights and children all. The knights demanded to be allowed to watch over their Knight Commander's new family, Ryan wanted to run drills with his new friends, Sam said that he didn't want to go back inside because it was *boring*. Tiggy proclaimed he wasn't done brooming, Kevin tried to eat three bees, and Gary was batting his glittering eyelashes at a tall knight who looked at the unicorn with confusion on his face.

"What a rockin' day this has been," Dylan said happily. "I like having fun even if I have no idea what's going on."

# CHAPTER 12
## The Beating Heart of Sam of Dragons

BY THE END OF the first week and a half, I was ready to die. If villains came to our home and demanded we surrender, I would have done so immediately, knowing I'd have peace and quiet in the dungeons for the rest of my days. If an assassin had stolen into the castle under the cover of night and found me defenseless in my bed, I would have bared my throat, begging for the knife. If the gods themselves had descended from the heavens, judging us and finding us wanting, I'd welcome the end of the world with open arms.

Unfortunately for me, none of these things happened.

No, it was far, far worse.

"Tell me you've figured out how to fix this," I begged as Morgan and Randall watched me with amusement. Part of it had to do with the way my voice broke, but I thought a bigger part of their humor had to do with the fact that I had *peaches* in my hair, a gift from Sam who'd thrown them at my head. This, of course, had caused the others to devolve into a food fight, Dylan included, who'd managed to spear four dinner rolls on Gary's horn, much to the unicorn's delight. I'd left them all under the watchful eyes of Joshua and Rosemary. It wasn't until I'd gotten to the labs that I realized I was sticky, and I wasn't in the best mood. "Tell me you've found a way to reverse this."

"We haven't," Morgan said. "At least not yet. You might need to prepare yourself that it won't return to normal until you've completed the ritual."

I sagged against the table in the middle of the room. Everything hurt. My muscles. My bones. My head, *everything*. I'd always thought myself fit, carrying on a strict regimen of exercise in order to keep myself in top shape. But a week with the kids had proven that I had no idea about *anything*, and I was paying the price for my hubris. I needed to sleep for days. The problem with that? Sam had decided that he needed to stay in my bed *every night*, which meant Ryan had to come too. Not to be outdone, Tiggy, Kevin and Gary had all agreed that where Sam and Ryan went, they were sure to follow. Kevin had taken to sleeping while hanging from the ceiling, announcing that he was now a bat, and that everyone needed to respect his decision. I'd asked after Joshua and Rosemary, wanting their help. They'd sent a note in response that read: YOU'VE GOT THIS! xx.

Suffice to say, the number of people on my shit list was growing daily.

"You look like you're handling this with your usual grace and aplomb," Randall said, and I *knew* he was mocking me, the ancient asshole.

I glared at him. "You think this is a joke?"

He rolled his eyes. "Of course not. It's quite serious. But if I can't laugh at you, who can I laugh at?"

Because *that* made things better. "You aren't even trying to fix this, are you."

"We are," Morgan said gently. "But this is deep magic, Justin. If it did come from Sam as we suspect, we're dealing with something we've never seen before."

"It's because of you," I said. "You and those damn dragons."

"I know you're not the biggest proponent of magic," Randall said gruffly. "Even when you were a child, you never appreciated the fantastic."

"You're blaming *me*?" I asked incredulously.

"Yes," Randall said.

"No," Morgan said hastily. "We don't blame you for that. This isn't your fault."

"Damn right it isn't," I snapped. "I didn't want this. I never *asked* for this."

"He says that a lot," Dylan said. I blinked, having forgotten he was there. It unnerved me how used to his presence I was becoming. I barely felt the sash at all anymore. "Which is cool, you know? Feels like a lot of weird things happen here. I like it."

"How kind of you," Randall said. "Got a good head on your shoulders."

"Thanks," Dylan said. "I'm pretty proud of my head. It's big."

I looked down at the table. There, laying open and pages ruffling, was Sam's grimoire. A grimoire was a wizard's greatest legacy, filled with everything from spells to descriptions of their day-to-day lives. I'd never looked through it, given that it was personal, but I'd be lying if I said I never wondered what lay inside, how often—if at all—my name was mentioned. The cover of Sam's grimoire was covered in gifts from the dragons: glittering scales and vibrant feathers, a remembrance of all he'd done. It was heady, being this close to it. I had to keep from grabbing it and rifling through its pages, trying to find all of Sam's secrets. It wasn't meant for me. Morgan could read through it given that he was Sam's mentor, but I didn't think even Ryan had looked through it.

"Anything in there that would help?" I asked.

Morgan sighed as he put his hands on the grimoire. "Not in the way you're thinking, though it isn't without its merits."

That didn't sound good. It didn't sound *bad*, either, but I'd take what I could get. "What do you mean?"

Morgan hesitated, causing Randall to mutter, "Oh, get on with it. You know the Prince won't leave until you do." He went to the door, opening it and leaning his head out as if to make sure no one was there, listening in. He shut the door once more, locking it for good measure. He pressed his hand against the wood. The air around his fingers rippled slightly, a wave of warm magic rushing over me. "There," he said, stepping away from the door. "No prying ears will be able to listen in."

"Ramos?" I asked. I'd seen the magician that very morning when he'd met with Dylan in my room. I'd gone into the bathroom to give them some space, pacing nervously until Dylan had knocked on the door to let me know they'd finished. I hadn't asked what they'd spoke about, but Dylan didn't seem too concerned.

"With his people," Randall said. "Dimitri is there to…" He glanced at Dylan surreptitiously. "To keep an eye on things, along with Lady Tina."

Dylan didn't seem to catch on to Randall's unsaid words. That didn't surprise me. I thought many things went over Dylan's head and was perturbed at the strange rush of affection I felt. I was tired. That's all it was. I was tired and my brain was malfunctioning.

"Sam is…thorough," Morgan said finally. "He always has been, but his grimoire is filled with many things I hadn't considered before."

Confused, I said, "I thought you read through it often." Wasn't that the point of having a mentor?

"I did," Morgan said. "When Sam was an apprentice. The goal of an apprentice's grimoire is to allow them to put their thoughts in order, to help them hone their voice in all things magic. Ever since Sam returned from the Dark Woods as an apprentice no longer, I've given him space to allow him to grow into his own. He knew there was still the chance I'd check it, and I think I failed him in that regard."

"Why?" Dylan asked.

Morgan sighed as he tapped the grimoire. "Because he was hurting, perhaps more than we thought. Randall, if you please."

Randall turned the book toward me, waving his hand over the page. A section of Sam's writing illuminated, the words wiggling on the page.

I began to read.

*….and I don't know how to make it stop, this feeling that things aren't quite right. What I've done is something people couldn't even begin to dream about, and it should make me feel good. Not because I'm better than them, but because it means I have something to offer that others can't. I'm going to be King's Wizard when Justin becomes king, and I only want to make him proud. But how can I do that when I feel like this? This power in me is bigger than anyone thinks. If I wanted to, I believe I could make anything happen, both good and bad. The only limits are my imagination. And that terrifies me. No one should have this much magic in them, but I do, and though I know I could never willingly do anything to hurt those who don't deserve it, what if something happens that's beyond my control? Ryan does his best to try and chase away the shadows, but I still see Myrin when I close my eyes, see us standing in front of the castle, Ryan laid out on the ground, dead because of me. And those Darks. All those Darks. It was close, closer than anyone realizes. I wanted them to feel every ounce of pain they'd caused me. I wanted them to* suffer. *What does that make me? I don't know if I want the answer. Magic is a gift, something Morgan has long taught me. But if that's the case, then why does this feel like a curse?*

I touched the words on the page, trying to parse through them individually and as a whole. My heart ached. Sam had never said anything, but then, had I asked? No. I'd been so relieved at winning back everything we'd lost, my father once again on the throne, that I'd taken Sam at face value.

"It's not your fault," Dylan said quietly.

I looked over at him. He studied me as he reached over and squeezed my hand. I didn't try and pull away, but neither did he. His palm was warm against the back of my hand. "What?"

He shrugged. "You can't be expected to know everything. This isn't anything you did. I know you're probably kicking yourself right now, bro, but you've been a good friend to Sam."

Nineteen days left before the ritual ended, but it was already like he could read my mind. That didn't bother me as much as it should have. I blamed the lack of sleep. I shook my head. "That's no excuse. For any of us. Sam was hurting. We should have known. Ryan..." I stopped, thinking hard. "He said something about it before the celebration, but I don't think he knew it was this bad."

"It's curious, though," Randall said, rubbing his beard thoughtfully. "Don't you think?"

"What is?" Dylan asked.

Randall nodded toward the grimoire. "Sam's writings are filled with Gary and Tiggy and Kevin. There are sections about Ryan that I could have lived without reading, especially when Sam devoted seven pages to the way Ryan's hair looked when he first wakes up."

I made a face. I really didn't want to read about that. It sounded obnoxious, and perhaps a little too personal.

"And the king is in here," Randall continued. "And Morgan and myself. Sam's parents. Sections devoted to Zero, Pat and Leslie. The Great White. David's Dragon. Ruv. There's even a delightful meandering story about kicking Lady Tina off a cliff, causing her to fall onto spikes and dying quite spectacularly. But it's this particular passage that says more than all the pages that came before."

"What do you mean?" I asked, knowing that when things went back to normal, I'd have to remind Sam he couldn't murder the captain of my personal guard. For the hundredth time.

"This is the only time he mentions Myrin by name," Morgan said.

Stunned, I said, "What? But Myrin is..."

"We know," Randall said. "Myrin is the source of much of his strife. So, it begs the question of why he's only mentioned this once? But that's not what struck me. What do you see about this particular passage?"

I looked down at it again, trying to find the secrets hidden within. I read through it once more, but when I finished, I still didn't know what Randall meant. When I told him as much, Randall said, "He mentions Ryan. But he also mentions you."

*I'm going to be King's Wizard when Justin becomes king, and I only want to make him proud.*

Heart in my throat, I asked, "What do you think that means?"

Dylan bumped my shoulder with his, hand still on mine. "It means he sees you as a safe space. I don't know all that happened with you guys, but if this is the only time he brought up the bad guy, it's pretty telling that he'd mention you and Ryan in the same place."

I shook my head. "Telling me *what?*"

Dylan laughed. "That he loves you, bro. That even when he's feeling low, he's still thinking about what you mean to him, and what he means to you. It's pretty great if you don't include all the sad parts. I totally get why you're Best Friends 5eva now."

"King Dylan is right," Randall said as I stood there in a daze. "Sam has the others, and they love him as he is, warts and all." He tweaked his nose. "And believe me, there are plenty of warts. He sees them as his future, but you, Prince? I believe he sees you as more than that. I think he's worried about letting you down." Randall smiled fondly as he stroked the page in Sam's grimoire, a look I'd never seen on his face before. "He's a stupid boy, and often more trouble than he's worth, but I can't find fault in his convictions."

"What a fucking moron," I muttered. "He doesn't need to be more than he already is. Was. Whatever. Why doesn't he know that?"

"Because our demons often take all the good in us and turn it into something rotten," Morgan said. "Especially when we're already feeling low. Trust us when we say we know that as well."

Apparently today was a day for firsts, because Randall wrapped an arm around Morgan's shoulders, kissing the side of his head sweetly. Morgan hummed under his breath. Centuries. They had centuries between them. I'd known them for years, but this was the first time I'd seen Randall so free with his affection. It threw me for a loop.

"What am I supposed to do?" I asked helplessly. "If we can't turn things back right now, how do I get through to him?"

"You gotta be there for him, bro," Dylan said. "You don't always have to know what to say. Sometimes, just being at his side will be enough. And when he's ready, he'll talk."

"How do you know?" I asked.

Dylan shrugged. "You're a good dude. I know you don't like others to think so, but you are. Sure, you can be mean, and you snore, but you—"

"I don't snore!"

Dylan chuckled. "Oh yeah, you do." His mouth went slack as he made an obnoxious grinding noise. "That's what it sounds like."

Back on my shit list. Pity. He'd been so close to moving to the short list of people I could stand for approximately ten minutes.

"But you care for him," Dylan said, staring at me as if daring me to interject. "You've both been through a lot, and he sees you as someone he doesn't want to disappoint. That's pretty great if you ask me."

"I didn't do anything to deserve it."

"He thinks so," Dylan said. "It's like my friend Digger always tells me. You love who you love, and no one can take that from you. You want to do anything you can to help them, even if you're not in a good place."

I nodded slowly. "Digger said that?"

"Yeah. Smart, right? He's cool like that. It's why he's one of my advisors. Good head on his shoulders. Well, most of the time. At my coronation, he thought it'd be a good idea to release doves when I was crowned king."

And even though I knew better, I asked, "What happened to the doves?"

Dylan laughed. "Oh, man, it was gnarly. He also decided to put the mascot of Yennbridge in the same box as a surprise."

"Which is?" They were pacifists. It was probably something soft and fluffy that wouldn't harm a single feather on the doves.

"Gremlins," Dylan said. "Nasty little things with really sharp teeth. There was a lot of blood and feathers and screaming. Crazy day."

I stared at him. "What. The *hell*."

"Right? Yennbridge signed an accord with the gremlins forty years ago and adopted them as our mascot instead of trying to exterminate them. The one that slaughtered the doves is named Craig. It's all right, though. As I always say, laughter is just one letter away from slaughter."

"And you think *Verania* is weird?" I demanded.

"It is," he assured me. "The weirdest."

I thought about snatching my hand back, but I didn't want to make a scene. That was the only reason. "What am I supposed to do with this?" I asked Randall and Morgan. "If we can't fix it, what was the point of telling me this?"

"Because you need to know," Morgan said. "Sam may only be a child right now, but that won't always be the case. If he wished all of this away when he placed his hand on the Damning Stone, it was only a temporary fix. In nineteen days, if all goes well, he'll get his memories back. All of them. Everything he's done or didn't do, he'll remember. This, Justin, was his escape from all of that."

I bowed my head. "We all fucked up."

"We did," Randall agreed. "But some of us—Morgan and me— more than others. I let myself become blind to his suffering, only focusing on how to use him to save us all. And that wasn't right. I know how you feel about me, Prince. I know you harbor resentment over what happened with Sam and what he did in order to take on Myrin, but believe me when I say Morgan and I have flagellated ourselves more than you know."

"If I could take it from him, I would," Morgan said, voice trembling. "I never…" He shook his head. "But I can't. The best I can do is make sure he knows he's not alone. And I need your help. He trusts you. He loves his parents, more than almost anything. But they're not who he seeks out at night when he's at his most defenseless. That's you, Justin. He may not remember you now, but he knows that with you he's safe."

"And there's no one better for it," Dylan said, sounding oddly proud. "Justin's awesome like that."

I scoffed, though it was without heat. "I haven't *done* anything."

"So you say," Randall said. "But I assure you, Prince, Sam thinks otherwise. It's clear from his writings and his actions that he sees you as his king. Yes, your father sits on the throne and Sam loves him dearly, but Anthony isn't his future. You are. And he would do anything to protect you."

I thought I knew this, deep down, and perhaps I'd known this far longer than I cared to admit. A king is not an island, my father had told me. He would have no hope of achieving anything good if he went it alone. Even Dylan seemed to have people he trusted to have his back. Granted, Digger and Ramos weren't exactly who *I'd* choose, but I didn't think I had room to talk. He had a best friend and a magician. I had the most powerful being in the known world, only now, he didn't have magic or his wits about him.

But did that matter?

Somewhere, locked away, was the Sam I knew. The Sam I'd grown up with. The Sam I had despised for so long that when it stopped, I was almost bereft at the loss of it. I could handle people disliking me. I could deal with antagonism, especially since I was the one usually dishing it out. But this? This felt beyond me, something so vast and grand, it knocked me breathless. I had done nothing to deserve such devotion. In fact, I'd done my best to stop it. But Sam—always and forever Sam—hadn't listened. He'd seen through the bluster and noise to the man underneath, and though I could have convinced myself I didn't want it, I hadn't.

Why?

The answer was simple: I *did* want it. I wanted it almost more than anything. Because a king is not an island. He couldn't be. And Sam knew that. He knew that without even being told.

The words were hard to force out, but I had to. I needed them to understand. "He…" I cleared my throat as Dylan intertwined his fingers with my own. It was soothing in ways I did not expect. I clutched at him as if I were drowning and he was the only thing that could save me. "He's annoying," I said gruffly. "A pest whose sole purpose is to drive me up the wall."

"But," Randall said.

I sighed. "But he's my wizard. And I would do anything for him."

"Far *out*, bro," Dylan said happily. "I love love. Friend love. Boyfriend love. Husband love. Family love. All of it. If we all laid down our arms and used *our* arms to hug, the world would be a better place."

"Oh my gods," I mumbled. "I hate every word that came out of your mouth. Never say something like that again."

"Nah," Dylan said, grinning at me. "I'm on to you now, Roth. You try and act like this stone-cold dude, but you've got a marshmallow center, just waiting for someone to crack you open and scoop it out and cover their face in it."

We all stared at him.

"What?" he asked. "You know it. I know it. It helps to say it out loud. You want to do it with me? Awesome! Hi, I'm Prince Justin of Verania, and I love my friends so much, my heart is going to explode." He nudged me. "You were supposed to say it with me."

"I like him," Randall said. "Reminds me of a man I knew in my youth. He could do the splits when we were caught in the throes of passion. It was quite the sight to see."

*Throes of passion*, I mouthed to no one in particular.

"We'll keep working on it," Morgan said, pulling Sam's grimoire back toward him. "There may have been something we missed. We've managed to trace the origins of the Damning Stone for centuries. Perhaps there's something there. With a little luck, we'll have the answers we seek."

"And if you don't?" I asked.

"Then this will play out until it's done," Randall said. "Regardless, you have decisions to make, Prince Justin. In nineteen days, you'll have to make a choice."

I glanced at Dylan, who apparently thought it was a good idea to try and pick up a beaker filled with a thick, glowing liquid. He brought it up to his nose and sniffed, face wrinkling in distaste. Then shrugged, brought it to his lips and—

Randall plucked the beaker from him. "I would recommend against that. It's my own personal concoction. You don't want to drink that."

"What's it for?" Dylan asked.

"Erections," Randall said, secreting the beaker away in his robes. "Causing them to last eight hours. Some of our plumbing doesn't quite work the way it used to. I'd hate to think what would happen if you drank it. Justin doesn't strike me as a power bottom."

"Righteous," Dylan said as I groaned. "I'm verse, so it doesn't matter to me either way. Power bottom? Check. Power top? Check. My dad taught me that a king must be willing to take *and* receive, but I think he was talking about something else, so that's okay. I also make a mean burrito and hold the record for eating the most eggs in a single sitting in Yennbridge. How many, you're wondering? Forty-two. I thought I was going to die and everything smelled like old quiche. What were we talking about again? Sorry, I got distracted. I'm just happy to be included."

Everything was going to be fine.

*****

"OH MY," DAD SAID, staring at Gary. "What is he doing?"

I had no idea, and I was fine with that. Joshua and Rosemary had decided that a game night was in order to keep the kids entertained. I had tried to beg off, wanting to be alone with my thoughts after our discussion with Randall and Morgan, but Dylan had immediately agreed to our participation. Since we were tied together (and he was much heavier than me), I couldn't leave. Rosemary and Joshua obviously didn't have the same problem, waving at us as they practically fled the throne room.

Gary had decided we needed to play charades. All well and good, except every time it was his turn, he ignored whatever he was supposed to make us guess, saying they were boring and far too childish for someone so magnificent. So he came up with his own. I'd reminded him that the hourglass we were using showed his time was up, only to have him snarl at me, saying *he* would let us know when he was done.

And now, Gary was on his back, legs kicking in the air, tongue lolling out of his mouth.

"Death!" Kevin yelled, walking around Gary in a slow circle, talons clicking on the stone floor. "You're dying! You're a princess who has been cursed because of your disregard for human life and are now suffering the consequences of your actions after spending a lifetime trapped in a tower!"

"Gary a broom!" Tiggy said. He and Dad were on a team. They were losing. Tiggy guessed everything was brooms. I wondered if he knew other things existed.

"You can't guess," Gary said out the side of his mouth. "It's not your *turn*."

"Aw," Tiggy said, folding his arms grumpily. "Tiggy play too."

Gary continued to writhe on the floor, Sam and Ryan sitting at my feet, whispering and laughing quietly to each other. Every now and then, Sam would tilt his head back against my knee, as if to make sure I was still there. Awkwardly, I reached down and patted the top of his head. I knew Dylan was watching me, but I ignored him. One thing at a time.

"Seizure!" Kevin exclaimed. "You're acting out having a seizure, which isn't very nice because some people can't control it, but for purposes of the game, that's what I'm guessing!"

Gary rolled over, front legs folded underneath him as he shook his backside, tail bouncing up and down.

"Nope," I said. "Nope, nope, nope. Gary, your turn is over. Time's up."

Gary glared at me murderously as he stood upright. "*Obviously*, I was an eighteen-year-old girl from a small village, having arrived in the big city with dreams of becoming a singer slash songwriter. But then I lost all my money because of an unscrupulous record executive and was left destitute. In order to make ends meet, I turned to dancing, assuming the name Brooklyn, not knowing the seedy underbelly was closing around me as I tried to make money to be able to afford bread and cheese to make toasties."

"That was going to be my next guess," Kevin said.

"We don't talk like that," I said in a stern voice. "Gary, stop spreading your legs. Kevin, stop sniffing Gary. Tiggy, stop eating the broom."

"My turn!" Dylan said. He jumped to his feet, reaching for the slips of paper resting in a bowl next to Dad. He grabbed one, stopping only when Dad said, "No, not that one. This one." He took the slip Dylan had, replacing it with another.

"Thanks, King," Dylan said.

Dad smiled at him, and it struck me then how happy he seemed, sitting on the floor, back against the dais as if he didn't have a care in the world. His crown lay forgotten on the throne behind him. He looked completely at ease, like he wasn't the king of an entire country, at least not in this moment. He was enjoying himself, and I knew how close it had come for me to never have something like this again. He must have felt me looking at him, because he arched an eyebrow. I shook my head, and he nodded toward Dylan, giving me two thumbs up.

He approved. Of me. Of Dylan. Of all of this. I was still angry with him, but it wasn't the fire that had burned the day of the celebration. Though it still sparked, it was muted, soft, barely keeping me warm. I didn't know what to do with it.

So I did nothing.

I just…let it go.

Especially when Dylan frowned down at the paper in his hands before nodding. He took a deep breath, dropping the paper to the floor. "Okay," he said. "I've got this. Back in Yennbridge, we do charades once a month. I'm pretty good at it, so we're probably going to win."

Dylan jogged toward the doors, going as far as the sash would allow before turning around and facing us. He shook out his shoulders. And then he marched toward us, head held high, each step careful and measured. He pantomimed waving at an invisible crowd, mouth moving silently as he grinned and shook his head. When he was halfway back toward us, he froze, eyes widening briefly. He pressed his hand over his heart, bowing low. Once finished, he marched toward us, knees practically reaching his chest.

I had no idea what the hell he was doing.

"A ghost!" Kevin said, apparently not understanding how the game was played. "You're a ghost who died in a horrible fire and now you're back to exact your revenge against those who you consider your enemies by eating their intestines and bathing in their blood!"

"I'm gonna marry the crap out of that reptile when I grow up," Gary whispered fervently.

Dylan reached us again, stopping before us. He acted out having a conversation. He looked strangely shy, rubbing the back of his neck and scuffing one of his boots against the floor. Then he smiled, wide and oddly beautiful, and Sam said, "Ow, Justin, you're pulling my hair! That hurt!"

I snatched my hand back, face heating up as I mumbled an apology.

Dylan raised his arms, his left forming a semi-circle waist high, the other stretched out and level with his shoulder, fingers curled inward. And then he began to sway. It took me a moment to realize he was *dancing*, his feet moving side to side as he spun slowly. I was impressed against my will. He was good.

"You're choking the life out of an assassin!" Sam exclaimed.

"Ooh," Ryan said. "That's a good guess. I was going to say he was churning butter, but I like yours better."

Dylan shook his head as he continued to move.

"You're dancing," I said.

He touched the side of his nose as he winked at me. Partially correct.

"King," Tiggy said, and we all looked at him. "King Dylan. Comes to Verania. Sees Justin. Happy. Justin pretty. King nervous. Wants to do good. Wants to ask Justin to dance. They do. King Dylan happy because of dancing and Justin. Happily ever after. The end."

I laughed. "I don't think that's—"

"That's right," Dad said, smiling at Tiggy. "You're very smart."

"I know," Tiggy said.

"Way to go, dude," Dylan said, holding out his fist, which Tiggy accepted gladly as he fist-bumped him back. "You're good at this."

"Tiggy good at everything," Tiggy said seriously.

I stood up. "That's not what the paper says." I scooped up the slip from the floor, looking down at it. "See? It says...King Dylan comes to Verania and is happy because of Justin even though he's nervous and wants to ask him to dance, so he does, and they live happily ever after, the end." I raised my head slowly. "Dad?"

Dad whistled as he looked at everything *but* me.

"*Dad.*"

"Yes, Justin?"

"Did you do this?"

"I have no idea what you're talking about."

I thrust the paper at him. "This is *your* handwriting."

Dad squinted at the slip. "Is it? Interesting. I wonder how that got there?"

Before I could retort, Ryan pushed himself to his feet with a determined expression on his face. He bowed before Sam, extending a hand clumsily, almost falling over. Then, explosively, he said, "Samwouldyoudancewithmeplease."

Sam blinked up at him. "What?"

Ryan coughed once. "Would you please dance with me."

I watched as Sam took Ryan's hand. "I'm not a very good dancer. My feet do things all by themselves."

Ryan pulled Sam up and put both his hands on Sam's shoulders, while Sam gripped his waist. They stood at least a foot apart, both of them beginning to shuffle side to side.

"Tiggy dance too!" Tiggy yelled, shoving Gary off him. He stood swiftly, looking around before frowning. "Who dance with Tiggy?"

"That would be me," Dad said, pushing himself up with a groan, knees popping. Tiggy grabbed his hand, pulling him toward Sam and Ryan.

"I want to dance with you," Kevin told Gary. "But it comes with a warning. Once we begin, you'll never be the same." He craned his neck, bobbing it up and down, wings folded up around his head as he made a strange clicking noise in the back of his throat. "I am a master in the language of love. Prepare yourself for the end of all you know."

"Oh," Gary breathed. "This is apparently a thing I really like."

No music played, but it didn't seem to matter. Everyone shuffled back and forth. If my father's advisors had chosen this exact moment to walk in, they'd probably hold an emergency meeting in order to discuss our collective sanity. Sam stepped all over Ryan's feet, Gary was doing backflips (why, I didn't want to ask) in front of Kevin as the dragon continued to click in his throat, and Tiggy decided it was better if he led, spinning my father out before snapping him back and proceeding to dip him low. "Tiggy dance *gooood*," Tiggy whispered.

I shook my head. Idiots, all of them. But they were my idiots, and this was the first time they'd been this quiet since everything had happened. I was fine with sitting where I was. Dylan, as it turned out, wouldn't have it.

He stood before me, a determined look on his face. I knew where this was going. I would tell him no, of course I didn't want to dance.

He extended a hand toward me, saying, "Justin? Would you dance with me?"

I opened my mouth to decline, to say it was ridiculous, especially since there was no music. But a strange thing happened. My brain highjacked my mouth, and I said, "Yes. Thank you."

Dylan looked as shocked as I felt. His hand closed around mine as he pulled me up. I wasn't ready, and I stumbled into him, the beads in his beard bouncing against my forehead. He chuckled quietly before turning his hand in mine, settling his other on my waist, just as he'd done when playing charades. It should have made me uncomfortable, this level of familiarity, and it did. Slightly. But he was strong, and he was warm, and I couldn't think of a single excuse to end this.

So I didn't.

We danced.

It wasn't good. Our knees bumped together, both of us apologizing over each other as we broke apart before coming together to try again. I wanted to lead. He did too. It felt like we were battling each other, each of us trying for dominance. I wasn't surprised to find he had moves, especially since I'd seen how he could handle a sword. Fighting, in a way, was like dancing. You moved back and forth, in and out. *It's also like sex*, my brain helpfully supplied. *Back and forth. In and out.*

I squeaked at the traitorous thoughts.

Dylan grinned at me. "What was that sound you just made?"

"Wasn't me," I said quickly. "I think Tiggy stepped on a mouse."

"No, I didn't!" Tiggy said as he lifted my father up above his head, Dad's arms and legs spread wide as if he were flying. Tiggy spun in a slow circle before spinning my father back down in his arms, setting him on his feet. Dad laughed so loudly I thought his throat would tear.

"Holy shit," I muttered. "How the hell did he do that?"

"You want to try?" Dylan said, looking me up and down. "I bet I could lift you. I'm pretty strong."

I rolled my eyes, refusing to even glance at his biceps. "That doesn't work on me."

"No?" Dylan said, leaning closer, his nose grazing my cheek. "Then what does?"

Dangerous, this. I was on the cusp of something significant and complicated, and I didn't know how to take the next step, or even if I wanted to. I was grateful he wasn't wearing one of his vests, instead having a billowing shirt that did nothing to hide the strength underneath. The swell of his stomach brushed against me, and I *refused* to let my knees go weak.

"Nothing," I finally said.

"I don't believe that for a second," Dylan said, and we danced and danced and danced.

By the time we parted, I was lost.

*****

I awoke that night because of a scream of terror. I shot up, hand going under my pillow, nearly slicing my fingers on the blade of the dagger. Dylan was up off the floor, looking around wildly, holding Ryan in his arms, shielding him from whatever was coming. The room was dark, the only light from the waning moon.

I looked down at the bed beside me.

Sam, tangled in the blankets, twisting back and forth, eyes closed tightly, mouth moving as he muttered, "No, please, no, please don't hurt them. Please don't take them away from me. I don't wanna be alone."

I pressed my hand against his forehead as Ryan asked what was wrong. I didn't hear what Dylan said in response, focusing solely on

Sam. I set the dagger down on the nightstand next to the bed before stretching out next to Sam. "Shh," I murmured in his ear, pulling him close. "Shh. You're okay. It's just a nightmare. I've got you. I'm here."

Sam's eyes snapped open. He looked around wildly before focusing on me, gaze slack and scared. "Justin?" he whispered.

"Yeah," I whispered back as Dylan lay Ryan back down on the bedroll next to my bed. I glanced across the room. Kevin's eyes glittered from where he hung from the ceiling. They closed, and he began to breathe slowly. I looked back down at Sam. "You're all right."

"I had a bad dream," Sam said miserably, face scrunching up as his chest hitched. "I couldn't find you because the bad man was chasing after me in the city."

My hand froze in his hair. "What bad man?"

"I don't know," he said as a tear leaked from his left eye, spilling down to his ear. "But he was big and scary and had *magic*." Then, as if he remembered something, he pulled up his shirt, revealing unmarked skin. He ran his hands over his chest and stomach frantically, and it took me a moment to realize what he was looking for.

Scars. He was looking for lightning-struck scars, a terrible gift from a dark man now gone into the stars.

"Sam," I said carefully. "Did the bad man have a name?"

He pulled his shirt back down, shaking his head. "I don't remember. But I could stop him. I could stop them all. I *knew* I could, but I didn't know how." He hiccupped wetly. "Why did the bad man want to hurt me?"

I lay down next to him, our faces on the same pillow. He turned his head toward me, his breath slightly sour from sleep. I didn't pull away. Not from this. Not from him, not now. "No one is going to hurt you," I told him, a promise I wished I could keep. It was foolish to say this out loud, but I meant it with every fiber of my being. "You want to know why?"

"Why?" he asked in a hushed voice.

"Because you have me," I told him. "I'm the Grand Prince of Verania, which means I know what I'm talking about. Anyone who tries to hurt you will have to go through me. And I'm good with a sword. Perhaps even the best."

He sniffled, wiping his eyes as I ran my hand through his hair. "You promise?"

"I promise," I whispered. "And when you have the promise of a prince, you know it's real."

"Justin?"

"Yeah?"

He gnawed on his bottom lip in indecision. Then he steeled himself and asked, "Are we really best friends?"

I closed my eyes. The Sam I knew wouldn't have asked. He would've told me that was the way it was going to be, whether I liked it or not. I was shocked by the wave of grief that washed over me, not just for him, but for myself too. So much time wasted that I could've been a better person to him. But my ego had taken over, filling my mouth with biting snark and evident disdain.

I missed him. The man he'd become. The man who'd given almost everything in the name of Verania.

I opened my eyes and said, "Can I tell you a story?"

"Yes, please."

"There once was a boy—"

"Boo," Ryan said from the floor. "Everyone knows stories start once upon a time."

Dylan snorted but didn't speak.

"Fine," I muttered. I gathered my thoughts and started once again. "Once upon a time in the Kingdom of Verania, there was a kickass boy born in the Slums of the City of Lockes. His parents were hardworking, and at times, life could be difficult, but they were alive and had all their teeth. Which was very important."

"Whoa," Sam said. "That's a good start. Everyone should try to keep their teeth." He blinked slowly, eyes never leaving mine. "What happened next?"

"This boy was annoying," I said. "He talked too much and caused calamity and destruction pretty much wherever he went. He grew up in the Slums, but one day, a wise man with curly pink shoes came to him and said, 'You are important. Your magic will be celebrated even though it probably shouldn't be because you might make my nipples explode.'"

Sam nodded. "That makes sense. Everyone knows magic can do that."

"Thankfully, the boy decided that exploding nipples weren't as important as moving to the castle and becoming a pain in the ass for—"

Dylan coughed pointedly.

"Becoming more trouble than anyone thought," I amended. "There, the boy met a knight and a prince and a king."

"Wow," Sam said sleepily. "That's a lot of people."

"It is," I said. "And the prince wasn't nice to the boy because he thought the boy was trying to take everything away from him. It was foolish for the prince to think this way, but he couldn't stop it, no matter how hard he tried."

"Boys are dumb," Ryan mumbled, half-asleep.

"They are," I agreed. "But the prince was perhaps the dumbest of them all. Because, you see, the prince was wrong. The boy was never trying to take anything away from him. The boy only wanted to make the prince happy, to feel like he had a friend, something the prince had never really had before."

"Was the prince lonely?" Sam asked.

I hesitated. "He...yes. I think he was. I think the prince was so consumed by what he thought his role was that he didn't make time for anything else. He didn't...he didn't have friends. He thought himself too important for that."

"Everyone needs friends," Sam said as I lay my hand on his chest. "If you don't have someone, then you're alone."

"But the prince didn't know that," I said. "At least not right away. Many things happened before the prince opened his eyes to the truth of all things. You want to know what he learned?"

"What?" Sam asked.

"He learned that it was better to have friends than it was to ever be by himself. That in the end, having something worth fighting for was more important than any crown. What would be the point of one day being king if you had no one to turn to?"

Sam reached up and touched my face, his small fingers dimpling my cheeks. "So he became friends with the boy?"

"Best friends," I said, swallowing past the lump in my throat. "In fact, they became Best Friends 5eva, which is capitalized, so you know it's true."

"Wow," Sam whispered. "And they lived happily ever after?"

I started to nod but stopped. "Not always. Sometimes, things happened beyond their control, and they had to learn to lean on each other when things were at their darkest. And the prince wasn't always the best person. But one day, after the boy grew into a man and left for the Dark Woods on an important mission, the prince realized that the life he'd led up to that point wasn't a life he wanted to continue. He didn't know how to put it into words, but he felt it all the same."

"Did the boy come back?" Ryan asked.

"He did. Eventually. And when he did, it was one of the happiest days in the prince's life, even though he didn't act like it. You see, even with all he'd been through, the prince still had a hard time admitting he was wrong. Many people thought he was frozen from the inside out, made only of ice."

"But they were wrong," Sam said, laughing quietly as he tweaked my nose.

I startled. "How do you know that?"

"Easy," Sam said. "Because if the boy loved him, then the prince loved him too. And even if he was the only one, the boy would know what he was talking about."

"Yeah," I said hoarsely. "The boy did know what he was talking about. He could see through the prince's actions to the very heart of him. And the boy found that the heart of the prince wasn't made of ice. It beat just like everyone else's, and the boy promised to never leave the prince again. And then they lived happily ever after, knowing that they would always have each other."

"That was a good story," Sam said.

"*Except*," Gary said loudly, "there was a lack of magical creatures in the story, which made it offensive and unbelievable. You really should've had a sensitivity reader before you went public."

I groaned as Tiggy began to chant, "Magical *rights*! Magical *rights*!"

"Go the fuck to sleep," I told them. Dylan chuckled, a soft sound that caused gooseflesh to spring up along my arms.

"Rude," Kevin said. But then he did just that, eyes closing as he swayed from the ceiling. A moment later, he began to snore. Tiggy and Gary followed suit, Gary mumbling sleepily that there'd better damn well be magical creatures in the next story, or he was going to bring the pain.

I looked down at Sam. His eyes were closed, and he was breathing slowly. I thought him asleep. I tried to get comfortable without waking him, but he opened his eyes as I sighed. "Justin?"

"Yeah?"

"You know how Ryan is my boyfriend?"

"Uh...yes?" They were eight. That couldn't mean much, right?

Even if there were glimpses of memory rolling through Sam—the bad man from his dreams, something that caused my blood to run cold— he couldn't remember what he'd had before, all that he'd done and been done to him. None of them could.

And yet, hadn't they still latched on to each other? Ryan and Sam. Tiggy and Gary and Kevin. Their world—and in turn, mine— had collapsed around them, turning them into these children without memory of everything we'd been through. By right, they should have been half out of their minds. They weren't. They were…happy. Well, as happy as they could possibly be, knowing that something wasn't *quite* right. It was strange to think that even with all they'd lost, they still had each other.

"Because I like him," Sam said. "He makes me happy."

"That's good."

"Do you have someone who makes you happy?"

Uh oh. I could see where this was headed. "Of course I do. I have my dad. I have you guys. That makes me happy."

He smiled as he shook his head. "That's not what I meant." He leaned closer, his face inches from mine on my pillow. He whispered, "Do you like boys or girls?"

Godsdammit. "You don't need to worry about that."

He wasn't to be deterred. "Because if you like girls, that's okay. A little weird, but okay. Just as long as you don't like Lady Tina, because she *suuuuucks*."

Yeah, Sam was still Sam, regardless of his miniature status. "I don't like Lady Tina."

"Good," he said. Then his eyes began to sparkle in ways I didn't like. "So you like boys? Guess what?"

"You should really go to sleep."

"Guess!"

"Sam."

"Fine," he grumbled. "I'll just tell you. It's a *secret*, though, so you can't tell anyone."

For a moment, I thought Sam was going to tell me *he* liked me, and I prepared myself for an attack by an eight-year-old Knight Commander. I'd hate to have to bitch-slap a child, but I would if Ryan felt the need to defend what he considered his. "I won't."

"You promise? Best Friend 5eva Promise?"

"That was capitalized, wasn't it?"

"Yep," he said, nodding furiously. "So you know it's true. My secret is…" Always the drama queen, the pause stretching out. "I know someone who *like* likes you."

I blinked. "You do? How do you know?"

Sam grinned. "Because he smiles whenever he sees you, and it's a happy smile that looks like it's coming from all of him, even his toes."

"Is that right?" I had no idea who he was talking about. No one ever looked at me that way. Or, if they did, it meant they were after something. It was about this time that I realized I had some very deep-seated trust issues. Not my fault, really.

"Yep," he said before yawning widely. "And you should take him on a date. Because when you go on dates, there's laughing and eating and holding hands and…and *kissing*, which is, like, so gross. That's what my mom says."

"So gross," I agreed. Then, without meaning to, I added, "Who is it?"

"He's in the room," Sam whispered fervently. "He's *laying right next to us on the floor.*"

I groaned. "Sam, you can't just—"

"It's King Dylan!" Sam said loudly before I could cover his mouth with my hand. "He like likes you and wants to take you on a date with laughing and eating and holding hands." He grimaced. "And kissing, I guess."

"Oh my gods," I muttered, face on fire.

"You should go on a date with him," Sam continued as if he weren't embarrassing the hell out of me. "Because I think you like him too. And if you do, that means he's a good person and you won't have to be alone anymore."

"I'm not alone," I told him, heart rabbiting in my chest. "I have you."

"I know," he said. "I'm pretty great. But I'm not everything. You need everything, Justin. And King Dylan is big and strong and has beads in his beard and tattoos! So many tattoos that he says are because of where he came from. I wish I could have tattoos." He brightened. "We should get tattoos!"

"Or we shouldn't do any of that," I countered.

"Nah," he said easily. "Maybe not the tattoos, but the date thing? Yeah, you should do that. Can I tell you another secret?"

I sighed. "If you must."

Sam dropped his voice once more. And even though we were breathing on each other, I had to listen hard to hear him. "King Dylan is cute."

I choked on my tongue, coughing roughly. "He's *what*?"

"Cute," Sam said as if *I* were the asshole. "He's big and strong and smart—" That was debatable. "—and he takes us on adventures with swords and lets us climb on him and never gets mad at us when we get too loud. That means he's perfect."

"Does it?"

"Yeah," Sam said. "And since *you're* perfect too, that means you would be perfect *together*."

"That's not how things work, Sam. And I'm far from perfect."

"Why not?" he asked. "Why can't you just say yes? Being old is dumb. You never do what you should because you worry too much about everything. When *I* grow up, I'm never going to let anything bother me because I'm gonna be happy all the time."

Oh, how I wished that were so. Swallowing past the lump in my throat, I said, "It sounds like you've thought about this a lot."

"I have," he said. "For *hours*. And since I have a boyfriend and you don't, I'm righter than you."

"Sam, I—"

He pressed his fingers against my lips. "Shush. I'm right. You're wrong. As your Best Friend 5eva, you have to listen to me."

I snapped my teeth at his fingers, causing him to squeal in delight as he snatched his hand back. "I have to, huh?"

"Yeah, that's how it works. So, you'll go on a date with King Dylan and we'll all live happily ever after, just like your story." He yawned again. "I'm tired. Gonna sleep now." He flinched slightly. "I don't wanna have more bad dreams."

"You won't," I assured him. "But even if you do, I'll be here to chase the bad dreams away."

He studied me for a moment before sitting up and leaning over me. I wheezed as his knee went directly into my stomach. "King Dylan! I told him just like you said! You get to go on a date with Justin."

"Heck yeah!" Dylan said from the floor. "Thanks, little dude! I owe you one."

"Damn traitors," I muttered as Sam laughed and laughed. "I hate all of you."

"Liar," Sam said, crawling back to his space next to me. He lay his head on my shoulder, his breath warm against my neck. "Justin?"

"Go to sleep."

"I *will*. But I have to tell you something first."

"What."

"Thank you," he whispered. "I feel safe when I'm with you. I know you won't let the bad man get me no matter how hard he tries." And then he was asleep, just like that.

I stayed awake, long into the night, watching the wonder that was Sam of Dragons.

# CHAPTER 13
## The King and I (Is Corn a Grain or a Vegetable? Fun Fact: It's Both!)

DYLAN STOOD NEAR THE ENTRANCE to the castle on the fifteenth day of the ritual, surrounded by a crowd of people, all vying for his attention. He smiled at each of them as they touched his arm, listening to everything they had to say. My people liked him. That had to count for something.

Except I was more nervous than I expected to be. I didn't know what the hell was wrong with me. I'd been on dates before, some by choice, others against my will, mostly thanks to Sam. At least this time around, I didn't think I'd have to worry about being threatened with fisting. Or so I hoped.

It absolutely did not help that Sam had gotten it into his head that I wouldn't know what to do, which meant he wanted to go on the date too. Which led to Ryan wanting to be involved. And Gary. And Kevin. And Tiggy. And, much to my dismay, Dad, Joshua, Rosemary, Morgan, and for some reason Randall, who told me in no uncertain terms that I needed to douche before going on the date. I banished him from Verania forever. He rolled his eyes at me. "Trust me," he said, an irritated curl to his lips. "Douche now and you don't worry about it later. No one likes shit on their—"

"*Ewww!*" all the kids cried as I glared at Randall.

"What?" he said. "Better they learn now than when it's too late."

"Gary's poop smells like cookies," Kevin said. "I'm okay with that."

This led to a discussion about why it was *not okay* to talk about such things. Kevin responded by lighting a table on fire. We managed to put it out, thankfully.

I banned them all from going on the date. I had enough to worry about as it was. While everyone seemed disappointed—what the hell was my dad doing? He had a fucking *kingdom to run*—Sam took it personally, pouting as he crossed his arms and glaring at me. But then Morgan had said he had the perfect idea, one that would allow them to be part of the date without interrupting.

"No," I said without hearing what the idea was.

Sam deflated, bottom lip wobbling. "But…but I *want* it."

Which is why I now had Sam's summoning crystal fixed to my ear, held in place by one of Gary's scarves, the lengths of which stretched down my back. I looked fucking ridiculous. Dad laughed at me when Sam had put it on me, saying that I should explain to Dylan it was a custom in Verania, that a prince going on a first date must wear the Crystal of Purity. They'd managed to turn the volume down on the crystal so only I could hear, but instead of making me feel better, I wished I'd never been born.

"This is Captain Amazing," a voice crackled in my ear. "Do you copy, Blue Eagle? Over."

It was also decided we should all have nicknames. I ignored him, glancing at Dylan as he showed the crowd the official greeting of Yennbridge, arms stretched out, spinning in a circle.

"Blue *Eagle*," Captain Amazing—AKA Sam—demanded. "Do you hear me?" Then, "Is this working? I think I broke it."

"It's working," I heard Randall say in the background. "Justin's just being a jerk."

"Fuck you, Randall," I snarled, causing a handsome member of the castle staff to stare at me as he scurried by.

"Hurray!" Sam said, the other kids cheering in the background. "We read you loud and clear, Blue Eagle. Over."

"I'm taking this off."

Silence.

"Do you hear me? I'm not going to wear this."

"Oh, were you talking to me, Blue Eagle?" Sam asked. "Because you have to say over when you're done. Over."

I ground my teeth together. "I'm over—"

"You're what? Over."

"I said I'm *over*—"

"I got that part," Sam said. "You're *what*. Over."

I grabbed the nearest banner and screamed into it. The same handsome member of our staff walked by me again, looking at me worriedly. Great. Fantastic. Exactly how I thought this was going to go.

I dropped the banner, taking a deep breath and letting it out slow. "I'm. Not. Doing. This. Over."

"Copy," Sam said. "Hold on." I heard them all whispering in the background, Dad laughing hysterically, Gary telling Kevin that humans were so damn stupid. Then Sam came back. "Blue Eagle? Over."

"*What?*"

Silence.

I threw up my hands. "Over! Over! Over!"

"My mom says that you should stop complaining and have fun. Over."

"Oh, *did* she?" I snapped. "Because *she's* not the one looking like a crazy fuck with a *crystal attached to their head.* Over."

"No cussing," Sam said sternly. "King Dylan doesn't like cussing. Say aw nuts instead. Over."

"Nope," I said, turning around toward Dylan. "Nope, nope, nope. I'm calling this off. This was a bad idea, and I don't have time to—" My words died on my tongue.

The crowd around Dylan was gone. Instead, Ramos the Pure stood in their place. They looked to be having a heated discussion. At least Ramos was, punctuating each word with a firm poke to Dylan's chest. Dylan's face was harder than I'd ever seen it before. He didn't look happy with whatever Ramos was telling him. I moved forward, hiding behind a large stone pillar, peering out around it as if the sash wouldn't give me away if they looked at it. I couldn't make out what they were saying, but I didn't like the expression Ramos wore. And I really didn't like that Dylan was just taking it.

Ramos had skulked along the edges the past two weeks, only appearing when Dylan had a question. He sometimes sat in on the meetings with our advisors, though he never participated. Morgan said he and Randall had invited him a time or two into the labs to discuss the situation at hand. Morgan promised me that Ramos was never left alone in the labs and didn't have access to their grimoires or the Damning Stone. Randall carried that on his person at all times. Dimitri acted as a guide for Ramos, but he hadn't had to do much, or so he said. "He prefers to stay in his rooms," Dimitri told me the day before.

"What's he doing in there?"

Dimitri shrugged, wings fluttering as he hovered near my face. "Writing. Reading. Nothing nefarious, at least as far as I can tell."

That did not make me feel better. I didn't quite know what to make of the magician. Dylan seemed to trust him, but trust could easily be turned into a weapon, one that could cause extraordinary damage if allowed. We'd seen that firsthand with Ruv and Lady Tina. I didn't know what Ramos's angle was, but he had to have one. I hoped to be proven wrong, but what he was doing to Dylan now certainly wasn't helping.

And that gave me pause, because when had I become so protective over Dylan? He could handle himself. He didn't need me speaking up for him.

And yet…

"Blue Eagle?" Sam asked in my ear. "What's going on? Are you kissing already? Gross! I mean, good job! Over."

"We're not kissing," I muttered, watching as Ramos stepped back, shaking his head. Dylan's mouth was a thin line as he folded his arms.

"*What?*" Sam yelled, causing me to wince. "What are you waiting for? Over."

I couldn't believe this was my life. "Fine. I'm going. I don't want to hear another word from you, understand? Over."

Sam laughed. "Yeah, okay. Over."

Steeling myself, I walked out from behind the pillar. Dylan must have seen me out of the corner of his eye, because he looked over at me. A slow smile bloomed on his face, causing my heart to trip all over itself. His gaze settled at my feet before *crawling* up my body. His smile froze when he saw what was attached to the side of my head. I wished I could go back in time and stop myself from ever being born.

Ramos, seeing that Dylan's attention was elsewhere, turned

toward me. The hard look on his face melted away, replaced by bland pleasantry. "Prince Justin," he said with a bow. "I've just heard the good news. You honor my king."

"Ramos," I said coolly as voices in my ear began to mutter. "How nice to see you again. You've been missing in action."

Ramos smiled, though it didn't reach his eyes. "It's best if I remove myself from the equation, to allow things to happen naturally." His eyes flicked to the crystal. "Better if we don't have little ears listening in to every single thing that happens, don't you think? Why, I was just telling Dylan that—"

"Bro," Dylan said. "You look... whoa. So gnarly."

I squinted at him. "You saw me five minutes ago."

"I did," he agreed. "But I was so taken aback by your...head decoration that I couldn't find the words. That scarf sure is...festive."

The scarf was paisley. It clashed with everything I had on, but Gary said that it was the only scarf he'd let me wear. When I'd suggested—quite pointedly—that I didn't need to wear a scarf, Gary had looked scandalized before promptly bursting into tears, wailing that the prince *hated* him, that he'd never felt so bad in his life, and he was going to find the nearest cliff and throw himself off of it. Wanting to avoid a full-blown meltdown, I'd acquiesced.

Gary's tears had dried immediately, and I knew I'd been played.

"Oh, this old thing?" I said stiffly. "It's...customary."

"Right," Dylan said, eyes wide. "Righteous. Won't step in the way of customs, then."

"Curious," Ramos said. "I'd never heard of such a custom before."

I smiled sweetly at him. "There appears to be much you don't know."

Ramos frowned, something black flashing across his eyes, there and gone before most would notice. But since I wasn't most people, I saw it clear as day. He wasn't happy. Good. Fuck him in his stupid face. "Well, I won't keep you, then. My king, are you sure you don't want your guard with you?" He glanced over his shoulder toward the gates that led into Lockes. "If you don't want me coming as chaperone, at the very least, consider taking a few of our people. You won't even know they're following."

Dylan shook his head. "We'll be fine. Justin knows the city. I'm in good hands."

"Kiss his face!" Gary yelled in my ear, causing me to almost fall down.

"Sorry," I said through gritted teeth. "Tripped over my own feet."

"Yes," Ramos said. "I can see that." He looked between us before sighing. "I'll leave you to it, then. King, please do take care of yourself. Prince Justin, I'm trusting you with him."

"We'll be fine," I told him. "You can go."

He looked like he was about to argue but bit it back down instead. Without another word, he bowed and left us as he went back into the castle, leaving me and Dylan alone.

"Prince eating flower?" Tiggy asked.

"Damn right," Gary crowed. "He's gonna eat a whole damn *field* of flowers, and we get to hear it!"

Not completely alone, as it were.

I forced a smile on my face. "Shall we?"

Dylan squared his shoulders, bringing one hand across his chest, sticking out his elbow toward me. I hesitated before reaching out and putting my hand through his arm. He smiled so widely I could barely breathe.

"I love love," Kevin said in my ear.

I worried about Dad's heart given how hard he was laughing.

\*\*\*\*\*

We DIDN'T HAVE A SPECIFIC PLAN in mind. At least I didn't. Sam and Ryan had tried to come up with ideas ("Walk through a park holding hands! Get ice cream that you feed to each other and make sure to accidentally get a little bit on his nose that you have to wipe off!").

I was nervous in ways I hadn't expected, and that wouldn't do. Yes, this was a date (one I'd been tricked into going on by a tiny wizard), but I'd been on dates before. I wasn't the nervous type. When I said jump, people asked how high. When I made a request, everyone scrambled to make sure it was fulfilled. I was the godsdamn Prince of Verania, and I didn't *get* nervous.

Except for, apparently, right this very second.

We left the castle behind, the sounds of the city washing over us. Lockes was alive in ways I hadn't taken the time to appreciate of late.

Crowds of people milled about, their voices bright and happy as they moved about their day. Vendors hocked their wares, shouting for all to hear that they had the *best* silk in the world or the *best* grain or the *best* fish, caught this very morning off the coast. Two buskers played a lute and a lyre, the sounds from their instruments melding sweetly with a woman singing about love and loss as she twirled, her dress flaring up around her legs. Children sat at her feet, watching her with wide eyes as she told them the story of her brave warrior whose ship had been lost in a great storm while trying to prove his loyalty to her.

We paused for a time in the crowd, listening to her sing. People kept their distance from us, though they periodically glanced in our direction, whispering to each other behind their hands. I did my best to ignore them.

When the woman finished singing, Dylan was the first to clap. Others joined in until the sound was a wall of noise, cheers of delight flying around us.

The woman startled when she saw us, face flushing slightly as she curtsied. Dylan left me standing alone as he walked forward, digging into his pockets before dropping coins of gold into the musicians' open instrument cases. He told them he'd never heard such lovely music before, and he hoped they made music for the rest of their days.

They looked at him in awe as he returned to me.

We moved on, my hand through Dylan's arm.

"I like this place," he told me as we continued through Lockes, people trailing after us though trying to act like they weren't. "The city isn't like I expected it to be."

I didn't know how to take that. "What do you mean?"

"It's loud," he said cheerfully. "The City of Light—my home—is nowhere near as big. It's a lot, but it's still pretty cool."

"Cool," I repeated.

Sam groaned in my ear. "Blue Eagle, he said something nice. You have to say something nice back. Over." Then, as if speaking to the others listening in, he added, "I *knew* he should've let us go with him."

Racking my brain, I blurted, "Your country sounds…."

Dylan looked over at me expectantly.

"Nice," I finished lamely.

"Oh boy," Kevin said. "That'll make his pants fall off. It's why I don't wear pants. I'm always ready for anything."

"It is," Dylan said seriously. "We may not have as many people, but we make do."

"I've got this," Ryan said in my ear, voice getting louder as if he were leaning close to the crystal somewhere in the castle. "Blue Eagle, he's proud of Yennbridge. Ask him more about it. Over."

"Ask him about smashing!" Tiggy said.

"Do you smash?" I said. "Wait, no, that's not what I—"

"Tiggy involved in love!" Tiggy screeched, causing me to wince.

"Do I what?" Dylan asked as he squinted at me.

I coughed roughly. "What?"

"You asked me if I—"

"Yennbridge!" I said loudly, causing people to look over at us curiously. "Yes, *Yennbridge*. We should talk about Yennbridge. And I want us to be *the only ones talking*."

Dylan looked around. "You want everyone to be quiet?"

"Yes," I snapped.

"Quiet!" Dylan yelled, and the crowd moving around us stopped all at once. Silence like I'd never heard before in Lockes settled over us. "Prince Justin has something to say about Yennbridge!"

I groaned as everyone stared at us.

"There," Dylan said, obviously pleased with himself. "Now everyone is listening. Go ahead. What were you going to say about Yennbridge? Something good, I hope. I've talked about it so much that it must feel like you've been there with the power of your imagination. This is going to be great."

I swallowed thickly, sweat dripping down the back of my neck as everyone waited for me to speak. I gave brief thought to shoving Dylan down and running back to the castle, but since that wasn't the mature thing to do, and the fact we were literally bound together, I didn't.

Barely.

"Um," I said, trying to find something innocuous that wouldn't offend a single person standing around us. "Yennbridge is…to the north?"

"It is," Dylan said, impressed. "You've got this geography thing down. Which is good, because I get lost really easy."

"Aw," a woman said, holding a squirming kid covered in what looked like raspberry jam. "It's like you two were made for each other."

"Three cheers for Prince Justin knowing geography!" a man cried. "Hip, hip, hooray! Hip, hip, hoo—okay, so apparently I'm the only one cheering. Now I'm embarrassed. This is not what I expected to happen when I woke up this morning."

"Say something else, Blue Eagle!" Sam said in my ear. "Make us *believe*. Over."

I ground my teeth together, wondering at the blowback I'd received if I sent a child to the dungeons. "Yennbridge sounds like a place where... people.... live?"

"Whoa," Dylan breathed. "That's exactly what it is. People *do* live there. That means a lot to me, bro. Thanks."

"Hip, hip, hooray!" the man yelled. "Screw all of you for not joining in. I finished it myself, and *none* of you can take that away from me! Prince Justin, you are *welcome*."

I pulled Dylan on, hoping people would finally leave us alone.

They didn't. Even more began to follow us, much to my dismay. I didn't know what I thought would happen. We should've stayed in the castle.

"I like Lockes," Dylan said as we made our way into an open market. Wooden stalls were covered in brightly colored banners. One had an open fire pit where meat cooked slowly, the fat dripping and hissing against hot coals. Another had windchimes hanging from it, the metal chiming like bells. "It's alive, you know? You can feel it wherever you go." He stopped in front of a stall where bundles of sage and thyme and dill lay on a green blanket. He picked up pieces of mint held together by a white ribbon, bringing it up to his nose and inhaling deeply. He sighed happily, holding out the mint for me to smell. "It's good," he said earnestly, and I was helpless to do anything but what he'd offered. "Clean. Makes your lungs feel like they're cold."

It burned in a good way as I inhaled sharply. Clean, cold. Just like he said.

He asked the vendor how much. The man sputtered that he wouldn't *dream* of taking a king's coin. Dylan wouldn't hear of it. The amount he left in payment caused the man's eyes to fill with grateful tears.

"Why do you do that?" I asked as we left the vendor behind.

"Do what?" Dylan asked, tucking the sprig of mint behind his ear. It looked ridiculous, but I couldn't bring myself to tell him that.

"Act like you do."

Dylan laughed, though he looked confused. "I don't know how else to act. I'm me. That's all I can be. Some people won't like it, but that's on them. I'm happy with who I am. Do I wish everyone liked me? Sure. But if they don't, that's okay. If you spend every second trying to be everything to everyone, you might forget how to be yourself."

"But everyone *does* like you," I muttered. "Poll numbers, remember?"

He shrugged. "So what? Numbers are just numbers. They change because people change. What they might want one day doesn't mean they'll want the same thing the next day. Doesn't mean they're wrong and I'm right. We could both be right. Or we could both be wrong."

"That doesn't bother you?"

He patted my arm. "Not really. Being a king isn't about being popular. It's about doing what's right for your people, even if they can't see it. For a long time, I thought being a king meant making everyone happy."

"And it's not?" I asked slowly. My father had said something similar to me when I was a child but hearing it from another king made it feel more real.

"Nah," he said. "Happiness, like choice, is fickle. What makes one person happy doesn't work for everyone. Can I tell you what makes me happy?"

Oh, this should be good. "Tell me."

"This," he said, waving his arm at the people and din around us. "Being out in the middle of all of it, taking everything in. Being cooped up in the castle really sucks. How am I supposed to know what people want if I never talk to them?"

"But what if they all want different things?"

He smiled. "They usually do. But sometimes, all people really want is for someone to listen to them. Everyone wants to be heard, no matter how big or small. And if you listen, you might end up hearing something that'll help guide you."

"Oh," I heard my father whisper in my ear. "Oh, what a lovely day this is turning into."

"That's what you do," I said, my thoughts jumbled in my head. "You listen."

Dylan nodded. "I try. It's tough, but I'm getting better at it so I can one day be the *best* at it. It's how you learn and grow." Then, "What about you?"

"What *about* me?" I asked, feeling strangely defensive.

"What do you like?"

"Brooms!" Tiggy yelled.

"Murder!" Gary exclaimed. "And also people complimenting my beauty."

"I also like murder," Kevin said. "But only people who deserve it."

"Knights and swords and armor!" Ryan cried.

"Best Friends 5Eva named Sam!" Sam added.

"Stuff," I said lamely. "And things."

"Stuff and things," Dylan said. "That's awesome. I also like stuff and things. It's so cool how much we have in common. Ooh, look! Bread!"

I stumbled as he jerked me toward another stall, this one filled with loaves of crusty bread. I watched as the woman behind the stall went into great detail with him about her business, down to the types of grain she used and the fact that the stone oven she used to bake the bread had been in her family for generations. He listened intently as if she was imparting timeless wisdom, interjecting only to ask about the amount of yeast she used. By the time he finished, the woman's pockets were heavy with coin, and Dylan had a bag filled with rye. He grinned at me, eyes alight as he took my hand—the sash now only a few inches long—and pulled me through the crowd. He glanced back over his shoulder at me, waggling his eyebrows.

He was simple. Even a few days ago, I thought that a fault, especially when that's all he appeared to be. Nice, yes, and more than a little gracious, but simple, which was a polite way of saying he lacked intelligence.

But he wasn't like that at all. Sure, he wasn't the smartest person I'd ever met—not by a long shot—but there was more to him than that. He was like the City of Lockes, in a way: all bluster and noise, overwhelming in the worst ways possible.

But perhaps, I admitted begrudgingly, in the best ways too. I loved my home. I loved the people in it. It was in the way they moved about the city, laughing and dancing and living, always living. Without them, I didn't think we'd have survived all that we had been through. I needed to remind myself of that more than I did. While we had been on the frontlines fighting in the name of Sam of Dragons and my father, we hadn't been the only ones. This was their home. And though things might not have gone back to the way it'd been before, they'd overcome, persevered, and made the most of it.

Maybe there was something to that, after all.

Dylan was happily distracted by almost everything. He'd be in the middle of telling me something, only to cut himself off and rush forward to greet a vendor selling snow globes, or to watch a troupe of actors called Cog and Sprocket performing a scene from The Butler and the Manticore, complete with well-made costumes. He laughed when they did something he found funny, hissed along with the crowd when the villain appeared. Then, of course, he'd see something else that captured his attention, pulling me along. He was a storm, and I was caught in it—in *him*—but for the life of me, I couldn't find reason to want to escape to safety. It wasn't a question of if I'd be dashed against the rocks, everything crumbling around me. He was a storm, yes, but I felt *safe* in his winds, in his lightning, in the way he crashed thunderously, his smile never fading. It was almost as if…as if…

As if I trusted him. As if he'd somehow worked his way past all my defenses and wormed underneath my skin, making a place for himself even though I'd wanted anything but.

Dylan stood in front of yet another vendor, selling what, I didn't know because I was in the middle of panicking. I kept my face carefully blank as I muttered. "Sam. *Sam.*"

Nothing. Maybe they were gone, having left us to it. It's what I wanted, right? But now that I had it, it only made things worse.

And then I remembered. "Sam, *over.*"

"I read you loud and clear, Blue Eagle," Sam said happily. "Over."

Oh, were we going to have so many words when I got back, count on it. I'd never let him hear the end of it. I was about to snarl my displeasure when I remembered I was running toward the one person who I knew could help me make sense of it all, the one person I could count on above all others. And he was only eight years old. The Sam I'd known for years was gone. He was still Sam. Arguably, he was still *my* Sam, but it wasn't the same. Grief, then, grief like a monster crawling its way through my chest, tearing through muscle, cracking my ribs as it closed its claws around my heart, digging in. Ryan. Tiggy. Gary. Kevin, all of them, all the people I had come to count on, all the people who had fought at my side, who'd lifted me up when all seemed lost, this group who made me want to pull my hair out daily.

I needed them, and they were lost to me.

Trying to hold back the worst of it, I choked out, "I don't know what to do."

I heard Dad start to speak, but Sam cut him off. "Of course you do," he said, laughing quietly. "You're Prince Justin. You're brave and smart and awesome and let me sleep in your bed so I don't feel bad. You can do anything."

"I miss you," I whispered, hating the way my voice broke.

"You do?" Sam asked. "That's okay. I miss you too. But when you come back, I'll be here. You don't have to miss me forever because I'm never going to leave you."

I closed my eyes. "Never?" I asked, knowing no one could promise such a thing.

"Never," Sam said.

"I—"

"Brought something for you."

I opened my eyes to see Dylan standing before me, hands behind his back. "What is it?"

He shook his head. "Nope. Not gonna tell you. Just open your mouth."

"Wow," I said flatly. "That doesn't sound like something I'm going to do at all."

He rolled his eyes. "Come on, man. Just trust me, okay? I wouldn't do anything to you that you wouldn't like. I got something for you to eat." He frowned. "You don't have any allergies, right? I know you don't like seafood, but that's okay because neither do I."

"How do you know that?" I demanded.

He shrugged. "Watching you. Whenever seafood is served for dinner, you always have something different."

"Why are you watching me eat?" I asked. It was perturbing, to say the least.

He squinted at me. "So I can learn what you like and don't like."

Okay, maybe not *that* perturbing. Mostly. I thought about telling him now, but he looked so earnest that I couldn't deny him. Knowing I'd probably end up regretting this, I closed my eyes and opened my mouth.

I startled when his thumb brushed my bottom lip, but I didn't pull away. "There," he said quietly, his breath washing over my face. "That wasn't so bad, was it? Thank you."

Before I could reply, he pressed something against my tongue.

A wooden spoon, filled with a sweet and buttery taste. It took me a moment to realize what it was. Corn. Kernels of corn mixed with warm liquid, almost like soup. I chewed briefly, swallowing it down. Not bad. Not the best I'd ever had, but still. Not bad at all.

I opened my eyes. Dylan stood less than a foot away, holding up a cup overflowing with corn. He looked pleased with himself as I licked my lips, chasing the taste. "Pretty good, right?" he asked. He nodded toward the vendor behind him. "Dude says it was a special recipe that he's spent a long time coming up with. Apparently, there used to be a certain type of corn growing in fields north in your country." His brow furrowed. "Said they used to make this particular variety by adding a secret ingredient, but that the person who came up with it was eaten by a dragon? That's pretty gnarly."

I wiped my mouth as the bite I'd taken hit my stomach. I started to tell him that people sometimes were eaten by dragons, especially if they insulted them to their faces when a thought trilled in the back of my mind like a little bird, singing a song I recognized but couldn't quite place.

A feeling of calmness washed over me, and for a moment, it felt like I was floating. "Whoa," I said, looking down at my hands. "That's weird."

"What is?" Dylan asked.

"I don't know," I muttered, gaping as I marveled over the fact that I had *ten whole fingers*. I didn't know why I'd never noticed before. Hands were amazing. The things they could do!

"Justin," a voice said in my ear, sounding urgent. Morgan? I whirled around, expecting to see the wizard standing right behind me. He wasn't. "Justin," he said again.

"Oh, right," I said, laughing loudly. "You're in my ear. Hey, Morgan! I sometimes like you but then I sometimes don't? How strange is that?" I frowned. That's not what I meant to say at all.

"Who's in your ear?" Dylan asked, cocking his head.

"Morgan," I told him. "And Sam and Kevin and Gary and Tiggy and Ryan and my dad and Sam's parents and Randall." I tapped the crystal. "This is a magic crystal that they can hear everything through. I did it because I was nervous about going on a date with you and didn't want to screw this—oh my gods, why am I *saying* this?"

"Justin," Morgan said. "You need to listen to me. The corn. Where did the corn come from?"

"The north," I said, lifting my hand and snapping my fingers open and closed in front of Dylan's face. He arched an eyebrow. "I thought we burned all those fields after Sam and Ryan were dosed with the truth serum that made them admit how much they wanted to fuck each other Why do you ask?"

"Justin?"

"Hi, Dad!" I said, waving at nothing. "I'm glad you're alive because I don't think I'm ready to be king, and also because I love you."

"Oh boy," Dad said. "Justin, you can't eat any more of that corn."

"Why not?" I asked, suddenly feeling like I could do anything. I wanted to find the tallest building in the city and jump off it, sure I could fly. I wanted to take off my clothes and dance in the fountain in the center of the square. "Corn is good for you. Did you know it's considered a vegetable but the kernels are a grain? It can also be popcorn. Isn't that amazing? *I* think it's amazing. Corn is awesome."

"You've been dosed," Dad said grimly. "With truth corn."

I laughed. "What are you talking about? I haven't been dosed with anything. I would know if I was. Sidebar: do you like the sky? I do. Sometimes, I like to lay on my back in the grass and watch the clouds go by."

"I need to speak with Dylan."

"Dylan," I said. "My dad wants to talk to you. You have to put your head against my head so you hear him."

Dylan didn't hesitate. He stepped up into my space, one hand on my hip, the other still holding the cup of corn. He pressed his ear against the crystal, and I heard every breath he took as his cheek scraped against mine, his beard tickling my chin.

"Ohh," I breathed. "This is making me feel things in my groin."

Dylan's eyes bulged. "It's doing *what*?"

"Dylan!" Dad yelled. "Don't eat the corn! Don't let Justin eat anymore, either. It's poisoned!"

Dylan reared back. In one swift movement, he pulled his arm back before flinging the cup of corn as hard as he could. The cup flipped, spilling its contents onto the ground. The mostly empty cup landed on top of a woman's head, causing her to shriek that she was under attack, that she'd *known* her comeuppance for stealing bodies from her brother's funeral business to sell on the black market was going to catch up with her one day, and woe, woe, woe was she!

Dylan cupped his face in my hands, gaze searching. "Are you dying?" he said, cheeks splotchy. "I didn't mean to poison you!"

"I'm not poisoned," I assured him. "I feel great! So great, in fact, that I'm thinking some thoughts better left unsaid, but I'm going to say them anyway." No, no, no, shut up, mouth, shut up! My mouth did not shut up. It said, "Did you ever climb trees when you were a kid?"

"Uh," Dylan said. "Yes? Why do you—"

"I want to do the same to you," I told him. "I wish you were a tree so I could climb you and sit in your branches." I slapped a hand over my mouth before I could make it worse, eyes bulging.

Dylan blinked. "You want to *what*?"

My hand fell away by itself, my body moving independent of what I wanted it to do. I said, "How great is it that I have my library card? Because now I can check you out."

"What," Dylan said.

But I, apparently, wasn't finished. "Was your mother a beaver? Because *damn*."

"Oh my gods," Dad mumbled in my ear as the sounds of children laughing their asses off bowled through my head. "Justin, maybe you should—"

I stepped away from Dylan. He reached for me, but I shook my head. I moved off to the right before walking past him. He tracked my every step. I glanced back at him over my shoulder. "Do you believe in love at first sight? If not, I can walk by again."

"This is the best day of my life," Randall said. "And I've lived many, many days."

"More!" Sam cried. "Do more!"

Dylan stopped me before I could walk by him again. His hands were big. Like, really, *really* big. He leaned forward, and I *knew* I was about to be kissed. I closed my eyes, puckered up my lips….

…and proceeded to kiss his sideburn when he turned his head toward the crystal.

We both froze. Froze, that is, until I pulled one of his hairs from out of my mouth.

Dylan said, "So. That happened."

"Oh my gods," I whispered, hoping this was a nightmare that I'd soon wake up from.

"What happened?" Dad asked.

"Uh," Dylan said, pressing his ear against the crystal. "Justin just...kissed my head."

"Good," Kevin growled. "Good."

"Your hair smells like autumn," I told him, unable to stop. "I want to live there."

"You...want to live in my hair?"

"Yes," I said as I sniffed him again. "It seems like a nice place."

"It's not poison," Morgan said as Sam and Ryan complained in the background that this whole thing was *their* idea, so they should be able to listen in. "Not in the traditional sense. He's not dying."

"Oh thank gods," I said, relieved. "I'd hate to die before I could tap that—*no*. I refuse! I refuse to say that Dylan's ass is fantastic and that I'd leave his hair and make a summer home in said ass. Gods*dammit*!"

"It's a truth serum," Morgan said, sounding like he was struggling not to laugh. "I don't know how it got into the city, but we've dealt with it before. There shouldn't be any long-lasting repercussions, but it'll need time to work its way through his system. It seems as if he's gotten a concentrated dose, so you need to prepare."

"You did this to me," I growled at Dylan. "You're lucky I want to hold your penis in my hand. Otherwise, you'd go to *jail*."

"Whaaaaat is happening," Dylan said.

"He's so cool," Ryan said. "That sounds like something I would say. Whaaaat is happening. See? I sound just like the king!"

"Bring him back to the castle," Dad ordered. "We'll deal with it here."

That was the best idea in a long history of good ideas. So good, in fact, that I knew I should do exactly that.

The problem, however, was I was high on corn and going back to the castle seemed like a travesty of epic proportions. I was out in the city, and I was feeling *fine*. I wanted to wander the city and get lost. I wanted to find a group of people and teach them all a dance that we could perform in a flash mob to celebrate the fact that we were all alive. And I *desperately* wanted to tell Dylan (much to my dismay) that there were at least sixteen things that I could do with my tongue that involved his ass.

I managed to hold that one back. Barely.

"No," I said, even as my brain screamed at me to shut the hell up. "We're not going back to the castle. I'm on a date for the first time in a long time, and I'm going to make the most of it."

"Justin," Dad said. "You need to listen to—"

"Oh no," I gasped, pulling the crystal off my ear and shoving it in my pocket. "How did that happen? Oh well. I guess we'll just have to keep on keepin' on."

Dylan stared at me. "Maybe we should—"

"Chase me!" I yelled, cackling as I tore through the crowd, people jumping out of my way to avoid getting knocked over.

I glanced back over my shoulder, grinning when I saw Dylan running after me.

I laughed until I could barely breathe.

*****

DYLAN WAS FAST, but I was faster. I heard him shouting as I ran through the streets, the sounds of the city blaring around me. People called my name, waving at me as I flew by them. I waved back, feeling lighter than I had in a long time. Why didn't *everyone* eat truth corn? It was the best thing I'd ever had. When I was king, I was going to decree that truth corn was now the national food of Verania, and everyone should partake. The young. The old. All those in between. Everyone should feel like I did now. There'd be no fighting, there'd be no war. No Dark Wizards with evil machinations, hellbent on taking over the kingdom. If everyone was on truth corn, we would all say what was in our hearts. Hands, I decided, should be used for hugging, not for killing. It was so obvious I didn't know why I hadn't realized it before. Everyone had to know.

Which is why I bellowed, "Hugs instead of swords! Hugs instead of swords!"

I waited for those around me to join in on my jovial chant.

One guy did. "Hugs instead of swords?" Yes, it was more of a question than agreement, but I'd take what I could get.

"You got it!" I cried. I stopped, grabbing him by the hand, pumping it up and down. I heard Dylan behind us, grunting as he pushed his way through the crowd, the sash pulling against my wrist.

"I…did?" he asked with a grimace.

"You did," I told him. "Congratulations. You're now my friend. Your name is Dave and I am going to come to your house and live with you."

"Wow," Dave said. "That sounds terrible. And my name is Trevor."

"I bet it is," I said. "Sorry, I gotta go. Bye, Dave!"

I darted down an alley, buildings looming up on either side of me. I planned on passing through the alley and turning right, but before I could, I stepped in something fetid and wet, my feet slipping out from underneath me. I landed face down in a pile of garbage, my nose buried in a rather pungent pile of *something* gritty that coated my face. I licked my lips. Coffee grounds. Yay!

I rolled over on my back, blinking up at the sliver of blue, blue sky I could see above the buildings. The sky was blotted out a moment later when a large shadow loomed above me. I squinted up at it as it cocked its head.

"Hello," I said.

"Oh shoot," the shadow said, sounding remarkably like Dylan. "What did you do?"

"Fell down," I told him. "I like running, but I sure as shit don't like slipping. But I'm good now. Come lay down with me."

"I'm not going to lay down in garbage," Dylan said.

I rolled my eyes. "You're no fun. Actually, you are, but I said that because you make me uncomfortable."

He crouched down beside me. "Bad uncomfortable?

I shook my head, coffee grounds sliding down my cheek. "You make my loins feel like they're on fire and holy *shit*, that was not something I wanted to say out loud."

"Um. Too late?"

I pushed myself up off the ground, causing Dylan to fall back on his ass. He sighed as he shook his head. I glared at him, even though I wanted nothing more than to sit on his face, right here, right now. "You did this to me."

"How was I to know that the corn is drugged? And *why* do people drug corn?"

"It's Verania," I reminded him.

He scrubbed a hand over his face. "That…actually makes a lot of sense."

I reached up and pressed my finger against his nose. "Boop."

"Oh my gods," he muttered, wiping away the grime I'd left on his face. Then, "That's what you all say, right? Oh my gods?"

"I'll make a Veranian out of you yet. Just wait. Pretty soon, you won't even question when we eat vegetables that make us spill our deepest secrets." Then, an idea hit me. It was so obvious I didn't know why I hadn't thought of it before. I leaned forward eyes wide as I dropped my voice to a whisper. "Hey. Hey, Dylan."

"What?"

"You should eat some truth corn too," I told him excitedly. "Then we can *both* tell each other everything." I gasped. "Or. *Or*. And stick with me here because it might get a little complicated. Ready? Okay. What if we—are you listening? Good. What if we did the sex right here, right now."

"The sex," he repeated dubiously.

I nodded. "Have you ever ridden a wild horse while trying to break it in? It's bucking and kicking and squishing your balls so much so that you want to get off?"

"Uh. Yes?"

*"That's what it's like to have the sex."* I frowned. "Hold on. That can't be right. Why would anyone want their balls to be squished?" I shook my head. "Whatever. Look! We even have lube!" I raised my hand, which was covered in a slimy wet substance that if I wasn't high as a kite, I'd probably demand that someone cut off my entire arm just to be safe. "The alley has provided for us. We must not reject its offering lest we suffer its wrath."

Dylan made a sound like he was gagging, a long *hrrrkt* that caused my own stomach to clench. "I'm going to throw up," he managed to get out, face paler than I'd ever seen it.

"No!" I cried. "Because if *you* throw up, then I'll have to…hup. Hup. *Hup*."

And then I vomited corn on the King of Yennbridge.

All in all, not one of my better first dates.

*****

HE MADE ME STOP next to a rain barrel, apologizing to the people whose nostrils flared, their faces twisting in horror at the terrible stench wafting off us. They backed away slowly before turning and running away without so much as a glance back in our direction.

"Bye!" I yelled after them, waving frantically. "I appreciate you!"

"Stand still," he muttered, grabbing a bucket next to the barrel. He filled the bucket with water before turning toward me, looking me up and down. He shook his head. "Sorry about this, bro."

I grinned at him. "Sorry about what?"

He dumped the bucket over my head, the water so cold, I yelped, a sound that I never wanted to make in public. My hair plastered against my head, the water running in rivulets down my face, soaking my clothes. "Great," I told him. "Now I smell bad *and* I'm wet. That was a good plan."

He snorted as he dipped the bucket once again. "Hey. Watch this."

I looked at him.

He turned toward me, eyes glinting with a light I at once found ridiculously erotic and evil in equal measure. Then in slow motion—*how*—he turned the bucket over his own head, letting the water fall onto him. Whereas I looked like a half-drowned lemur, he was anything but. The afternoon sun caught the droplets of water, causing them to glitter as they splashed down onto him. I gaped as he shook his head side to side, his dark hair flipping back and forth, water soaking his clothes, molding them to his powerful frame. I decided right then and there that I would let him stick anything in me, but I somehow kept that thought to myself.

Especially when the bucket slipped from his grasp and fell down on top of his head, covering his face.

I burst out laughing, wrapping my arms around my waist. I bent over as I cackled, struggling to breathe. What a fucking dork. I wiped my eyes as I looked back up in time to see him pulling the bucket off his head. He wasn't laughing. Instead, he was looking at me with something akin to wonder.

"What?" I asked, looking behind me, trying to find what had captured his attention. I turned back around when he cleared his throat. "What happened?

He shrugged as he dropped the bucket on the ground. "I've never heard you laugh like that before."

"I do laugh, you know," I snapped at him.

"I know," he said. "But never like that. And never with me."

I thought the truth corn's grip on me was starting to lessen, because that old familiar irritation started to burn in my chest. "I'm not made of ice, no matter what anyone else thinks."

"You're not," he agreed. "And maybe it's the truth corn—"

"Which you fed me against my will!"

"—or maybe, just maybe, you're actually starting to like me. Just a little. Who knew all it would take was corn?"

I opened my mouth to tell him that I absolutely *did not like him.* But since I wasn't completely free of the corn, I said, "Maybe. Just a little."

He smiled as if amused.

I squinted at him. "Can I tell you something?"

"I don't know, bro," Dylan said. "I think it doesn't matter if I want you to or not."

Good. He was learning. "When you first showed up, I wanted to kill you. Like, really, really kill you. Put my hands around your throat and throttle you until you're dead and then throw your corpse out onto the streets to be picked apart by birds."

"Wow," he said. "That wasn't what I expected you to say at all. Huh."

But now," I continued, "I kind of want to hold your hand and think about what your face tastes like." I groaned. "That came out wrong. Let me try again. Dylan."

He took a dangerous step toward me. "Yes, Justin?"

I licked my lips. They tasted like coffee garbage and bile. "I'm sorry I vomited on you."

Another step. "And?"

I couldn't move. "And I apologize for the running away thing."

"*And?*" His knees bumped against mine, and he was all I could see.

"And," I whispered, running a hand down my chest. "I want to stick my—ugh. Is that…is that a banana peel?" I pulled said banana peel off the front of my shirt. "What the hell?"

Dylan laughed as I dropped the peel to the ground. He took my elbows in his hands and leaned forward. I thought he was going to kiss me. He did, but not in the way I expected. He kissed my forehead, just once, his nose in my hair. He inhaled deeply before backing away, coughing. "You smell terrible."

"And *you* missed my mouth," I told him. "Obviously, none of us are perfect."

"Not like this, bro" he said, and a warm arc of electricity ran down my spine. "When I kiss you, I want it to be because you want me to, not because of what the corn is making you say."

It might have been the most romantic thing anyone has ever said to me. Which, unfortunately, spoke volumes as to the current state of my love life. It certainly didn't help that I could now *smell* me, and it was a travesty of epic proportions. "But it's making me tell the truth," I muttered.

"I know," Dylan said. "Which is how I know you like me now." He grinned razor sharp. "And if you think I'm not going to use that against you, then you sorely underestimated what I'm capable of."

"Oh no," I whispered.

# CHAPTER 14
## Before Working Out, Make Sure You Stretch!

TRUE TO HIS WORD, he became relentless.

In the week following our first date, King Dylan of Yennbridge waged an all-out war on my defenses, taking no prisoners. I thought I could handle it. I thought I could remain cool and aloof no matter what he threw at me.

I was wrong.

It started the next day. I remained shut up in my room, not wanting to face the others after all they'd heard. I needed to find a way to salvage this. My pen raced over the parchment, writing out a decree that anyone who spoke of truth corn would immediately have their tongue removed from their mouth, no questions asked. And that didn't even begin to cover what I planned to do to the vendor who'd sold the corn. He would know suffering by the time I finished with him.

I paused my fiery proclamation when I heard grunting behind me. I turned around and immediately choked, the pen falling to the desk.

Dylan *had* been sitting on the bed behind me, reading *The Butler and the Manticore*. I didn't know where he'd found it, sure that I'd burned all the copies in the castle.

He was still reading, but he was also shirtless and doing one-armed pushups, the book held in his other hand as he lowered himself to the ground before pushing himself back up. The muscles in his arms and back strained, sweat trickling down his tattoos, his earring jangling as he moved up and down, his pelvis hitting the ground before the rest of him.

I stared hard.

"Oh, hey," he said easily as he looked up at me, sticking out his bottom lip and blowing air, flicking a lock of hair off his forehead. "How are you?"

"What are you doing?" I whispered feverishly

"Working out," he said. "And reading. The manticore is about to confess its true feelings for the butler." Without looking away from me, he lowered himself toward the ground once more, the muscles of his ass on display. "Oof, bro," he moaned. "So good. Can really feel it burn all over."

I jerked back toward the desk, almost falling out of my chair. "Bully for you," I said through gritted teeth. I started to get back to work, but the grunts and groans coming from behind me were obscene. I managed to write a few more words before I decided I should *probably* check on him again, just to be safe.

Big mistake.

He'd stood up from the ground and was now facing away from me. He spread his legs out before bending over, one hand flat against the floor, the other still holding the book open. He looked at me between his legs, hair hanging down around his face, the beads in his beard falling against his chin. "Hello, again. You all right? Wanna come stretch with me?"

"Yes, please," I whispered. Then, louder, "I'm *busy*."

He moved his hips side to side. "Of course. My bad, bro." He stood upright again, turning to face me, the slope of his stomach falling over his low-slung trousers. "You know what's cool?"

"What?" I asked, mouth very dry.

"I can do the splits." And then he did just that, still holding the book open as he hit the floor. He bounced once, twice, as he turned another page. "Good book. A little racy, but still good."

I turned back around and screamed into my hands.

*****

THAT WAS ONLY THE BEGINNING.

Dinner, while normally a boisterous affair—especially with five children who got more food on their clothes than in their mouths—turned into an excruciating event. Dylan, in his infinite wisdom—had for some reason decided torture was the correct way to wear me down.

And not physical torture. I could have handled that.

No, this was something far worse.

"Oh wow," Dylan said with delight. "Sausages. Haven't had these in quite a while." I watched in horror as he speared the biggest one before passing the plate along to Randall, who stared at him with barely disguised interest. But Dylan didn't seem to notice, especially when, after making sure I was watching, he managed to stick almost the entire length of the sausage in his mouth, lips wrapped around it. He didn't gag. He didn't choke. Instead, he winked at me before pulling it back out.

"Oh my," Randall said. "That was impressive. Tell me, King. Do you often fellate your food in front of company? Or is this just a special occasion?"

"No," Ramos said, eyeing his king with disdain. "Perhaps King Dylan would like to remember *where we are*."

"I can do it too!" Sam said. "Look! I fellate just like King Dylan." He bit down on the sausage with a mighty chomp, chewing aggressively. "And I don't even know what that means!"

"Oh my gods," Morgan muttered, looking slightly ill. "Perhaps we should—"

"That's not how you do it," Gary said, nosing at his plate until his sausage rested on the edge. He pursed his lips before sucking in a sharp breath. The entire sausage was sucked into his mouth, and he swallowed without chewing. "Like that."

"Uh oh," Kevin breathed. "It's happening again. Hi, penis!" Then he raised his voice until it was high-pitched. "Hi, Kevin! Thanks for noticing me. I was feeling awfully lonely hidden away!"

Tiggy tried to swallow a sausage too. I didn't know if I was relieved or horrified when he started choking. He stood up, punching himself in the stomach. The sausage shot out and bounced off the side of Ramos's head.

I sank low in my seat.

Dad said, "What a terribly fascinating meal."

"Novices," Dimitri scoffed. He fluttered down to the table near the plate stacked with meat. He struggled to lift one, arms wrapped around it as his wings flapped furiously. With all that I'd witnessed in my life, I was strangely comforted by the fact that I could still be horrified in a matter of seconds.

"Sam," Ryan said. "Watch. Watch!" Then Ryan threw a sausage up in the air, opening his mouth. It hit his cheek and bounced before it fell to the floor. He frowned down at it.

"That's okay," Sam said, patting his arm. "You'll learn how to fel—"

"Nope," I said, slamming my hand on the table. "Sam, knock it off. Ryan, don't throw food. Tiggy, nice aim. Gary, stop sucking up sausages. Kevin, put your penis away. Dylan, you need to—*why are you licking your fingers?*"

He pulled his index finger out of his mouth with a wet pop. "Greasy, bro. Gotta make sure I lick it all up." And with that, he stuck his thumb in his mouth, tongue swirling around his knuckle.

I was doomed.

*****

SOMEHOW, IT GOT EVEN WORSE after that.

Dylan decided that after showering, he should only wear a towel for at least an hour. When questioned, he said, "I like to air dry. Good for the skin."

"That's not a thing," I groused as he lay back on my bed, the towel low on his hips. I didn't know what to do with my hands, so I shoved them under my armpits, pinching myself viciously.

"Sure it is," he said, patting his soft belly.

"Then why the hell haven't you done it before?"

He chuckled lazily. "Dude, it's called decorum."

"Dude," I mocked. "You, like, have no idea what you're talking about."

"Oh no!" Dylan exclaimed. "My towel is coming undone all by itself! How weird. Well, not *that* weird. It's Verania, after all."

I turned to flee. Somehow, my feet didn't get the message and I tripped against my desk and fell to the floor. I lay there, blinking up at the ceiling.

"You all right?" Dylan asked from the bed.

My groan went on for years.

*****

AND EVEN WORSE.

"Now, little dudes," Dylan said, standing on the training fields, a line of eager faces staring up at him. "I think it's time you see what a real sword fight looks like." He furrowed his brow. "While fighting should only be a last resort, it's important that you know how to defend yourself and others. And since Justin lost last time, I'm gonna give him a chance to make us even."

"You *cheated*," I growled.

"You hear that?" Dylan asked the kids, cupping his ear. "That's the sound of someone who doesn't know when they've been bested. That's okay! You should be confident in your abilities, even if you're going against someone far more adept."

Oh, he was testing the limits of my patience, so much so that my skin thrummed with it. I'd learned at a young age to never, *ever* go into a fight pissed off, because anger leads to mistakes.

But I was furious, and therefore, couldn't be bothered to listen to reason.

"That's his mad face," I heard Sam whisper as I picked up a discarded wooden sword, one used for practice. It was chipped, but it'd do for what I had planned.

"Is he gonna kill the king?" Ryan asked, sounding worried.

"Probably," Gary said. "But that's okay. Run him through, Justin! Wear his intestines on your head like a godsdamn *crown*."

"No," Tiggy scolded, petting Gary's mane. "Intestines stay inside. Not outside."

"I have intestines!" Kevin exclaimed, laying on his back in the grass, the sun warming his stomach. "They're wrapped around all my hearts. Isn't dragon anatomy interesting?"

"In a moment," I told Dylan coolly, "we begin. I won't go easy. I won't hold back."

Dylan grinned as he flipped his sword up in the air, catching it by the hilt behind his back. Fucking pacifists. "Counting on it, bro. Let's put on a show, huh?"

Without giving him warning, I twisted my wrist in a circle, pulling the length of the sash taut. I jerked it toward me, causing Dylan to stumble forward. He took three hard steps, the muscles in his thighs quivering. I didn't give him a chance to recover. I rushed forward, going low. I fell to the side, right hand digging into the earth as I swept my leg out in a flat arc, wanting to knock him off his feet. It should have worked.

It didn't.

He jumped over my leg, grabbing onto the sash and pulling as hard as he could. The sash tightened around my wrist as I flew upward, crashing into his chest, my sword trapped between us as he trapped me in a bear hug, his face inches from mine.

"No one told me there would be *sexy* sword fighting," Gary said. "Why do people kill each other when they could do this instead?"

Dylan grinned, leaning forward like he was going for a kiss. Dazed and distracted, I didn't notice his true intent until it was almost too late. Instead of kissing me (something I didn't try and stop, what the fuck), he gripped me by the shoulder, pushing and spinning me away, the sash wrapping itself around my body. He came, then, before I could regain my bearings, sword horizontal to the ground. Dylan lashed out, and I barely managed to block it, the impact against my sword causing my arm to vibrate.

He jumped just out of reach, waiting as I spun in a quick circle, unwrapping myself from the sash.

He was strong, that much was clear, stronger than I was. I needed to use that against him. He arched an eyebrow as I stretched my neck side to side. I scoffed. "Do let me know when you've started."

"Oh," he said, lips quirking. "You'll know when I've started, bro. Consider that a warmup."

I was startled into laughter, and his expression softened. "Huh," he said. "I made you laugh. Again. But hey, who's keeping track?"

"Fuck off, *bro*," I snarled. I lunged at him. He raised his sword and parried neatly. But he wasn't as fast as I was, and by the time he'd turned half-way around, I slapped the flat of the wooden blade against his ass, relishing in the way he yelped.

"Started yet?" I asked, breathing heavily but in control.

He turned slowly toward me, and his smile was so dark, it knocked the breath from my chest. "If that's the way it's gonna be." He darted forward, feinting left, but then going right. I didn't fall for it, deflecting the blow from his sword. Without warning, he attacked again, sword up and falling swiftly. I barely managed to raise my own sword in time, the blades sliding along each other, wood shavings falling toward the ground. Not allowing him to recover, I kicked out at his left leg. He grunted as he fell to one knee in front of me.

"That's how you should be at all times," I growled at him.

"On my knees?" he asked, eyes dancing. "All you needed to do was ask, Prince." He lowered his other leg until he was on *both* knees. I raised my sword above my head, meaning to bring it down on top of him. He rolled to the side, the blade hitting the dirt and becoming stuck. I pulled it as hard as I could. It came loose, and I fell backward. Dylan caught me, my back against his front. His breath was hot in my ear when he said, "Oh look. I feel like we've been here before." I shivered when his beard scraped against the side of my neck.

"We have," I said, struggling to keep my voice even. "Which is why you should be ready for my dag—"

He shoved me away, sword slapping against the back of my left hand, causing the dagger I'd pulled out to fall to the ground.

"And that, little dudes," he told the kids, "is why you should *never* be so cocky that you—"

He never got to finish as I tackled him. I wasn't proud of it, but he left me little choice. We hit the ground roughly, legs becoming tangled as we rolled along the grass. I came to a stop on my back, a dandelion pressed against my ear. I panted as Dylan lay on top of me, sweat dripping off the tip of his nose onto my cheek. He grinned down at me, and I—

"Now *kiss*," Gary hissed.

"Hey," Dylan said easily. "How are you? I'm good, if you were wondering."

"Get off me!"

"Make me," he said, earrings dangling down toward my face.

His eyes bulged comically when I kneed him in the nuts. Wheezing, he rolled off me, pulling his legs up to his chest as he rocked back and forth. "Not...*cool*," he choked out. "I *use* those, bro!"

"Not tonight you don't," I said, pushing myself up. I bowed in front of the kids. They clapped politely. "And that is how you win a sword fight."

"By fighting dirty," Sam said. "Got it."

I blinked. "What? No, that's not—*oof.*"

Apparently, it was Dylan's turn to tackle. He hit me like a godsdamn brick wall, but before we crashed once again into the ground, he twisted *both* of us, so this time, I landed on top. His strong arms wrapped around me, holding me in place.

It was only then I realized he wasn't angry. He wasn't seeking revenge. If anything, it looked like he was having the time of his life, laughing as if he didn't have a care in the world.

"So serious," he whispered. "You're okay, Justin. I promise. I wouldn't do anything to hurt you."

And strangely, I believed him.

"*Now* kiss," Gary said.

*****

WHEN ONE IS BOUND TO ANOTHER via a magical sash, one has to make the most of it to keep from going insane. Granted, this wasn't a problem that many people would have to face, but since I did, it was time to change tactics, especially since the person I was bound to had decided to change the rules of the game. I *never* meant to get used to him being there every night and every morning, much less give a damn about him. Unfortunately, he'd somehow charmed his way past my defenses, and that wouldn't do. Dylan wanted to play with fire? Fine. He would have no one to blame but himself when he got burned.

We had one week left. I was the godsdamn Prince of Verania. And I was going to war.

*****

I STARTED SLOWLY, not wanting to spook him by coming on too strong. I touched him more in one day than I had since I'd met him. Little things, my hand on his arm when he was talking to me, squeezing his shoulder as he sat on my bed, reading yet another book. He looked surprised at these tiny moments, but he covered it up quickly. Once, I sat next to him on the edge of my bed, leaning close, my chin on his shoulder. His chest hitched, and I hid my smile.

My hand brushed his as we walked through the castle, my pinkie finger hooking with his for only a second or two before falling away.

"Dylan?" I asked at breakfast, the kids around us laughing loudly.

He looked over at me, a quiet smile on his face.

"Can you pass me the—oh, never mind. I can get it." I stood from my chair, reaching over him to a plate of fruit on the table to his right that I had no intention of eating, given the amount of disgusting pineapple piled high. "Oh no," I exclaimed as I lost my footing, landing in his lap. "I'm so *sorry*. I slipped. I'm such a klutz."

He grunted as I shifted my hips, his hands going to my waist. "You need to be more careful, bro," he said seriously.

I laughed obnoxiously. "Oh, you're so *funny*." I trailed my fingers down his arms. "But I must say, this seat is much more comfortable than mine. I think I'll stay right here, if it's all right with you. You don't mind, do you?"

"Uh. No?"

"Good," I said sweetly. "Hold on. I need to get more comfortable." I wiggled around, causing him to gasp. "Are you all right?"

"Fine," he said through gritted teeth.

"I'm eating here," Randall muttered.

"We all are," Dad said as he plucked the fork from Gary's mouth to keep him from stabbing Ryan in the back of the neck. He glanced over at me with narrowed eyes. He knew what I was doing. I stared back, daring him to try and call me out. "Perhaps our guest would like to not have someone sitting on their lap for the duration of a meal."

I hooked my arm around Dylan's neck. "He's fine. Right, Dylan?"

Dylan swallowed thickly as I plucked a grape from the plate, popping it into my mouth and groaning. I bit down hard, juice squirting onto Dylan's cheek. I reached up and wiped it away slowly before sliding my finger into my mouth and sucking, cheeks hallowing.

"Whoa," he breathed. "Bro, that was... I don't know what that was."

"A travesty of epic proportions?" Randall offered.

But Dylan only had eyes for me.

\*\*\*\*\*

"It's the gym," I told Dylan as I led him toward the lower levels of the castle. "The knights use it to work out. I haven't been going as much I as normally do." I flashed him a smile. "I've had someone to distract me."

He nodded furiously. "Right, right. Hey, question."

"Yes?"

"Do you...ah. Is that what you normally wear when you work out?"

I looked down at the boots on my feet, rising up to my shins, and the old pair of trousers that didn't quite fit as well as they'd used to, from a time when I was skinnier than I was now. I'd cut off most of the length of the legs of the trousers until the bottoms only reached mid-thigh. The strings that tied the seam together couldn't quite close all the way. The top of my ass was on full display, something I'd grinned at in the mirror while Dylan was in the bathroom.

And that was all I had on. It was obscene, and I didn't give two shits about it.

"Oh, this old thing?" I asked, turning in a slow circle, stepping over the length of sash between us, stretching my leg as far as it would go, trying to keep from wincing as the trousers pulled against my balls. "Of course. What else would I wear?"

Dylan cleared his throat. "Something a little less...I don't know. Revealing?"

I blinked at him, hand going to my chest. "Do you not like it?"

"No, no," he said hastily. "It's...ah. Just the bee's knees. I don't want you to get cold."

"Oh, don't worry about that," I purred. "I like to let my nipples breathe." Turning away, I mouthed *nipples breathe?* What the fuck was I *saying*? Gods, I needed to be careful with this. It didn't help that three of our waitstaff had walked into walls at the sight of me walking through the castle and violating at least three decency laws.

We reached the gym, the sounds of the knights loud through the door. Taking a deep breath, I pushed the door open and walked in as if I didn't have a care in the world.

The conversation immediately died a fiery death as everyone turned to look at me, jaws dropped, eyes bulging.

I ignored them, leading Dylan into the gym. I smiled at a pair of knights with large dumbbells in their hands. The knight on the left dropped his weight on his foot, causing him to yelp and jump around in a circle. I struggled to keep from laughing, not wanting to break form.

"It's nice, isn't it?" I asked Dylan. "Only the best for the knights of Verania. Now, as you so graciously reminded me a few days ago, we need to stretch to make sure we don't hurt ourselves. I'm not as limber as I'd like to be, so maybe you could help me?"

He wiped the sweat from his brow. "Sure, sure. I got you. What did you have in mind?"

I clapped before I grabbed him by the arm and led him toward the middle of the room. "Here's what we'll do. I'll lay on the ground on my back, and you can help stretch out my legs. Is that something you're comfortable with?" I frowned. "It'll mean getting really, really close, and I don't want to make you do anything you don't want."

He nodded furiously. "I can do that. I can do that so good. Yeah, back in Yennbridge, I help everyone stretch. I might even be the best at it."

"Oh, wonderful," I said with a sigh as I lowered myself to the ground on top of a sparring mat, never looking away from him. "So long as I'm in good hands, I'd be forever grateful." He towered over me, breathing harder than he'd been only a moment before. I lay on my back, raising my arms above my head. "Oof, I'm so tight. I hope you're ready for that. You need to go slow, okay?"

"Oh my gods," one of the knights muttered. "I normally have to pay to see things like this."

"Shut *up*," another knight snarled. "They'll hear you and stop! I need this. I *need this*."

"But you're straight!"

"I know! I'm just as confused as you are. I always heard sexuality was fluid, but I didn't know it was *this* fluid."

"Maybe I could help you with that," Dylan said gruffly.

"Would you?" I asked. "That's so nice of you. Okay, so you come down here with me. We'll start with my legs." I raised my right leg toward my chest, the hemmed trousers filling in places in my body I didn't know existed. "Press it against me as hard as you can. Don't stop until I tell you. Make me feel it."

A poor knight wheezed, squeezing his water bottle so tight, it sprayed up into his face.

Dylan practically collapsed on top of me, catching himself with his hands on either side of me, his chest pressed against my raised shin. I chuckled and squirmed as he gripped my leg. "Sorry," I said, sucking my bottom lip between my teeth before letting go. "I'm a little ticklish."

"Do we throw money at them?" a knight asked. "Because I really feel like we should throw money at them."

"Prince Justin!" another knight yelled. "If the king can't do it, I volunteer! I volunteer so hard."

"No!" his friend shouted. "Pick me! I'm literally the best at stretching! Everyone says so."

The other knight scoffed. "Bullshit. You're *literally* incapable of speaking correctly, much less stretching out a twink."

"I'll do it," Dylan said, mouth in a thin line as he glared at the knights.

Oh, he was too easy. I was going to enjoy this.

I groaned loudly when Dylan pushed against my leg, the muscles in my thigh burning pleasantly. "That's it," I said, rolling my head side to side. "Yes. Yes! Oh my gods, push harder. *Harder.*"

Dylan did just that, grunting as his face rose above mine, a lock of his hair hanging between us. "That feel good?"

"So good," I moaned, gripping the mat so hard, my knuckles turned white. "I can feel it all over. Wait, here. Let me help you." I moved one of his hands to my ankle, the other to the back of my thigh. His hands dug in, gooseflesh sprouting along my arms. "There. That's better. Now push."

He did. I was almost swallowing my own kneecap as my ass lifted off the floor.

The knights were no longer working out, more interested in the show happening right in front of them. For a moment, I worried that I'd gone too far, but Dylan's pupils were blown out, his eyes almost completely black, and any doubt I might have had washed away as if it'd never been there at all.

He moved on to the other leg, pushing it against my chest. "Oooh," I said. "I feel that one. You're really good at this." I tweaked his chin, tugging on the beads in his beard. "I'm so lucky you're here."

He stayed on top of me far longer than was necessary, pressing my leg against my chest. "Dylan?" I asked.

"Yeah?"

"I think that's good. Thank you. Shall we move on? I have an idea for what we should do next to make sure I'm *really* limber."

"Yes," a knight whispered aggressively. "That. Do that."

I pushed Dylan off me, rising to my feet. I turned away from him. "Let's work on my back. Here. You come up right behind me, okay?" I bent over, keeping my legs as straight as possible as I put my hands flat to the ground. I bounced my ass, once, twice, before looking at Dylan between my legs. "Come on! Don't be shy."

He almost knocked me over with how fast he moved, his hips bumping into my rear. "What...what do you want me to do?"

"Get a good grip on me," I said, blood rushing to my face. It wasn't the most comfortable position, but I was too far into it to stop now. "One hand on my hip, the other flat against my back."

He did as instructed, leaning over me, careful to keep most of his weight off me. He pressed down on my back, and I said, "Holy shit. I'm gonna feel *that* tomorrow. I don't know if I'll be able to walk straight by the time you're done with me."

Dylan fell down next to me.

I looked over at him, hands still flat against the mat. "Oops. You slipped. But that's okay. It's your turn, isn't it?" I moved quickly, stepping over him, my feet on either side of his chest. I sank down, my ass a few inches above him, my crotch almost in his face. I hovered there for a moment before falling back on my hands, crab-walking away from him, stopping at his feet.

"I've been working out wrong my entire life," a knight muttered.

"Here," I said, grabbing Dylan's leg. "Let me help you. After all, what are friends for?" I pushed his leg up against his chest. Unfortunately, I then became distracted by how thick his thighs were underneath his trousers.

"Wait!" Dylan cried, and I froze, thinking I'd taken this too far. I was about to ask what was wrong, but Dylan sat up, and in one fluid movement, lifted his thin shirt up and over his head, tossing it to the side. He arched an eyebrow as he lay back down on the mat, his many tattoos bright in the sunlight streaming in through the windows. "There," he said smugly. "That's better. Wouldn't want it to get dirty. Go on, bro. Let's see what you've got."

Uh oh. I was in trouble.

"Question," a knight asked. "Are we going to have an orgy? Because I thought Ryan said we couldn't do that in the gym anymore. He didn't like how sticky the equipment got."

"He's not here," another knight reminded him. "If you don't tell him, I won't."

That...wasn't part of my plan. At all. I raised my head to snap at them, but then Dylan put his hands on top of mine, pulling his leg back against his chest, and any and all rational thought disappeared from my brain. It hit me, then, that I was dressed like one of Mama's boys while laying on top of the King of Yennbridge, surrounded by a group of horny knights, all in the name of trying to prove said king didn't know who he was messing with.

I might have made a mistake.

Especially when Dylan said, "Wow, bro. You're really working my hamstring. I can feel it all the way down to my glutes." Never in my life had being called *bro* been so terribly erotic, and I wondered at my moral and mental deficiencies. I, as it turned out, was *not* a good person, and even though my plan was backfiring spectacularly, I couldn't bring myself to stop.

"Yeah?" I muttered. "You feel it in your glutes?"

"Like you wouldn't believe," Dylan panted. "You're stretching me out, bro. I'm going to be so loose by the time you're done."

"Oh my *gods*," one of the knights breathed. "I love going to the gym."

Dylan made me switch to his other leg, and it was about this time I realized I was covered in sweat, even though I hadn't done much. My hand slipped on his leg, and I started to fall forward. Fortunately, my reflexes kicked in. Unfortunately, that meant I stopped myself from collapsing on top of him by grabbing his junk.

His not inconsiderable junk. Someone seemed to be enjoying himself.

I jerked my hand up as if scalded. "All done!" I said hysterically as I jumped up. "Great! That went well. Hurray. Now we're done."

Dylan grinned at me as he rose from the mat, cocking his head like an evil golden retriever. "What? We're not done. We're just getting started."

That's what I was afraid of.

The next hour was a test in patience, one I failed spectacularly. Dylan made it his mission to stand as close to me as possible, apparently having no concept of personal space. This was supposed to be *my* game, but he was turning the tables on me quite easily.

He stood behind me as I lifted dumbbells, his hands on my arms, his breath in my ear as he counted off.

He stood in *front* of me as I did pullups, my groin rising to his face and falling, rising to his face and falling.

Not to be outdone, I decided that sitting on his back while he did pushups was the proper course of action. It took only seconds to realize that wasn't probably the best move, especially when my weight didn't seem to hold him back at all as he pushed himself up off the ground at least two dozen times. I tried to keep count, but I kept getting distracted by the way his skin shifted over the muscles in his back.

Our audience didn't leave. If anything, it grew, more knights coming into the gym as if they didn't have anything better to do. I saw money changing hands, and I really didn't want to know what the hell they were betting on.

And then Dylan seemed to think it was time to cool down, which meant dragging a towel across his chest and down his stomach for at least nine minutes (though, time didn't seem to be working as it normally did, so it might have been six seconds or twenty hours). When he'd finished this extremely unnecessary display, he flipped the towel around his neck, holding onto the ends, his biceps bunching up. He looked around, smiled at the knights in various stages of arousal, and said, "Hey, thanks, guys. Exactly what I needed. Justin, you limber enough or do I need to give you a private lesson?" And with that, he walked toward the doors, whistling a jaunty tune.

It took me longer than I cared to admit to remember I had to go *with* him, seeing as how the sash still bound us together. Cursing, I stalked after him, wondering how the hell I'd gotten this so wrong and *why*, exactly, I wanted to ruin him for anyone else.

\*\*\*\*\*

THAT NIGHT, I TOSSED AND TURNED, unable to fall asleep. My mind was exhausted, but the rest of my body didn't seem to get the message. I was conscious of every breath Dylan took in ways I hadn't been before. Every inhale, every exhale was like a whispered song in my ears.

"Stop kicking me," Sam mumbled sleepily. He rolled away from me, his cold feet pressed against my shins. I touched the back of his head, and he murmured quietly before falling back to sleep. This was the fourth night in a row without any nightmares waking him and I hoped that meant he'd moved beyond them. Five days. In five days, things would go back to normal. Or, at least, as normal as things were in Verania.

What that meant for my future, I had no idea. I never expected to be this far into the binding ritual and not know what I wanted when it was over. Dylan wasn't…he wasn't as he first appeared, a douchey frat bro who upended everything I thought I knew. I'd made the mistake of underestimating him, and that was on me.

And if I was being honest with myself, the idea of the ritual ending and us parting ways wasn't sitting right. Somehow, someway, I had gotten used to his constant presence, and while I'd enjoy having a moment to myself, I didn't know how long it'd last. What would happen if he left?

Or—and somehow scarier—what would happen if he stayed?

I rolled over away from Sam, looking down at Ryan, laying spread-eagled, mouth open as he snored quietly next to Dylan. I raised my gaze to the king, only to find his eyes open and watching me.

"Hi," I whispered, embarrassed at being caught.

He didn't speak. Instead, he reached up and touched my fingers hanging off the side of the bed. I closed my eyes, his touch gentle and kind.

"I know what you were doing," he said, voice low.

I couldn't look at him. "Oh? At least one of us does."

"Can I tell you something?"

I nodded.

"I didn't want to come here."

I opened my eyes and breathed and breathed.

"I didn't want to come here," he said again. "I didn't want to leave my home behind. I didn't want to try and woo a prince I'd never met in a kingdom I'd never been to."

"But you said…" I started weakly. "Your parents. You said you wanted what they had."

"I did," he said. "I do. More than you know. But I told Ramos that it wasn't fair to me. Or to you," he added quickly, in case he thought I'd argue. It hadn't even crossed my mind. "But he said that the pact was in place, and that I had to do my duty for my country. It would be for the greater good. My people would prosper."

I swallowed past the lump in my throat. "I'm sorry."

"I'm not done," he said, though there was no censure in his voice. "Let me finish. You talk and talk, but now it's my turn. Please."

I squeezed his hand, letting him know I was listening.

"I didn't want this," he said. "It worked for my parents, but that didn't mean it'd work for me. I was a...disappointment, to them. I heard more than once that my head was always stuck in the clouds, and that a king needed his feet firmly planted on the ground. I didn't know how to tell them that I was doing as best I could. I'm not the smartest. I'm not the bravest. I'm just...me. And I didn't know how to be anyone else but who I was."

Anger then, quick and biting at people I'd never met, people I'd *never* meet because they'd passed beyond the veil. I tamped down on it as best I could. He didn't need me talking shit about his dead parents. That was low, even for me.

"I tried," he said. "I really did. I tried to be who they wanted me to be, but I know I wasn't good enough. You want to know what I realized?"

"What?"

"That was on them," he said, and I marveled at how it was a statement of fact, not something said in resentment. I didn't know if I would be as magnanimous. "They loved me, and I loved them. Of course I did; they were my parents. And maybe they were right when they said they were worried about leaving Yennbridge in my hands."

"No," I said. "No. Never that."

He smiled softly. "Thanks, bro. But I figured that out for myself. I knew the type of leader I'd be. I wouldn't be my father. I wouldn't be my mother. I'd forge my own path, and even if I had to walk it alone, I knew I'd do so with a clear conscience. No one can prepare you to wear a crown. They think they can, and they'll try their hardest to teach you everything they know, but the moment you become king, everything changes."

"I'm scared of that," I admitted. "I don't..." I shook my head, gripping his hand like he was the only thing that would save me from drowning. "I don't know if I'll be good enough."

"I didn't think you were either. No offense."

"Please tell me there's a but after that," I muttered. I tried to pull my hand back, but he wouldn't let me go.

"There is," he said. "A big one. Because now that I've gotten to know you, I know you'll be the best king Verania has ever seen. And

I'm not the only one who thinks so." He nodded toward Ryan. "Faith, Justin. It all comes down to faith. You may not have it in yourself, but you have people who more than make up for that. Ryan. Gary. Tiggy. Kevin. Your father. Morgan and Randall, though I know you have your issues with them. And Sam. Your wizard. Why do you think when he's scared and confused, you're the one he seeks out? It's because he has faith in you. Not just as his friend. Not just as his brother. As his king. He fought for his country. He fought for your father. He fought for his friends and family. And you, bro. He fought for you because he had so much faith in the man you are that he couldn't stop."

My eyes stung, and I desperately wished my Sam was here so I could hold on to him and never let him go. It was funny, really, in a sad way: I didn't appreciate what I'd had before it'd been taken from me. Oh, he was still here, feet pressed against the back of my legs, but it wasn't the same.

"And that," Dylan said, "is how I knew that you were more than you made yourself out to be. Prickly, maybe a little mean, but the people you've gathered around you aren't here because you forced them to be. They're with you because they choose to be. And if you could garner that type of faith, then you will be the king your country deserves." He chuckled, a low rumble that crawled lazily from his throat. "And that helped me to understand you, and all that you are."

"I don't deserve them," I mumbled.

"You do," he said. "More than you know. We're not like them. We're not Ryan and Sam. I told you once that we're not bound by fate, or have a destiny written in the stars. But that—"

"But that doesn't always have to be important," I finished for him, the memory of his words like a shooting star. "We could try this because we choose to, and that's all you could ever want."

"It is," he agreed. "And I want to try. With you. I don't know what's going to happen when this is over. I don't know what we'll do. But I do know one thing."

"What?"

"I like you," he said simply.

Three words, and I thought I'd never heard anything so humbling, so profound. I took them in, holding them close. They warmed me, calming the storm in my head. How it could be so easy for him, I didn't know. But if he could be this brave in the face of the unknown, then I had to do the same.

"I like you too," I whispered. A weight I hadn't even known was crushing me lifted off my chest. And in its departure came relief, bright and warm.

He laughed. "Oh, I know. The whole gym thing kind of gave that away. Nice try, though."

I groaned. "That wasn't one of my better ideas."

"Nah," he said. "I think it was one of your best, but I'm probably a little biased."

"What do we do now?"

He was quiet for a long moment, and I thought he'd fallen back asleep. I looked down at him again to see him rubbing his chin thoughtfully. "Now? We take it one day at a time. That's all anyone can ask for. But I'm in this, Justin. I'm in this all the way. And I hope you are too. I think we could be something amazing." He seemed to grow nervous, eyes darting to my face then away. "Only if you want to, though. I can…I'll respect whatever decision you make. I probably won't like it, but I've dealt with disappointment before. I'm happy with myself for the first time in a long time. And even though I know I'd be happier with you, I'll make sure that Ramos knows you did nothing wrong. You deserve all the joy in the world."

I stood at a precipice. Before me, the great unknown. Behind me, shelter and safety. I could back away. It would be so very easy. Faith, like living, was complicated. We hid ourselves away, afraid of taking chances because we'd been hurt before. But here he was, laying all his cards on the table and hoping for the best. I didn't know how or why he'd seen past all of my defenses to the heart of me. I could count on one hand the number of people I had like that in my life.

What if I had one more?

And so I jumped into the unknown and fell, the wind rushing past my face. I'd never felt so free in my life.

"We're going to have to figure out how to run two kingdoms," I said. "I think we'll have to divide our time between Yennbridge and Verania." The more I spoke, the more confident I sounded. "We might even be able to convince Randall to allow us to use Castle Freesias as a base of operations, since it's closer to Yennbridge than Castle Lockes. It's a lot of snow and ice, but I'm sure we'll get used to it." He sat up slowly, gaze intense, but I couldn't stop talking, no matter how hard I tried. "I know Yennbridge has its customs, but you're king, right? We don't have to get married right away. We can take our time until we're ready, and this will grow and grow until it's a fire like we haven't seen—"

He kissed me.

He kissed me, and I gasped into his mouth. He took that as an invitation, tongue sliding against mine, his hand coming up to cup the back of my head, holding me in place. I tried to deepen the kiss, frantic that I was dreaming, but he gentled it slowly, moving on to kiss my cheeks, my forehead, my eyelids. I breathed him in, lost in my freefall.

"Yaaay," I heard a voice whisper, and we broke apart to see Tiggy watching us, Gary snoring against his chest. "Good job," Tiggy said, smacking his lips. He closed his eyes and breathed slowly.

"I'm going to make you so happy," Dylan whispered to me, brushing my hair off my forehead. "No matter what we do, no matter where we go, you're never going to know one day more without me by your side."

And because I was still me, I said, "That sounds annoying."

He laughed. "Heck yeah, it does. I can't wait."

That night, we fell asleep, his hand holding onto mine.

# CHAPTER 15
## Too Good to be True

I WANTED TO KEEP IT SECRET, this new thing between us. Not because I was embarrassed that I'd been proven wrong quite spectacularly, or because I didn't want people to know that Dylan made my heart flutter in my chest. No, I wanted to keep it quiet because I knew that I'd never hear the end of it once word got out. I knew it'd spread through the City of Lockes like a wave of fire, anyone and everyone having an opinion whether asked for one or not. That was one of the many problems with being royalty: everything I did was in the spotlight, and people would be watching me closely, knowing that my future also belonged to them. Once it was out in the open, there'd be no taking it back. I worried it would put pressure on us we weren't ready for.

With four days left until the ritual was over, I thought I could use the time to work out the logistics of what Dylan and I had started under the cover of darkness. I opened my eyes the next morning, stretching languorously, my back popping, my jaw cracking as I yawned. I turned my head to the left, expecting to see Sam snoring and drooling on my pillow. He was gone. I blinked slowly and rolled over to look off the side of the bed. The blankets where Dylan and Ryan had slept were folded, the pillows sitting on top.

I sat up and frowned. Where the hell did everyone go? At the very least, I'd expected Sam and Ryan to have woken me up by now, demanding that we do *this* or go *there*. Kevin wasn't hanging from the ceiling. Tiggy and Gary weren't cuddled up against the wall. The light from the morning sun filtered in through the window. It was still early, which made the absence of my friends all that more concerning.

I was about to get up from the bed when I heard voices from the other side of the door, muffled but...angry? Whoever was on the other side sounded like they were in the middle of an argument.

I rose from my bed, knees popping as I headed for the door, following the sash. I paused with my hand on the doorknob, the voices louder. I pressed my ear against the door.

"—and I have *rights*," a voice was saying angrily. "He is *my* prince, and I demand to have an audience with him."

"Of course," Dylan said, sounding confused. "I'd never want to keep you from Justin, bro. He's, like, so rad."

I sighed as I shook my head.

"But it's early," Dylan continued. "I don't think he's awake yet. Maybe give him a few minutes? I can let him know you stopped by. Maybe you can meet with him later, huh? No one likes meetings first thing in the morning."

I jerked open the door, causing two pairs of eyes to fall on me as I stepped out into the hall.

Dylan grinned at me. He held a tray of breakfast foods: eggs and sausages piled high on a plate next to a carafe of pungent coffee. At the edge of the tray sat a vase with golden flowers sticking out of it. The blooms were familiar, looking as if they'd been plucked from Rosemary's garden.

"Sam and Ryan made it," Dylan said proudly at my unasked question. "With some help from the others. Didn't want to wake you so I could keep it a surprise." He glanced down at the tray. "I think I got most of the eggshells out of it, so it should be somewhat edible. If the sausages are crunchy, don't ask why. It's probably better you don't know."

"Kevin burned them, didn't he?"

Dylan winced. "He's way into being vegetarian. Did you know that a small dragon can make you feel guilty for eating meat? Because *I* didn't know that."

I chuckled, stepping aside to let Dylan into the room. He apparently decided that I needed to be kissed on the cheek as he passed by. I allowed it, even as my face warmed, his beard scraping against my chin. "Morning," he said quietly.

Before I could reply, another voice said, "My Prince, a word, if I may."

I looked back out into the hall. A man stood there, and it took me a moment to place him. One of my father's advisors, the man who'd taken offense when Ramos had called Verania a red-headed stepchild. I groaned inwardly, not wanting to discuss whatever was on his mind. It was far too early, and I was still rubbing the sleep from my eyes. But since he was one of my father's advisors, that meant he'd one day be mine too. I couldn't ignore him, even though the pull of Dylan in my room alone was growing stronger by the second.

"What is it?" I asked.

The man glanced over my shoulder into the bedroom before lowering his voice. "In private, Prince. I have news that cannot wait."

"What news?" I asked. A thought struck me. "Is it my father? Is he—"

"He's fine," the man said quickly. For the life of me, I couldn't remember his name, which felt like a shitty thing. He'd been with my father for years. It took me a moment to remember what he even did. He was in charge of the day-to-day infrastructure of the City of Lockes, making sure the potholes in the streets were filled, the garbage pickup running smoothly.

"Then what do you need?" I asked.

He took a step back. "To tell you what I have to say without anyone listening in." He looked pointedly behind me.

I sighed as I leaned back into my room. "I'll be a minute," I told Dylan as he set the tray down on my desk.

"Cool," Dylan said. "That'll give me time to scrape off the sausage. I think there might be some parts that aren't charred."

Shaking my head, I closed the door, the sash sliding through the crack with ease. The advisor looked nervous as he stopped next to an open window near my room that looked out onto the city. I joined him, the sash tugging pleasantly against my wrist. Smoke curled from chimneys, Lockes beginning to wake for yet another day. I inhaled deeply, knowing today was going to be the first day of the rest of my life. Soon, Sam and the others would return to normal, and once the ritual was completed, Dylan and I would be free to make our own choices. I couldn't wait to see what we did.

But first.

"What is it?" I asked, trying to keep my voice even. I wanted to be in the room with Dylan, but my father's voice whispered in my ear, reminding me that being a king meant listening to those who needed me. "Is something wrong?"

The man hesitated before shaking his head. "I don't know. But I figure it's better to be safe than sorry."

I frowned. "Out with it. I don't have all day."

"You know me," the man said. "I wouldn't be here if I didn't think it was important."

"Right," I said, squinting at him. "I know you. You're…"

The man threw up his hands. "Keith. My name is *Keith*."

"I knew that," I said. I hadn't known that. "Of course you're Keith. Who else would you be? You're so…you."

"Thank you," Keith said, wiping the sweat from his brow. "That might be the nicest thing you've ever said to me."

Yikes. But since I was a new man, I went for magnanimity. "And I meant every word."

"I know you did," Keith said. "You're the most wonderful prince Verania has ever seen. You're kind and gracious and when you speak your subjects hang on your every word, as they should."

"Thank… you?"

"I wouldn't be here if it wasn't important," he said again. "I know there are protocols in place, a chain of command, but I fear that chain has become corrupted."

That caught my attention. "How so?"

"Ramos," Keith breathed. "He's not who you think he is."

A chill ran down my spine. I hadn't seen Ramos since he'd stood with Dylan before our date. When I'd asked later why Ramos had seemed so perturbed, Dylan had waved me off, telling me that was how Ramos usually was. "And who is he?"

"A snake," Keith said. "Hidden in the tall grass, waiting to strike. I…I don't have any proof, but I know something's wrong."

"In what way?"

He shook his head. "You know what I speak of. Think about it, my Prince. They come here, claiming your father signed a pact agreeing to give you away to the first born of Yennbridge."

I narrowed my eyes. "He didn't agree to *give me away*. I'm not going anywhere, no matter what's decided."

"Yes, yes," Keith said hastily. "Of course. You're so wise, so knowing. But doesn't it strike you as strange that your father doesn't remember signing his name to such a serious document? And that doesn't even begin to cover how Morgan didn't know about it. What if there's more to it than we've been told?"

"Spit it out," I said irritably. "You're trying my patience."

Keith leaned forward, dropping his voice until it was barely a whisper. "What if your father was magicked into it? What if the reason he can't remember is because he was *forced* to forget?"

I paused, mulling his words over. "By whom? Dylan was barely older than I was when this occurred. And Ramos wasn't the Yennbridge magician at that time."

"Or so he says," Keith whispered. "What if that's all a lie? What if he's been behind the scenes this entire time, pulling the strings until his puppets danced the way he wanted them to? Think of it, Prince Justin. Ramos admitted that he'd tried to become a wizard, only to be refused by Randall. So he leaves Verania and goes north, becoming the magician of Yennbridge. And then he returns here, now an advisor to the king. It's all part of his master plan."

"For *what*?"

"To take over Verania!" Keith exclaimed. "And *yes*, I don't have tangible proof of this, but come on! Think, my Prince. If he's addled the king's mind, erased his memories—or worse, planted *new* ones— we'd have no choice but to believe him. And now he's here, ready to enact his devious machinations, to destroy all that we've worked so hard toward."

"The pact was written on the skin of a sphinx," I reminded him. "There's no way to forge such a thing."

Keith rolled his eyes. "Did you know that before it was mentioned? Because *I* didn't know that."

He had a point, as much as I hated to admit it. "It's magic," I said. "It's not supposed to make sense. Trust me, I've lived with it long enough to realize that. It's better to just smile and nod."

"You've thought about it," Keith said. "I know you have. Anyone with half a brain would realize that something's off about this entire mess. And don't even get me started on how it turned your wizard into a child. That doesn't—"

I slapped my hand over his mouth. His eyes widened. "Who told you that?" I hissed.

He reached up and took my hand in his, squeezing gently until I dropped it. "I'm not stupid, Prince. Sam and Ryan are sent on a secret mission along with Gary and Kevin and Tiggy, and then out of the blue, there's suddenly a small unicorn and dragon? An extremely tall and wide boy? Two children who hang off you wherever you go? It's obvious. I don't know why no one else can see it."

I thought about telling him he was wrong, that he was seeing things that weren't there. But he didn't appear to be an unintelligent man, and his words had begun to worm their way into my head. "Have you told anyone else?"

He shook his head. "Regardless of what others think, I know how to keep a secret. I wouldn't have the position I do if I couldn't."

"Good," I said. "Make sure you keep it that way." I paused, mulling it over. "Why come to me with this? Why not Morgan or Randall? Or even my father?"

"Because I know you," Keith said. "I saw your bravery after the fall of Verania. I stood with you at the Port. I know you're the king this country needs. Which is why I hope you'll hear me. My loyalty lies with Verania, and you. I only want to keep you safe. If Ramos is the puppet master, that means King Dylan is one of his puppets. Either Ramos has warped his mind into doing his bidding, or King Dylan is in on it."

I blinked. "What?"

"Think, Prince Justin," Keith said. "Think as hard as you ever have in your life. We're not like them. We're not magic. We've worked hard to get where we are. We've had to fight tooth and nail for every happiness we have. You, as the King-in-Waiting. Me, signing off on fixing potholes in the streets. And while I would *never* think our jobs were the same, we both want our home to prosper, so in that way, we *are* the same." He gnawed on his bottom lip. "And I mean that with the utmost respect."

I'm sure he did. It wasn't sitting well with me how similar our thoughts had been. I hadn't trusted Ramos, even for a moment, but I'd been distracted as of late by Dylan. "And you think…what? That Ramos is trying to fool us all into doing exactly what he wants in order to take over Verania?"

Keith nodded furiously. "Once you're wed to King Dylan, the kingdoms of Verania and Yennbridge would become one. For all we know, that could be *exactly* what Ramos wants." He hesitated. Then, "I really didn't want to have to come to you with this, but I couldn't hold back any longer. Not when…" He frowned. "Not when you seem to have fallen under the king's spell. Not that I think it's magic," he added quickly. "It's just…"

"Out with it," I snapped.

Keith took a deep breath. "I know you were…lonely."

"Tread carefully," I said through gritted teeth.

Sweat trickled down between his eyes, sliding down the side of his nose as his lips pursed. "I don't mean that as a slight. You're on this…this pedestal, one that towers above all the rest of us, as it should be. But I know such things can make you feel like you're cut off from everything else. It's why I never, *ever* called you the Ice Prince, especially since I know the pressure one such as yourself is under." He looked eager. "I've had words with anyone who speaks about you in such a way. No one talks about you like that and gets away with it."

"It's not *that* many people."

"Right," he said. "Of course not. Only a few. But it does beg the question, Prince Justin. Ramos and Dylan admittedly studied Verania, studied *you*. They learned all about you, and for what?"

"To get to know me as a person before presenting themselves to the court?"

"That's what they *want* you to think," Keith said fiercely. "I know this might hurt to hear, but my Prince, what if Dylan *isn't* under the thrall of Ramos? What if he's playing a part, knowing how you—in your loneliness—would react to the attentions of a reasonably handsome man? What if he's using you for their evil plans?"

I laughed. I didn't mean to, but the absurdity of it all was too preposterous to take seriously. "Dylan," I said, still chuckling. "You think *Dylan* of all people is evil."

"I do," Keith said. "I know how it sounds."

"Do you?" I asked. "Because I'm not quite sure about that."

"I'm asking you to trust me," Keith said. "I've been your father's advisor for years. I earned my position. I would never want to see harm come to him, or you. I have lived in service of Verania and will continue to do so for as long as you'll have me. Which is why this brings me no joy. For all we know, magic is already in play. What if you've been manipulated, and you haven't realized it?"

I scoffed. "No one manipulates me. I'm the Prince of Verania."

"And the best we've ever had," Keith said. "I know you see King Dylan as a…well, to be honest, I don't know *exactly* what you see in him, but that's neither here nor there. But what if I'm right?" He frowned, glaring down at the sash around my wrist, gaze crawling along it as it disappeared into my room. "Is it more plausible that a king from a foreign land comes to sweep you off your feet? Or that they have dark designs on us all? Isn't it better to be cautious, after all we've been through? For all we know, he could be another Ruv. And we all know how that ended."

Pointed that, and barbed, but not without merit. We'd all been fooled by Ruv. He'd worked to earn our trust after the debacle that was Vadoma's introduction of him. Even Sam, who saw villains everywhere he went, had fallen for it.

But I still couldn't find a way to reconcile that with what I knew of Dylan. Granted, I'd only known him for a month, but what if Keith was right? Hadn't we distrusted Ramos from the start? Hell, Gary and Tiggy had all but proven he acted like every single villain that had tried to take from us. And here we were, inviting them into our home. It really would be the perfect plan. Instead of attacking us from the outside, they were coming from within, Dylan getting under my skin in ways no one else had before, even Ryan. The thought of being betrayed in such a way stole the breath from my chest.

And yet…

I'd seen the way Dylan smiled at me, the way he'd never let anything get him down, no matter my ire or the path he'd taken to get to this point in his life. I'd felt the way his hand fit into mine, like it was made for it. And how he'd kissed me the night before, soft and sweet, like I was something to be treasured. No. No, I couldn't believe it. I wouldn't. Because the alternative meant I'd been played so stunningly that it threatened to turn my lungs to dust.

Then Keith said, "A trinket."

"What?" I asked, dazed.

"A trinket," he repeated. "A bauble. A gift given to you from the King as a sign of his intent. Perhaps it's been cursed with dark magic, to allay all your fears and worries. Have you been given such a thing?"

I laughed. "Of course not. I would know if…if he'd…"

The heart. The stone heart he'd carved out of citrine and gifted me. The one I'd meant to throw away almost immediately, but had, for some reason, held onto it. Even now, it sat upon my desk, one of the first things I saw in the morning, one of the last before I closed my eyes at night.

"What is it?" Keith asked in a low voice.

"Nothing," I said faintly. "It's…" If the Damning Stone could take away magic, what if a different stone could do something else entirely? I thought back over the last weeks. I hadn't felt any different, right? I couldn't cast magic, but I knew what it felt like. I'd had years of experience with it, whether I wanted it or not. It couldn't be. Because if it *was*, it meant Dylan was no different than Myrin. Ruv. The Darks.

Which meant I'd have to kill him. Him and Ramos.

"I don't want to hurt you," Keith said, sounding miserable. "I never want that. You're important to us all. And I would have come to you sooner, but I couldn't be sure. I still can't. That being said, there are only four days left in the ritual. I couldn't let the deadline come without saying anything. You deserve to know the truth." He looked away. "Fear, Prince Justin. It's all about fear. Making us scared of the unknown. I fear for you, for our home. Fear, like hope, is a weapon, one, if wielded in deft hands, can bring about the end of all we know."

"I appreciate your counsel," I said. "You've given me much to think about. Keep this to yourself. Tell no one."

"I won't," he promised. "Whatever assistance I can offer, you need but ask." He smiled, his eyes troubled but kind. "You deserve to be loved, my Prince. Never forget that. You deserve to be loved, but you also deserve to know the truth. I'll leave this in your capable hands. If you ever have need of me, I'll be there, by your side."

Touched, I patted his arm. "Thank you, Keith."

He nodded gratefully, turning to leave. He stopped before he got too far away, glancing back at me. "You should know that they are already calling you Dystin." He made a face. "Like, Rystin, except with a D. Shameful, that. You're a person, not one half of a whole. I won't allow people to write egregiously erotic fanfiction about you. I've already tried to put a stop to a pornographic play put on in Mama's brothel about your group called Justin Does Verania where the character based upon you is at the center of a gang-bang, but I haven't had much success."

The skin under my right eye twitched painfully. "There's a what?"

"I haven't seen it," Keith said. "Just heard the stories. It's…well. Apparently the production values are exquisite, but the first few rows of seats are given umbrellas to keep from being sprayed with bodily fluids."

"I can't believe I'm going to say this, but that might be the least of my problems."

"Of course," Keith said, bowing low. "I don't want to add to the considerable weight you already carry, but we can't lose you. Not now.

Not ever." With that, he hurried down the hall, disappearing around a corner.

I sagged against the wall, rubbing a hand over my face, trying to clear my head. I needed Sam. I needed Ryan. I needed Kevin and Gary and Tiggy. But I didn't have them, not as they once were. I'd never felt more alone in my life. I told myself that Keith had to be wrong, but I couldn't get the two most onerous words in Veranian language out of my head.

*What if?*

I hated the *what if*. It was too big, too wild. I dealt in absolutes, regardless of what ridiculous situations I'd found myself in in the past. I'd grown in these last years, but even then, I'd tried to hold on to the practical side of myself even in the face of the extraordinary. If Keith was right, then I'd lost myself in the throes of whatever had sprouted between Dylan and me. I couldn't imagine Dylan being as what Keith potentially said he was. But then, did I really know him at all?

I moved until I stood in front of my bedroom door, hesitating with my hand on the doorknob. Inside, Dylan waited for me. When I opened the door, he'd turn and smile in that way he did whenever he saw me, a mixture of hope mixed with no small amount of awe. No one had ever looked at me that way before. If Keith was right, then I didn't know how I'd survive such a betrayal. Not again.

I leaned my head against the door, trying to calm my racing heart. I thought through every interaction Dylan and I'd had, trying to find any hint of deception. Nothing, as far as I could tell. He was simple, really, in all the best ways. An open book, willing to share whatever was going on in his head, whether I wanted to hear it or not. Had I really been so fooled by a pretty face? At the first sign of positive attention thrown my way?

I couldn't believe it.

But what if?

Fixing a smile on my face, I opened the door. Dylan stood in front of my desk. He looked up at me and grinned, just as I knew he would, eyes crinkling. "Hey, so good news and bad news. The good news is that I was able to scrape most of the sausage. The bad news is that there's no sausage left because it was all burned. But the eggs are edible! Well, parts of them are. Apparently they decided to sprinkle cinnamon on them. I thought maybe it was a Veranian thing, but then I tried it, and it was like someone punched my feelings. Bro, it is *not* good."

"The stone," I said. "The heart."

His smile widened. "Still here." He nodded to where the stone sat on my desk, next to the tray. "It's not much, I know, but you've kept it." He sounded pleased. "That's pretty epic."

"And you carved it yourself," I said slowly. "No one else helped you."

"Nope," he said. "All me. For better or worse."

"And it's just that? A stone?"

He cocked his head. "Just a stone. Found it on one of my walks. They're all over the place." He rubbed the back of his neck. "It's not... expensive, but then I thought it didn't need to be, because it's the intention that matters most."

I searched for any sign of deception. I wasn't surprised when I found none. Either he was telling the truth, or he was one of the best liars I'd ever met.

I closed the door behind me, stalking toward him. He laughed as I wrapped my arms around him. He hugged me back tightly, his face in my hair. "Morning hugs are my favorite type of hugs."

"Don't hurt me," I whispered against his throat. "I couldn't take it if you did."

I felt him stiffen, and I couldn't look at him when he pulled away. He put his hand underneath my chin, pushing my head up gently. "What was that?" he asked.

I shook my head. "Nothing. Just..."

He frowned, glancing over my shoulder at the door before looking back at me. "Everything all right? That guy seemed really eager to talk to you. Prince stuff, huh?"

"It's fine," I said. "Nothing to worry about."

"You sure?"

No. No, I wasn't. "You'd never..." I stopped, unsure of how to continue.

"I'd never what?" he asked, leaning forward and kissing my forehead.

"Do you trust Ramos?"

He blinked as he pulled back. "Ramos? Yeah, I do. I mean, I know he's a little...out there, but he's always had my best interest at heart. He's more rigid than I'd like, but it helps to keep me in line." He laughed quietly. "You may not believe this, but I get distracted pretty easily."

I rolled my eyes. "What? No. Of course not."

"Ha ha," he said dryly. He sobered. "Why are you asking about Ramos? Has he done something?"

Yes. He'd brought Dylan into my life and made me think there was something more than what I'd built for myself. Dylan, who had made me believe I could one day be a king this country deserved. Dylan, who had gotten past every one of my defenses through sheer force of will. Dylan, who had spent the last weeks distracting me.

If Ramos was a villain, he'd used the one tool at his disposal I had no chance against.

I couldn't stand the thought.

"No," I said. "He hasn't done anything." I smiled again, though I felt like screaming. "Let's see about those eggs."

Dylan laughed, and I prayed to the gods that my fall wasn't already written in the stars.

*****

TRY AS I MIGHT, I couldn't keep Keith's words from taking over my brain.

I watched Dylan closely, looking for any sign of subterfuge as we went about our day in the castle, waiting for the moment when he would reveal himself to be a master villain capable of bringing Verania to its knees.

"Oh, now you've done it," he hissed, eyes ablaze. "You never should have crossed me. I will bring about the end of all you know. You want to know what it means to suffer? I'll show you."

"Never!" Ryan cried, shoving Sam behind him. "You'll never take him from me! We are the knights of Verania! We'll kill you *dead*."

Dylan took a step toward them as Sam peered over Ryan's shoulder. "I will have the boy," Dylan said. "And there is nothing you can do to stop me." He cackled evilly, head rocking back.

"Annnnnnd *scene*," Gary said.

Tiggy collapsed onto the floor of the throne room, setting down the lantern Gary had made him hold, telling him that the lighting needed to be *perfect*, or the entire hastily put-together production of

The Evil King from Far Away would fail, and would Tiggy really do that to him?

Gary pranced forward, hooves clicking along the stone. "I have notes. Sam, you played the role of the damsel in distress quite well, though I'm going to ask you for a bit more. I need to *believe* you're scared. Give me tears."

Sam nodded. "Got it. Boys can cry too because we have tear ducts like everyone else."

"And Ryan," Gary continued. "Your bravery in the face of the evil king trying to take your one true love needs some work. You can't cry, but I want to see the pain on your face."

Ryan frowned. "I have questions. Why am I called Knight Delicious Face in the script you wrote?"

"I don't know," Gary said. "I heard someone say it, so I stole it for my own. But that's wrong, so I'll properly attribute it to the person who said it so we may lift them up and celebrate their creativity. That person is—Kevin, I'm not feeling properly fanned. I'm the *director*. If I faint because of the heat, this entire production will fall apart, and the blame will fall entirely on you."

"Yes, my queen," Kevin said, hurrying toward Gary. He stopped next to him, bringing up one of his wings and fanning Gary.

"Ah," Gary said, his mane fluttering around his head. "That's better. I look amazing. Dylan, you were perfectly evil. Maybe even the evilest thing I've ever seen."

Dylan grinned down at him. "Thanks, little bro. I was worried because I've never acted in a play before. I wasn't quite sure how to find the proper motivation. The character description you gave me just said BAD GUY WHO DOES BAD THINGS."

"That's because I'm a genius," Gary said. "Though, I will say you ad-libbed part of your lines which, in a community theater production would be fine, but here? That's *not* okay. See that it doesn't happen again. Actors are replaceable. That being said, you were the only one who showed up to audition for the role, so we'd have to replace you with a yam."

"Stupid yams," Dylan muttered, scuffing his boot on the floor.

Gary whirled around, stalking toward the dais where I sat slumped on my chair. Dad and Morgan had been watching too, but then Dad had said he'd be right back, asking Morgan to follow him. They'd gone into a storage closet near the back of the throne room ten minutes ago and hadn't come out yet.

"Justin?" Gary asked, stopping before the dais. "Thoughts?"

"I don't care," I told him.

Gary nodded slowly. "Thank you for your constructive feedback." He sneezed, but it came out sounding like *you ungrateful dick*. "I appreciate it, and everything about you." He sneezed again. This time, it sounded like *you don't know shit*. He sniffled daintily. "Excuse me. My seasonal allergies are wreaking havoc upon my body." He cleared his throat obnoxiously, and somehow, it still came out like *I will fuck you up, you philistine*.

I rolled my eyes. "Perhaps you should get that checked out."

"Script supervisor!" Gary cried. "I need my script supervisor. We're in rewrites, everyone! Take five, but do *not* get out of character."

Tiggy grumbled as he pushed himself up off the floor, pulling out a ream of papers from his pocket. "Do this, Tiggy," he muttered. "Do that, Tiggy." Then he grinned. "I like being included!" He picked up Gary, rubbing his back as they went off into the far corner to confer, Kevin frantically fanning them both as he trailed after them.

Sam and Ryan sat on the floor, Sam poking Ryan in the face as Dylan came over to the dais, smiling at me. He looked at me as if I were the sun. I swallowed thickly as he hopped up on the dais, crouching down near my chair. He settled his hand on my thigh, squeezing gently. "How was I?"

I shifted in my seat. "Evil."

He laughed. "Yeah, I didn't even know I had it in me. It's fun being the bad guy, at least for a little while."

I stared at him. "Really? You've never been a villain before?"

"Nah. It seems like too much work." He shrugged. "Always needing to have an evil plan for everything. I'd rather be happy and help people than be mad and hurt them."

I hesitated briefly before dropping my hand on top of his. "Can I ask you something?"

"Of course. I'm an open book."

I thought hard. "Say you were a bad guy. A villain who wanted to take over the kingdom. How would you go about it?"

He rubbed his chin thoughtfully. "Well, I'd wouldn't do it how Gary wrote. It's a little on the nose, you know? Being so comically evil doesn't allow for the element of surprise." He chuckled. "No, I'd probably go about it a different way. Get people to trust me. Make them think I'm good. The best, even. And then, when they least expected it, I'd turn on them."

Talk about being a little on the nose. "And then what?"

"I'd hit 'em where it hurt. After lifting them up and making them feel special, I'd use what I learned about them against them." He shook his head. "Man, it's a good thing I'm not evil. No one would suspect me, and I'd always win."

"Yeah," I said weakly. "It's a good thing you're not evil."

His smile drooped. "Are you okay? You're acting a little—"

One of the great doors creaked open, the royal announcer scurrying into the room. He almost tripped over his feet before saying, "Prince Justin! Lady Tina has requested an audience."

"Gross!" Sam yelled. "Why is she still alive?"

"Send her in," I said as Dylan stood next to my chair, his hand on my shoulder.

The announcer nodded before spinning on his heels and ran out the door. A moment later, Lady Tina entered. She wore her armor, her thin sword hanging off her hip. Sam stuck his tongue out at her, and she flipped him off. Which, of course, caused Sam to bellow that if I was *really* his Best Friend 5eva, I'd drop her into a vat of boiling oil.

She stopped in front of the dais, bowing once before looking up at me. "Prince Justin, thank you for granting me an audience." She glanced at Dylan. "King Dylan, I'm pleased to see you here as well. I have news."

I sat forward eagerly. "Are we under attack?"

Lady Tina squinted at me. "Um, no? At least not the last time I checked which was three minutes ago."

"Then why are you here?"

"As I said, I have news." She reached into a leather satchel at her waist and pulled out a scroll. "The new poll numbers are in."

Hurray. I couldn't wait to hear how badly people thought of me again. Just what I needed. I sighed, motioning for her to continue.

She nodded as she unfurled the scroll. "The new numbers are about you and your father. We thought that keeping our focus on the pair of you would give us a better idea of what we're looking at." She looked around. "Where is the king?"

"He'll be here momentarily," I said. "He needed Morgan to help him with something. You may proceed."

"King Anthony's numbers have remained the same. He is nearly universally beloved by all, and most agree he's helped bring the City of Lockes and Verania itself back to its former glory. Many approved of his forward-thinking ideas, and of the seven hundred and forty-six people polled, ninety-seven percent said that he is the best thing to have ever happened to anyone ever."

"Good," I said. "I'm pleased to hear it. I know he will be too." I took a deep breath, letting it out slow. "And for me?"

"I'm pleased to inform you that your approval rating is now at seventy-six percent."

I blinked. "Come again?"

"Dystin fever has taken over Lockes," she said gleefully. "Of those polled, ninety-nine percent believe that King Dylan has brought out your softer side and made you appear to be more human. The remaining one percent were aggressively against your coupling, saying that the king from Yennbridge deserved better." She frowned. "One enterprising gentleman wanted King Dylan to know that he can...ah. That he can peel a banana using only his teeth and tongue."

"Wow," Dylan said. "That's wicked awesome. We should invite him here and—"

"Seventy-six percent?" I said, confused. "I haven't done anything."

"The numbers don't lie," Lady Tina said. "Dystin is the greatest thing to hit Lockes since Rystin. Everyone thinks so. Would you like to hear a sampling of the semi-erotic fanfiction that your personal guard has written?" She scowled. "Fair warning, it was a round-robin story where everyone contributed, and Deidre has recently discovered what she calls the joy of object-insertion. Her part of the story is... well. Unpalatable is probably the best way to put it."

"Yes," Dylan said promptly. "Yes to all of that. I want to hear it *now*."

Lady Tina cleared her throat. "Once upon a time, the extremely handsome King of Yennbridge came to the City of Lockes with his twelve-inch member. The Prince of Verania quivered at the sight of his kingly bulge, and—"

Sam and Ryan screamed in horror.

"Perhaps," I said through gritted teeth, "we can save that for another time."

"Aw, man," Dylan said as he pouted. "I wanted to hear more about my big—"

"Even the tabloids are on board," Lady Tina said, pulling out a newspaper from her satchel. She handed it over. I glanced down at the blaring headline. LOVE IN LOCKES? THE ICE PRINCE IS MELTING!

Below it, a drawing from our date in the city. My nose was perhaps too big, and my eyes certainly weren't set as far apart as the artist seemed to think. This, however, did nothing to take away from the fact that I'd been drawn as a melting ice sculpture, a puddle of water at my feet as I gazed adoringly up at Dylan. The sash was wrapped around both our wrists, little red hearts drawn floating above it. Dylan had been drawn as a tremendous figure, strong and imposing. But the artist had somehow captured the light in his eyes, and his smile was soft and warm.

The contents of the article were, in a word, fawning. It described Dylan's attributes in gushing prose, saying that while his intelligence was questionable, he was the paragon of manly virtue, the kick in the ass I so desperately needed. The reporter had cited anonymous sources in the castle, saying that Dylan and I were usually locked away in my room. *And what goes on behind closed doors in the castle isn't something this reporter usually speculates on,* the article read (and oh, they were such *liars*), *but I would be remiss if I didn't mention that Prince Justin is apparently a rather…vocal lover. If the castle's a-rockin, the royal staff know not to come knockin'. And if my sources are correct, our fair prince has certainly found his royal chambers plundered by the visiting king's exuberance. I spoke with three of the prince's former flames, and all agreed the prince is a very generous lover before he kicked them out and pretended they didn't exist. Will King Dylan find himself in the same position? Or will he try a few* different *positions in order to keep the prince happy? Only time will tell!*

"Oh my gods," I groaned.

"Whoa," Dylan said, reading over my shoulder. "That's not cool."

Relieved, I said, "Thank you. I know it's invasive, but freedom of the press is important, even if it's mostly shit."

"What? No. I don't care about that. I'm upset because that's weirdly homophobic. Why do queer men need to be put into preconceived sexual roles based solely on our appearance? I mean, sure, it's awesome to be on top, but sometimes, I want to be filled with….what? Why are you looking at me like that?"

"Oh my *gods*," I groaned again, this time for entirely different reasons.

"Story ideas," Lady Tina breathed. She coughed roughly. "I mean, many happy returns and whatever. I'm pleased to bring you this good news. I think we—"

A muffled shout from behind me followed by a crash.

I was up and moving even before I realized it. Something was wrong. My father and Morgan hadn't returned, and the sound seemed to come from the storage closet. I ran toward it, visions of Ramos standing above my father ready to take his life filling my head. I would tear him limb from limb. Fuck him and his evil plans. He messed with the wrong family.

I practically knocked the door down trying to get in.

I stopped at the sight before me.

The storage closet wasn't big, mostly filled with decorations used for any celebration we had, along with the oppressive stench of cleaning supplies. A bucket lay on the floor next to a row of newly polished swords.

But I paid it all no mind.

Because my father *wasn't* battling for his life.

A wet *pop* that would haunt me for the rest of my days came when Dad pulled his mouth away from Morgan's, his beard in disarray, his hair sweaty and matted down on his forehead. Morgan looked no worse for wear and didn't even have the temerity to act like he'd been caught mauling my father.

"No," I said as my stomach twisted slickly. "No, no, no. Oh my gods. My eyes. My fucking *eyes*."

"Oh, hush," Dad said, and he was practically *panting*. "I was doing inventory, and Morgan offered to help."

"With his *mouth*?" I demanded as Dylan crowded behind me. "We have staff for that!"

Dad frowned. "To help me with their mouths? Honestly, Justin, we might need to have a talk about proper boundaries between employer and employee."

Morgan sighed. "I don't think that's quite what he meant."

"What's happening?" a little voice asked, and I looked down to see Sam and Ryan crowding against my legs. "Why is everyone sweaty?"

"I can answer that," Gary said, his horn nearly goring my leg as he walked between them. "When a king loves a wizard, sometimes they go into closets to—"

"You're *asexual*," I snapped at Morgan.

He squinted at me. "Do…do you not understand what that means?"

"He knows," Dad muttered as he straightened his shirt. "He's being obstinate on purpose. As the King of Verania, I order you to close the door and let me finish the inventory."

"You're in so much trouble," I snarled at him. "You go to your room until I've calmed down enough to talk to you. If I tried to do it now, I'd end up saying things we'd both regret."

Dad stared at me. "What."

I winced. "Right. Sorry. You're the parent. Which means you can't go into closets to make out! Do you know what that *does* to me?"

"I have no idea," Dad said. "And honestly? I don't think I really care. I love Morgan. Morgan loves me. If I want to go into a closet to make out with him, I—"

I slapped my hands over my ears. "Oh my gods, stop talking!"

Morgan snorted. "Make out. Oh, Anthony. You do have a way with words."

Dad grinned at him. "I also have a way with my—"

Whatever horror Dad was about to say out loud was cut off when the great doors opened once more behind us with an ominous groan, followed by the royal announcer shouting for Dad and me. I pushed my way through the others in front of the door, trying to see what fresh hell had befallen us now.

"Raincheck," I heard Dad say, to which Morgan replied, "Counting on it."

The announcer stood in the middle of the room, bent over with his hands on his knees as he panted. Lady Tina was next to him, frowning down at him as the announce babbled incoherently.

"What is it?" Dylan asked as we stopped in front of them, the others gathering behind us. "What happened?"

The announcer shook his head as he tried to catch his breath. "Randall," he managed to gasp. "He's been attacked!"

"*What?*" Morgan growled, and I'd never heard such a tone in his voice before. He sounded furious. "Is he alive?"

The announcer nodded, mouth twisted down. "In the labs. A knight found him. He's injured, but awake."

Morgan nodded before whirling around, robes flaring around his feet as he stalked back toward the storage room.

"Lady Tina," Dad said, voice deep. "Stay with the children. Guard them with your life. Do not let them out of your sight. Byron, find Rosemary and Joshua Haversford and bring them here." The announcer nodded and ran from the throne room. Dad turned to Dylan and me. "Dylan, take Justin to his rooms and don't—"

"Fuck that," I snapped. "I'm going with you. I'm not going to hide away, especially when we don't know what's happening."

Dad looked like he was about to argue. I arched an eyebrow, daring him to. He sighed instead, shaking his head. "I don't know how you can't see it."

"What?"

"All that you are," Dad said, squeezing my shoulder. "With us, then. Eyes open, watch each other's backs."

"Anthony."

We turned to see Morgan carrying four swords. He tossed one to my father, who caught it deftly by the grip, the steel flashing. Morgan gave two more to Dylan and me, keeping the last one for himself. "Do you even know how to use that?" I asked him.

He nodded grimly. "Magic isn't all that I can do. Randall made sure of it." He swallowed with an audible click. "He's okay," he said, more to himself than anything else. "He's going to be fine."

"He is," Dad said. "And whoever did this will suffer the consequences. You have my word."

I had a sinking feeling I knew who it was. I glanced at Dylan, who was testing the heft of the sword by swinging it back and forth, the sash stretched between it. I barely noticed it anymore. It had become part of me, connecting me to this man I'd once despised for all he'd represented. I had opened myself to him in ways I'd never done with anyone else. I didn't know if my heart could recover if it turned out he was part of this.

He must have felt my gaze on him, because he looked up at me, smiling tightly. "I've got your back," he said. "Whatever happens, I'm here. You won't go through this alone."

No, I didn't think I'd survive him at all.

# CHAPTER 16
## Shit Gets Real

THE CASTLE WAS ABUZZ as we hurried down to the labs. Regardless of if they'd already heard of the attack on Randall or not, the sight of the four of us rushing through the halls of Castle Lockes with swords drawn wasn't something that happened very often. Anyone we came across, Dad barked orders to protect those who couldn't fight until they heard from him again. No one questioned him. They wouldn't. Protocols had been implemented after Myrin in case the city once again came under siege. Everyone knew what to do and where to hide, weapons drawn to protect the children and the elderly who lived in the castle. I saw a maid pull out one of the biggest daggers I'd ever seen from underneath her dress as she herded an older couple out of the hallway.

We might have survived all that had come before but we'd never forgotten what we'd been through. Whoever it was—Ramos or someone else— would be surprised to find this wasn't the Verania that had existed before the Dark Wizard had risen. No one would go down without a fight. This was our home. We would defend her until our last breath.

Through my anger and confusion, a dark wave of grief rolled over me. Sam and Ryan should've been at my side, ready to deal with whatever had come. Gary and Tiggy and Kevin too. But they weren't, and it caused my heart to stutter in my chest. Four days, I reminded myself. In four days, they'd come back to me, come back to us all. I would see to it. If that meant killing Ramos, then so be it.

And if Dylan was part of it, well. I cared for him. But I loved my friends. He wouldn't harm one hair on their heads, not while I still stood.

We reached the floor where Morgan and Sam's labs were located. The hallway in front of the door was crowded with knights, all of whom parted to make way for my father who led the charge, Morgan huddled close to his back, myself and Dylan following after them. I gasped in relief when I heard Randall's cranky voice say, "Would you get your damn hands off me? I'm fine."

We burst into the doorway. Randall sat in a chair, the healer behind him, trying to put his hands in the wizard's hair. Blood trickled down the side of Randall's hair, a droplet falling off his ear and onto his shoulder, splattering on his robes.

"What happened?" Morgan demanded, pushing by Dad to get to Randall. The healer grumbled as he took a step back, Morgan taking his place. His eyes widened at whatever he saw on the back of Randall's head. "You're injured."

"Obviously," Randall muttered, though he didn't try and tell Morgan off like he'd done with the healer. "I'm all right. I'll take care of it myself once my head clears." He snorted. "Medicine. Bah. Who needs it when you have magic?"

"Who did this to you?" Dad asked, looking around the labs. I followed his gaze, trying to see if anything seemed out of place. I couldn't find anything, at least not until a cupboard door rattled as if something was trapped inside. A tiny voice raged that someone needed to open the door *right this second*. I went to it, pulling the cupboard opened. Dimitri burst through, wings buzzing angrily.

"Someone *swatted* me!" he cried, eyes narrowed as he flew up above our heads in a dizzying circle. "I'm the King of the Fairies. Whoever did this will face my significant wrath!"

"You have my word," Dad said. "I won't let this go unanswered. Tell me. Leave nothing out."

Randall frowned as he stood up, hand going to the back of his head. He pulled it back, and his fingers were shiny with blood. "Came up from behind me," he muttered. "Got a good hit in too, the coward. If you're going to fight someone, have the balls to face them head on."

"Ramos," Dimitri snarled. "Where is he?"

Dylan grunted as if punched in the stomach. "Ramos? Was he

here?"

Dimitri buzzed in front of his face like an angry wasp. "Randall and I were distracted, going over everything we could find about the Damning Stone to ensure once the ritual ended, the magic would be returned. Ramos was here with us."

"Where is he?" Dylan asked, looking around.

"He obviously attacked us!" Dimitri exclaimed. "It was all part of his plan in order to…well, I have no idea what his plan is, but it's nothing good."

"Maybe he was attacked like the rest of you," Dylan said, though he sounded unsure. "He wouldn't…" He stopped, shaking his head. "I know him." He looked at each of us in turn, gaze finally settling on me. "I trust him, okay? He would never do anything to hurt us. He knows how important this is."

"Then where is he?" Dad asked, not unkindly.

"I don't know," Dylan said, and my heart hurt with how it sounded like he was pleading with us. "But I wouldn't have brought him if I thought he'd do something like this, whatever this is. I wouldn't put any of you at risk." He looked at me. "You believe me, right?"

I wanted to say yes more than anything. But a seed of doubt had blossomed in my chest, and I stood there stupidly, mouth opening and closing.

Before I could force out words that wouldn't crush Dylan, Randall spoke instead. "I know Ramos," he muttered. "Foolish, hard-headed. I never liked him. Always thought he should be given more than he'd earned. But I can't imagine him doing something so severe. What would be the point? Not if…" His eyes widened as he began to pat down his robes. "No, no. Where is it? Where *is it*?"

"What?" Morgan asked as Randall pulled out his pockets. "What are you looking for?"

Randall exhaled heavily as he dropped his hands. "The Damning Stone. It was on my person when I was struck. It's been stolen."

We all stared at him.

"You're telling me," Dad said slowly, "that a stone filled with magic from a unicorn, a magician, and two of the most powerful wizards in existence has been taken?"

Randall glared at the floor. "Yes. That's what I'm saying." He shook his head. "But that doesn't make any sense. That level of magic would tear someone apart. I doubt even I could handle all that power.

Morgan either. Sam is another story entirely, but we know he didn't take the stone."

Morgan slumped into Randall's abandoned seat, looking dazed. "Anthony, we need to lock down the castle. Now. We must find the stone before someone tries to use it."

Dad barked an order at the knights gathered, telling them to close off the castle, allowing no one to leave. The knights snapped to attention, bowing before fleeing into the castle. We heard them shouting, and a moment later, warning bells began to ring from somewhere above us.

Dylan looked miserable as he stared down at the sash around his wrist. And although that seed of doubt was blossoming, I went to him, taking his hand in mine. He startled, frowning at me. "You don't believe me."

"I don't know what to believe," I admitted, squeezing his hand. "It doesn't look good for Ramos." He started to speak, but I overrode him. "That doesn't mean he's involved, but we have…trust issues, when it comes to this sort of thing."

Dylan scowled, and it struck me then that I'd never seen him angry before. He pulled his hand from mine, leaving me feeling bereft. "That's fair," he said, voice low. "But I would never do anything to hurt you." He folded his arms. "Any of you. Ramos…he cares for me. He's the only one who stood up to my father on my behalf. He wouldn't do something like this. He…" Dylan trailed off, a strange expression crossing his face.

"What is it?" I asked gently.

He scratched the back of his neck. "We…haven't been exactly honest with you. We didn't lie," he added quickly, "but we didn't tell you everything."

My blood turned to icy sludge as Randall's head jerked toward Dylan. And though Dylan had inches on him, and at least fifty pounds, Randall loomed over Dylan, and the air around us thickened with magic. Even though Randall was older than shit, he was still the Head Wizard, and he was furious.

"Speak," he growled. "Before I make you."

Dylan took a step back, and he looked so impossibly young, my heart ached. "I…"

I couldn't stand it. I couldn't stand how lost he looked, how scared. It reminded me of how Sam had been after his first battle with Myrin in the desert, terrible scars covering his body. I hadn't been there for the fight, but I'd seen the aftermath. An aftermath that was still with him to this day, even though he'd forgotten all about it. Praying to the gods that I wasn't making a dire mistake, I went to Dylan, moving between him and Randall until I was all Dylan could see. I cupped his face with my hands, thumbs brushing against his cheeks. He trembled as I leaned forward, kissing him sweetly. He reached up, pressing his hands against my own, holding me in place.

"I believe you," I said quietly. "I trust you. But if you know something, you have to tell us. It's not just about Ramos. It's about my friends. My family. My people. I made an oath to keep them all safe, and I can't fail them now."

He blinked slowly. "You believe me?"

I nodded. "Please don't make me regret that."

I laughed when he crushed me against him, rocking me back and forth. He lifted me off my feet, spinning me in a circle, my legs almost hitting Randall, who grumbled that love was the most disgusting force on the planet while still somehow sounding amused.

"I'm going to make you so happy," Dylan whispered as he set me back on the ground. "You hear me, bro? You and me, we're going places. And I can't wait to see what we find."

I kissed him again. "Damn right. And if it's Ramos, we'll deal with it. If not, we'll figure that out too. Together."

"Ah," Dad said as I stood beside Dylan, taking his hand again. Dad smiled at the both of us. "I see that things have worked out as well as I'd hoped." He moved until he stood before us, one hand on my shoulder, the other on Dylan's. He grinned at me before looking at Dylan. "This is my son. I love him more than anything, which is why when I say I approve of this, you know I trust you. You're a good man, Dylan. A good king." He gathered us up in his arms, and chuckled when Dylan clutched back tightly. "Yes. A very good king. Our world will be in safe hands because of the pair of you. I just know it."

"This is all lovely," Dimitri said as we pulled away. "But we have a big problem here. If the stone is in play, it could bring about the end of all we know. We can't take the chance that someone will use the magic within."

"Ramos thinks my parents were murdered," Dylan said, and the air was sucked from the room. "By magic. Our healers couldn't figure out what was wrong with them. One day they were healthy, and then the next, they were both just…gone. It took only a day or two." He tried to smile, but it cracked right down the middle. "Yennbridge was…well.

In a state of panic, after. Losing one would have been hard enough, but the loss of both the king and queen? It devastated us. I assumed the throne, but I didn't know who I could trust. Ramos thought..." He shuddered. "He thought that if something *did* happen to them, we needed all the protection we could get." He looked at Randall. "He spoke of you. Said that we needed to get in your good graces so that you could help us. Help *me*, especially after Dad told him about the marriage pact right before he died."

Randall frowned. "Why didn't you just ask that in the first place?"

"Because he knew you didn't like him," Dylan said without censure. "He said your last meeting didn't exactly go well."

"Understatement," Randall muttered. He sobered as he shook his head "Ramos was...I didn't think he had what it took to become a wizard. His magic was too weak. I've found in my years that it's better to be blunt than to string someone along. He...didn't take well to my refusal. He demanded that I teach him, allow him to take the Trials. I knew it would kill him if he tried, so I told him no. He was quite angry with me." Randall winced. "I could have gone about it a bit better, but I thought I'd gotten through to him."

"You're not infallible, Randall," Morgan said. "We've all made mistakes we wish we could take back."

Randall hung his head. "I know. But when *we* make mistakes, it's something else entirely. People have suffered because of our actions. If this...if this *is* Ramos, what does that make me? I failed you. I failed my cornerstone." He swallowed thickly. "And I failed Sam, because I saw him as an opportunity to correct all my past wrongs. For a time, I thought him nothing more than a weapon, and I treated him as such. It doesn't matter what the gods thought, or what they had planned. I didn't want to believe that our destiny had already been written, even as the stone path beneath our feet began to crumble. That nothing could have been done to change what had happened."

"He's so much more than that," Morgan said. "Who knew that when I found Sam in that alley, boys of stone around him, that he'd become all that he has? He is the better part of us, Randall. We've taught him as best we could, but he took the tools we'd given him and made them his own. There is no one like him in all the world. I thank the gods every day for allowing me into his life, even as I struggle with what our actions have wrought. But he hasn't done it alone. He's had you. And me. But we pale in comparison to Ryan. And Kevin. And Gary and Tiggy. And to Justin."

Randall steeled himself, squaring his shoulders. "Which means it's our time. Our time to protect him, to protect them all. Whoever has taken the stone, be it Ramos or someone else, we need to act quickly before it's too late."

"Where do we begin?" Dimitri asked. "I need to warn my people, to prepare in case this spreads beyond the city."

Dad nodded. "Go. Do what you need to. Protect the forest. We'll send word once we know anything."

Dimitri nodded before rising, wings fluttering. He spread his arms as he began to spin in a circle. A moment later, he vanished, leaving behind air swirling with glitter.

Randall raised his hand, flexing his fingers. A low roar filled the labs as a hole opened up, the edges ragged and sparking as cold air washed over us, bits of snow and ice swirling through the portal. "The dragons," Randall said as he stepped toward the hole. "Pat. Leslie. The Great White, if that old bastard will listen to me. I'll do what I can to bring them here." And with that, he stepped into the hole. It closed behind him with an electric snarl, a snowflake landing on my cheek and dripping down my face.

"Wasn't there another dragon?" Dylan asked.

I shuddered. The emo snake dragon monster thing. "Zero's asleep in the desert and won't wake up for a hundred years. It's better not to ask too many questions about that."

Dylan grinned at me. "It's Verania."

I snorted. "Yeah, that about sums it up."

Dad said, "If he's in the castle, we'll find him." He glanced at Dylan. "And if it's not Ramos, and he's been taken too, we'll do what we can to save him."

"We can't let him get to Sam," Morgan said. "Whoever this is, they may think Sam is part of this. We need to keep him safe, and the others."

"They're with my personal guard," I said. "Joshua and Rosemary too. They'll protect them."

Morgan looked relieved. "We need to hurry. Join the knights in the search of the castle. If we're lucky, whoever has the stone hasn't yet left."

We all headed for the door, but stopped when Dylan said, "Hold on a second."

I turned to look at him. "What is it?"

He frowned, looking down at the sash. I could see his mind working, and though I wanted to snap at him to get a move on, I waited. I told him I trusted him. I needed to prove that.

After a long moment, he looked up at me. "You changed."

I blinked. "What?"

"When I brought you breakfast. I came to your room, and you were fine. But then after you spoke with that advisor, something changed. You weren't like you normally are. You were more closed off. Like you were when I got here."

I winced, but he wasn't wrong. And he'd picked up on it, though he hadn't pushed. I was well-matched. I wondered if the gods were laughing at me.

"Which advisor?" Dad asked.

It took me a moment to remember his name. "Keith."

Dad's eyebrows rose up his forehead. "Keith. The infrastructure advisor? What on earth would he need to meet with you for?"

I paused, thinking back through our conversation. "He warned me," I said slowly, a feeling of unease rising through my chest. "Said that I shouldn't trust Ramos. Or Dylan. That Ramos was a snake in the grass, waiting to strike. That Dad might have been magicked, which is why he didn't remember signing the marriage pact." I grimaced. "And that Dylan might be trying to do the same with me."

Dylan burst out laughing. "No way. He did? That's awesome. Not the whole I might be a bad guy thing, but that he thought I could do magic." He raised his hands, wiggling his fingers. "See? Nothing. I tried to do a card trick once, but then Digger tackled me and I forgot all about it. He does that a lot."

Gods help the day I ever met Digger. "Keith said that it might be the stone heart you carved for me."

Dylan stopped laughing. "What the heck? It's just a *rock*. I found it on the ground! The only power it has was to make you think I'm awesome." He shrugged. "Which it did. Hurray!"

"It wasn't just the rock that made me think you're awesome," I muttered, and immediately regretted that entire sentence.

Dylan grinned. "Oh really? What else was it? It was the handstand, wasn't it? You saw me do a handstand and thought man, I need to get me a piece of that."

"If I say yes, can this conversation be over?"

"Yep."

"Then yes, it was the handstand."

He pumped his fist in the air. "I *knew* it."

"Justin, could you maybe flirt later?" Dad asked, sounding amused. "Not that I'm not enjoying myself, but I think we're in a bit of a hurry here."

I threw up my hands. "If you'll recall, this is all your fault."

Dad patted my arm. "Yes, yes. And I feel just awful about. How dare I play a part in bringing you the happiness you so deserve. The audacity. I apologize profusely. I don't know what I was thinking."

"I'm going to marry your son," Dylan announced as if the world wasn't already upside down. "Not today, and probably not next week, but I'm gonna marry him so hard." He waggled his eyebrows at me. "You should see what else I can do while standing on my hands."

"Tell me," I demanded. Then, "No, wait. Stop. Stop it *right* now."

"Oh boy," Morgan said. "While I appreciate Justin wanting to explore Dylan's finer virtues, I don't think now's the time for that."

"We should go on a double date," Dylan told my father, and not for the first time, I wished the ground would open up and swallow me whole. "You and Morgan. Me and Justin. Have you ever had onion rings? They're better when you take out the onions."

Dad had to keep me from banging my head against the wall. "Deal. Once everything is back to normal, we'll do just that."

I looked at my dad in horror. "What? Are you out of your damn *mind*? We're not going on a double date!"

"The King of Yennbridge has made a request," Dad said. "And who am I to deny him?"

Kings were a mistake. Every single godsdamn one of them. "Where is Keith's room?" I asked, desperate to change the subject. "If he knows something more, we need to get to him first."

"Fifth floor," Dad said. "West wing."

"Heck yeah," Dylan said. "Let's rock this thing and save the world." And with that, he pushed by us, leading the charge from the labs.

"I can't believe I have to marry him," I said as the sash began to stretch.

"You don't have to," Dad said. "Especially if that's not what you want."

I looked at my father. "I said that wrong. I meant I can't believe

I *get* to marry him." The sash pulled tight, tugging me along, leaving Dad laughing after me.

*****

KEITH'S DOOR WAS LOCKED. Dad knocked, but no one answered.

Morgan frowned as he bent over to peer at the lock. "I think I can open this. Give me a second to—"

Dad managed to pull Morgan out of the way just in time as Dylan bellowed, slamming into the door, the wood cracking in its frame as the door slammed open, hanging off its hinges. He looked back at me over his shoulder. I didn't speak, afraid that anything that came out of my mouth would be highly inappropriate given our present company. It was unbecoming of a prince to say that he hoped that he could be banged the same way, especially when said prince stood next to his father.

"Stop being ridiculous," I hissed at him as I walked into the room. "It's not fair because I can't do what I want to you right now."

Dylan flexed his considerable arms, kissing each bicep with a loud smack. "You like that?"

Gods help me, I did. "Absolutely not."

He chuckled. "You're such a liar. I can't wait to pick you up and put you against a wall while I...holy fricken *crud*."

Holy fricken crud indeed.

Because Keith's room wasn't what I expected. Oh, it was small, with room for a large bed that reached from wall to wall, and a chest of drawers on the opposite side. A rug lay on the floor at the foot of the bed, and atop it, sat a small table with a book next to a framed drawing of...

Me.

And...Keith? His arm wrapped around my shoulders, his face in my hair as I smiled like I was so in love, I could hardly contain it.

It wasn't the only one.

In fact, every inch of the walls was *covered* in drawings of me in various poses, some extremely salacious that I absolutely did not pose for. Whoever had drawn them had been very generous with my...well. With my fucking junk.

Interspersed with these drawings were articles from every major paper in Verania. I stepped forward slowly, and I saw the articles were all about me. Everything good, bad, and all in between. The walls were covered in what felt like my entire history in the public eye.

"Bro," Dylan breathed. "Why didn't you tell me you dated one of your father's advisors? I mean, it's cool and whatever. We all have history, but I think I'm getting a little jealous?" He frowned as he rubbed his chest. "Yep. Definitely jealous. But congrats on your penis. We're really going to need to work me open in order for that to fit."

"What in the actual *fuck*?" I whispered feverishly.

"It would seem our prince has an admirer," Morgan said, sounding like he was trying not to laugh. "He's...quite thorough." He flipped through the book on the table before his eyes widened and he slammed it shut. "No one should read this. It's...ah. Let's just say that Keith has a very active imagination about what he'd like to do to Justin."

But because he was Dylan, he rushed forward and grabbed the book. I saw his eyes darting back and forth as he read, his smile growing larger. "Wow. He *does* have an active imagination. Respect. Also, what's felching, and why does he spend three paragraphs talking about that's what he wants to do to you?"

I slapped the book out of his hands. "Stop reading terrible erotica when we're trying to not die!"

"Hey," he said seriously. "No judgement, remember? I respect your kinks. If you tell me what felching is, I'll see if that's something I'm comfortable with you. It's important to discuss boundaries before we push against them."

"And now I'm extremely uncomfortable," Dad said.

"*Dad.*"

He rolled his eyes. "What? I am."

"This isn't good," Morgan said as he studied the wall. "Keith appears to be fixated on Justin."

I scoffed. "Oh, really? What gave that away? Please, Morgan. Continue to give us your extremely valuable insight."

Morgan ignored me. "Did you know about this, Anthony?"

Dad shook his head. "Of course not. If I had, I'd have done something by now. I've never even heard Keith mention Justin outside of duties of royalty." He grimaced as he glanced at a drawing where I seemed to be a nude contortionist, bending in ways that were not humanely possible. "He's certainly thorough."

"You want me to talk with him?" Dylan asked me. "I can, if you want. I won't hurt him, but I can get him to back off."

I put my fist in my mouth and screamed.

"Whoa," Dylan said. "He wrote that you could do that in the book. He must know you really well. And now I'm jealous again. Feelings are hard. I respect your autonomy, but if we're going to be together, I want to be the only one putting things in your mouth."

"Still here," Dad reminded him. "Still very uncomfortable."

Dylan nodded. "My bad. I'll only talk about sticking things in your son when we're alone."

"I have no one to blame but myself," Dad muttered. Then, "I have a feeling I know who took the stone."

"Oh, really?" I demanded, waving my arms wildly. "What gave you the first clue?"

"Who is it?" Dylan asked. "Who took the stone?"

We all turned slowly to look at him.

Dylan brightened. "Ohhhh. Right. Keith. That makes sense. Ish. Why would he take the stone if he can't use it? And what does that have to do with Ramos who may or may not be the bad guy even though I don't think he is?"

"Who the fuck knows," I growled. "But I'm going to kill him myself. Any of them. All of them. No one keeps a drawing of me licking my own asshole and gets away with it."

"Can I keep it?" Dylan asked. "For science."

"Yep," Dad said. "Now I'm done." And with that, he practically ran from the room. Morgan sighed and followed him, leaving Dylan and me alone.

"So," Dylan said after a beat.

"So," I said through gritted teeth.

Dylan clapped his hands in front of him. "So you have a stalker. Is it your first? I've had eleven, so if you need any advice, I'm your man. And that advice is do *not* engage. The moment you do, that's when they think they have an in, and then you're tied up surrounded by black candles while they chant in a weird language before trying to take your blood and inject it into themselves."

I gaped at him.

He nodded solemnly. "That was a bizarre eighteenth birthday. But we had cake without candles after I was rescued because I was still trying to get over being kidnapped, but it's all good. I love cake. Give me all that frosting."

"I like you," I said helplessly, to myself or him, I didn't know.

He softened. "Oh, hey, thanks. I really like you too." He smiled as he looked down at the floor. "Maybe even a little more than that."

Oh, my heart stuttered in my chest. "But I swear to the gods, if you don't focus, I'm going to do at least seven of these things on the wall to you."

He squinted at me. "Before I decide, can you tell me which seven? Because there's one over there that I have my eye on. You don't have to wear the garters, but the feather boa? Heck yeah."

"Yes, fine, that one," I said. "But the others are going to hurt!"

He shrugged. "Cool. I'm down. We'll need to have a safe word. Gary told me it's okay to use Sam's name, but that feels a little weird. Why would I call out someone else's name during our bone sesh?"

"Bone sesh," I repeated, wondering if it was too late to take back my admission of feelings.

He snorted. "Oh, I'm sorry, my Prince. I didn't mean to offend your delicate sensibilities. What I should have said instead of bone sesh was lovemaking."

I gagged. "Gods, that was somehow worse. Stop it. We have to be serious."

"I can be serious about more than one thing at once. And I'm *very* serious about our future relations." He grinned as he took a step toward me, a trickle of sweat dripping down the back of my neck. He stopped in front of me, only inches away. I could feel the heat rising off him. He leaned forward, his beard scraping my cheek. His lips brushed against my ear, causing me to shiver as he whispered, "Let's go save the day so we can be… serious about a couple of other things that involve less clothing. You know, as a little treat."

I nodded weakly. "Yeah. Okay. That sounds good. Let's do that."

He pulled back. "Great! Now that we have a goal, we can move forward. Digger always said that it's easier to do hard things if you get a hard thing when you're done."

I hadn't quite figured out if Digger was a genius or a moron, but with the way Dylan looked me up and down, I was beginning to lend credence to the former. I was so fucking screwed. At least figuratively. For now.

Dylan followed me out of the room. Dad and Morgan stood in

the hallway, Dad's head bowed as Morgan whispered to him. Morgan stopped when he saw us, and Dad lifted his head. "Morgan is of the mind that I need to go into hiding for my protection."

"You should," I admitted. "But what are the chances you're actually going to listen to him?"

Dad hummed. "Slim to none. If I go, you go, and I know you won't do that." He kissed Morgan on the cheek. "I know you're worried, but I can't let you all face this alone. I am the King of Verania. It's my duty to protect my people. I won't hide away when they're in danger."

Morgan shook his head, but he looked defeated. "I can't have anything happen to you."

Dad took Morgan's chin in his hands. "It won't because you'll be at my side. I have faith in you, Morgan. I have faith in all of us. We'll—"

A knight rounded the corner at full speed, armor clanging as he skidded to a stop in front of us. Neil, Ryan's second in command. He panted as he bent over, hands on his knees, face red from the exertion.

Dad stepped toward him. "Neil? What is it?"

"The throne room," he gasped. "The children."

"No," Morgan whispered.

"What happened?" I demanded. "Are they all right?"

Neil shook his head. "Someone took Sam and Ryan's kids. Joshua and Rosemary said the throne room filled with shadows like night had come. They got lost in the dark, and someone struck Joshua upside the head. He's fine, but he's pissed off. Rosemary too. They're waiting for us downstairs."

"Magic," Morgan breathed. "How....?"

"Sam and Ryan's kids?" Dad asked with a frown.

"Godsdammit," I growled. "He thinks—Neil, those aren't their kids."

Neil looked confused. "That's not very nice. Just because they adopted them and named them after themselves doesn't mean that they aren't a real family who—"

"You absolute *idiot*!" I cried. "That *is* Sam and Ryan and Gary and Kevin and Tiggy. They were magicked into children when I bound myself to Dylan!"

Neil sputtered. "*What*? Why didn't you just say that in the first place? The knights and I already put together funds for their unisex baby shower, and you're telling me it's all a lie?" He groaned. "How am I supposed to trust anything ever again? Though, strangely, it does make sense now."

"It does?" Dylan asked incredulously. "Because I have no idea what's going on."

"It's Verania," we all said at the same time. I really wished we'd stop doing that.

"What about Lady Tina?" Morgan asked. "She was supposed to be guarding them."

Neil shook his head. "I don't know. She's gone too, so it seems as if she was taken along with them."

A loud roar filled my head, and anger I hadn't felt in a long, long time flooded my veins. Neil flinched as I charged toward him, only stopping when Dylan grabbed me around the waist, lifting me up off the floor. I kicked my legs, bellowing at the ceiling. Dad put his hand against the wall as he sagged, Morgan pale, hand over his mouth.

"Where?" Dad asked faintly. "Where were they taken?"

Neil opened his mouth to reply, but before he could, a tremor rolled through the castle, causing dust and bits of stone to fall from the ceiling above us. Dylan stumbled, dropping me back on the floor. I took off like a shot, my father and Morgan shouting after me. I expected the sash around my wrist to pull tight, but it didn't. I glanced back over my shoulder to see Dylan running after me, a determined look on his face.

"With you!" he shouted after me as the castle shook again. "I'll follow your lead."

We raced through the castle, hitting the nearest stairs and heading up, trying to avoid everyone descending. "Get to the dungeons!" I snapped at them, almost taking an elbow to the throat. "Once you're all in, barricade the doors. Don't let anyone by until you hear from me or my father."

We managed to reach the floor where my room was without coming across anyone trying to stop us. My mind whirled. Ramos. Keith. Lady Tina. The kids. I couldn't make the pieces fit, but it didn't matter. I knew what I had to do. If anyone else was assisting whoever thought they could fuck with Verania, then may the gods have mercy on their souls.

I slammed open the door to my room, going to the armoire that held my weapons. I threw the doors open, the left creaking loudly as the hinges busted. There, sitting in its scabbard, the sword my father had gifted me. *My* sword. The sword of a king. I pulled it free, the steel glinting in the light pouring through the window. I took my other sword out and tossed it to Dylan. He caught it deftly, flourishing it once before nodding.

I went to him, pressing my forehead against his. "I need you," I whispered. "I need you to help me."

He bared his teeth, eyes alight. "Anything for you."

"You stay by my side. Never lose sight of me. We're going to offer no quarter for those who stand in our way. I know you believe in pacifism, but—"

He shook his head against mine. "Not when it comes to protecting your family." Then, "*Our* family, because they're mine now too. Let's go cause some trouble."

I grinned ferociously at him. I didn't know if the gods had set him in my path, but if they had, they'd chosen wisely.

The castle rumbled again as we left my room behind.

# CHAPTER 17
## The Wrath of the Gods

WE FOUND MY FATHER and Morgan with Joshua and Rosemary, standing at the front entrance of the castle, looking out onto the city of Lockes. They were all silent, a contingent of knights and Dylan's guard surrounding them. The knights all had their swords drawn, but they hung limply at their sides. Dylan's guards—the dancers who'd filled the hall upon his arrival—held their sashes tight between their hands like garrotes.

I skidded to a stop beside them, Dylan bringing up the rear. His people looked relieved, rushing toward him and demanding to know if he'd been hurt.

I ignored them, looking out into the city. The gates to the castle had been closed, and from Lockes, bells rang in warning. I didn't need to see the streets of the city to know that if they'd done as we planned, they were already seeking shelter. I jostled my father. "Why are we all just standing here? What are we going to do?"

But Dad didn't answer, looking off into the distance with a stunned expression. I frowned, waving my hands in front of his face. Morgan grabbed my arm, pulling me toward him. I stumbled, but he caught me by the chin, turning my face east, toward the city wall. I saw what they were staring at, and any and all rational thought left my head.

"Oh my gods," I heard Rosemary breathe as my mouth dropped, my knees going weak.

Because there, towering over the City of Lockes, shadow stretching long, was a monster.

It was absurdly large, at least twice as tall as Kevin had been, and vaguely human shaped. It had arms and legs, but it appeared to be made of black stone, lines of red-orange fire shot through its entire body. It didn't seem to have a neck, its head a circular lump of rock. Its eyes glowed red, wisps of flames rising around them. It opened its mouth and roared, the sound so loud, it blotted out everything else. I slapped my hands over my ears to try and muffle it, but my teeth rattled in their gums as my skin vibrated.

"Well, nuts," Dylan said as the echoing roar began to die. "That's not what I expected. Huh. Well, I suppose that it's Verania. Did I do that right? It's Verania?"

"What the hell is *that*?" one of the knights shouted as he cowered. "Oh my gods, I'm gonna die. Today was supposed to be my last day before retirement. We all know what happens to people on their last day before retirement!"

"Morgan?" Dad asked, gaze never leaving the monstrosity towering over the city. "If you know what this is, now would be a really good time to say so. And while you do, I'd also appreciate the plan I know you have about how to destroy it."

Morgan put his hand to his throat. "I have absolutely no idea."

Dad sighed. "I was afraid you were going to say that."

I choked as a memory shot through my head like a shooting star. "Holy shit, Sam was *right*?" What was it he'd said? We'd be trapped by a monologuing villain who's trying to awaken some ancient god that sleeps beneath Verania. Gods, I was going to fucking *murder* him for willing this into existence. After we saved him, of course, and after I'd ordered that he never be out of my sight again.

Everyone turned to look at me. "Justin?" Dad asked.

I glared at my father. "This is your fault."

Dad blanched. "*Me*? I didn't do this!"

"You asked Sam what's the worst thing that could happen!" I cried. I waved my sword at the monster. "Well guess what. There's the fucking *worst thing that could happen*."

Dad sniffed. "Oh. Well, then. You may continue." He rubbed his chest as he grimaced. Before I could start to panic that he was about to have another heart attack, he said, "Do you feel that?" He tapped his hand against his chest. "It's…here." He raised his hand to his head. "And here."

I didn't know what the hell he was talking about until Morgan nodded grimly. "I feel it too. It's…fear."

I gaped at them. "Of *course* it's fear! There's a giant monster standing right the fuck *there*. If you're not scared, there's something wrong with you."

Morgan shook his head. "It's not that. It's more. Look." He pointed out toward the guard surrounding us with a trembling hand. They were the bravest Verania had to offer, those who would charge into battle without a second thought.

Now, though, it looked as if their bravery had left them entirely. Some had dropped their swords to the ground, crouched on their knees, their hands over their heads. Others were wailing, tears streaming down their faces. Even Dylan's guard was affected, falling to their knees and screaming at the ground. I didn't know what the hell was wrong with them. I shouted at them to get the fuck up, but they ignored me.

"What's wrong with them?" Dylan asked.

Dad looked at me with wide eyes. When he spoke, his voice was hoarse and small, as if coming from a child. "I've never been more scared in my life. Justin, I don't think I can do this." He glanced down at the sword in my hand. "Good. You have my gift. Guess what? You're king now. I wish you every success. I'm gonna go hide. Bye." He tried to flee back into the castle, but I grabbed him by the arm, pulling as hard as I could.

"What are you doing?" I shouted in his face as the monster roared again. The sound hit us like a wave, and Dad screamed as he jerked his arm from my grasp, hands covering his face.

I gaped at him as I took a step back. This wasn't my father. I'd never known him to be scared of anything, and yet, here he was, shaking like a leaf caught in a hurricane.

"We have to run," Morgan muttered. "We have to run as fast as we can. Maybe it'll go away if we ignore it. Yes, that sounds like it'd work." He rocked back and forth. "Yes, yes, we run and it'll all go away."

Without a second thought, I said, "Sorry about this," before I slapped him hard across the face.

His head rocked to the side, the imprint of my hand forming on his cheek. Rosemary and Joshua sobbed as they clutched each other, and Dad hopped from one foot to the other, wheezing in terror. Morgan froze before turning his head back toward me, eyes clearer than they'd been only a moment before. "Fear," he gasped. "It's fear. Magic.

Can't fight it. Taking over." He shuddered as he curled in on himself, beginning to rock again. "Justin, it's coming from the monster."

I took a step back, awash in unreality. I too was scared, but it wasn't affecting me like it seemed to be with everyone else. And it couldn't be just those who used magic, because my father and the knights were hit just as hard. I glanced back over my shoulder to see Dylan hadn't been overcome, either. If anything, he looked confused as he tried to soothe his people to no avail. They cowered before him as if they were afraid *he* was going to attack them. He frowned as he reached for them, flinching when they screamed, the sash stretching between us.

The sash.

I stared down at it, turning my arm over to look at my wrist. The Sash of the Grand Hunt didn't feel any different than it had before. "It couldn't be," I muttered, rubbing against the fabric. I didn't have magic. Dylan didn't either. But the sash did.

What if it was keeping us from feeling what everyone else was?

"Morgan," I said, still looking at the sash in wonder. "Could this...?" I didn't know how to finish. But it didn't matter, because Morgan was lost to his terror, pupils blown as he moved to hide behind my father who was still trying to make himself as small as possible. They clung to each other, weeping quietly.

Randall was supposedly coming with the dragons, but I didn't know how long it would take. For all I knew, he was afflicted as the others were, cowering in Castle Freesias and waiting for it all to end. If he was, then we...

We were alone.

I gripped the hilt of the sword so tightly I thought my fingers would snap. I closed my eyes and remembered how I'd felt standing in front of my people in the port, promising them I'd protect them, that I wouldn't let those who tried to take from us do so without retribution. I'd been angry then. Angry and lost and afraid. Hope, I'd said, was a weapon. I'd believed it then, hadn't I? I'd believed it because I'd had to hope that we would see this through, that no one, not the gods, not the Darks, *no one* would be allowed to fuck with our home.

I raised my head, a calm washing over me that I did not expect. I felt tethered to the earth, to Dylan, grounded, my head clear. I knew what I had to do.

I was the godsdamn Prince of Verania.

And I was *pissed the fuck off.*

"Dylan," I said, his head jerking toward me at the hardness in my voice. "It looks like it's up to us."

And oh, how he smiled. Whatever would come, we'd have this moment. I went to him, kissing him with all the strength I could, pouring every piece of me into it. He gripped the back of my head as his teeth tugged on my bottom lip. I laughed wildly as he pulled back. "With you," he said. "No matter what."

I took his hand in mine and turned toward the monster. I raised my sword above my head and screamed so loudly, I thought my throat would tear. Dylan raised his own sword and did the same. Our cries echoed, mingling together like a symphony.

And then we ran toward the gates, not looking back, even as my father shouted my name.

*****

THE STREETS OF THE City of Lockes were flooded in fear, people running, slamming into each other in their hurry. A woman tried to pull her child along with her, but someone crashed into them, breaking her hold on her son. The boy fell over, raising his hands above his head. A large man wasn't looking where he ran, face tilted up toward the sky. Dylan managed to grab the child in time before the man crushed him. The boy's mother hissed at him as she snatched her child back, turning and fleeing into an alley.

"It's okay!" Dylan called after her. "I know you didn't mean it. Have a good day!"

It took us time to reach the front gates that opened up into Lockes. Terror like I'd never seen before covered the city in a heavy shroud, afflicting anyone and everyone aside from Dylan and myself. People cowered together, tears streaming down their faces as they tried to make themselves as small as possible.

I too was afraid, but it was a negligible thing, drowning in the anger that roared within me. I felt like I was on fire, and it brought with it a clarity I hadn't felt in a long time. I felt alive in ways I hadn't in the last year, vital and strong. Part of it had to do with Dylan, following me without question. I didn't know what I'd done to deserve his loyalty, but it only further stoked the flames that burned within me.

I would have done this alone had I been called to, but I *wasn't* alone. I promised myself if we survived this, I'd do whatever it took to let Dylan know he was cherished and maybe one day, not so far in the future, I'd look upon him and tell him the words I'd said to no other aside from my father.

Not *if* we survived this.

When.

The knights guarding the front gate flinched when we appeared, swords drawn, a sharp wind rushing over us, causing my clothes to billow around me. A pang hit my heart, deep and cold, knowing Sam would be enjoying the hell out of this. After he was rescued, after everything went back to normal, I'd tell him of this moment, tell him that yes, Dylan was at my side, teeth bared and at the ready—a part, a piece of a whole—but it was Sam I thought of. He had proven me wrong, and though I fought against it with all my might, he'd gotten past my defenses to the heart of me, to the scared boy prince underneath. I was not an island. I was a prince who needed his people in order to take another step.

"Open the gates," I thundered. The knights wailed in terror but did as I ordered, crashing into each other in their haste. The gates groaned mightily as they opened, revealing the grounds in front of the castle, grasses swaying. In the distance, the Dark Woods stood ominously. I hoped Randall and Dimitri found what they sought. We'd need them if we had any hope to survive what came next.

"Ready?" Dylan asked me.

"Ready," I said, and when he smiled at me, I knew if we survived, it would be love I felt when I gazed upon him.

He took my hand in his, and we left the City of Lockes behind.

*****

"Mistake," I muttered weakly. "Everything I've ever done has been a mistake."

The fear monster towered above us, blotting out the sun as we approached. It made no move to attack as its gigantic head swung toward us. Though not the biggest thing I'd ever seen—the Great White held that honor—it was still a great beast, and I didn't know how well our swords would do against it, especially when we got close enough to see it seemed to be made of fiery black stone. The heat emanating from it was overwhelming, causing my hair to plaster wetly against my head as sweat trickled down my face in rivulets.

It stood on the training fields, the ground beneath its feet blackened and charred as if every step it took had lit the earth on fire. Behind it and the fields, a massive crater had appeared in the ground as if the monster had crawled from the depths of Verania. How long had it been hidden beneath us? Where had it come from? Who had called it? And how the hell could we destroy it?

I had answers for none of my questions, but it didn't matter. People were counting on us. We would do what we had to in order to ensure Lockes stood at the end of the day.

"Whoa," Dylan breathed, looking up at the monster. "That's not something you see every day. Question. What are we going to do if it tries to step on us?" He grimaced. "No offense, but I'd really rather not be squished. I think my head would pop like a grape."

"At least it'd be over quickly."

He laughed. "Look at you, bro. Optimism. Cool. I approve."

I rolled my eyes as the monster growled above us. "Any ideas?"

He glanced at me before looking back at the monster. "A few, but they all involve running as far and as fast as we can. Pretty sure we could get to Yennbridge in a month if we started now and didn't stop."

"You think?"

He shrugged. "Yeah, but then I'd feel bad about leaving everyone behind, so we might as well kick this thing's ass. Even if we die, at least we'll get a gnarly song sung about us by the Bard. Weird Thursday, though."

"It's Tuesday."

He groaned. "Oh man, that makes it even worse."

Before us, on the ground, sunlight. Three more steps, and we'd be in the shadow of the monster. I saw movement between its legs amongst the training dummies. I thought I heard the voice of a child, high-pitched and scared, and any fear I might have felt in the face of such a beast left as if it had never been there at all, replaced by cold resolve.

And so we stepped from the sunlight into the shadow, the heat increasing, causing the air to shimmer in front of us. I waited for the monster to attack, but it didn't. Instead, it stared down at us, eyes endless pits of orange and red. A piece of its neck broke off, falling toward the ground like a meteor, the ground shaking underneath our feet as it hit the earth, throwing up a wave of dirt and burning grass. It made a strange noise—like a grumbling mewl—as it watched every step we took.

"*Justin!*" a voice screamed, and I jerked my head toward the shed near the training dummies. The door to the shed hung open, and I thought I saw movement within. Keeping one eye toward the sky, I ran toward the shed, Dylan following me. The monster growled so loud, my skin vibrated, the hairs on my arms standing on end.

"Why isn't it attacking us?" I heard Dylan ask behind me, but before I could answer, my throat closed at what I found inside the shed.

Sam of Dragons. Knight Commander Ryan Haversford. Knight Tiggy. Lady Gary the Tyrannical. The Beast from the East. All still children, and bound together with vermilion root that covered them up to their necks. They all looked relieved to see us, though stricken with fear. Dylan stood at the door guarding us as I sank to my knees in front of them. I didn't see Ramos or Lady Tina or Keith, but one thing at a time.

Tears streaked Sam's face as I touched his cheeks, pressing my forehead against his.

"Justin," he whispered in a choked voice. "Justin."

"Are you all right?" I asked them as I pulled back.

"*No,*" Gary snarled. "Do I look all right? I swear to the gods, if my mane is messed up, there is going to be *hell to pay*. You think looking this good is easy? It's *not*."

"We were kidnapped," Kevin said miserably. "And then monsters came." His eyes filled. "I want a snack and to go *home*."

"I'm trying to be brave," Ryan said with a sniffle. "But it's hard when you're little."

"Tiggy brave," Tiggy said. "Tiggy also scared. My brooms okay?"

"Your brooms are fine," I assured him. "I know you're scared, but I need to you to listen to me. I'm going to get you out of here. When I do, I want you to run for the forest. Run and hide in the trees. Don't look back."

"What about you?" Sam asked as I began to hack away at the vermilion root. It broke off in pieces, falling to the ground.

"I'm going to stop this," I muttered as another piece of root fell off.

"Don't you worry about me. The forest, Sam. You know it better than anyone. You don't remember, but you went there once and returned with something unexpected. The forest will protect you. I need you to lead the others away."

"But—"

"*Sam*. There's no time to argue."

Ryan was freed first. Instead of collapsing in on himself or running as fast as his little legs could carry him, he turned to help me, grunting as he pulled on the vermilion root, hair bouncing as the cords on his neck jutted out. He squawked as a large section of the root came free, causing him to fall back on his rear. Tiggy stood, the root cracking around him as he sneered. He pulled up Kevin and Gary with him, gathering them in his arms, holding them close.

Sam came last, and as the root fell away around him, he launched himself at me, wrapping his arms around my neck, his knees digging into my stomach. I hugged him back as his face went into my neck, his breath hot and wet. "You came for me," he whispered, clutching at my hair. "I knew you would."

"Always," I whispered back.

"Bro," Dylan said loudly. "I don't know who you are, but you need to stay back. I'm armed, and I will stab you in your *face* if you take another step."

"Ah, there's no need for such things," a voice said, and *now* came the panic, *now* came the fear, bright and glassy and all-encompassing. My vision grayed out as I stood slowly, Sam's legs wrapping around my waist as the others huddled behind me.

Because I knew that voice. Not as well as the boy I held, but well enough. It wasn't possible. He'd been destroyed. Sam had seen to it, or so we'd thought.

"It's him," Sam whispered feverishly. "The man from my dreams. *He's here.*"

I felt as if I were floating on the surface of a vast ocean as I went to the doorway, Dylan standing in front of the shed, gripping his sword tightly.

And there, standing only a few feet away, was the Dark Wizard Myrin.

He looked as he had before he'd descended on Verania, like Morgan, though as if seen through a hazy lens. His eyes were the same, but off, vacant and pitch-black. His black beard curled down onto the chest of his red, flowing robes. His feet were bare, toes flexing in the grass. His hands were clasped behind his back, head cocked as he watched us with vague disinterest. The monster above us shifted, and a beam of sunlight fell upon us. I blinked against it, trying to clear my vision.

Myrin, who had once been consumed by David's Dragon in a cosmic plane, smiled, gaze crawling over me before focusing on Sam. "Oh," he said as a twisted smile formed on his face. "We've been here before, haven't we? Do you remember, Sam of Dragons? You, with your faith in those you'd gathered around you. Me, the necessary counterpoint. I found you in Mashallaha, the boy anointed by the gods. I wasn't impressed. You were such a little thing, though perhaps a bit more now than then. I saw your bravery, foolish though it was. I underestimated you, then, trying to tear your lightning-struck heart from your chest. I failed, as I failed every time after. But that is in the past. I won't fail again." He took a step toward us.

"No," Sam whispered. "No, please, no."

"I mean it, bro," Dylan snapped. "Not another step."

Myrin ignored him. "You can't beat me. I am in your head. I am in your nightmares. I am in your *blood*, because you've always been like me, haven't you, Sam? Your little friends can't see it, but I can. I know the darkness within you, the magic you struggle to contain. We're the same. We always have been. Morgan and Randall knew it. It's why they kept so much hidden from you. They knew what you could become, and though they tried to fight it, they can't stop what you're supposed to be. I feel it rising in you." His nostrils flared. "I can *smell* it on you. Yes, even though you look as you do now, you're still in there, somewhere, locked away. But fear not, because I am the key, and you know it." He raised his hand toward us, palm toward the sky, fingers curling as he beckoned. "Come, child. Come with me, and I will leave your precious city standing. It's always been about sacrifice with you. Give yourself to me, and I will let your family live to fight another day."

"Not real," Sam muttered against my throat. "Not real."

I cupped my hand to the back of his head, trying to keep him from looking at the man who'd followed him into his dreams. "You won't ever touch him again."

Myrin smiled in such a way that my breath was stolen from my chest. It was like his brother's, though without the unending kindness. This was dark and warped, a disgusting parody of Morgan of

Shadows. "And you," he said, bowing mockingly, hands flourishing. That discordant feeling washed over me again. I could see him as clear as anything, and yet something still felt off. "The Grand Prince of Verania. The would-be king. How delightful it is to see you up close. I don't believe we've ever had the pleasure." His smile grew so wide, I thought his cheeks would split. "What do you think will happen here? That you'll somehow emerge victorious and save the day?" He shook his head slowly. "Oh, my dear boy. How mistaken you are. Your hubris will be your undoing."

"We killed you once before," I growled. "We can do it again."

Myrin laughed quietly. "Obviously it didn't take. What more do you think you can do to me? I am eternal. Not you, not the gods, and certainly not Sam will be able to stop me now. I bided my time, and my day has come."

"Not real," Sam said, sounding urgent. "Justin, not *real*." He sat back in my arms, grabbing my face and turning it back toward Myrin, positioning my head so that it looked at the ground near Myrin.

"Sam, not now." Something was wrong, but I couldn't quite place it. I could see Myrin clear as day. He looked as I'd remembered, but it wasn't the same. It wasn't—

"Shadow," Sam said, fingers digging into my cheek. "Justin, *shadow*."

And then I knew what he was trying to say. My own shadow was a black lump that moved as the children shifted at my feet. Dylan's own shadow looked fierce, bigger than he ever was in life as he sought to protect us.

But Myrin didn't cast a shadow. There should have been one, the bright beam of sunlight falling upon his shoulders. There wasn't. It was as if Myrin wasn't...

"Real," I said. My eyes widened. "Dylan, he's not *real*!"

Dylan glanced back at me, brow furrowed. "What?"

I set Sam down beside me. He immediately took my hand in his, squeezing so hard, I thought it'd leave bruises. The other children gathered around him, terrified, but holding on to each other, Gary and Kevin squirming in Tiggy's arms as the giant towered over them, ever watchful.

"Stay here," I told them, taking a step away even as Sam begged for me to come back.

Myrin's smile faded as I stalked toward him, my sword coming up. Dylan tried to stop me, but I shrugged him off. I only had eyes for Myrin. I stopped only a foot away from him. He had a few inches on me, but I was no longer afraid of him. As the monster loomed over us, as Sam screamed for me, I looked Myrin up and down, shaking my head.

"We're not afraid of you," I told him as his eyes narrowed. "We once were. We once thought you'd win. That you'd take everything from us. You almost did. But you failed because you didn't know what we were capable of. You thought we would cower before you. We didn't. And even though you're in our heads, you failed. You're *dead*."

"I am *everything*," he hissed at me.

"Not anymore. You're nothing but a memory, one that will fade long before our end. You don't get to touch my best friend again."

Myrin laughed wildly. "I already have. My marks are upon him, a reminder that I am infinite. Once I'm done with you, I will show him the true meaning of darkness. I'm—"

"Oh my gods, shut the fuck *up* already!" And with that, I stabbed him in the chest.

My sword went right through him. Instead of blood gushing from the mortal wound, the area around my blade rippled as if I'd thrust it into a lake. Myrin grimaced, mouth open wide as his head rocked back, tongue snaking out and running over his teeth. He made a strange noise, almost like the yelp of a grievously injured dog. Then his head snapped forward once more.

Myrin was gone.

In his place, stood my father, his crown sitting askew on his head. "Justin," Dad said, tears trickling down his cheeks. "What have you done? Why have you hurt me this way?" He reached down and touched the steel of the blade through his chest. He coughed harshly, a burst of blood dribbling down his cheek. I took a stumbling step back, falling over. I would have hit the ground had it not been for Dylan, holding me up, my back against his chest, his chin hooked over my shoulder.

"No," I moaned. "No, no, no—"

"You've killed me!" Dad cried. "Justin, why would you do this? I love you, I love you." He took a step toward us, the hilt of the sword now bobbing up and down. He began to jerk his head from side to side. One moment, he was my father, crying out for me to save him. Then he was Pete, Sam's guard. "You did this," Pete said, voice broken and weak. "I tried to help you, and you let me die. Why, Sam? Why, Justin? Why would you do this to me?" He bowed forward, bending over the sword. When he looked back up, I cried out in horror. Knight Commander Ryan Haversford glared at me, face twisted. "You think I cared for you?" he asked, his teeth coated with blood. "I never did. I used you to get what I wanted. Sam and me, oh how we laugh behind your back. When he's fucking me, I remember how weak you were, how you never could be what I wanted. You really think I could ever love someone like you?" He laughed harshly. His face became a blur and he shot up feet in height. Tiggy glared at me balefully. "I smash. I smash you *dead*."

Then his skull split in half as a unicorn's horn broke through. Dylan's hold tightened around me as he pulled me back, the kids moaning as a unicorn fought its way out of Tiggy's body. The giant's chest shattered with a horrifying crunch as a hoof shot through it. Before the unicorn could be free, it changed again, sprouting the black wings of a dragon as the beast rose before us. "I'm gonna fuck you up, little sheep," the dragon growled.

And then it all collapsed in on itself, and the figure fell to its knees. The wings melted as the scales glittered in the sunlight, the black and red sloughing off, revealing dark human skin underneath. When it looked up at us again, my blood ran cold as my sword fell to the ground.

Sam of Dragons smiled, that same smile I'd seen countless times before. He rose before us, robes billowing, dark eyes ablaze. "I've thought about this," he said with a chuckle, even as his counterpart whimpered behind me. "So many times. Remember when you brought me here? You wanted to teach me a lesson. To keep my hands off what you considered yours. You drew your sword, and oh, did I feel the hatred in your heart. You would've killed me, I think. Had it not been for that damn dragon, you would have run me through with your sword, and not felt even a twinge of remorse. What does that make you?"

"Not real," Dylan whispered in my ear. "Not *real*."

I knew that, deep down. But hearing this false Sam saying things I'd only thought in my secret heart was enough to render me immobile. He wasn't wrong, not completely. I didn't think I would have killed Sam on that summer day so long ago, but he was right. I *did* want to teach him a lesson. I'd worked my ass off every day to become the man the people needed me to be, and Sam could come here and do the same so effortlessly? Anger flooded me, but it wasn't at this interloper. No, it was at the child behind me, the child who was begging for me to listen to him. And didn't I always do just that? I did, and look where it'd gotten me. Look at what that trust had led to.

"Yes," the Sam-thing breathed. "Yes. I can feel it. You remember too, don't you? I took everything from you, and you did nothing to stop me. What kind of king do you ever think you could be? You're a coward, Justin. A weak little boy who thinks he deserves the crown for simply being *born*."

My vision narrowed as if I stood on the outskirts of a great tunnel. The voices of my friends faded until all I could hear was the mockery before us. Even Dylan's hold on me seemed distant, far away.

"You're scared," the Sam-thing whispered, whether out loud or in my head, I didn't know. "A little boy playing dress up. You aren't the man you think you are. I see it all, the thoughts in your head. How conflicted you are. How angry. How *frightened.* End this. Pick up the sword. Turn, and end this. Finish what you started on that day. It'll all go away if you just—"

"Suck my *butt*!" a voice cried, and I blinked slowly as if waking from an awful dream. I looked down to see my Sam standing in front of me, little hands curled into fists. He looked furious, his teeth bared.

"Yeah!" another voice said. "Suck our entire *butts*!" Ryan joined him, grabbing Sam's hand.

"You don't win," Tiggy said, joining his friends, Gary and Kevin glaring at the apparition before us. "*We* win because we together."

"And wouldn't you know," Gary growled, "I just happen to have a one-way ticket to Gore City with your damn *name* on it."

"I would threaten you too," Kevin said, "but Gary just made me feel tingly inside, and I'd rather focus on that." He nuzzled Gary's cheek. "Threaten him again. Only do it harder."

"I'm going string your intestines like a *garland*!" Gary bellowed.

"Ooh," Kevin said. "Hi, penis!"

Dylan moved until he stood beside me. He smiled at me. "You see?" he whispered. "Never alone." He kissed my hair before looking at the Sam-thing. "We're not scared of you, bro, or whatever you are. We're together, and nothing can stop us."

The Sam-thing screamed as it charged toward us, hands outstretched like claws.

Tiggy moved before we could stop him. He dropped Kevin and Gary and bellowed, "*TIGGY SMASH!*" His fist flew and struck the creature in the face. The Sam-thing exploded into black dust that buffeted against us. Tiggy looked around wildly. "Did Tiggy win?"

He threw up his hands and began to cheer. "Tiggy won! Yay Tiggy!"

The monster above us roared. But the tenor of it had changed. Oh, the anger was still there, but for the first time, it sounded as if it had been injured, like we'd hurt it somehow.

We whirled around, Dylan shoving us away just in time as the monster brought a fist down onto the shed, crushing it, the shockwave knocking us off our feet. I hit the ground roughly, groaning as the hilt from my sword dug into my back. I sat up in a daze, ears ringing. To my right, Sam had landed on top of Ryan. Beyond him, Tiggy pushed himself off the ground, standing above Gary and Kevin as he glared up at the monster.

Dylan grabbed my hand, pulling me up. He'd been hurt, a gash leaking blood on his cheek. "I'm fine," he said, jerking his head back when I reached for his face. "Don't worry about me. We have to—"

"King Dylan."

He turned. I stood on my tiptoes to peer over his shoulder.

There, standing beneath the fear monster's feet, was Ramos the Pure.

Godsdammit, I hated being right.

Or was I? Ramos looked unsteady on his feet, swaying side to side, his eyes glazed over. He seemed to be having trouble focusing, looking at us and then down at his hands as he brought them up to his face, turning them back and front. But he was real. He had a shadow.

"Ramos," Dylan said, taking a step toward him. "What have you done?"

Ramos wiggled his fingers in front of his face before dropping them. He grinned at Dylan. "Hello, King. I worry about you."

Dylan stopped as the monster growled down at us. "What do you worry about?" Dylan asked, bending down slowly to pick up his sword. I glanced around for mine and was relieved to see Tiggy had picked it up, standing above the other kids, protecting them. I jerked my head back toward the castle. He nodded at me, and began to back away slowly, the children clutching at him.

"Everything," Ramos said, and he chuckled as he rocked his head side to side. "If I'm good enough to help you be the king I know you are. When your parents died, I felt so alone. I…" He frowned. "I loved your father. More than even he knew. I only wanted the best for him and your mother. I loved her too, in my own way."

"Then why are you doing this?" Dylan asked, and he sounded so heart broken, I could barely stand it.

"Doing this," Ramos repeated. "I'm not doing anything. They left me, Dylan. They left me and you, and I'm so angry at them." I startled when a tear slipped down his cheek. "When you were a boy, you were so headstrong, so set in your convictions. I told your father you would make a great king, if only he gave you a chance. But he didn't believe me." He shook his head. "I was furious with him. That wasn't the man I'd come to know and love." He grimaced as he crouched down toward the ground. He plucked a blade of grass, turning it over between his fingers. "He didn't believe in you. I argued with him. I told him you needed to forge your own path to become the king Yennbridge needed. You couldn't be your father. You had to be your own man."

"And then you killed them," Dylan said, his bitterness so palpable, I could taste it.

Ramos gaped at us. "Of course I didn't kill them. I've never killed anyone in my life. You don't hurt the people you love."

"You're hurting me," Dylan said, taking another step forward. "All of this. Can't you see? You're hurting my friends, which means you're hurting me."

"Dylan," Ramos said. "Dylan, Dylan, Dylan. I'm not…" He stood back up like a puppet, strings being pulled from somewhere above him. His body spasmed, a tremulous thing that seemed to crawl from his toes up to his shoulders. "I'm *not*…"

"Trust me," I whispered in Dylan's ear. He nodded and I walked around him to stand at his side. Out of the corner of my eye, I saw Tiggy slowly herding the others away. The monster seemed focused on Ramos. Good. Any distraction would do. "Ramos."

He looked at me with vacant eyes. "Prince Justin."

"What do you think of me?"

"You're not good enough for my king," Ramos said promptly. "No one is. I put Dylan above all others. It wouldn't matter if you were the kindest prince in all the world, I'd still think you weren't fit to stand in Dylan's presence. But you're not kind. You're mean. You don't appreciate what's right in front of you. I don't know how you'll be king when you don't even seem to know who you are."

"What would you have me do?" I asked, now sure of what was going on.

"Finish the ritual. Tell Dylan you don't care for him and let us return to Yennbridge. He deserves better than you. He deserves the sun and the moon and the stars."

"I can't do that," I said evenly.

Ramos cocked his head. "Why?"

"Because I *do* care for him. And maybe that's selfish of me, because you're right. I'm not the best person. Dylan deserves better than anything I could offer him." I felt Dylan looking at me, but I ignored him. This was too important. "But I promise you, I will spend the rest of my days making sure he knows how wonderful he is. I don't know what we are right now, but I know what we could be if given the chance. I've spent too much of my life worrying about who I'd become, what others thought about me. I wish I could say I don't anymore, but that would be a lie. And yet, I know Dylan deserves everything you want for him and more. If you'll trust me, I will do whatever it takes to prove myself to you."

Ramos frowned. "I'm being selfish, aren't I?"

I shook my head. "Not when it comes to Dylan. You only want what's best for him, don't you?"

"I do," Ramos whispered. "That's all I ever wanted."

I held out my hand for him. "Can you trust me?"

"Ye-es?" he whispered.

I curled my fingers. "Then please, Ramos, give me the stone."

He studied my hand for a long moment before coming to a decision. He reached for me and—

"Oh, come *on!*" another voice cried, causing Ramos to flinch. And then my father's advisor appeared out from behind the monster's right leg, looking harried and furious. His red hair sat in angry tufts on his head as if he'd been yanking on it, eyes narrowed into slits. Spittle glistened on his lips as he snarled at Ramos. "Damn truth corn. I *knew* we'd given him too much!"

"He's been dosed," I whispered quickly in Dylan's ear. "Poisoned. He's not himself. I hope."

Dylan nodded but didn't speak, sword at the ready as Keith slapped Ramos across the face.

"Useless," Keith snarled in Ramos's face. "You're *useless*. If we didn't need your magic, I'd have killed you a long time ago." He grabbed Ramos by the shoulders, shaking him roughly, Ramos's head snapping back and forth. Keith froze as if remembering who else was here. He turned around slowly, wringing his hands. "My Prince," he said. "This isn't what it looks like."

"Really," I said. "Because it looks like you've poisoned the King's Magician. Do I even need to tell you the damage you've done? By rights, Yennbridge could wage war against Verania because of you."

"No!" Keith cried. "It was never supposed to get this far. I didn't…" He choked. "I didn't want it to come to this, but you left me no choice!"

"I saw your room," I told him. "I know you…care for me." Understatement, that, but I didn't think it would help to say as much.

He blanched, eyes darting to me then away. "I love you," he said, causing my skin to crawl. "I've loved you for years. I stood idly by while you fawned over that damn knight, because I knew it wouldn't last. How could a commoner think he could breathe the same air as you? And don't get me started on *Sam*." His hands curled into fists at his sides. "Sam, who everyone loves, Sam who came into our home like he *belonged*. And I saw it, my Prince. I saw it clear on your face. You hated him. You hated everything about him." He stared at me as if challenging me to dispute his claims.

Which I couldn't. "I did," I said. "I did hate him. But that didn't have anything to do with him. It was about *me*. I was selfish. I thought he was trying to replace me."

"He *was*," Keith spat, eyes wild. "He diverted your father's attention, he made himself a home in a place where scum like him don't belong. Everyone loved him. It didn't matter how much danger he put us all in, they still thought he was something special." He began to pace. "He took from you! He took Ryan, took your father, took *everything* you were owed. And finally, *finally* when I thought our problems were solved with matters of the gods and destiny, he managed to overcome that too. Oh my gods, I fucking *hate him so fucking much*. Damn half-breed who thinks he can—"

"Not cool," Dylan said. "Bro, I don't know who you think you are, but we do *not* judge people because of the color of their skin. That's messed up, man."

Leave it to Dylan to champion against systemic racism while a monster towered over us. If we survived this day, I was going to show him just how appreciative I could be.

Keith's eyes bulged from his head. "And *you*. Justin didn't even *like* you when you first appeared. Everyone could see it! You've bewitched him, somehow, and I won't let you take him from me. He's *mine*."

"Or," Dylan said, "you could let him decide what he wants.

Because he's his own person. And even if you've got the largest collection of erotic Justin art I've ever seen, that doesn't mean you have any ownership over him."

"The *largest?*" I demanded. "You've seen more?"

Dylan shrugged. "Saw some in one of the booths on our date. Didn't want to point it out because it involved a lot of tentacles. It took the phrase *go screw yourself* a little too literally."

"I don't know what to do with that," I said faintly.

"I respect that," Dylan told me. "And, since we're sharing, I'll say that I'd probably still like you if you had tentacles."

"Thank...you?"

"You can't have him," Keith said, taking a step toward us. Above, the monster rumbled threateningly. "You think you're something special just because you're a godsdamn king. Well guess what, *Dylan.* You may be a king, but I have a god." He turned his head up toward the monster and raised his voice. "Those damn kids are trying to escape! I command you to stop them!"

I turned, ready to run towards my friends. But before I could move, the monster roared. The air whistled as the monster brought down its hand, slamming it into the ground behind the children. They screamed as dirt and dust kicked up around them. The monster dug its hand into the earth, circling it around the huddled kids. Tiggy slammed the sword against its thumb, but the blade glanced off it in a shower of sparks. The monster pulled its hand back, leaving the kids standing on a patch of ground surrounded by a deep hole. It was too wide for all of them to jump safely. Tiggy could probably make it, and take a couple of them at a time, but I knew he wouldn't leave the others behind. They clung to his legs, faces buried in his clothes. Tiggy's face twisted as he raised the sword above his head. "Smash you!" he shouted. "Do again, and Tiggy smash you *goooood.*"

I turned back toward Keith, whose crazed grin chilled me to the bone. "Why are you doing this?"

Keith's smile faded into something vicious and dark. "It all started when my father left and didn't come back. It crushed me in ways I can't even begin to—"

I couldn't help the laughter that bubbled its way from my throat. "Are you *serious?*"

"Maybe don't piss off the man controlling a monster," Dylan muttered.

I shook my head, still laughing. "No, it's fucking ridiculous. You know how many people who've tried to hurt us because of daddy issues? It's the same. It's always the same." My laughter died as my anger took over. "Every single time, it's someone like you, thinking they're better than everyone else, that they're owed more than what they've made for themselves. You know what? I'm sick of it. When I'm king, everyone is going to be required to go to godsdamn *therapy*. Mandatory therapy so these idiots will work through their issues in a healthy way, rather than summoning fear monsters to try and make up for all their shortcomings."

Dylan nodded sagely. "That's cool, Justin. You'll always know wealth when you take care of your mental health."

"Sweet molasses," I muttered. Then, "I'm going to steal that, just so you know."

Dylan bumped my shoulder with his. "What's mine is yours."

Oh, how I wished the City of Lockes wasn't under attack so I could put my face on his face. Instead, I squared my shoulders, looking at Keith. Changing tact, I said, "I'm sorry you felt you had no other recourse but to try and kill everyone I love by bringing a monster to fight for you. That's...." Absolute bullshit, but that wasn't the diplomatic thing to say to an insane stalker. "...not the best way to go about it, but hey, what do I know? I'm only the Prince of Verania." I smiled at him. "You've opened my eyes. Thank you. You can tell your monster to go back where it came from."

Keith narrowed his eyes. "You believe me?"

"Yep!" I said cheerfully. Or, rather, as cheerfully as imminent death allowed. "I believe everything you've said, so no need to say anymore. You have my apologies in that I didn't see you for what you were."

Keith looked relieved. "Wow. That was nice of you to say. I feel better now." He scratched the back of his neck. "It's hard, right? And just when I finally thought I was getting through to you, the king from Yennbridge shows up and makes a mess of everything!"

"Exactly," I said. "You almost got through to me because I knew you existed before he ever arrived." That was a lie. I shuddered to think what he meant by getting through to me. I hadn't noticed anything, but now I wondered if he'd followed me through the castle or worse, jacked off on my clothes without my knowledge. Two extremes, but I blamed Sam for that. "Thank you for opening my eyes. We should go back to the castle now where we can live happily ever after." I waggled my eyebrows on him. "Get to know each other a little better."

"I know you're joking," Dylan whispered to me, "but since honesty is important to any relationship, you should know I'm getting a little jealous."

I barely kept from screaming at him. Progress.

"Yes," Keith breathed. "That. Let's do that. I know it probably doesn't look like it, but I'm a very generous lover. You know what they say about red heads who top. Once we finish, you'll be ginger bred."

Dylan said, "I don't get it. Why would he be a cookie?"

I hated everything. "That...sure is something. I can't wait to witness...all of that." I nodded up toward the monster. "So, what say we just chalk this up to a misunderstanding, huh? We all have bad days. Send that thing back to where it came from, and I'll make sure everyone knows you didn't mean it."

He nodded, but then paled. "I...I want that. But I don't know if my cousin would allow it."

I blinked. "Your cousin? Who the hell are you talking about?" I shook my head. "It doesn't matter. Just listen to me. We—"

Except I never found out if I'd gotten through to him. Because as he reached for me, Keith suddenly jerked forward as a thin sword burst through his chest, the blade glistening wetly. I gasped as he fell to his knees, blood bursting from his mouth as he said, "Well, that can't be good." And then Keith fell face-down on the ground where he didn't move. The sword was pulled from his body, steel grating against bone.

Lady Tina DeSilva shook her head as she wiped the sword off on his clothes. "Good help is so hard to find. I thought family wouldn't betray me, but I can see I was mistaken. What's the point of cousins?" She looked up at me and smiled as the monster roared above us. "And now, I will tell you my plans to take over the Kingdom of Verania."

"Dun dun *dunnnn*," Gary said from behind me. "Oh, and I'm still really scared, but fuck you, Lady Tina! Right in your stupid fucking *face*."

# CHAPTER 18

# Yeah, Yeah, Like You All Didn't Hate Her to Begin With

I COULDN'T BELIEVE IT.

Even though she stood right in front of me, Keith's dead body at her feet, I still couldn't believe it. I didn't *want* to believe it.

"No," I whispered.

"Yes," she said primly. "Surprised, aren't you? I thought you would be."

"But," I sputtered. "You…me…*why?*" Then, "You know what? I don't care. Fuck this and fuck you." I started to charge toward her, meaning to pummel her until there was nothing left, but Dylan grabbed me, holding me back.

Lady Tina eyed me up and down. "Tsk, tsk. I'd hold off, if I were you." She patted the monster's leg, hissing as it singed her skin. "I summoned him, which means he's under my control. I've always wanted a pet, but after our cat mysteriously disappeared when I was a child, mother wouldn't buy me another one." She sighed. "Poor Mr. Fluffies. Cats do land on their feet, even if their feet explode when you drop them from atop a building."

"I *trusted* you," I snarled at her.

"I know," she said. "And I love you for it." Her eyes widened to an obscene degree. "Oh, Justin," she said, voice pitched high and trembling. "I feel so terribly sorry for my part in Morgan's death. Ruv, he was *controlling* me with his magic. He made me bring Sam and Ryan to that house." Her chest hitched. "I never meant for anything to happen the way it did. Please, won't you believe me?" She scoffed as the act melted. "If I'd known you were that easy, I would've gone after you years ago." She made a face. "I can't believe I shipped you with Ryan for so long. Such a disappointment."

"What in the actual *fuck*," I growled.

She shrugged. "I'm a fan, Prince. Or, I was. And while some fans are fine when they don't get what they want, I'm not one of them. You blew your chances with the dreamiest dream to have ever been dreamed. I was the president of the Ryan Foxheart Fan Club Castle Lockes Chapter. Rystin was…everything to me. And while it took me a little longer to warm to you than it did to Ryan, once I saw past all the noise and bluster, I knew you'd be his perfect match. And then *Sam* had to get in the way and ruin everything."

"Boo!" all the children hissed.

"Let me at her!" Gary cried. "I'm gonna stab her in her *brain*."

Lady Tina made a face. "With his stupid horse and even stupider half-giant. I thought everyone would see through his ridiculous façade, but they didn't! They bent over *backwards* for him, all because Morgan and Randall decided he was someone important. Instead of sending him back to the Slums where he belonged, they welcomed him with open arms." She snorted. "Can you imagine? Someone from his lowly station granted an audience with the King of Verania, all on the word of a godsdamn *wizard*."

"I'm going to end you," I promised her.

She startled briefly before recovering. "I had such high hopes for you. Whether you realized it or not, we're kindred spirits. Don't lie, my prince. You hated him just as much as I did."

She wasn't wrong, and it pained me to see that someone like her had seen it. Keith too. The thought that I'd had played any part in this made me nauseous. "That doesn't give you the right to do what you've done."

She shrugged. "Doesn't it, though? Just because *you* were too much of a coward to take care of the problem yourself doesn't mean the rest of us aren't. I thought you'd see it my way. I really did. But then Sam somehow infected you too." She bared her teeth in a furious snarl. "Wherever he goes, calamity is sure to follow, and he brings the rest of us with him to clean up his damn messes. And we're supposed to be *happy* about it? We're supposed to *revere* him because the gods ordained him as a savior?" She laughed bitterly. "All I ever wanted was for you and Ryan to get your happily ever after. But you couldn't even do *that* right. And then Ryan fell under Sam's spell, and you followed like a little lap dog. Oh, you tried to make everyone believe you still reviled everything about him, but I *know* you, Prince. I've stood by your side for the last year, watching you lower yourself for him. You came to care for him, and try as I might, I couldn't get you to stop. I couldn't save you."

"I don't *need* to be saved," I snapped. "Sam didn't do anything to me that I didn't want." Another lie, but fuck her. "And in the end, he stood with me when all seemed lost."

"Yes," Lady Tina simpered. "Your Best Friend 5eva. We know. We all *know*. We hear about it incessantly. Gods, you're all pathetic. And what's a fan to do when their fandom descends into chaos and the characters start changing motivations out of nowhere?" She spread her arms wide as the monster grumbled angrily. "We create a new fandom out of the ashes. One where everyone does what we want, when we want."

"Cripes," Dylan said. "You really need to vet your staff better."

"Not helping," I muttered.

"Oh. Right. Sorry. You may continue."

"You won't get away with this," I told her through gritted teeth.

She rolled her eyes. "Of course I will. Everyone is cowering in fear because of me." She eyed us speculatively. "Except for the two of you. I suppose it's the sash, but that can be remedied quite easily. Ramos?"

"Yes, Lady Tina?" Ramos said.

"Remind me what happens when the sash is severed before the ritual ends?"

"Those bound will die, Lady Tina."

"Oh," she breathed. "That's *right*. They would die. Thank you, Ramos." She jerked her head toward him. "Concentrated serum from the truth corn. Makes him subservient. Aren't vegetables fun? I would give credit to the woman that came up with it, but seeing as how she was eaten by Kevin, that doesn't matter."

I took a step toward her.

"You really want to take the chance?" Lady Tina asked me, pointing her sword at the sash. "One wrong move, Prince, and you'll both be dead." She glared balefully at Dylan. "Dystin. What a travesty. And yet, once again, you *fell* for it. I mean, my gods. *Look* at him!"

Dylan shuffled his feet. "Aw. That's a low blow, bro."

She rolled her eyes. "As if a Prince of Verania would *ever* consider dating an idiot frat boy. You're beneath him. You haven't earned the right to breathe the same air."

I snatched the sword from Dylan's hand, pointing the blade toward her. "Say something bad about him again. I dare you."

Dylan grabbed the sword back from me. "No, *I* dare you."

Lady Tina laughed. "You? What are you going to do to me? You're a pacifist."

He grinned at her, razor sharp. "Yeah, well, I'm gonna pass my fist right into your face."

"I'm going to do you so gross later," I whispered.

His brow furrowed as he looked at me. "What?"

I coughed roughly. "Nothing. Never mind. Ignore me."

"See?" Lady Tina said. "Sam has infected you. You've even started talking like him. That won't do. If you won't submit to me, then you'll suffer along with the rest of them. Never, *ever* mess with a pissed off fangirl. We will *ruin* you."

A roar from above, but not from the monster. I turned my face toward the sky to see a great hole tear through the fabric of reality. I was stunned into immobility when two ice dragons burst from the hole, fangs bared in a furious snarl, feathers quivering. The bigger of the two—Pat—opened her wings, catching an updraft, causing her to soar high into the sky, her blue feathers glittering in the sun. I raised my hand to shield my face against the bright light, making out a figure riding upon her back.

Randall. Randall had come.

Leslie, the other dragon, folded her wings at her side, hurtling toward us. At the last second, she opened her wings, the ground rumbled beneath our feet as she landed, legs on either side of the children. They stared up at her in wonder as she curled her head down toward them, eyes flashing. Sam reached up with a trembling hand, pressing his fingers against her snout. "Oh dear," Leslie said. "You're much smaller than you used to be." Her tongue snaked out, brushing against Sam's cheek, who grimaced but didn't try and stop her. "Taste the same, though. Hello, little Sam. I'm pleased to see we weren't too late."

"You know me?" Sam asked in awe.

"I do," Leslie said. "I know you very well, my love. We have come to your aid because a dragon never forgets their promise."

"I'm a dragon too!" Kevin cried. "Will you be my mother?"

"I already am," Leslie assured him, covering them all protectively with her wings. "Fear not, children. We will protect you."

I heard a dragon bellow, and I looked up to see Pat dive-bombing the monster, who rumbled as it tried to swat her and Randall out of the sky. She flew deftly, avoiding the monster's attack with ease as Randall's beard and robes trailed behind him. "Save them!" Randall shouted down at us. "Get them as far away as you—"

The monster clipped Pat's neck, causing her to fall in a tailspin. Leslie gasped as her mate plummeted toward the earth. She raised her head, the feathers on her skull beginning to rattle, sounding like frozen bones banging together. The feathers glowed with an ethereal blue light, and Leslie's jaws opened wide. The temperature dropped suddenly as blue fire shot from her mouth, crystalizing as it hit the ground and froze solid as she tilted her blast upward, creating a ramp. Pat hit the tip of the ice and slid down it until she landed next to Leslie, Randall hanging on for dear life.

Pat lifted herself to her feet, nuzzling Leslie. "Thank you, even though I had it."

"Of course you did," Leslie said. "Doesn't hurt to make sure."

Randall hopped down off Pat, a thunderous expression on his face. I felt his magic gathering as he raised his hands above his head. The monster swung down at him, and I screamed for my friends. But then the monster's fist crashed into a barrier that formed above Randall, rippling with energy. Part of the monster's fist broke off, sliding down the barrier and landing in the grass. The monster roared in pain as it lifted its injured hand back up.

"Can't hold it," Randall muttered, sweat dripping down his face. "The fear. It's eating away at me. We must hurry."

"Yes," Lady Tina said. "I suppose we must. Gods only know who else is coming. Might as well get this over with. Ramos, I'm thinking three sculptures. The sun will do the rest."

"Yes, Lady Tina," Ramos said, reaching into his robes. He pulled his hand out and opened it. There, sitting on his palm, was the Damning Stone.

Lady Tina clapped as she jumped up and down. "Oh, this is going to be so much fun! Not only does Ramos have his own magic, useless thing though it is, but he also has the magic of a unicorn. Of Morgan of Shadows." She squealed. "And of Sam of Dragons, the most powerful wizard in an age. And even better? He can harness *it*. A little loophole, something he didn't tell you about. Because a *wizard* can't use the magic in the stone, but a magician? Yes, they can use it just fine. I think you'll really love this next part."

Ramos whirled his hand above the stone. Light poured from it, so bright it was like he held the sun in his palm. He pulled his free arm back, and then thrust it forward above the stone. A sharp *crack* followed as the air grew thick with the stench of magic. Randall had no time to react. Neither did Pat or Leslie. The magic struck them head on, immediately turning them to ice. Randall stood frozen, hand outstretched as if to ward off what he couldn't stop. I watched as a droplet of water fell from the tip of his ice-blue fingertip.

The children cried out in horror as I stared dumbfounded, Dylan tensing at my side as he tried to shove me behind him.

"There," Lady Tina said. "That's better. Now, where were we? Ah, yes! My plans for Verania. I'm so glad you asked! Did you know how many books there are in the library? Thousands upon thousands, some going back millennia. Most look like they haven't been touched in an age." She frowned. "Except for the half-dozen copies of *The Butler and the Manticore*. Those had dog-eared pages, which is *offensive*."

"I think your idea of offensive is seriously skewed," Dylan told her. "Like, you have no idea, lady-bro."

She ignored him. "All this history, just waiting for someone like me to discover it. It's how I found the incantation to raise this big guy." She smiled dreamily up at the monster, who blinked slowly, its eyes on fire. "You'd think such books would have been locked away or destroyed before they could be used. What do you all say to excuse your awful existence? Oh, right! It's *Verania*. As if that should explain away everything."

"I won't let you destroy my city," I said.

She laughed. "What? Ew. That's so gauche. Why in the name of the gods would I destroy Lockes? No, that certainly wouldn't do. I'm going to install myself as Queen of Verania and remake the city in my image, a place where fans can gather without judgment to discuss our favorite ships and all the gossip we could ever want."

I scoffed. "That's the stupidest thing I've ever heard of."

She smiled at me. "I thought you'd have a place in my new world, but I can see there's no hope for you. That's all right. With Ramos, I'll have an unlimited well of magic at my disposal, and everyone will love me." Her smile widened, all teeth like the gaping maw of a shark. "If they don't, well. I'll straight up murder them myself. A good queen knows when to delegate, and when to take matters into her own hands. I will be feared, because with fear comes respect. You taught me that, Prince. I thank you for your contributions."

"I'm nothing like you," I snarled at her.

"Yes, yes," she said, waving at me dismissively. "So you try and tell yourself. But you know it, and I know it. It's why they call you the Ice Prince." She paused. Then, "Well, that was mostly my doing. You'd be surprised just how many people are willing to spread rumors about royalty. It's like they have nothing better to do."

"You won't win," Dylan told her.

"Ugh," she said with a twisted grimace. "I'm bored with you now. I have so much work to do. I'm thinking walls of pink. An entire *castle,* all pink. It's going to be so delightful, and we'll have tea and cakes and people from the Slums will be forced to battle each other to the death for my amusement."

Something in the distance caught my eye. Behind her, behind the monster, a white blob was rising from the Dark Woods. It took me a second to realize what I was looking at, and my heart jumped into my throat. The tide was about to change, and I couldn't let her know. "And the others?" I asked to distract her. "Your contingent. Were they in on this too?"

She snorted. "Please. As if those bitches have the vision I do. They think *small,* Prince. They're happy just to act as your guard." She made a face. "There was a time I thought Deidre would be on my side, but she's more interested in practicing with her weapons. Such a waste. That being said, we do have a history, my girls and me. I'll give them a choice. Join me or die. And then I'll…"

As Lady Tina droned on about whatever-the-fuck, I whispered to Dylan, "Get ready."

"For what?" he whispered back.

"To *run.*"

"Are you listening to me?" Lady Tina demanded. "I'm trying to tell you why I will remake Verania in my image, where everything is wonderful and no one tells me what I can't do!"

"Yeah," I said. "You keep telling yourself that. I'm sure that's going to work out well for you."

"What the hell is *that*?" Gary said, and I grabbed Dylan by the arm, pulling him toward the kids.

Lady Tina stopped mid-rant, her captive audience no longer paying her any mind. She turned to see what the kids were staring at as Dylan and I ran past Randall and Pat, leaping over the divide that led to the children. I almost brained myself on Leslie's frozen wing.

I scooped up Sam in my arms as Dylan did the same for Ryan. Tiggy picked up Kevin and Gary. "*Jump!*" I shouted at them, shoving them away from what was coming.

They did, Tiggy going first and clearing the divide with ease. Dylan went next, Ryan gaping over his shoulder toward the sky as the monster began to turn. "I'm scared," Sam whispered into my ear, his breaths light and quick.

I put my hand to the back of his head. "I know. I am too, but I won't let anything happen to you."

"Because you love me?"

"More than you know," I said, before jumping across the divide. I almost didn't make it, the heels of my feet hanging back over empty air. I started to fall back, but Dylan's arm shot out and gripped my bicep, jerking me forward.

I opened my mouth to thank him, but the words died when Lady Tina said, "Well, shit."

The monster had barely begun to turn around when a dragon god slammed into it, wings spread so wide, they looked endless. The Great White's claws closed around the monster's neck, bone against rock, a cascade of sparks falling like rain. The monster reached up and grabbed the dragon's wings, pulling down as hard as it could. For a moment, I thought the wings would tear and all would be lost. Instead, the dragon's claws dug in, one underneath the monster's chin, forcing its head back as it opened its mouth. The Great White reared up, jaws wide, tongue flickering out.

"*Run!*" I bellowed.

We ran as fast as we could as white fire burst from the Great White down into the mouth of the monster. The lines of flame that covered the monster's body turned as white as a full moon. Someone screamed, but I didn't know if it was Sam or Ryan or me. I glanced back over my shoulder in time to see the Great White lift from the monster as it *expanded*, its torso filling like a balloon.

And then it exploded.

The shockwave slammed into us, knocking us all off our feet. Sam was torn from me as I hit the ground, large boulders raining down around us. I sat up in a daze, my vision filled with white. It took me a moment to realize I wasn't dead. No, the white had come from the great dragon before me, on the ground, shielding Pat and Leslie and Randall from the hellfire that rained down around them. Rocks like meteors crashed into his back, causing the Great White to roar in pain and anger.

Smoke and ash billowed around me, making it hard to breathe and to see even a few feet on either side. "Sam!" I cried, pushing myself up off the ground. "*Sam!*"

No response. Shaky on my feet, I stumbled forward, rounding a rock I thought had been the monster's nose. I followed the sash and found Dylan on the ground, unmoving. I collapsed next to him, hands going to his chest, his face. I nearly choked on the relief when his chest rose again and again. Aside from the gash on his face, he had a lump on the top of his head but didn't seem to be hurt more than that. I cupped his face, thumbs against his cheek. "Wake up," I muttered. "I need you to wake up. Please."

"Grand Prince of Verania," a deep voice rumbled behind me.

I turned slowly to find a gigantic head peering down at me, eyes glowing brightly. I'd never been this close to the oldest creature in Verania. He was almost too big for me to comprehend. His eyes narrowed as his nostrils flared, a hot wave of air bowling over me. "Where is he?" the Great White asked. "Dimitri said Sam was in danger. What has been done with him?"

"I don't know," I said frantically. "I had him, I lost him when the monster exploded. The others too. Gary. Kevin. Ryan. Tiggy. They have to be here somewhere."

The dragon said, "We will find them." He raised his head, mouth open as he sucked in a deep breath. His cheeks expanded and air rushed from his mouth, causing the thick cloud of smoke and dust to swirl away.

Dylan groaned, eyes fluttering open, unfocused. He tried to sit up, hand going to the knot on his head. "What happened?" he whispered.

"We were saved," I told him, pulling him up. He was unsteady on his feet, so I wrapped his arm around my neck, trying to hold him up.

He paled as he looked around. "Um, Justin?"

"Yeah?"

"That's a big freaking dragon."

"I am," the Great White agreed as he lifted his wings. "Thank you for noticing. You must be the King of Yennbridge. I would say I'm pleased to meet you, but that'd be a lie. I've only been asleep for three months. Everyone knows I need at least four in order to function. I am not amused."

"Oh," Dylan said weakly. "It can talk too. Neat. Hey, Justin?"

"Yeah?" I mumbled, trying to keep him from sinking back to the ground.

"No offense, but Verania is *weird*, bro. Like, cool and stuff, but I'm pretty sure I have a fear of large reptiles that I'm only figuring out now, so."

The Great White seemed pleased. "Good. Justin, I approve. You may keep him."

I was startled into laughter. "Great. Thanks. Exactly what I was hoping for. That means so much to me, you don't even know."

The Great White blinked. "Really?"

"*No!*" I snapped at him. "Gods, what the hell is wrong with you? We need to find the kids!"

"Rude," the Great White said with a sniff.

I glared up at him. "You really need to stop hanging out with Sam."

"Yes," he said with a sigh. "As soon as I said it, I regretted it." He twisted his neck, looking down at Pat and Leslie and Randall frozen beneath him. He pressed his snout carefully against the tip of Randall's frozen finger. "Now you've gone and done it, you old fool." But even I could hear the rough fondness in his voice for his former protégé. "How you've survived this long, I'll never know. I'll make you well again. I promise."

"Ryan!" Dylan called. "Can you hear me? Tiggy! Gary!"

"Sam!" I shouted. "Kevin!"

No response. Fear bled into my ribcage, real fear that had nothing to do with the monster who lay in pieces around us. I didn't see Lady Tina or Ramos, and I hoped the former had been squashed flat. If the same had happened to the latter, then so be it. I didn't blame him, but I had bigger things to focus on.

And that was a mistake.

Because we'd barely made it a few steps before a shrill voice rang out. "Are you fucking *kidding* me? Do you know how hard it was to summon that thing? I had to feed it the blood of eight innocents!"

We whirled around to find Lady Tina standing next to Ramos, who swayed on his feet, hands raised above him, a bright blue barrier snapping and crackling above them. They were on the other side of the Great White, barely visible through his massive legs. Lady Tina looked no worse for wear, though her rage was clear as day. Her face was twisted obscenely, her hair having fallen out of its braid, hanging limply on her shoulders. She stalked forward, snarling as she collided with the barrier. "Ramos! Let me *through*."

"Yes, Lady Tina," Ramos said, dropping his hands. The barrier snapped out of existence.

The Great White snorted. "This is the cause of all this strife? This petulant little girl?"

"Ex*cuse* you!" Lady Tina shouted. "I am a *woman*. And you won't be able to stop me!"

The Great White smacked his lips. "I think you'll find you're sorely mistaken. Greater than you have tried, and all have failed. You are not Myrin, little girl. He at least had a bit of finesse about him, even if he was lost to the shadows. You are nothing. And in a moment, the only time I'll think of you again is when you pass through my intestines toward my anus three days hence. I'm very regular."

For a moment, Lady Tina looked afraid. And then it melted into a sticky-sweet smile. "Ramos. I don't like how big this thing is. Make it smaller."

The Great White laughed. "He is a magician. What do you think he could possibly do to me?"

Eyes widening, I turned back toward them. "She's got Sam's magic!" I cried.

The Great White jerked his head toward me. "What?"

Ramos held the stone, hand a blur above it as he muttered under his breath. The stone flashed once, twice, a green light rising from it like a flowering plant. The air sizzled as the light rocketed toward the Great White, striking his neck. One moment, the dragon towered over us. And the next, an obscenely comical *pop!* filled the air, and the dragon disappeared.

"What did you *do*?" I demanded as Dylan panted in my ear.

A tiny squeak near my feet. I looked down to see a small white lizard scrambling in the grass. It blinked up at me with black eyes, and

I was stunned when little wings raised from its body.

"No," Lady Tina said. "I'm *not* Myrin. I did what he wasn't able to. I've defeated the dragons of Verania." She tilted her head back and cackled. If I didn't hate every fiber of her being, I'd be impressed at how evil she sounded. I was going to have so many trust issues after this. And that didn't even begin to cover how Sam was going to be able to say the four words I dreaded most coming from him.

*I told you so.*

But first, we had to survive what happened next.

"*Justin!*"

I looked left to see Tiggy running toward us, feet pounding the earth. "Catch!" He brought his arm back over his head before thrusting it forward. The sun caught the blade of my sword as it hurtled toward us. I managed to pull Dylan down just in time before it skewered us both. It landed ten feet to my right, blade piercing the ground, the hilt quivering.

"You no catch," Tiggy said.

"You threw the sword at me! How the hell was I supposed to catch that?"

Tiggy ignored me as he ran in front of us, bending over and scooping up the Great White mid-stride. He blew by us, shouting over his shoulder, "Tiggy help! Find others. You *smash*."

"Fuck yes I'm gonna smash," I growled, pulling Dylan toward my sword. "I'm gonna smash until there's nothing left *to* smash."

"This is so sad," Lady Tina said just as we reached my sword. My fingers circled the grip tightly as I pulled it from the earth. "But I'm done with you now. We have so much work ahead of us, and I fear you won't listen to reason."

"Reason," I said, voice dripping with scorn. "You know *nothing* about reason, you fucking twat."

She sniffled daintily. "That was certainly uncalled for. You know you've lost the argument when you devolve into name calling. I'd hoped that you'd see it my way, but I know now you're beyond saving. Worry not, Prince. I'll look back fondly at our time together. You were part of my first fandom, after all, and a fan never forgets."

I raised my sword toward her as Dylan did the same. "It's over, DeSilva."

She smiled a terrible smile. "For you, yes. Finally. Ramos. *Kill them.*"

And for a moment, Ramos hesitated, Damning Stone resting on his palm. He looked at us, at his king, his eyes briefly clear. "My King," he gasped. "I can't...fight it. Please. Run."

"I'm not leaving you," Dylan said, pulling himself to his full height, looking every inch the king he was. "You're my friend, and we don't leave friends behind."

"Blah, blah, blah," Lady Tina said. "Ramos, do it, and do it *now*."

Ramos tried to fight it. I could see that plainly. He fought with everything he had, but Lady Tina's control over him was too great. The stone began to glow as he swirled his hand above it. Magic began to build, and the moment before Ramos thrust his hand over the stone, I saw the regret that filled him, painful and absolute.

"No," Dylan whispered right as Ramos completed his spell.

"I'm sorry," Ramos said. "My King. I'm so sorry."

He jerked his hand over the stone in a slashing motion.

Without thinking, I shoved Dylan as hard as I could. It would have worked. Ramos's magic would have passed between us, but I'd forgotten one important thing.

The Sash of the Grand Hunt.

It stretched between us as Dylan fell away, the fabric rippling in the wind. The hairs on my body stood on end as the magic struck the sash, and a bright burst of agonizing pain like nothing I'd ever felt before bowled through my body as the sash tore, breaking the bond between Dylan and myself.

Above my own screams, I heard Dylan's as we both writhed on the ground. It felt as if massive hands had wrapped themselves around my insides, squeezing my organs until they threatened to pop. Trying to rise above it, I dug my hands into the ground, pulling myself toward Dylan as my body began to seize. Bright lights flashed before my eyes as my vision tunneled. It was getting harder to breathe, each inhale like I was swallowing fire and ice all at once.

The last of my strength left. I fell flat onto the ground, grass poking against my ear.

And then I began to die.

It was strange, really. My heart slowed. My breaths grew shallow. I felt regret, but it was a trivial thing, faraway. I was never one for wishes upon the stars. It had seemed trite and ridiculous, better suited for boy wizards. But here, now, at the end, I wished for a great many things. For Dylan, the man I'd come to care for beyond measure. For my father, whose face I'd never see again. For Randall and Morgan, two men who had made the ultimate sacrifice against one they loved most. Ryan, who had seen through my armor in ways no one else had. Gary and Tiggy and Kevin, three of the most unexpected creatures I'd ever had the pleasure to know.

And Sam.

I hoped he would somehow survive this day knowing that no matter what I'd done to him in the past, no matter how angry I'd been, I'd learned to love him as my friend. As my brother.

Dylan turned his head toward me, eyes growing vacant. "Justin," he murmured, trying to reach for me, but too weak to do so. His hand fell into the grass, palm toward the sky, fingers curling as if beckoning me. The sash lay severed between us, dull and lifeless. "I'm sorry."

"No," I choked out as another bolt of pain lanced my head. "You... can't..."

But I couldn't finish.

My heart stuttered in my chest as I rolled over onto my back, looking at the clouds hanging overhead. For a moment, I thought I saw constellations, stars raining down around me, but that couldn't be right. The stars only came out at night, and the sky was blue, blue, blue. It could only be the dying gasp of my mind, struggling to find meaning in my ending.

I gathered the last of my strength and spoke one last word in a reverent whisper.

*Sam.*

A star alighted in front of my face. It reached out to touch me, fingers in my eyebrows. "He is coming," the star said, sounding eerily like the King of Fairies.

Movement out of the corner of my eye, off to my right. The star pushed against my cheek, turning my head. I saw little feet. Little feet attached to little legs. Little legs that rose to—

"I'm here," a soft voice said as a figure crouched over me. "I won't ever leave you." Stars swirled around him, and as I began to fade, I realized they weren't stars at all. Fairies. All of them fairies, spinning around the head of a child. "Thank you," the boy said. "For believing in me. I heard you. I won't forget this time."

He moved away, and I tried to call for him, tried to bring him back, but my voice was gone. I watched as Dimitri settled on his shoulder as the boy frowned down at the remains of the sash. He picked either end up, bringing it close to his face, tongue sticking out between his teeth as he studied it. "I can do this," he said quietly.

"Yes," Dimitri said. "You can."

"How do you know?"

"Because you're ordained by the gods. There is nothing that you can't do."

The boy nodded. "My magic is gone."

Dimitri patted his cheek. "Not gone, merely contained. Call for it, Sam. It will hear you. And we'll be with you every step of the way. It's the least we could do for all that you've done for us."

Once upon a time in the Kingdom of Verania, there was a kickass boy born in the Slums of the City of Lockes. His parents were hardworking, and at times, life could be difficult, but they were alive and had all their teeth. Which was very important.

But he was more than he knew, more than anyone thought possible. This brave boy carried the weight of the world on his shoulders, his heart so vast and wild, it could only be lightning-struck. He had suffered, this boy. He had lost much, but still he stood, shoulders squared, brave and true. I loved this boy, this man he'd become, more than I'd ever said. I couldn't imagine a world without him, and as I took my final breath, I promised him that I'd love him for all of time.

My Best Friend 5eva.

As my vision faded, I watched as this boy pressed the ragged, burnt edges of the sash in front of his face, gripped tightly in his hands. "I wished," he said, voice loud and clear, "for impossible things. For a home. For a place to belong. For people who would love me for who I am and not for what I could do. I found my home. I found my family. My people. And no one will take them from me."

"No!" Lady Tina screamed as she ran toward him, sword raised above her head. "You can't do this! Verania is *mine*!"

Sam of Dragons said, "You stupid girl, I *am* Verania." He smiled, and in it I saw the man he'd once been, lovely and strong. "Flora. Bora. *Slam*."

And then he smashed his fists together. The fairies exploded in a light so bright, I thought the entire world could see it. I gasped in a harsh breath as my chest expanded, ribs cracking. My head rocked back as my heart beat thunderously, my legs jerking as if electrified. A wave of cleansing air caused my hair to whip about my head, and I inhaled again and again and again.

I pushed myself up as glittering smoke swirled around me. I flinched when a large shadow appeared in front of me, but then a hand gripped mine, familiar and warm. Sam—*my* Sam—grinned at me as he helped me stand. I gasped when I saw he was taller than me again, his robes of green and gold billowing around him. He laughed when I lunged at him, and his arms wrapped around me and held me close. "Good hug," he whispered in my ear. "The best hug, really."

"How did you…?"

His cheek scraped against mine as he pulled away, but not before kissing my forehead. "You," he said. "You believed in me. You and the others." He shook his head, shaggy hair hanging around his face. "I heard you, in here." He tapped his chest. "All of you. You needed me as much as I need you. I see that now."

"We're not islands," I whispered to him.

"No," he said. "We're not. We're together, and nothing will take that away from us." He turned away from me, walking through the smoke, the lights of the fairies beginning to blink around him. I started to follow him but stopped when a hand closed around my ankle. I looked down and saw Dylan staring up at me, looking confused.

I could do nothing to stop the way my chest hitched, the way my voice broke when I said his name. I pulled him up as quickly as I could, kissing him for all I was worth. He grunted into my mouth in surprise and laughed when I frantically kissed every inch of his face I could reach.

"Bro," he said. "We almost *died*. How wicked is that? I can't wait to tell Digger. He's going to be so mad he missed all of this."

"Fucking Digger," I muttered. Then, "I can't wait to meet him."

Dylan grinned. "Yeah? He's probably gonna give you shit, but that's how you know he likes you." He started to say something else, but stopped, mouth agape as he stared over my shoulder. I turned to see what he was looking at.

Sam walked amongst the remains of the fear monster, head held high. He moved underneath Leslie, hand raised, fingers trailing along the ice, a warm blue glow trailing in their wake. The ice cracked and shattered, Leslie shaking her head, nostrils flaring. "Sam," she said. "Hello."

"Hey, Leslie, long time no see."

"Right? I was just saying the other week we were due for a visit. You'll have to come to us, next time. Too many things happen when we leave the mountains." She turned her head and sighed. "Oh, Pat. My love. Look at you."

"All will be well," Sam said as he continued on, Leslie and the fairies trailing after him. I watched as he moved on to Pat, doing the same as he'd done to her mate. The ice around her wings snapped, large, jagged cracks forming over her entire body. The ice split apart, and Pat growled as she shook her head.

Leslie nuzzled her side, her right wing going over Pat in the approximation of a hug. "There you are," Leslie said.

Pat turned her head, pressing her snout against Leslie's. "I told you we should've stayed home."

Leslie laughed, a low, deep rumble. "Yes, you did. But then we'd have missed out on all the fun."

"Fun," Pat mumbled. "You have a ridiculous idea of *fun*." Then, "Are you all right?"

"I'm fine, dear. Sam helped."

Pat peered down at him, standing under her head. "Sam."

"Pat."

I thought she'd snap at him, but instead, she licked his cheek. "Never scare me like that again."

He laughed. "Eh. No promises. You know how it is. Something always happens."

"You should really stop that," Pat admonished him. "We're not getting any younger."

"You look good to me, girl."

She preened, though she looked pissed off as she did so. "As if I care what you think." Then, in a quieter voice, "I really, really do."

"I know," he said, patting the scaled skin on her cheek. "Thank you for coming to help us."

Pat snorted. "Like we'd leave you to get in trouble on your own. Someone needs to watch out for you."

He turned away from her and moved toward Randall. He stopped in front of him, frowning. "I'm sorry, my friend. I never meant for this to happen." He pressed the tip of his finger against Randall's outstretched hand. The ice shuddered and shook before sloughing off in wet chunks. Randall blinked slowly, mouth twitching as his teeth chattered. He sagged forward, Sam catching him before he could fall.

"You ridiculous boy," Randall muttered, face in Sam's hair.

"You ridiculous, foolish boy. Thank you." Sam tried to pull away, but Randall wouldn't let him. "Someone once told me that hugs are supposed to last at least a minute."

"Sounds like pretty good advice if you ask me," Sam said, gripping the back of Randall's robes.

Eventually, they parted, and Sam turned to face what lay before him.

Ramos lay on the ground, eyes closed, though he still breathed. The Damning Stone glittered in the grass near his hand.

Next to him, Lady Tina, armor dented, eyes blinking, mouth opening and closing wordlessly.

Sam shook his head as he stepped toward them. He crouched over Ramos, pressing a palm against the magician's forehead, fingers in his hair. Sam breathed in and out and pulled his hand away as Ramos's eyes fluttered open. "What happened?" Ramos whispered.

"Nothing we couldn't handle," Sam said cheerfully. "You all right, dude?"

Ramos frowned as he sat up, hands going to his head. "I...think so." He paled as he dropped his hands. "I almost..."

Sam nodded. "You almost. But it wasn't you. We know that. No one blames you, Ramos the Pure. You were a victim the same as the rest of us."

"My King?" Ramos asked in a trembling voice. "Is he..."

"Fine," Sam said. "And looking like he's about to tackle you, so. You know. Get ready for that."

Dylan rushed forward, bending over and picking up Ramos like he weighed nothing. Ramos wrapped his legs around Dylan's waist as the king rocked him back and forth. "I knew it," Dylan said. "I *knew* you were cool, bro."

Ramos laughed. "Of course I'm cool. I'm your magician, after all."

Sam picked up the Damning Stone, bouncing it in his hand. I came to his side, looking down at it. "Such a small thing, isn't it?" Sam muttered. His fingers began to close over it when someone shouted his name.

We turned in time to see a tiny unicorn hurtling toward us, followed by a small dragon, a dashing and immaculate boy, and a half-giant. Sam was knocked off his feet as Gary collided with him, both going down in a tangle of limbs. Sam laughed happily, his hands in the unicorn's mane as Gary threatened him with immense bodily harm for scaring him like that, don't you know what that does to my *complexion*, and why, why, *why* would you do that to me?

Kevin looked nervous as he fluttered his wings in front of Pat and Leslie. "Hi! I'm glad you're not ice anymore!" He spun in a circle, claws leaving divots on the ground.

"My *baby*," Leslie breathed. He screeched as Leslie nuzzled him, knocking him to his side, her snout grazing against his belly as his tongue lolled from his mouth.

"Whoa," Knight Commander Ryan Haversford said, eyes wide as he stared down at Sam. "You're so *big*. How did you grow up so fast?" His face twisted into something heartbreaking. "Does that mean you won't be my boyfriend anymore?" He scuffed his feet against the dirt. "Because that sucks and I don't like it." He crossed his arms and pouted. "Stupid grownups. I'm still gonna love you, and you can't stop me."

"I know," Sam said lightly. "You told me once on top of a tower that you wished for me. I've never forgotten. Look." He opened his hand, revealing the stone.

"Sam go boom?" Tiggy asked, touching Sam's hair as Kevin jostled Gary for a place in Sam's lap.

"Sam go boom," Sam agreed. He looked up at the sky, tears streaking his face. I worried for a moment that something was wrong. Worried, that is, until I saw Sam smile. "Hold on. Things are about to get a little strange."

And with that, he closed his hand over the stone.

"Ooh," Kevin said. "I feel all tingly again!"

Sam opened his hand once more, and in his palm, lay nothing but sparkling powder. Sam breathed in, and Sam breathed out, and then he threw the powder into the air. It arced in the sunlight, glittering as it fell back toward the earth. It struck Tiggy first, landing in his unruly hair. His entire body began to ripple before he expanded upward and outward, shooting up at least three feet, his clothes tearing before reforming as the half-giant choked out, "I...I remember. Tiggy a knight! Tiggy Knight of Brooms!" He pumped his fists as he jumped up and down.

Gary was next, horn taking on an otherworldly glow as if it contained all the stars in the universe. His body stretched, mane and tail lengthening until he once again became the unicorn we'd known for years. He blinked slowly, lips pulled back over his teeth. "I'm me," he whispered. He began to prance. "Hell fucking *yes*, I'm me again! Oh my gods, I am going to fuck the nearest thing I can find. I have a mighty need to find a warm hole to stick my entire face in!"

I grimaced. "Maybe we should have left you as you were."

He turned on me, eyes ablaze. "You listen here, you oozing scab of a human being. I am a godsdamn *unicorn*, and I demand you treat me as such."

I grinned at him. "Missed you too, Gary."

He sniffed. "Of course you did. I'm the light of your life. Honestly, Justin, your obsession with me is unbecoming of a prince."

"Don't need no mens!" Tiggy shouted as he hugged Gary so hard.

"Yes, kitten," Gary agreed, and I startled when I saw his eyes fill. "We don't need no mens, but I'm happy to have you all the same."

We were all practically knocked flat as Kevin suddenly towered over all of us, the spikes along his back sharp and deadly. His red underbelly shook as he laughed. "That's better," he said. "I don't like being so close to the ground. Gary! Yoo hoo, *Gary*. I have that warm hole you were looking for. Get ready, because by the time we're finished, you're gonna be permanently cross-eyed when I—Moms!" He growled as he dove between Leslie and Pat, the former cooing over him, the latter rolling her eyes but still smiling.

Sam knelt down in front of Ryan as the last of the powder fell around him. Sam cupped his face, Ryan's eyes wide. "I'm scared, Sam," Ryan whispered.

"I know," Sam said quietly. "But you have me." He lowered his hand, pressing it against Ryan's chest as the remains of the Damning Stone settled in his hair. Ryan closed his eyes, and groaned when his youth melted away, the muscles in his arms and legs expanding, the curve of his jaw sharp, his hair bouncing as he grew. Sam stood as Nox, as Ryan Foxheart, as Ryan Haversford closed his eyes tightly, lips pursed. He opened one eye. "Did it work?" he asked, voice much deeper, though tinged with nervousness.

Sam tackled him. Ryan grunted as they fell to the ground in a tangle of limbs and tongues that I absolutely did *not* need to see.

I was about to tell them to cut the shit when a loud cry came from the direction of the castle. I raised my head to see a great many people running toward us, knights and lords, ladies and children, all led by my father and Morgan, Dad leading the charge. I ran toward him, and the relief I saw on his face was so breathtaking, I almost fell to my knees. Instead, I leapt the last six feet, crashing into him. His arms wrapped around me, his face in my neck as he spun me in circles. "My son," he gasped. "My boy. You did it. You saved us."

"Had a bit of help," I said, and laughed when he smacked a kiss against my cheek as he set me back down on the ground.

"Did you?" he asked. "I knew you would. I'm sorry that I—"

I shook my head. "No, it doesn't matter. It was that…that thing. It wasn't you."

He studied me for a moment. Then, "I can see it in you, now. Look at you. You've found your fire again."

I grinned. "Let's hope it sticks around this time. Can't have something attack us anytime I need to get my ass in gear."

Morgan's hand brushed along my back as he continued on. I glanced back to see him stop in front of Randall, hands shaking as he reached for him, touching every inch as if to make sure he was real. Randall rolled his eyes, but hugged Morgan just as hard.

"Who did this?" Dad asked me as the crowd began to form around us. "Was it Ramos?"

A dark lance of anger pierced my chest. "No," I said. "It wasn't. He was being used just like the rest of us. It was Keith." I took a deep breath. "Acting on behalf of his cousin, Lady Tina."

"*What?*" Dad snarled, every inch a king. "How did she…" He shook his head. "There's time for that later. Does she still breathe?"

"Last I checked." And because he needed to know, I added, "I don't think the rest of my guard had anything to do with it. We'll need to interrogate them, but I think they didn't have any part in her plan."

Dad nodded grimly. "Good idea. Better to be safe than sorry. Take me to her, if you please."

We walked side by side, the crowd around us parting as they tittered, the word already spreading for who was to blame. I knew that rumors would run rampant, but we'd get ahead of them. There would be those who'd question how we didn't suspect Lady Tina was going to betray us, but the truth would come out, eventually.

Ryan stood with Gary and Tiggy, Kevin above them. Ryan snapped to attention, fist going across his chest as he bowed for my father. "My King," he said as he stood upright once more. "I'm at your command." He laughed when Dad hugged him. "Good to see you too, sir."

"Sam?" Dad asked as he pulled away.

We turned in time to see a god grow before us, his massive body covering us all in shadows. As one, we began to walk toward him.

Pat and Leslie parted as the Great White lifted his head, revealing Sam standing in front of him, hands curled into fists, knuckles white and bloodless. He tensed as he heard us approach but didn't turn around.

"Sam," Dad said quietly, resting a hand on his shoulder. Sam jerked his head toward us, and for a moment, something black crossed his face before it melted away as he sagged. "Are you all right?"

Sam nodded tightly. "I…" His face twisted. "I'm angry. So angry. I don't know how to stop." He wiped his eyes as Randall and Morgan joined us, the fairies buzzing about around our heads.

"Myrin," I said quietly. "The fear monster showed us Myrin."

Morgan's hand went to his throat as Randall frowned. "What?"

"It wasn't real," Sam said bitterly. "Just a manifestation of what I was scared of most." He waved his hand at the remains of the monster. "Whatever that was, whatever Lady Tina summoned, it showed the darkest parts of us."

"He's gone, Sam," Ryan said, gathering Sam up in his arms. "You saw to that. It was just a nightmare."

"I know," Sam said, voice muffled. "But I…" He shuddered. "I think I need some help. I can't keep going on like this. I need to be free of him, once and for all."

"We'll get you the help you need," Randall muttered. "Hell, I think we could all do with some therapy about now."

Sam laughed wetly as he pulled away from Ryan. "Yeah. That'd be a good start." He smiled as he looked at all of us. "But do you know what this means? We won because of the power of friendship!"

"Hurray!" Tiggy crowed.

"Oh my gods," I mumbled as Dylan appeared beside me, taking my hand in his. "You're so embarrassing."

"Sam."

We all turned to see the Great White staring at us with enormous eyes. Sam walked toward him as the dragon lowered his hand toward the ground. Sam touched his chin. "Thank you," he said. "Thank you for coming once again when I needed you most, GW."

"I told you not to call me that," he rumbled. "I'm pleased to see you as yourself once more. What would you like to do with her?"

He lifted his head, and there, pinned to the ground under one of his claws, lay Lady Tina.

She looked furious, her face splotchy and covered in sweat. She batted her hands against the claw to no avail, shrieking when she saw us standing above her. "*I'll kill you!*" she screamed, spittle flying from her mouth. "I am Lady Tina DeSilva! I'll kill *all of you!*"

"Noisy little thing, isn't she?" Leslie asked as Pat growled at the pinned woman.

"You want me to eat her?" Kevin asked, tongue flicking between his lips. "I can still be a humanitarian if you'd like. Already ate the corn lady, so it's not a big deal."

For a moment, I thought Sam would agree. A black part of me hoped he would, that he'd tell Kevin or any of the other dragons to bite her fool head off. He certainly looked like he wanted to. But I was strangely relieved when he eventually shook his head. "No. We're not…that's not who we are. As much as I want to see her dead for all she's done, we're better than that." He crouched down next to her as she struggled. "You tried, didn't you? You tried. You tried to take from me again and again. Morgan. Ryan. My family. Why?"

Joshua and Rosemary pushed their way through the crowd, Joshua pale, Rosemary's hand going to her mouth as her eyes filled. Dad shook his head at them, and they watched, waiting for what would come next.

"Because I hate you," she snarled up at him. "I hate *everything* about you. You don't deserve anything you've been given."

Sam sighed. "That's not for you to decide. It never was."

"Kill me," she whispered. "I know you want to. I can see it on your face. Do it. *Do it.* Show them who you really are."

"Nah," Sam said easily. "You're going to stand trial for your crimes against the crown. And if I have my way, you'll live a very, *very* long life pooping in buckets in the dungeons." He leaned forward, voice dropping. "And the toilet paper is *single ply.*"

She bellowed her outrage as Sam pressed a hand against her forehead. She tried to bite him, but he was stronger than she ever was. A faint whisper of magic pulsed around us as Lady Tina's face grew slack, her eyes closing, chest rising and falling.

"There," Sam whispered. "That should shut you up for a little while." He stood up, his father and mother lunging forward and shielding him from the rest of us. Ryan joined them, the members of this little family whispering words of love and peace in Sam's ears.

"Knights," Dad ordered. "Arrest Lady Tina. Put her in as many chains as you deem necessary."

The knights did as they were told, lifting Lady Tina from the ground as the Great White pulled away. The last I saw of her was the flash of her blonde hair as she was carted back toward the castle.

"Weird day," Dylan said.

"Yeah," I said. "This was a bit much, even for us."

He bumped my shoulder with his. "I can handle it, bro. In case you were wondering."

I swallowed thickly. "Yeah?"

He nodded. "Yep. If this is the worst that can be thrown at us, I'm good with it." He let my hand go, wrapping his arm around my shoulders. "I don't scare off that easily."

I leaned into him, his chin resting on top of my head. "Good."

Ramos said, "You shattered the Damning Stone."

We all looked at him, but he only had eyes for Sam. Sam's parents let him go, though they didn't go far. Joshua glared at Ramos as if daring him to blame Sam for anything.

"I did," Sam said.

"How?" Ramos asked. "I'm grateful. You…" He shook his head. "The sash was severed. My king and your prince should've died."

The crowd began to mutter.

Sam shrugged. "Couldn't have that, dude. Justin is my best friend. Dylan is his boo, and I'd never let them go."

"My *what?*" I demanded, outraged as Dylan chuckled in my ear. "You take that back right this second!"

Sam snorted. "Oh, please. You've been infected by *love.*" He waggled his eyebrows at me. "Just think! We now get to have sleepovers where we get drunk on apple wine and talk about our men before we have a pillow fight."

"Dylan," I said solemnly. "I'm sorry, but I have to break up with you because I'm *not* going to do that."

"Yeah, no," Dylan said. "I'm on to you now, Roth. You're stuck with me for a very long time."

Strangely, I couldn't find a single thing wrong with that.

"Thank you," Ramos said. "I don't know how you did it, but thank you. I can see now why they call you the most powerful wizard in an age." He bowed toward Sam. For a moment, he was alone in his action.

But then I did the same, because he needed to see just how much he meant to all of us. Dylan followed suit. And then Ryan did the same. Gary. Tiggy. Kevin. Joshua and Rosemary. Pat and Leslie. The Great White. Randall. Morgan, with a quiet smile. The crowd that had amassed behind us began to bow silently, along with the fairies as they buzzed above us

My father took a step forward as Sam's lips trembled, eyes wet. Dad brought his fist across his chest and bowed before Sam. "You honor us," Dad said toward the ground. "I'm so very pleased with you, Sam of Dragons. Thank you for all that you have done. Verania owes you a debt that I will spend the rest of my life making sure is repaid."

Sam tilted his face toward the sun and smiled.

# CHAPTER 19

# Wherein King Dylan Gets that Good, Good Prince Dick

THREE NIGHTS LATER, I found myself in my room at my desk. Dylan sat behind me on my bed, back against the headboard, long legs crossed as he flipped through one of my books. I tried to ignore him, but I could feel his gaze on me every now and then, heated yet soft. This was the first time we'd been alone since the battle at the training fields, and I was more nervous than I cared to admit. If all went the way it was supposed to, at midnight, the ritual would end and the sash could be removed. For some odd reason, I wasn't looking forward to it as much as I'd thought I was. We needed to talk about what came next, whatever that would be.

Whatever magic had fallen over the City of Lockes had been broken with the destruction of the fear monster. Thankfully, the damage to the city had been minimal, mostly coming from people attempting to flee. We'd been fortunate that there'd been no loss of life, and only minor injuries, the worst of which was a broken rib on a man who had fallen over a trash bin.

None of us had seen Lady Tina since she'd been chained in the dungeons, though the dungeons guards had told my father and me that she was quite incensed, ranting and raving that she'd have her revenge before someone had finally seen fit to muzzle her. The other members of my personal guard had been shocked to learn of her betrayal, Deidre promptly bursting into tears during her interrogation. I was satisfied that none of them had known about what Lady Tina's plans were. I had assured all of them that they could remain in their positions, warning each one that if I even got a *whiff* of something off, my response would be swift and severe.

I laid down my pen, stretching out the cramp in my hand. I'd been at it for a couple of hours, documenting everything that had happened. Dad said it was important our history be written down for all the generations who came after us, in the hope that those who followed in our footsteps would know of what we'd done and learn from any mistakes we had made.

Luckily, Sam had decided not to give me *too* much shit over Lady Tina's actions. And by that, I mean he only brought it up fifteen times a day. It could've been worse, so I'd take what I could get. In the end, he wasn't wrong.

"You couldn't have known," he told me at dinner the night before, watching as Ryan and Dylan goaded each other on to see how many cherry tomatoes they could fit into their mouths at one time. I couldn't believe those idiots were ours.

"I should have," I muttered bitterly. "If I'd listened to you after Myrin, none of this would've happened."

"Maybe," Sam said. "But you wanted to believe in the good in her. I can't blame you for that." He paused, considering. "Well, not too much, anyway."

"Gee, thanks."

"You're welcome." He looked at me. "Don't be so hard on yourself. Trust me. Been there, done that. It'll tear you down, if you let it. We're better than that."

I closed my eyes, not trusting myself to meet his gaze. "How can you even stand to look at me?"

I felt his hand on mine, squeezing gently. "Because I love you," he said, and I opened my eyes to find him smiling at me. "I know that's hard for you to hear, but I mean every—"

"I love you too."

He blinked. "Whoa."

I sighed. "Yeah. I'm not proud of it."

"You just…threw that out there. Give me some warning next time. Gods, Justin." He didn't pull his hand away, and I turned my own over so our palms pressed together, fingers intertwining. "Thanks, though.

I think I needed that."

"Don't get used to it," I muttered, fighting a smile.

"I wouldn't dream of it," he said. He looked over at Dylan and Ryan, expression softening. "What are you going to do now?"

"I don't know," I admitted. Dylan laughed loudly, and I never wanted it to stop. The sound echoed off the stone walls and ceiling, and my heart stumbled in my chest. "I'm not…" I shook my head.

"What?" Sam asked.

I lowered my voice. "It's not…what you and Ryan have."

Sam rolled his eyes. "Of course it's not. It belongs to you and Dylan. You don't need to be like us because you need to be like *you*. Do you love him?"

"No," I said too quickly. Then, "I don't…isn't it too soon?"

Sam shrugged. "For who? There's no rule book about this sort of thing, dude. And even if you don't yet, that's okay. You'll get there, I know you will."

"With Dylan?"

He looked at me, brow furrowed. "Do you want it to be with Dylan?"

I hesitated. Sam didn't push, watching and waiting.

So I took a deep breath and said, "I think so. But what if I screw this up?"

He leaned over, laying his head on my shoulder. I turned my face into his hair, breathing him in. "You'll make mistakes," he whispered. "But if you can forgive yourself for them and grow from it, you'll be all right. I have faith in you, Justin. You deserve happiness after everything you've been through. We all do. Sure, we don't know what's going to happen tomorrow, but if we spend all our time worrying about what might happen, we'll forget to appreciate what *has* happened."

"Can't have that," I muttered as Tiggy declared himself the winner through a mouthful of at least two dozen cherry tomatoes. Then Gary said something that caused him to spray tomato all over Morgan, and I didn't want to be anywhere else.

"Can I give you some advice?" Sam asked.

"If you must."

He snorted and turned his face toward my throat. "Don't let things go unsaid," he told me. "You'll regret it if you do. It can be terrifying, but Dylan needs to hear how much he means to you. Don't leave him guessing."

"And how do I do that?"

"You'll figure it out. You always do."

"Faith, huh?" I said as Dylan caught my eye and winked at me like a dork.

"Faith," Sam agreed. "Believe in him, Justin. Because I know he believes in you."

And it was Sam's words that filled my head as I turned in my chair to look at Dylan sitting on my bed. His forehead was scrunched up as he read, his tongue stuck out between his teeth. He looked relaxed, almost soft. He wore a pair of loose-fitting trousers, his toes curling and flexing, one hand resting on his bare, thick stomach, the other holding up the book. His tattoos appeared to be moving in the flickering candlelight, the metal in his ears and nose flashing as he cocked his head down at the book. I turned inward, parsing through the complicated feelings he brought out in me. Annoyance yes, because he could be the most aggravating man I'd ever met. But strangely, this was eclipsed by how protective I felt over him. I couldn't stand the thought of anything hurting him. I forced myself to imagine a day not so far in the future where I'd have to say goodbye to him as he left for Yennbridge. It didn't sit well with me. In fact, it hurt more than I cared to admit. I didn't want him to go. He would have to, one day, but what did that mean for us?

I opened my mouth to ask if the book was any good. Instead, I said, "I don't want to marry you."

He held up a finger, eyes darting side to side as he continued to read. "Hold up, bro. About to finish this chapter. Annnnd….done." He snapped the book closed, setting it on the nightstand next to the table. He folded his hands on his stomach and gave me his full attention. "Okay. You may continue. You don't want to marry me."

I blanched. "I…it's not as if…it's far too soon to…you can't just *say it* like that."

"Say it like what?" He grinned. "Exactly like you did?"

I groaned, rubbing a hand over my face. "I didn't mean it like that."

"Like what?" He appeared to be enjoying my discomfort far too much.

"I don't want to marry you *yet*," I said stiffly. "We still have a long way to go before that should even be a consideration. For all we know, we're not compatible in the slightest."

He nodded. "Oh, definitely. I'd hate to get married to you and figure out that we're not...how did you put it? *Compatible*."

I scowled at him. "You're not funny."

He chuckled. "A little bit." Then he sobered. "So, you don't want to marry me. *Yet*. I'm okay with that."

I startled, not believing it could be that easy. "You are? But Ramos said..."

"I know what he said. And you reminded me once that I'm a king, which means I can shape my own future. We don't have to do anything we're not ready for. And if anyone gives us any guff over it, we'll deal with it then."

*Guff*, I mouthed to no one in particular.

He ignored me. "No one else gets to decide what we do. That's up to you and me. And I know that can be scary, but I think we can do it." He looked down at his hands. "Remember what I told you shortly after I arrived?"

"You told me a great many things," I reminded him. "Most of which I didn't want to hear."

He snorted. "Yeah, there was that. But I told you that we're not bound by fate or have a destiny written in the stars."

"That doesn't always have to be important," I said, picking up the dangling thread of memory. "We could try this because we choose to."

"And that's all I could ever want," Dylan finished. He looked back up at me, eyes dancing. "I want to try this. With you."

"Why?" I asked, suddenly needing to hear it from him. It wasn't a feeling I was used to, but I didn't stop it. I couldn't, even if I'd wanted to.

"Because you make me happy," he said, as if it were that easy. And maybe it was. "I had a good life before I came here. I'd still have a good life if I went back without you. You aren't all my happiness, Justin. That wouldn't be fair to either of us."

"But?" I whispered.

"But," he said slowly, "I..." He shook his head. "The life I led without you isn't a life I want anymore. Maybe this won't work. Maybe in a week or a month or even a year from now, you'll decide I'm not what you want."

"I won't—"

"And it'll hurt," he continued. "It'll hurt a lot, but I'll remember you fondly for the rest of my days. You've taught me so much, bro. About what it means to be a king. About what it means to be a good dude, to have people you would do anything for. I'm not the same person I was before I met you, and I'll always be thankful for that, no matter what happens to us."

"I don't want that."

He winced. "Ouch."

"No," I said quickly. "That's not…" I stood from my chair. He tracked my every move, eyes darkening, breath slightly quicker. "I'll…" Why was it so hard to say, even now? Why the hell was I holding back? He'd earned the right to hear the truth from me, no matter how scary it was. If he could be as brave as he was, perhaps it was time for me to do the same. "I'll want you. A week. A month. A year from now. *Years* from now. I'll want to be by your side. I'll want to look over and find you next to me."

"Whoa," he breathed. "That was super intense. Frick yeah."

"Think you can handle it?" I asked, taking another step toward the bed, the sash shortening the closer I got. Sweat trickled down the back of my neck as my skin buzzed. Please say yes. Please say yes.

"You?" he asked, gaze crawling the length of my body as he looked me up and down. "Pretty sure I'm up for it." He grinned, but it faded slightly. "Are *you* sure? I know I can be a little…me."

Gods help me, I was. "I happen to like how you can be a little…you."

"Do you?" he asked, eyebrows arching almost to his hairline. "And what, exactly, do you like about it? Be specific."

"I like the way you talk," I said, stepping closer. "I like the way you laugh." Another step. "I like the way you think and fight and dance. I like waking up and knowing you're close and then going to sleep as I listen to you breathe. I like groaning after you say something ridiculous."

"You can hypnotize frogs by placing them on their backs and rubbing their stomachs. Isn't that rad?"

I groaned as I reached the foot of the bed, and he laughed. "I like the way you smile. I like the way you fit in with my family like you've always been part of it. I like how the craziest shit can happen, and you're still game, even if it might mean we'll die horribly."

"It's Verania," he said with a shrug.

"It is," I agreed. "So am I. I'm Verania, warts and all, and you've never let that stop you." Might as well go for broke. The only thing stopping me was me, and I was tired of it. I wanted more. I wanted to *ask* for more, and even though I'd rather face a hundred Myrin's than say it, bravery wasn't always about what you did to survive. It could also be about taking that last step into something grand, even if you didn't know if the ground would be there to meet your feet. "I like you, Dylan. Probably more than like. And I want to see where that goes, if you'll have me. I know I haven't been the easiest person to like. I put you through shit you didn't deserve, and I'm sorry about that. You... you made me see that I could have something more, if only I could reach for it. And I want to, I want to so badly. I think...I think we could be something amazing. You're right. We're not fated. This isn't destiny. It's us, because we choose it to be. I choose you. Do you..." I swallowed thickly. "Could you ever see yourself doing the same?"

He studied me for a long moment. I tried not to fidget, but it was no use. So much felt like it hung in the balance, and whatever he said next would either make my path forward clear or send me on a different road entirely.

Finally, he said, "I think I could do that."

I exhaled explosively. "Really?"

"Oh yeah. In fact, I know I can."

My knees knocked against the footboard as I lunged onto the bed. I fell face first into his feet, and silently cursed my stupidity. I didn't move, cheeks on fire as his feet tapped against my shoulders. He chuckled as the bed shifted, hands coming under my arms and pulling me up on top of him, my face brushing against the hair on his stomach and chest. A great swell of relief crashed over me as his arms wrapped around me, holding me close. One hand went to the back of my head as I settled on top of him, breathing him in, chin resting on his shoulder. He let me lay on top of him for a minute before he dropped his hands to my shoulders, pushing me back slightly until our faces were inches apart. His skin felt heated underneath my hands, fingers curling into the hairs on his chest. The beads in his beard tapped against my nose as he leaned forward, kissing my forehead. Then, without pulling away, he said, "I like you too. Probably even more than like. I might even go as far to say that I'm pretty sure I'm on my way to loving you."

I kissed him. I couldn't not. He'd said what he had as if whispering a great secret, and I wanted to swallow it down, keeping it safe within me. His tongue brushed against mine as the kiss deepened. I gasped into his mouth as I felt his hardness beginning to grow against my own, his hips grinding up against mine lazily. His mouth pulled from my own as his teeth scraped against my cheek before nipping at my jaw. "Now," he breathed against my ear. "Should we find out how compatible we are?"

"Yeah," I said roughly. "That. Let's do that."

I felt him smile against the side of my head. And then I was flipped over, the room spinning dizzily as he loomed above me, hands on either side of my head. His gaze darkened as he peered down at me, the ends of his beard brushing against my chin. "Fair warning," he said easily. "I can get a little…mouthy. Some might even call me risqué."

I laughed though I didn't mean to. "*You*? Come on. You don't need to try and do something you're not comfortable with. I'm good with whatever you—*oh my gods*!"

My back arched off the bed as he twisted my nipple. Not so hard that it hurt, mind you, but enough so that I felt it, an arc like lightning snapping through me. "Here's how it's gonna go," he said affably. "I'm gonna use this sash and tie your arms to the headboard. And then I'm gonna worship your body before sucking your cock. Fun fact! I don't have a gag reflex. And, right before you're about to come, I'll stop. You're probably going to be a little pissed, but that's okay. You'll get over it because you're gonna watch me work four fingers in my asshole and once I'm ready, I'll ride you into the mattress until I come on your chest. Sound cool, bro?"

My eyes bulged as I gaped at him. "*What*?"

"Yeah," he said more to himself than me. "That sounds real cool."

"No," I said. "Seriously. *What*."

"Don't worry about it. Just think of it like a sword fight, except with our dicks."

"Who the fuck *are you*?" I wheezed.

He straddled my waist, hands pressed against my chest as he circled his hips, the pressure against my cock so insistent, I thought I'd lose my godsdamn mind. "I like surprising you," he said seriously. "And man, are you in for a surprise. Just you wait and see. The things I'm gonna do to you… But," he said, eyes narrowing, "only if you want to. Consent is important, and if you change your mind at any point, all you have to do is say so, and I'll stop."

"You have consent," I choked out. "All the consent."

"Good," he said. He ground his ass down viciously before clapping his hands. "Let's get this show on the road. Hands clasped, if you please, and above your head."

I practically punched him in the face with how quickly I moved, reaching back and pressing my palms together, fingers gripping the slat at the bottom of the baseboard. He looked pleased as he wrapped my wrists with the sash, cinching my wrists tightly. He used the slack from the sash to tie me to the headboard. I could get free if I wanted to, but for the life of me, I couldn't bring myself to do it. I wasn't quite sure if this was real or the product of my fevered imagination.

He finished and pulled on my hands. They moved only a few inches before the sash tightened. He looked pleased with his handiwork. "There," he said, eyes glittering in the low light. "Now I get to do what I want with you."

"Holy shit," I breathed.

He sat back on my waist, one hand going to my chest, expertly flicking open the buttons of my shirt. He'd done this before, and I wanted to snap and snarl at the jealousy that bubbled in my head. I pushed it away. Whatever he'd done before didn't matter. If this went the way I thought it might, I'd benefit from his experience. Screw whoever else he'd fucked. He was with me now, and the way he was looking at me drove the thoughts of anyone else from my head.

Once he'd finished with the buttons, he opened my shirt, the edges falling away until my torso was exposed. He ran his hands up and down my chest, my stomach, fingers digging into my side causing me to burst out laughing as I tried to squirm away. "Sensitive," he said quietly. "Good to know." He bent down over me, like he was about to kiss me. He stopped before I could reach him, his breath warming my face. He kissed my cheek, and I tried to turn to meet him, but he wouldn't have it. He bit down on my earlobe, tugging it gently. He let it go before gripping my face, tilting my head back.

My breath was ragged as he licked my neck, sucking the skin until I knew there'd be a mark later. For the life of me, I couldn't find the words to make him stop. I didn't *want* him to stop. He moved on from my throat, kissing his way down my chest before growling against my skin and sucking on my right nipple. I cried out as his teeth scraped flesh. It hurt, but it was a *good* hurt, something I'd never experienced before. He worried the skin before moving to the left, doing the same thing again. He blew hot air against my wet nipple, causing gooseflesh to prickle along my arms and neck.

He did as he'd said he would. He worshipped every part of me that he could reach. He brought his legs back as he laid down between my own, his considerable stomach against my cock. Every breath he took increased the pressure until I was half out of my mind. He trailed his tongue down my chest to my sides, as if he needed to trace every part of me. I pulled at the sash holding my wrists, frustrated when I couldn't grab his head. He chuckled as he moved lower, his beard causing the muscles in my stomach to tense. He scooted down the bed further until his legs hung off the end, his face above my crotch. He looked up at me with dark eyes. When he made sure I was watching him, his fingers played with the hem of my trousers as he mouthed the line of my dick through the fabric.

"Nice," he muttered as he nosed my dick. I didn't think he even blinked. "Big enough that I'll feel it tomorrow, but not so big that I won't be able to do this again right away. I can't wait to sit on it."

"Oh," I gasped. "That's…that's…" I had no idea what that was because his saliva was soaking through my trousers, and I couldn't think of anything that didn't involve me testing his claim that he didn't have a gag reflex.

He opened my trousers and pushed them down until they were at my knees. I thought he'd fuck with me more, but instead, he pulled down my underwear, my dick slapping against my stomach as he shoved the hem underneath my balls. He didn't touch me even though I was straining for it. He brought his face down near my dick. I could feel the breath from his nose along the length as he swiveled his hips into the mattress. Just when I was about to snap at him to get the fuck on with it, his tongue flicked out against the head of my cock, a line of heat that he repeated again and again. My eyes rolled back in my head as he used his mouth to pull my dick up before swallowing it down whole, his nose in my pubes.

Fun fact: Dylan did *not* have a gag reflex.

I bowed off the bed as his cheeks hollowed, eyes still on me as his head bobbed up and down. Words fell from my mouth, begging for more, godsdamn you, more, and he grabbed my balls, fingers curling into my sac. My hips lifted of their own volition, and he pulled off. "Yeah," he said, voice hoarse. "Do that. Hit the back of my throat, bro. I can take it. I'll tap out if I need to." He descended once more, his free hand gripping my thigh, urging me on. I fucked into his mouth, his throat closing around the head of my dick as he *sucked*. Just when I thought it was going to be over far more quickly than I'd hoped, he pulled off, going lower and nuzzling my balls as he lowered my

trousers and underwear. He took one into his mouth as he dropped a
finger between us, tapping against my hole. He didn't try and push in,
merely rubbing his finger against it as he took both of my balls in his
mouth. Spit dribbled down his chin as he let them go.

Dazed and turned on more than I thought possible, I watched as
he sat up, stroking me once, twice, three times before squeezing and
letting my dick fall back against my stomach. He sat up on his knees,
hands going to the ties of his trousers. He pulled on one of the strings,
his excitement evident. Once his trousers were untied, he reached in
and pulled out his dick. It was dark and lovely, shorter than my own,
but fatter. I whimpered at the heavy ring through the head of his cock.

"Oh yeah," he said, tugging on the ring, his dick jutting out proudly
from a dark nest of wiry hair. "Forgot you didn't know I had that.
Surprise. Got it a few years ago. It's gnarly, bro. You're gonna love it
when I'm fucking you. But we'll save that for later. Here, open your
mouth." He moved until his knees were on either side of my chest, his
trousers tight against his thighs. He lifted his dick and tapped the ring
against my lips. "Come on, bro. Open up. You can tug on the piercing,
if you want. Feels good."

Have you ever had a visiting king sit on your chest demanding you
suck his pierced dick? Because *I* have. And since I was nothing if not
diplomatic, I did as he asked.

The ring felt awkward against my tongue, and it took me a moment
to figure out what to do with it. I captured it between my teeth and
pulled gently. His head rocked back as he groaned, chest heaving. I
did it again before taking the head in my mouth, tongue swirling in
and over the ring. "Yeah," he muttered darkly as he began to thrust
his hips. "You're good at that. Fuck, bro. That mouth of yours." He
pushed in further, and I took him in as far as I could before gagging.
He pulled out, letting me catch my breath before he did it again. My
throat relaxed around him. Just when I was getting a handle on it, he
pulled out again, raising his hips until his dick slid against my face, his
balls hitting my chin. My tongue darted out, tasting the clean skin as
the ring through his dick rubbed along my forehead.

He climbed off of me, dick bobbing in front of him as he got
off the bed. He stood next to the bed, hips wiggling side to side as
he stepped out of his trousers. He tossed them onto the floor before
standing above me, head cocked. It was the first time I'd seen him
completely nude, and I was *not* unimpressed. He looked strong, his
thighs like slabs of rock, his wonderful stomach jiggling as he rubbed

his hands up and down his torso, watching me hungrily. I choked on my tongue when he flexed his arms behind his head, the hair in his armpits dark and curly.

I'd never been on display like this before. I'd never not been in control. And though part of me tried to fight against it, I was overwhelmed by *want*. I didn't want him to stop.

Once he was done showing off, he leaned over the bed, kissing me deeply, tugging on my bottom lip before saying, "You got oil?"

"In the nightstand. Hurry the fuck up."

"Patience," he said, gripping my cock and jacking me off. Pressure built and I was sure I was about to come. But he seemed to know I was almost to the edge because he let go of me. I watched as he opened the drawer, pulling out a small jar of oil. He opened it up and sniffed it before grinning at me. "It smells like almonds. Which, if you think about it, is pretty cool seeing as how you're gonna nut in me."

"Why are you like this?" I asked weakly.

He brought the vial back, setting it near my head. He then went to the foot of the bed and pulled my trousers off and dropped them to the ground. He climbed over the edge of the bed like a feral animal on the hunt as he nosed my dick before licking up my chest. He stopped at my mouth. I surged up and kissed him. He grunted into my mouth, tongues sliding together wetly. He broke the kiss, panting in my face. "You know what's going to happen next, don't you?"

I nodded, not trusting myself to speak.

"Say it," he said, as if daring me. "What did I tell you was going to happen next?"

I bristled. He thought I wouldn't do it. Well, fuck him, because *I* wanted to fuck him. "Four fingers," I said through gritted teeth. "You're gonna get up to four fingers."

"Yep! Because you can't spell fingering without fun."

"Uh, what? Yes, you can. There's no *u*."

"Aw," he said, batting his eyelashes. "There's no one like you, either."

I barely kept from bashing my head against his. "That doesn't make any godsdamn—"

"Oh, yeah," he said, eyes darkening. "You forgot the last part. I'm gonna get up to four fingers in my ass, and you're gonna *watch*."

He grabbed the oil before twisting around on top of me, facing toward my legs, his dick rubbing against mine. He grabbed both our cocks, grip loose as he jerked us both off. He let go before dipping his fingers into the oil and pulling them out, the viscous fluid stretching before breaking. He looked back at me over his shoulder. "Don't close your eyes. You'll want to see this, bro."

If someone had told me a month ago that I'd be turned on at the word *bro*, I'd probably have demanded they be tortured in the dungeons for the rest of their lives, the idea was so preposterous. But here I was, practically begging for him to say it again.

He sat forward on the bed, one hand going between my legs as he brought his oil-coated fingers back behind him. The sound I made when he began to finger himself open wasn't something I was proud of. He knew what he was doing, knew what it looked like. I almost demanded he remove the binding at once, but then the first finger slid in all the way to the second knuckle, and all rational thought fled my mind. He groaned as he rocked back on his finger, fucking himself. It wasn't long before a second finger joined the first. He panted as he dropped his head, hair hanging down around his face, fingers scissoring as he worked himself open. Then a third finger followed. "Yeah," he mumbled. "Been too long since I've done this. Can't wait for you to fuck me, bro. Make it so I can't walk tomorrow. Everyone will know what we did, you thought about that?"

I hadn't, and I didn't give a fuck. The animal part of me, the part that wanted to rut against him until he smelled like me, liked the thought. That probably wasn't the most reasonable reaction, but frankly, I was already too far gone to care, especially when he did exactly as he'd said he would: the fourth finger entered him, leaving only his thumb against his ass. He sat up onto his fingers, riding himself as he looked back at me, face covered in a sheen of sweat. "Almost time," he assured me as I gaped at him like a fish. "Gotta make sure I'm ready for that prince dick, you know?"

The filth streaming from his mouth left me breathless. This was the guy who'd said *cripes* and *aw, nuts*. I wouldn't underestimate him ever again. "Yeah. Sure. Whatever you need to do."

"There," he said with a sigh, pulling his fingers out of his asshole obscenely. "Think that's good. Hey."

"What?" I said, tearing my eyes away from his hole.

He grinned at me as he turned around, once again straddling my waist. "You good to go?"

"If you don't sit on my cock in the next five seconds, I will order you *executed*."

"Aw," he said, rising up and gripping my dick with a slick hand, coating me with oil. "Listen to you. It's adorable how you think you're in control." His grin turned evil when I writhed underneath his grip. "Yeah, you're not in charge of anything. Here? Right now? I am. And I'll decide when I sit on your cock." He gripped the head of my dick and *squeezed*, thumb sliding over the slit until I begged for him to stop. To prove his point, he didn't, and by the time he lifted his ass, minutes later, I was spitting and snarling at him, cursing his name. The sash held me tight. I wondered if I'd have abrasions by the time we finished. I almost hoped so.

The relief I felt when he pressed my dick against his asshole was overwhelming. Overwhelming, that is, until everything blotted out when I entered him. He groaned as he lowered himself, thighs quivering, sweat trickling down his chest. I wanted to fuck up into him as hard as I could, but he pressed his hands against my hips, holding me down. It felt like an eternity before his ass rested against my thighs, a blissful expression on his face. He didn't move, not right away. For a long moment, he just sat in my lap, clenching his muscles and causing me to bite my lip so hard, I tasted blood.

And then he began to move. Slow, not rising up and down but swiveling his hips in a delicious circle. "Yeah, bro," he muttered, reaching up and twisting his own nipple. "That's it. That's what I wanted." His dick jerked as his eyes fluttered closed. "Yeah, got that good prince dick, huh? Sure did. Feel it in my gut."

"Oh my gods," I whispered, half-out of my mind.

He opened his eyes, the pupils blown out as he sucked his bottom lip between his teeth. I needed to kiss him, and he knew it. He leaned forward, stopping a hairs-breath away from my mouth. His tongue flicked out, brushing against my lips. I surged forward, kissing him as hard as I could. He laughed darkly into my mouth before pulling away, falling back with his hands on either side of my legs. He moved his feet until they were flat against the mattress, the bones of his ankles digging into my sides.

"You might want to hold on to something," he warned me, and before I could ask him what the hell *that* meant, he began to move, and I gripped the headboard, holding on for dear life. He gasped as he rose and fell, his dick slapping against my stomach—leaving a sticky smear—before bounced up against his own. The jewelry in his belly button and ears jangled as he fucked himself on my dick, and I began to drift, sinking into the pleasure he took from me. Every fall of his hips brought new filth from his mouth, telling me that was it, gods, Justin, it burns so good, come on, come on, I want to come on you. His head fell back, the cords in his neck jutting out in sharp relief, and I couldn't form a single coherent thought. I'd never seen anyone more fierce and lovely than he at that moment. Regardless of where the road took us, I'd remember this moment for the rest of my days.

Especially when he leaned forward, back bowed, teeth gritted as he wrapped a hand around his dick and jerked himself off. "Oh," he breathed. "Oh shit. You're gonna get it now. You ready, bro?"

He didn't wait for an answer. Heat splashed against my chest and neck as his orgasm ripped through him, mouth open in a silent scream. It was all I could take, and my vision whited out as I came, my hips stuttering as I fucked my way through it.

He collapsed on top of me into his own mess, my dick still in his ass. He shuddered, his face in my throat. I felt his hot breath washing over me, and I didn't want him to move. He kissed my neck gently, hands running up and down my sides before he reached up and untied me from the headboard.

My arms tingled painfully as the blood returned, and I hugged him close, barely grimacing at the sweat on his back.

He panted as he raised his ass, letting me slip from him. The cool air hit my cock and I whimpered at the loss of his heat. He didn't seem inclined to move off me, and I didn't mind in the slightest.

Once our breathing returned to normal, he lifted his head, stretching out until his legs tangled with my own. "Hey," he whispered, kissing the tip of my nose. "Thanks for that."

"Thanks," I repeated. "You're thanking *me*."

His brow furrowed. "Yeah?"

I rolled my eyes. "If anyone needs to be offering thanks, I think it should be me. Also, two questions: what in the fuck was that, and when can we do it again?"

He laughed as he slid off, lying next to me on his stomach, his arm across mine. He turned his head on the pillow we shared, blinking sleepily at me. Because I could, I kissed his cheeks, his chin. He hummed as I kissed between his eyes, breathing him in. "That," he murmured, "was wicked awesome. And yeah, bro, we'll do it again soon. And again. And again."

"And again and again," I told him, grinning when he chuckled.

My smile faded when he grimaced. "What's wrong? Did I hurt you?"

"Nah," he said. "Just the gross part after."

It took me a moment to realize what he meant, and I flushed. "Uh. Yeah. Give me a second. Stay right here, okay? Don't move."

"Not going anywhere, bro. Legs don't work."

I rose from my bed, muscles burning as I hissed at the cold floor. I went to the bathroom, and was startled to see the crazed grin of my reflection in the mirror. My hair was in disarray, and there was no mistaking that I'd been ridden hard. I wetted a cloth, wiping myself off before returning to the bed.

Dylan still lay on his stomach, the shadows from the candlelight flickering across his back, his tattoos once again looking sentient. My heart rose into my throat, and I couldn't look away from this man, this wonderful man in my bed. Shaking my head, I went to him, climbing on top of him. He grunted when I cleaned him off carefully, not wanting to cause him any discomfort. "Aw, cripes," he said.

"Cripes," I muttered. "Good to know we're back with that."

"What?" he asked, raising his head to look at me.

"Nothing," I told him. I threw the cloth to the floor beside the bed before grabbing the oil and setting it back on my nightstand. I thought about dressing in my sleep clothes, but no children would be sneaking into our room this night (or so I hoped). Dylan reached for me and I took his hand, allowing myself to be pulled back into bed. He made quite the show of pulling the comforter over us, wrapping me up until I was safe and warm. I tried to turn over away from him to fit my back against his front, but he wouldn't let me. He positioned me until we faced each other, one of my legs between his. He closed his eyes as I played with his hair, tugging on the dark locks.

"Sorry about that," he whispered.

My hand stilled in his hair. "About?"

He shrugged. "I get a little dirty when I'm horny."

"That's not as big a problem as you seem to think."

He opened one eye. "Yeah?"

"Yeah. In fact, I will insist upon it. Maybe not every time," I added quickly. "But hell, Dylan. I didn't know you had it in you."

He laughed. "Oh, I had it in me, all right."

I groaned, playfully punching his arm. "You know what I meant."

He captured my hand, kissing my knuckles before holding it

against his chest. "I did. I do. And man, I can't wait until I get to do the same to you."

I swallowed thickly. "Yes. That. Let's do that." I paused, considering. "Maybe not tonight."

"Tomorrow," he said.

"Because we have so many tomorrows."

"We do, don't we? That's gnarly, bro. We'll have all the tomorrows we could ever…" He stopped, eyes widening.

"What?" I asked, hoping he wasn't injured. "Did you—"

"The sash," he whispered.

"What about the—" I looked at my wrist and was stunned to see it bare. I raised my head and found it laying on the pillow above us, unattached. It looked like nothing special, just a discarded cloth. I startled at the strange grief that clamped around my heart. It must have been after midnight, on the thirtieth day. The ritual was over.

"Hey," he said, sounding concerned. "It's all right, Justin. We're okay."

I laughed wetly. "I know. I just…I can't believe I'm going to say this, but I'm not ready for it to be over." I winced, knowing how ridiculous I sounded. "Stupid, right?"

He watched me before shaking his head. "No. Not stupid. I get it. It brought me to you, and now…" He looked a little unsure, lost.

And I couldn't have that. "And now we no longer have need of it," I said firmly. "Because it did what was required of it. It bound us together. But we don't need it anymore."

"We don't?" he asked hopefully.

"No," I said, kissing his forehead. "Because while it's done, what it represented is still here. You and me."

"You and me," he said, and the relief in his voice sent me soaring. "Together."

"Together," I agreed. "Sleep, Dylan. I'll be here when you wake up."

"Promise?"

"I promise."

He closed his eyes once more. I thought he'd dropped off quickly, but then he said, "I think I'd like to be with you forever."

Nine words, nine simple words, and yet I doubted I'd heard

anything more profound. I took them in, holding them close, parsing through each and every one until I knew that I felt the same. There was no doubt. No hesitation. I liked when I was with him. I liked who *I* was when I was with him. We didn't need each other, no; we'd lived entire lives without realizing the other existed. What we had was more than that. We *chose* each other, and that felt more monumental than I expected. And so I said, "I'm going to make you so happy. I swear it. And though there may be days when you want to make me tear my hair out, or when you think I need to remove the stick from my ass— *no,* you shut your mouth right this second. You don't get to make that dirty when I'm being sincere."

He snapped his mouth closed, grinning ruefully.

I waited a beat to make sure he'd stay silent. Then, "But no matter what happens, so long as we remember we've got each other's back, we'll be okay. So yes, Dylan, I think I'd like to be together forever too."

He touched my face, thumb brushing underneath my eyes. I leaned into it, letting my head sink into the pillow. "I can't wait to wake up with you," he whispered, and then his eyes closed, his breath evening out.

I watched him for a long time after he slept. I expected to drop off soon after, but I didn't. I catalogued every inch of his wonderful face, disbelieving he was mine.

And then my mind—as it was wont to do—began to think ahead, about what came next. I looked around my room, taking in the familiar space. My entire life had been decided in this castle, in service of my country. It didn't weigh as heavily as it had before, but it was still there. I thought it always would be. I would be king, after all. One day.

But maybe not as soon as I'd expected.

Because an idea began to form in my mind, one terrifying yet exhilarating. I thought on it far into the night, and eventually, when my eyelids became too heavy, I knew that no matter what happened, whatever I—*we* decided, I wouldn't be alone.

I wasn't an island, after all.

# CHAPTER 20
## The Decisions We Make

I FOUND MY FATHER the next afternoon in the castle gardens, listening to Rosemary as she told him of the new flowers she'd planted, and her plans for expansion. She wanted to open the gardens to anyone who wished to visit. "I want this to be for everyone," she told him, looking slightly nervous as she did so. "This is a place of love and healing. It has brought me such peace, and I'd like to share that."

Dad smiled at her. "That is a fantastic idea, Rosemary. Would you like to be the one offering the tours? No one knows the gardens as well as you."

She beamed at him. "I'd be honored, Anthony. I'll put together a proposal and have it to you by the end of the week."

He squeezed her shoulder. "I look forward to it. Anything you need, ask. I'll make sure you have everything you desire to make your plan a reality."

She kissed him on the cheek before turning around and heading toward the doors. She smiled at me, patting me on the arm as she left without another word.

Dad glanced at me, brow furrowing. "Ah," he said as his forehead smoothed out. "That's what's different. Your shadow isn't with you. I take it the Sash of the Grand Hunt fulfilled its purpose?"

"And then some," I said. "Wait, that's not what I meant. Holy shit. Ignore me."

Dad chuckled. "As if I could ever do that. Come here."

I went, relishing his arm across my shoulders as he held me close. We walked through the gardens slowly, exclaiming over the bright flowers Rosemary had brought to life. "Your mother would love what this place has become," Dad said, reaching out and rubbing his fingers against a bright yellow flower petal. "She'd be pleased at all that we've created."

"Because we didn't do it alone," I said.

"Precisely. We built this life with those we love at our sides. And yes, we've fought for that same life, but in the end, hasn't it been worth it? Look at all we have. Our friends. Our family. Our kingdom, safe once again."

And I said, "I'm not ready to be king."

He paused, still holding the flower petal. He sighed as he let it go, turning to look at me. I tried to stand tall and proud, but this was my father. He didn't need it from me. What he needed was my honesty, my truth. He looked at me expectantly, suffused with warmth and love.

I took a deep breath and let it out slow. "You've taught me so much. Even with the weight of the crown, you never lost sight of what's important." I looked away. "After...after Mom, you could have lost yourself to your grief. I don't think anyone would have blamed you if you'd done so."

"I loved her," he said. "I love her still."

I nodded. "But she's gone. And you've found new love."

"I have," he said. "Have you made peace with that?"

I rolled my eyes. "All I care about is that he makes you happy."

"He does."

"Then that's all that matters. Morgan is...good, for you. I don't think I realized how much until recently."

"Hmm," Dad said. "I wonder why that is."

"Yeah, yeah," I muttered. "Let me have it. You were right, and I was wrong."

Dad laughed. "That's not what I meant, Justin, though I'm relieved to hear it." Then, "You know I'd have supported you no matter what decision you'd have made, right?"

I sighed. "Yeah, Dad. I know."

"Good. So. What have you decided?"

I looked at him, this great man with a fierce heart. I owed him so much more than I could ever repay, and the pride I felt at being his son filled me with a bright light, akin to the sun. I loved him as my father. I loved him as my king. I wanted him to be proud of me, which is why what I had to say next was so hard. "Dylan. He's my future. Or, at least he's part of it."

"I see," Dad said. "And does he feel the same?"

I smiled at the memory of us waking up next to each other, and what followed after. Turns out I could take it just as good as I gave, my name on Dylan's lips like a prayer. "He does," I told my father. "Improbably. Impossibly, he does."

"Not so impossible," Dad admonished gently. "He knows you. He's witnessed you at your best and your worst, and still, he didn't flinch. I couldn't ask for a better man to be my son's partner in all things. Cherish him, Justin. Cherish every moment you have together as if it'll be your last."

"I will," I said, and I'd never meant anything more.

"But that's not what you speak of, is it?"

I shook my head. "You've taught me so much about what it means to be a man. A king. And I will be forever grateful for it."

"But…"

I pushed through my worry. "But I need to stand on my own. To make my own mistakes, both big and small. You've watched over me for years, and while I appreciate every moment we've had together, I need to see what else is out there before I wear the crown. I want to be the king you think I can be. And I will, one day. Not yet, though. I still have much to learn."

Dad's eyes were wet as he smiled at me. "And how will you achieve this?"

"I want to go with Dylan to Yennbridge," I said. "Not forever, of course, but if Dylan and I are going to…wed one day, our kingdoms will be joined. And I can't be a good king to a place and people I've never seen before. While Dylan will be their rightful ruler, I still owe it to him and Yennbridge to learn all I can about his home. I can't think of any better way than to go with him." I looked down at my hands. "If you'll let me."

Dad was quiet for a moment. "This is truly what you want?"

"It is."

"Have you told him yet?"

I shook my head. "I wanted to talk to you first. I think Dylan will—"

"Oh," my father said. "I have no doubt Dylan will find great joy in your decision. But I wasn't speaking of him."

"Then who are you—Sam."

"Yes," Dad said. "Your wizard. I can only imagine the amount of sputtering he'll do, all while threatening the King of Yennbridge within an inch of his life."

I laughed though my stomach twisted. "He *would* do that, wouldn't he?"

"He would," Dad agreed. "And will. Have you thought about what you'll tell him?"

I grimaced. "I'm sure he'll make his opinions known whether I ask for them or not. All of them will." I shuddered at the thought of Gary's reaction. I hoped he wouldn't invite us on a one-way trip to Gore City.

Dad laughed brightly. "Yes, I expect that'll be the case. We don't seem to keep things to ourselves these days, do we?"

"They'll understand," I told him. "Sam, especially. I think. But even if they don't, I need to do this. Not for them. Not for Dylan. Not even for you. It's for me."

"As it should be," Dad replied. "What if they want to go with you?"

I shook my head. "Sam…Sam needs help, more than I can provide. Ryan told me they're already looking into therapists for him. Like me, he needs something more to find himself. And he knows it, too, which makes it easier." I frowned. "I should have been a better friend. I didn't see what was right in front of me, how much he was hurting."

"Because he didn't want us to see," Dad said. "Not because he didn't trust us, but because he didn't want to burden us."

"He wouldn't," I said fiercely. "Not with this. He needs to take care of himself. And not just because he'll one day be the King's Wizard. But because he's my friend, and I want to see him better."

"You're sure about this."

"I am," I said firmly. "I don't want to leave you. Any of you. But I can't be the king I know I can be if I'm stuck inside these walls. There's an entire world out there, and I need to explore it, to see what I can find." My tongue thickened in my mouth. "You can see that, can't you?"

"I can," Dad said, tugging me close once more. "And though I'll miss you every day we're apart, you have my blessing. Yes, my son. Go. Find yourself. We'll be here waiting for you upon your return."

I hugged him tightly. "I'm gonna have a few words with Morgan," I muttered into his throat as he rubbed my back. "Someone needs to keep an eye on you in my absence."

"I'm sure he'll take to the task with great relish. You should see how he's monitoring my diet. Dictator, he is. I like mead."

"In moderation," I said sternly. "We—*I* need you around for a long time to come."

"And so it shall be," Dad whispered, and as the sun shone down upon us in the blooming gardens, I closed my eyes and breathed him in.

*****

DYLAN WAS, IN A WORD, ECSTATIC.

"Holy *geez*!" he yelped. "Are you serious?"

Amused, I nodded. "You're okay with this?"

He gaped at me before sputtering, "Okay? Am I *okay*? Heck *yes* I'm okay with this! Bro, I left Yennbridge as a single man and I'm returning with *you*? What about that could *possibly* not be okay?" He spread his arms out in a circle before spinning dizzily. "Best. Day. *Ever*."

I snorted. "Well, that was easier than I thought it'd be."

He stopped, squinting at me. "You thought I wouldn't want this?"

I shrugged awkwardly. The thought had more than crossed my mind. I knew he cared for me, and I him, but this? This was big. "I'd hoped you would."

"Justin," he said seriously as he approached, hands cupping my face as he stopped in front of me. "There's nothing I want more than to have you at my side. Never, ever doubt that, bro."

Relieved, I said, "Good. That's…good."

He laughed as he hugged me, lifting me off my feet and spinning me around. "Oh man, I have so many things to show you in Yennbridge.

How do you feel about milking goats? It's a little weird at first, but since I have first-hand knowledge of how you grip fleshy appendages, I'm not worried."

I glared at him as he set me back down. "Never say something like that again. What the fuck is wrong with you?"

"Absolutely nothing," he said, kissing me sweetly. He pressed his forehead against mine. "Is this real? We're really gonna do this?"

"We are," I said, smiling slightly. "It's not permanent, but if we're going to make something of this, then I want you to know I'm all in."

"I can't wait to tell Ramos. He thought we'd stay here for a while before making a decision. He's a little homesick, I think." He scratched the back of his neck. "I am too, if I'm being honest." He looked worried as he added, "Not that I don't love Verania. I do. I just…"

"Miss home," I finished for him.

"Yeah," he said. "Weird, right? All I've known my whole life is Yennbridge, and I couldn't wait to get out of there, at least for a little while."

"And now?"

He grinned. "And now, I can't wait to go back. Digger's gonna freak out in the best way. I'm going to show you everything. The City of Light. My home. My castle." He waggled his eyebrows. "My bedroom. In fact, I think we should start there."

"Oh? And why is that?"

"Because I want to see you spread out in my sheets," he growled. "Your cock hard, my name on your lips."

The maid who found us screwing in the closet really didn't need to scream as loudly as she did. What a drama queen.

\*\*\*\*\*

I WAITED TWO MORE DAYS, just to be sure this feeling I had wasn't a fluke. When I woke up on the third morning after the ritual had ended and found myself in the same frame of mind, I knew it was time.

We began making plans with Ramos, who seemed surprised but pleased I'd be joining them in returning to Yennbridge. "You honor us, Prince Justin," he said with a bow before I departed. "And while I'm not…happy with postponing any potential nuptials, I trust my king in all things, including this." He took the Sash of the Grand Hunt from Dylan, folding it carefully before storing it away.

"Give us time," I told him, Dylan grinning like a fool as he looked back and forth between us. "We'll get there."

Ramos nodded. "I expect you will. When?"

"How soon can you and your people be ready?" Then, "Randall might allow us to use his magic to travel back instantly, if you'd prefer."

"No," Ramos said. "That won't be necessary. We'll use the time it takes to travel to get to know each other a bit better and to teach you our customs, without the prying eyes of an awaiting people. That being said, I'll send notice ahead of us so that they may anticipate our return. Their king has been sorely missed, and I know they'll be happy we're returning sooner than we planned. Give me until week's end. We can leave then, if it suits you."

I kissed Dylan before leaving them to it. I made my way through the castle, fingers trailing along the stone walls, memorizing everything I could. I felt a little ridiculous, but this place had been the only home I'd known, if you ignored the time spent at the Port. I would miss her, and the people who lived within her.

I found Sam where I expected him to be, in the labs with Randall and Morgan. Ryan was out with his knights, bringing Tiggy into the fold. Gary and Kevin had gone to watch, telling us they'd made glittery posters with his name on it so they could cheer him on as he beat all the knights senseless.

Sam looked up from his grimoire as I entered the labs. He smiled at me. It wasn't as heavy as it'd been even a month ago. While not exactly at peace, I knew he'd find the path forward with a little help. I worried that this would hurt him more than necessary, so I needed to proceed with caution.

"Prince Justin," Randall said, arching an eyebrow. "How… expected."

Morgan cuffed the back of his head. "Don't be rude. Honestly, Randall. How you've survived this long, I'll never know."

"Squats," Randall said. "Onto penises. Have I ever told you about the time in my youth when I met a trio of triplets who moonlighted as gymnasts? They were very bendy and didn't have the social boundaries most find acceptable."

"Oh my *gods*," Sam groaned. "Just when I thought we'd escape without bringing up incest, you had to go and do that. What the fuck, Randall."

"Love is love!" Randall bellowed as Morgan shoved him toward the door.

"Gross," Sam muttered as I went to the door, meaning to close it behind them. I stopped when Morgan leaned back in, glancing at Sam before looking at me.

Somehow, he knew. Either he saw it on my face or he'd heard it from Dad already, but he knew. "You're doing the right thing," he said quietly. "I'll look after your father. I'll make sure he knows he's loved every day. The others, too."

"Thank you, Morgan."

He nodded and left, dragging Randall down the hallway. I closed the door behind them just as Randall went into great detail about his orgy.

I turned and leaned against the door, looking up at the ceiling and trying to calm my racing heart.

"Hey, dude," Sam said. "What's up? You look spooked. Ignore Randall. Half his stories are full of shit. I'm hoping the triplets one was too." He paused, tapping his chin thoughtfully. "Though, now that I think about it, I wonder if there's a spell to replicate Ryan? Can you imagine? Three Ryans rubbing up against each other all dashing and immaculate while I watch? Fuck yeah. Wait. Is that weird? I don't know if that's weird." He grinned at me. "But if I told Ryan to go fuck himself, he literally could."

"Nope," I announced. "Absolutely not. You keep your deviancy to yourself. I'm the godsdamn Prince of Verania, I don't need to hear about your disgusting…would that work on Dylan?"

He laughed, sounding freer than he had in a long time. I hoped it would stay that way for a long time to come. "I'm sure it could. Let me run a couple of tests. I'll let you know what I come up with." He looked down at his grimoire before lifting his gaze back to me. "What are you doing down here? Is everything okay?"

"It is," I said, pushing myself off the door and walking around the table where he sat. I looked over his shoulder down at his grimoire, giving him time to close it in case he didn't want me to see what he'd written. He snorted and sat back, leaning into me as I glanced through the pages. Tales of our adventures written in his familiar scrawl. He certainly had a flair for prose, even if he made me sound much greater than I was. I couldn't find fault in that. If that's how he saw me, then I'd found the best wizard a King-in-Waiting could ask for. "I wanted to talk to you."

He closed the grimoire as I took a step back, fingers sliding over the dragon scales and feathers the book was bound with. He spun around in the chair, giving me his undivided attention.

I didn't know how to start. How to tell this man who meant more to me than almost anyone that I was leaving him behind? Nothing I thought to say seemed to encompass all I'd mean. I'd never had problems with words before, but now? Now I couldn't even make a sound.

He reached up and took my hand in his, tugging gently. "Justin?"

I cleared my throat, heart thrashing about in my chest. I wasn't second-guessing my decision, but this was proving to be harder than I expected. I began the only way I knew how, with the truth. "You're my Best Friend 5eva."

The smile he gave in response was bright and happy. "Hell yeah, I am."

I squeezed his hand. "And no matter what happens next, nothing will change that."

His smile faded. "What's going to happen next?"

I watched him closely as I told him of my plans. He didn't try to interrupt, didn't grow outraged or furious as I had thought he might. He listened, taking in everything I said, and though I knew he would run through the conversation over and over again in his head, he let me finish. He never let go of my hand. If anything, his grip tightened as if he thought I'd float away.

"And though I know we'll be apart," I said in conclusion, "it's not forever. I'm not done with you yet. We have so much work ahead of us, but I know we'll rise to every challenge that comes into our path. Nothing we do is set in stone. We decide our own futures."

"Stone crumbles," Sam whispered.

"It does," I agreed. "But we won't. Because you're my friend. You're my family. And one day, our world will look upon us to lead. I want to make sure I'm ready for that."

He gnawed on his bottom lip as he blinked rapidly. "And you think going to Yennbridge will help you?"

I shrugged, a heavy lump in my throat that I forced myself through.

"I don't know. Maybe it won't. Maybe I'll come back and be exactly as I was before. Or maybe I'll find what I'm looking for. Either way, Verania is my home. *You're* my home. I won't ever forget that no matter how far apart we are. And think, it's not as if I won't get to talk to you, if you can give me your summoning crystal. We can talk every day, if you'd like." Going for broke, I added, "Because I want that too. Even if just for a few minutes."

He rose from his chair. "Incoming," he warned me. "I'm going to hug you so fucking hard your liver will squirt out your nose."

I opened my arms, gladly. "If you must."

I gave as good as I got, and if it went longer than three minutes, it was nobody's business but our own. We both wiped our eyes as we finally pulled apart. "If you tell anyone what has transpired here, I'll—"

"Make pointed threats that you'll never follow through on?"

He knew me too well. "Exactly that."

"Your secret is safe with me. Well, okay, that's not true in the slightest, because I'm going to tell Gary, and then *he'll* tell Tiggy and Kevin, and then everyone will know about an hour after that, so. Hurray for feelings!"

I didn't try and stifle my laughter. "Hurray for feelings, indeed."

He sobered, looking down between us at our joined hands. "This is what you want?"

"It is. I'm…" I shook my head. If I couldn't tell him this, then who could I tell? This man knew everything about me, whether I'd wanted it or not. And now that I had it—had *him*—I never wanted to go back to the way I used to be. "I'm a little scared," I admitted. "How do I know if I'm making the right decision?"

He raised his head. "What does your heart tell you?"

"The opposite of whatever my brain says."

"Yeah," he said dryly. "I might know a thing or two about that. I think we often confuse our head and hearts, especially when they seem to be at odds. But if we allow ourselves to overthink everything, we run the risk of growing stagnant in indecision." He jostled my arms slightly. "You know this is the right thing to do." His eyes were wet when he added, "And though I'll miss you when you're gone, I…I'd say that maybe we could go with you, but you want to do this alone, don't you?"

I shook my head. "I'd love to have you by my side." Visions of the City of Light on fire as some villain monologued about his daddy issues filled my head. "Mostly. But you need to focus on yourself right now. That's the one thing I want the most."

He made a face. "Yeah, there is that. We found a therapist, I think. He seems pretty cool, but I haven't had the chance to tell him about the time I accidentally turned Gary into a butterfly, so we'll have to see how it goes."

We both shuddered. For something so small and delicate, Gary the butterfly had somehow managed to maim the three men who'd tried to capture him with a net. It'd been an odd morning to say the least.

"And the nightmares?" I asked carefully. From what the others had told me, they'd remembered every moment of their sojourn back to childhood. Gary and Tiggy and Kevin seemed no worse for wear. Ryan took it in stride as he always did, but Sam? Though he seemed lighter than he had before, I wasn't sure where he stood now.

"Still there, though not as frequent, at least so far," he said. "But it's not…I know they're not real. At least I'm not trying to crawl into bed with you anymore."

"That doesn't make them any less terrifying."

He laughed hollowly. "No, I don't suppose it does." He shook his head. "Seeing the façade of Myrin like that…I don't know. I thought it'd make things worse."

I blinked. "It didn't?" That was news to me.

"Not in the way I thought it might," Sam said. "Even when he stood before us, part of me knew it couldn't be real. I saw what happened to him with the Star Dragon, the relief he felt right before his end. He had…he paid for his crimes in the most cosmic sense possible. Even if he still held onto his rage, the gods wouldn't have allowed it."

"The gods," I said bitterly.

"Yeah, they do like to fuck with us, don't they? I can't wait to tell the therapist that, just to see the look on his face." He tugged on a loose string on the sleeve of his robes. "Is it…weird that I'm almost excited about going to therapy?"

"Not weird at all," I said. "I'm happy that you're asking for help. That's all I could ever want. And if it doesn't work out with this one, you'll find another. Don't let it fall by the wayside. It's important, Sam. *You're* important, and not just to me."

"It helps more than you know. Thank you."

"Think nothing of it," I said. "Therapy is—"

"Not for that, though I appreciate it." He frowned, and I waited, not wanting to push. Eventually, he sighed and said, "You were my safe place. Even though I didn't know who you were, I knew you'd watch over me. That you'd never hurt me. I don't know *how* I knew that, but I did."

"Of course you did," I said roughly. "I'd never let anything happen to you, not on my watch."

He sniffled. "Is Dylan the one?"

I shrugged even as my face heated. "Who the hell knows?"

He laughed at me. "Oh, cut the shit, man. He's pretty great."

"He is, isn't he?"

"He has to be," Sam said. "To deserve you. Can I threaten him? Give him the ol' shovel talk."

I glared at him. "Absolutely not." Then, "Maybe a little, just to make sure he knows what he's getting into."

"Deal," he said immediately. "And no take backs."

"I wouldn't dream of it."

He hesitated, studying my face. I never looked away. Not from him. Never him. "You're going to come back, right?"

"Yes," I said. "I'm coming back. I don't know when, but when I know, you'll be the first I tell."

"Damn right," he muttered. "I'll hold you to that. We've got a kingdom to run. And believe it or not, I've got a list of six hundred and forty-seven things I've thought of in order to ensure we become the most successful King and King's Wizard Verania has ever known."

"Only six hundred and forty-seven?" I teased. "You're slacking, Haversford."

He flipped me off. "I only started on it two days ago. Give me time. It'll grow."

"I'm sure it will. Want to show me what's on the list?"

He looked surprised. "Are you sure? You don't have somewhere else you need to be? Because it's probably going to take hours."

"For you? I've got all the time in the world. Come on. Show me this list that's probably going to make me want to scratch my eyes out and banish you forever."

"Promises, promises," he said, and then he was off, blabbing at a mile a minute. I listened to everything he said, and though half his ideas were illegal and most certainly blasphemous in ways I couldn't even begin to articulate, I took them all in, treasuring every piece, every part.


*****


THE REST OF THE WEEK PASSED by in a blur of packing and planning. I spent half my days with my father's advisors, most of whom made their worries known about me traveling so far away without a guard. They'd subsided when I'd reminded them that it'd been the *leader* of my personal guard that had betrayed us all. And then my father told them—in a tone that allowed for no argument—that I had his approval, not that he deemed it necessary. "Justin knows how to handle himself," Dad said, his advisors sinking lower in their seats. "And I trust Ramos the Pure and King Dylan to watch over him. They know very well that if something were to happen to my son, there'd be no end to my wrath."

Ramos smiled blandly, sitting back in his chair without a word.

Dylan, on the other hand, had something to add. "Like, I get you're freaked," he said seriously to the men and women who watched him with barely disguised disdain. "Totally get that. But I have good news! From what I can tell, we don't have monsters hiding under our city that can be summoned and make everyone scream and run." His brow furrowed. "I think. Anyway, Justin is gonna be great because he'll have me. I really, *really* like him, so." He glanced at me. "Sam says you're my boo, so I gotta take care of you."

"I will see to his execution myself," I muttered, annoyed when Dylan and Ramos and my father saw right through my threat and laughed. Any retort I could have thrown at them lost its heat as I fought a smile.

The other half of my days were spent in my room, packing as much as I could within reason. I didn't know how long I'd be gone, and when I began to fill my fourth suitcase, I wondered why I needed so much damn stuff. I thought back to all the times I'd gone on the road with my friends, with nothing but a pack on my back. Those were the days I'd felt freer than I ever had in the castle, and while I was never going to shirk my duties, it wasn't time for me to rise, not yet. Dylan watched me with wide eyes as I began to unpack, going through everything and deciding on what was necessary. In the end, I took a few spare changes of clothes—including formal wear—and riding boots. I managed to fit it all into one suitcase, and when I finished, I breathed a sigh of relief. Then I remembered one last thing. I went back to my desk, grabbing the crystal heart Dylan had carved for me. I placed it on top of my clothes before closing the suitcase.

"Don't worry about it too much," Dylan said. "If anything, you can use my tailor when we arrive in the city. Or you can just wear my clothes, though they probably won't fit very well. And now that I've said that out loud, I really, really want that, and also to suck you off right this second."

"If you must," I said, ever magnanimous, hands already going to my trousers.

Later, after I'd given Dylan what he called That Rockin' Dicking ("Capitalized so you know it's true. What? Why are you laughing at me like that?") we lay in bed, me on top of Dylan, playing with the hair on his chest. He made a happy noise as I traced the tattoos on his arms with my tongue, hand going to the back of my head. "Tomorrow," he whispered.

"Tomorrow," I agreed. Then, "You sure you're okay with this?"

"With what?"

I hesitated. "Me. Going with you."

"Oh yeah, bro," he said. "So okay. In fact, even more than that. There's nothing I want more."

"Truly?"

He shrugged. "I like looking at you. I like hearing you talk. I like hearing you laugh and growl and snark. Why wouldn't I want you with me?" He frowned as he gripped my chin, lifting my gaze to his, thumb moving over my bottom lip. "Are *you* sure? Can't have you do anything you don't want to do."

"I do," I said firmly. "You're part of it. Maybe even the biggest part. But I'm doing this for me, too. I've spent so much of my life doing what was expected of me. Do this, Justin. Go there, Justin. Smile, Justin, you're the Prince of Verania." I nipped at his jaw, causing him to squirm deliciously. "I want to see who else I am. Or who I could be."

"I like that," he said quietly. "This will be so good, Justin. I promise."

I lay my head against his chest, his hands rubbing my bare back. "Tell me more," I whispered, eyes growing heavy. "Tell me more about Yennbridge."

As he spoke—ever prideful of his home—I began to drift. I floated on a wave of his wonderful voice and found myself at peace. When I slept, I dreamed of the sun and the stars, and with me, my friends, my family, my loves.

*****

WE GATHERED AT THE FRONT of the castle, Ramos and Dylan's guard already waiting for us at the front of Lockes. The caravan I'd be traveling in was made up of thirty horses, ten covered wagons pulled by oxen and a couple of carts carrying back gifts from my father for Yennbridge. My suitcase had already been packed away next to Dylan's.

Rosemary and Joshua hugged me first, both telling me they'd miss me, and that they expected to speak to me at least once a week. Rosemary tucked one of her flowers—a daisy—behind my ear, saying it was for luck before they both stepped back.

Randall came next, muttering to himself about the foolishness of monogamy. He held out his hand for me to shake, but I knocked it to the side and hugged him. He allowed it for a few seconds, even bringing his arms up to pat me on the back before stepping away, telling me that I was lucky I was the prince, because he'd killed men for less.

Morgan followed, and laughed quietly when I hugged him too. "Fear not," he whispered in my ear. "Your father is in good hands. I'll make sure he eats what you and I decided he can. He won't like it, but he doesn't have a choice in the matter. I'd like to keep him around for many years to come."

I nodded against him. "You're good for him."

Morgan pulled back, looking amused as he arched a bushy eyebrow. "I'm glad you think so. I love him, Justin. I've been given a second chance at life, and I won't let a moment be wasted. But, no matter what happens between us, he is your father first."

I shook my head. "He spent my entire life putting me first. It's time for him to do something for himself."

Morgan bit his bottom lip. "And you think he should…do me. For himself."

"Godsdamn wizards," I grumbled as Morgan laughed and stepped back.

Dad looked between us curiously as he came before me, resting his hands on my shoulders. He leaned forward, pressing his forehead against mine. "My boy. My beautiful boy. Though my heart is heavy, I know this is only temporary. You've earned this, Justin. I have never been prouder of you than I am at this moment. And I know she would be too. You have proven yourself over and over again, and Verania is lucky to have you as their future."

A tear slid unbidden down my cheek. "Because of you "

"Perhaps," he said. "Or maybe you did it all on your own."

I glanced at my friends, waiting their turn. Sam looked like he was ready to knock my father down just to get at me. "I was never alone."

Dad smiled. "No. I don't suppose you were." He fiddled with my shirt as if he couldn't bear to let me go. "You packed everything?"

"Dad."

"Your toothbrush? Oh, what about underwear? You know how you like a fresh pair of—"

"*Dad.*"

"Like he's going to need underwear," Gary told Tiggy. "I just happened to be walking by the prince's room last night and heard several reasons why Justin won't need underwear. Did you know the prince is a screamer?"

"Respect," Tiggy said as I ground my teeth together. "Dylan ate his flower."

"And how," Gary said. "Shame, really. All that hot foreign king flesh, and I didn't even get to sample."

"Not too late for that," Kevin said, eyeing Dylan aggressively. Dylan, for his part, took it in stride and decided that flexing his arms was the appropriate thing to do.

"I'm just as big as he is," Ryan said, flexing his own arms, trying to step in front of Dylan.

"Oh, man," Sam breathed. "The things I'm gonna do to you are better left unsaid seeing as how my parents are standing right here."

"Like that's ever stopped you," Joshua said dryly.

"Though we really wish it would," Rosemary said.

Dad smiled, turning his face toward the sun. "Yes. No matter how far our travels take us, we're never alone."

The others descended upon me, Tiggy lifting me up off my feet, hugging me so hard, my back cracked. I didn't try and stop him, or even Kevin when he licked my cheek with an extraordinarily wet tongue. Tiggy set me back down, and Gary loomed in front of me, nostrils flaring as he leaned closer, his horn jutting dangerously close to my forehead. I grimaced when his lips attached to my cheek, sucking a disgusting kiss. "There's more where that came from if it doesn't work out with the hot king. You know what they say: once you go unicorn, with my spunk you'll be adorned."

"Yes," Kevin growled. "Good. Rhyming makes it sexier."

I shoved Gary away which, of course, caused him to rant and rave about the rights of magical creatures, and just who in the fuck did I think I was?

Ryan and Sam came last, hands joined. I expected more tears, at least from Sam. I was a bit perturbed to see him smiling sunnily, as if he didn't have a care in the world. "You take care of yourself," he said. "And don't forget to call when you get a moment."

"Sure," I said slowly, trying to keep the hurt from my face. I didn't know why he seemed at ease with our parting. Maybe he'd gotten it all out when we had spoken in the labs. Still, it didn't sit right with me. "Are you okay?"

He laughed. "Never better."

I nodded. "If you're sure. Ryan, take care of him for me, okay?"

"Of course," Ryan said. "I don't think you'll need to worry about that."

"If you need me, all you need to do is—"

"Yeah, yeah, yeah," Sam said, spinning me around and shoving me toward Dylan. "Need to get moving. You're wasting daylight. Bye, everyone! Bye! Bye, Ramos! Bye, Dylan! Bye Yenners whose names I didn't bother to learn because that was an ancillary detail, sort of like those two people who found me after I returned to Verania and never saw again. Bye! Farewell!"

Dylan grinned at me as I stopped in front of him. He held out his hand toward me. "Are you ready?"

I looked back at my people. They smiled, Sam nodding obnoxiously. I turned toward Dylan again. I took his hand and said, "I'm ready."

*****

AN HOUR LATER, we found ourselves on a dirt road, heading north toward the Dark Woods. Dimitri was going to meet us at the edge of the forest, providing us passage through it with his fairies. We were supposed to meet Grundle, his new boyfriend, and though I was sure that was an introduction I'd like to avoid, I didn't want Dimitri to abandon us in the middle of the Dark Woods.

I frowned down at the crystal in my hand. A gift from Randall, one he said wasn't normally given to non-wizards. He'd said he had cast a spell upon it, and all I needed to do was think of the person I wanted to speak to, and it should work.

"Sam," I muttered. "Sam. Sam."

The crystal stayed dark. Annoyed, I shoved it back in my pocket. I was worrying too much. I needed to focus, but I couldn't get Sam's good-bye out of my mind. I was irritated that he'd been able to let me go so easily, though I shouldn't have been. For all I knew, he was in my room, hugging my pillow as he sobbed for me to return.

"All right?" Dylan asked.

I looked over at him. He bumped my shoulder as we trailed after the caravan. "I'm fine," I said with a sigh. "Just...I don't know. Did Sam seem weird to you before we left?"

His mouth twitched. "He always seems weird to me. I thought it was just a wizard thing."

"There is that," I said. "But..." I shook my head and forced a smile on my face. "It doesn't matter. They'll be all right."

"Oh," Dylan said. "I expect they'll be more than all right."

I narrowed my eyes at him. "What are you talking about? What did he say to you? I swear to the gods, if he told you about the time we made out, I'm going to turn around and go back to Lockes and stab him with my sword. It wasn't my fault! How the hell was I to know that the succubus had infected us both with its magic?"

"Wow," Dylan breathed. "He didn't say anything about that at all. Uh oh. I think I'm jealous again. Come on, Dyl. You got this. Don't think about Sam and Justin eating each other's faces and...darn. Too late."

I shoved him away as he laughed. "Fuck off. It wasn't even *good*." This was a lie. It'd been very good, much to my dismay. Granted, most of that had to do with magic, and by the time the curse of the succubus had worn off (after Ryan had lopped off its head while threatening me at the same time) I demanded someone bring me a bar of soap so I could cram it in my mouth to rid myself the taste of wizard.

"Oh, because *that* makes it better," Dylan said. "But seriously, bro. Don't worry about them. I'm sure you'll be...surprised."

That stopped me in my tracks. "What are you talking about?"

"Uh," he said, eyes darting side to side. "I...don't know? Don't listen to me. I have no idea what I'm saying. In fact, let's not talk anymore at all and just walk in silence until we get to Yennbridge."

"Dylan."

"Aw, cripes," he muttered as he scratched the back of his neck. "I suck at surprises."

Before I could ask what that meant, a large shadow crossed over us. I looked toward the sky, raising my hand to shield my eyes against the sun. I could make out a black and red smudge against the sky, wings spread wide. And then the dragon reared back, and I gasped when I saw Tiggy and Sam riding atop Kevin.

"Oh, good," Dylan said, obviously relieved. "They're right on time. I wonder where...oh. There they are."

I looked back in stunned silence to see what he was pointing at. Behind us, coming up the road in a fast clip, dust kicking up behind them, was Ryan, riding bareback on Gary, whose mane fluttered in the wind.

The ground rolled beneath our feet as Kevin landed next to the caravan, the horses side-stepping in fear as they shook their heads side to side. Tiggy picked up Sam, and leapt off Kevin's back, landing in a crouch on the ground as Gary and Ryan reached us. "You'll never get to do that again," Gary told him as Ryan slid off his back. "In fact, next time—if there *is* a next time—I'm going to be the one riding you."

"Yesss," Kevin hissed. "Add a new item to our bakery. Knight Commander Ryan Haversford Glazed Bread. Guess what the glaze is going to be?"

"Frosting?" Tiggy asked as he set Sam on the ground.

"Yes, kitten," Gary said. "So much frosting, Ryan is going to be *gagging* with it."

"Already gagging," Ryan said with a grimace.

"What are you doing here?" I demanded as Sam walked toward me looking nervous. Ramos smiled behind him as he motioned for the others to continue on towards the Dark Woods.

"Don't blame me," Sam retorted. "I was all for letting you go off into the world without your Best Friend 5eva, even though I knew you'd cry yourself to sleep every night because you missed me so much."

Suddenly, our dismal parting made more sense. "You planned this!"

"*I* didn't plan shit," Sam said easily. "That's all on your boo."

I turned slowly to glare at Dylan, who seemed to find something very interesting to look at that wasn't me. He even started to whistle.

"Dylan."

He winced. "Uh, yeah, so don't get mad, bro. But I know how much your friends mean to you, and I know I kinda wished Digger was with me when I came here, because honestly? Going somewhere new is scary as heck." He shrugged awkwardly. "I didn't want to put you through that. So I asked Sam if they wanted to come along."

"And we said yes immediately," Gary said. "Because we love you so much."

"And also because we want to sample the international cuisine," Kevin said.

Gary nodded furiously. "Yep, yep, there is that too. And by cuisine, we mean butt sex."

"Hurray for butt sex!" Tiggy crowed, pumping his fists in the air.

"I got that," I snarled at him. "Of all the…" I deflated as Sam eyed me warily. "You just had to insert yourself into this, didn't you?"

"I will insert my—"

"Kevin! Now is *not the time.*"

"Sorry, sorry." Then, in a whisper, "So much insertion."

Sam looked unsure as he wrung his hands. "I mean, if you don't want us to come, we can always go back."

"What about your therapy?"

"We have free healthcare in Yennbridge," Dylan said. "He can go to my therapist if he wants, or we can find him another."

I stared at him. "You're in therapy?"

"Of course I am," he said. "I'm in charge of an entire country, bro, remember? Gotta take care of the ol' noodle. As I always say, once you go to therapy, your mind will never atrophy."

"You've *never* said that," I growled at him.

"Sounded like I did, though, huh?" He grinned at me, wild and beautiful.

"We need to work on your rhyming scheme," Kevin said. "I've often found that it's easier to do when you don't wear pants."

"Kevin, knock it off. Dylan, stop taking off your pants. Ryan, *no one* asked you to flourish your sword. Gary, get your damn horn away from my man. Tiggy, you're perfect." I took a deep breath. "And Sam."

"That's me," Sam said hopefully. And then he tried to give me the Big Sam Eyes that worked on almost everyone. Unfortunately, it worked on me too. Godsdammit.

I hugged him as hard as I could. "Of course I want you with me," I whispered in his ear. "Of course I do. But are you sure? What about Morgan? Randall?"

He relaxed against me, clutching at my back. "They said it'd be good for me, and I agreed. Get out of Verania for a little while. Clear my head. And if we have need of them, they'll be there in an instant."

"You're going to therapy," I told him as I pulled back. "That's non-negotiable."

"Deal." He smiled. "So, does that mean we can go too?"

"Well," I said, drawing out the word just because I could. "It *is* a long way back to the castle. And you know the Dark Woods almost as well as the fairies. Chances are Dimitri will say something to piss me off and he'll abandon us. Might as well have someone who knows where they're going." I sighed the weary sigh of the put upon. "Who am I to dash your silly little whims?"

"You do it all the time," he reminded me as his smile widened.

"Yes, well," I said, "*someone* has to keep you in check. Might as well be me. For all I know, I'd have returned to Castle Lockes and found nothing but rubble because of you. This way, I can at least be sure we have a home to return to."

"That was one time! And I fixed it after!"

"Twelve people nearly died," I reminded him. "*I* nearly died."

He waved at me dismissively. "Like I'd let you cross the veil without me. You're stuck with us. Forever."

"Only you can make that sound like a threat," I muttered.

"Bro!" Ryan said to Dylan. "*Bro.* We get to go with you!"

"Heck yeah, bro!" Dylan cried. "Let's celebrate!" They began to dance around each other, shaking their hips obscenely.

"I brought a *lot* of oil," Sam whispered to me. "In case you need to borrow some."

He looked surprised when I laughed so hard. I bent over, clutching my sides. I couldn't stop it even if I wanted to.

"Uh," Sam said. "Dylan? I think I broke your boo."

"Nah," Dylan said. "That's just how he gets when he's happy. Pretty rad, huh?"

I wiped my eyes as I stood upright, a weight rising off my shoulders I hadn't even known was there. I felt lighter, my heart thump, thump, thumping in my chest. I felt vital, alive in ways I hadn't felt in a long time. "Come on," I said, wrapping my arms around Sam's shoulders and leading him toward the caravan in the distance. "We're going on an adventure. And there's no one else I'd rather have at my side." And I meant it with every fiber of my being.

Dylan fell into step beside me, taking my hand in his. Ryan did the same to Sam on the other side of him. Gary and Kevin and Tiggy brought up the rear, chatting happily about how much chaos they planned to cause, ignoring me when I glared back at them.

As we approached the Dark Woods, Dylan turned his head and whispered in my ear, "This is it, you know? This is what's important. You. Me. Our friends. I can't wait to see what we'll find. This, Justin. This is our happily ever after."

And you know what?

I believed him.

*****

AT LEAST, THAT IS, until we arrived in Yennbridge. Little did we know about what waited for us there. Because plans were being made by those in shadows who would do anything to bring an end to all we held dear. There would be running and screaming and billowing robes and a ridiculous bro named Digger, all centered around a dark design to steal the throne from the rightful King of Yennbridge.

But that…well.

That's a story for another day.

TJ KLUNE is a New York Times bestselling, Lambda Literary Awarding-winning author and an ex-claims examiner for an insurance company. His novels include *The House in the Cerulean Sea* and *Under the Whispering Door*. Being queer himself, TJ believes it's important—now more than ever—to have accurate, positive, queer representation in stories.

www.tjklunebooks.com

# OTHER WORKS BY TJ KLUNE

THE BEAR, OTTER AND THE KID CHRONICLES

Bear, Otter and the Kid

Who We Are

The Art of Breathing

The Long and Winding Road


TALES FROM VERANIA

The Lightning-Struck Heart

A Destiny of Dragons

The Consumption of Magic

A Wish Upon the Stars

Fairytales From Verania

The Damning Stone


GREEN CREEK

Wolfsong

Ravensong

Heartsong

Brothersong


AT FIRST SIGHT

Tell Me It's Real

The Queen & the Homo Jock King

Until You

Why We Fight


HOW TO BE

How to Be a Normal Person

How to Be a Movie Star

IMMEMORIAL YEAR

Withered + Sere

Crisped + Sere


Extraordinaries

The Extraordinaries

Flash Fire

Heat Wave


STANDALONES

Olive Juice

Murmuration

Into This River I Drown

John & Jackie

The Bones Beneath My Skin

The House in the Cerulean Sea

Under the Whispering Door

Printed in Great Britain
by Amazon

79711169R00224